Dragon's Mate

The DragonFate Novels #4

DEBORAH COOKE

Copyright © 2020 Deborah A. Cooke

All rights reserved.

ISBN-13: 978-1-989367-43-8

Books by Deborah Cooke

Paranormal Romance

The Dragonfire Novels
Kiss of Fire
Kiss of Fury
Kiss of Fate
Winter Kiss
Harmonia's Kiss
Whisper Kiss
Darkfire Kiss
Flashfire
Ember's Kiss
Kiss of Danger
Kiss of Darkness
Kiss of Destiny
Serpent's Kiss
Firestorm Forever
Here Be Dragons: The Dragonfire Novel Companion

The Dragons of Incendium:
Wyvern's Mate
Nero's Dream
Wyvern's Prince
Arista's Legacy
Wyvern's Warrior
Kraw's Secret
Wyvern's Outlaw
Celo's Quest
Wyvern's Angel
Nimue's Gift

The DragonFate Novels
Maeve's Book of Beasts
Dragon's Kiss
Dragon's Heart
Dragon's Mate

The Prometheus Project
Fallen
Guardian
Rebel
Abyss

SHORT WORKS
An Elegy for Melusine
Coven of Mercy
A Berry Merry Christmas

CONTEMPORARY ROMANCE

The Coxwells:
Third Time Lucky
Double Trouble
One More Time
All or Nothing
Christmas with the Coxwells

Flatiron Five Fitness:
Just One Fake Date
Just One More Time
Just One Night Together
Just One Hometown Hero
Two Weddings & a Baby
Just One Second Chance
Just One Silver Fox (2021)

Flatiron Five Tattoo
Just One Snowbound Night
Just One Vacation Night
Just One Unforgettable Night
Just One Christmas Night

For information about Claire Delacroix historical romances, please visit:
HTTP://DELACROIX.NET

Dear Reader;

Dragon's Mate is the third paranormal romance in the *DragonFate* novel series. Dragon shifter Hadrian feels the spark of his firestorm as the *Pyr* are preparing for a final battle against the Fae Queen—only to discover that his destined mate is a swan maiden and an assassin sent by Maeve to kill him. Hadrian also needs to harness his legacy as an ice dragon to see the day saved, and Rania holds the key to that. Hadrian and Rania's romance is a battle of wills and an enemies-to-lovers story, with the lives of her bewitched brothers hanging in the balance. Rania trusts Maeve completely, since the Fae Queen has raised her, but Hadrian knows that Maeve will break her promise to Rania. I loved watching these two gradually learn to trust each other—it's no spoiler that Maeve does betray Rania, but will Hadrian and Rania be able to work together to defeat the Fae Queen's plan? This book was a roller coaster ride to write and I hope you enjoy reading it.

At this point, I'm not sure whose story is next in the series. I'm going to work on the possibilities and will put the next book up for pre-order after it's completely. Please subscribe to the blog on my *Dragonfire* website or sign up for my newsletter to make sure you don't miss the next *DragonFate* novel. My dragons all live on this website:

http://DragonfireNovels.com

Look under the *DragonFate* tab for resources specific to this series. You'll find a link there for the Pinterest pages for *DragonFate* where you can see some of my inspiration. Also, there's a List of Characters, which is updated after each addition to the series.

To keep up to date with my books, please sign up for my monthly paranormal romance newsletter, *Dragons & Angels*. You'll hear about sales on ebooks, be notified of new releases, and have the chance to download free bonus content exclusively for subscribers.

I hope you enjoy Hadrian and Rania's story! Until next time, I hope you have lots of good books to read.

All my best,
Deborah

Dragon's Mate
The DragonFate Novels #4

PROLOGUE

Saturday, November 30, 2019—Vermont

The moon was so new that there was only a tiny slice of silver in the sky. Thorolf was watching over his fellow *Pyr*, Alasdair, who continued to struggle with nightmares after being tormented by the Dark Queen. Thorolf's son, Raynor, and mate, Chandra, were both asleep as midnight approached, and Alasdair was, too.

Being on watch had to be the most boring job ever. There was nothing on television, because Kristofer's farm was so far out in the country, and Thorolf had surfed the 'net on his phone long enough. He was in the kitchen, wishing there were more chips, and debating the merit of driving into the closest town to get some.

Even out here in the sticks, there had to be some shop open at night. This was America, after all.

And Thorolf had a serious case of the munchies. He felt like he hadn't eaten for a week, even though that wasn't the case at all. The *Pyr* had dined like kings at Thanksgiving, thanks to Rhys' amazing skills in the kitchen, and there were still leftovers. It was all healthy, though, and Thorolf yearned for salt and fat. His body, he was convinced, needed regular infusions of junk food.

The night was still, but then, it probably always was out in the country like this. Nothing had happened in the paranormal realm since Rhys had busted out of Fae with his mate. There hadn't even been a good dragon fight since Thorolf had gotten to town. He was restless as well as hungry.

Thorolf could see Rhys' truck from the kitchen window. The keys were on the counter, as if to tempt him. How long could it take? Down the driveway, drive a couple of miles into town, find a place and return. Twenty minutes, if he drove faster than the speed limit. Thirty, tops. He'd pick up some new kind of pickle for Chandra. The dragonsmoke barrier around the house was thick and deep—he'd breathed it with the other *Pyr* and thought Kristofer had insisted on it being excessive. He understood, though, the need to protect a pregnant mate. Chandra was starting to show, too.

What could go wrong in half an hour?

No one would ever know, if he hid the empty bags from the chips.

His choice rationalized, Thorolf was tugging on his boots when Alasdair awakened with a scream of anguish. "They're coming," he cried, seizing Thorolf's arm so hard that it hurt. "They're coming!" Before Thorolf could ask what the heck he was talking about, Alasdair raced out to the patio, leaving the door open behind him. He shifted shape in a shimmer of blue, becoming a dragon of hematite and silver, soaring into the night as he breathed a brilliant plume of fire.

What was that about? Thorolf swore, torn between responsibilities. Should he follow Alasdair or remain on guard? He hated when he needed to be in two places at once: there was no good choice. He peered into the sky, still able to discern Alasdair's silhouette.

Why hadn't that scream awakened anyone else?

"Dude!" He called Hadrian in old-speak. *"Your cousin's AWOL."*

"What was that?" Quinn rumbled sleepily. *"What's wrong?"*

"What? How?" Hadrian demanded from the other end of the house.

Thorolf could hear footsteps, but Alasdair was disappearing fast. Despite his injuries, that *Pyr* was making good time, wherever he was going. Where *was* he going?

"Alasdair!" Thorolf cried, wishing he could cast his old-speak better. He jumped when Chandra touched his arm.

"Go," she said softly. "We have the dragonsmoke barrier."

Thorolf knew the dragonsmoke barrier wouldn't stop the Fae, so he hesitated. "Are you sure?"

Chandra nodded, her gaze trailing after Alasdair. "The other *Pyr* are here. Go before he's lost."

Thorolf didn't delay any longer. There was another brilliant shimmer of blue light on the patio as he shifted into a dragon with moonstone and silver scales, then he lunged into the sky. *"Alasdair!"* he roared in old-speak. *"Get your sorry butt back here!"*

But Alasdair seemed to be flying to the moon. He didn't respond or slow down, much less turn back.

At least he had back-up. Thorolf felt the presence of another *Pyr* and glanced over his shoulder to see Hadrian's emerald and silver scales gleaming in the moonlight. A team effort. Thorolf liked that. Hadrian wasn't just Alasdair's cousin and the closest of all the *Pyr* to that dragon, but he kicked butt. Between the two of them, they'd get Alasdair back to safety.

With the excitement, Thorolf even forgot about chips.

The Circus of Wonders was parked in an empty lot on the lower East Side of Manhattan, between performance locations. The tents were packed away and the trailers were nestled close together, as if huddling against the winter wind.

Rosanna, who ran the Circus of Wonders, couldn't sleep. She felt a prickling on the back of her neck, the same kind of premonition she often had when a shifter in need stumbled into the circus. Those interactions weren't always easy, as the abused or hunted tend to be slow to trust. She paced in her trailer, smoked half a pack of cigarettes, and waited impatiently.

It was in the early hours of the next morning when the assault came out of the blue.

Or out of Fae, as it were.

There were a dozen blinding flashes of silver light, all occurring simultaneously throughout the makeshift camp. Before Rosanna even got the door of her trailer unlocked, several propane tanks had exploded. Trailers were rocking, many in flames, and she heard the screams of trapped friends. She ripped open the door to find wolves with their tails on fire, Fae warriors slaughtering whoever they could reach, corpses on the ground, and too much blood.

Fae warriors couldn't be mistaken for any other kind, with their blond good looks, taut bodies and ruthless savagery. Their weapons shone with an eerie silver glow, one that Rosanna had learned to despise.

Ivan—the biggest of the bear shifters—reared over a Fae warrior and snarled, taking a swipe at the intruder with one lethal claw. The Fae warrior danced backward, moving quicker than light, then stabbed Ivan in the gut with his dagger of silver fire. Another two Fae warriors jumped Ivan from behind, slitting his throat and stabbing him in the back.

Ivan's mate, Natasha, and his twin sons, Bernard and Helmut, joined the battle in their father's defense, but it was too late. Ivan staggered, and the Fae flung him into the harbor before slaughtering the rest of the family. It happened so quickly and was so vicious that Rosanna was shocked.

Worse, there was carnage everywhere she looked. Djinns flitted through the battle in agitation, and even they were slashed to ribbons. The air shimmered blue as circus members shifted shape, and more explosions rent the air as trailers burned.

Animals were being released, but those that couldn't shift shape—the elephants, tigers, monkeys and snakes, among others—were uninjured, at least. Their freedom would make trouble for the circus, though, and Rosanna worried that they'd be hurt. The automatons were all running even though they weren't plugged into any electrical source, spilling music and patter into the air in a crazy cacophony. Lights were flicking on and off all over the camp.

Rosanna shifted to her demon form to join the battle. No sooner had she stepped out of her trailer than a Fae warrior ambushed her from one side. His blade sliced one of the horns from her head, then he vanished into a silver sliver of light. She felt her own blood on her cheek and was sickened.

She knew with complete certainty in that instant that her cousin, Lilith, was dead. Rosanna shivered, hating her gift of foresight in that moment, then was furious.

How dare Maeve choose who would live and who would die?

Rosanna shouted and jumped into the fray, kicking the knife out of one Fae warrior's hand. He spun and snatched it up, then slashed at her. She ducked, he flashed past her and struck down a werewolf, then turned on her again. The Fae moved like lightning, cutting down shifters on all sides, until one, obviously the leader, gave a shrill whistle.

"Leave the rest," that Fae said. "Someone has to be a warning to the Others that remain." He laughed and the warriors returned to the portals they'd sliced between realms. "Alaska calls."

Alaska? What—or who—was in Alaska?

The Fae vanished as one, sealing the portals and leaving bloodshed and death behind them.

The entire attack couldn't have lasted a minute.

Rosanna could hear sirens in the distance—the last thing she needed was trouble with human authorities, but there wasn't enough magick in the world to make this disaster disappear. She saw Caleb run into the park in his wolf form and stop cold to stare. He was fast, but he hadn't been fast enough to make a difference.

The Circus of Wonders had to pack up and move, and they had to do it immediately.

Something was wrong.

Wynter could smell trouble, and her nose was the sharpest in her pack. Not that her skills meant much in a wolf shifter pack—her gender meant she could never be alpha and as much as that bit, the defense of the pack was the responsibility of everyone.

She rolled out of bed silently and rose to her feet, listening. The Alaskan pack slumbered in Kirk's big log lodge, each wolf shifter in his own room, many with their mates. The house was filled with the sound of steady breathing.

She heard someone inhale and moved to the doorway of her room. She could see Logan's silhouette in the great room below. He was standing guard this night and must have sensed something as well. As she watched, he prowled toward the windows that overlooked the forest. Wynter took a step forward and he spun to look, his eyes gleaming in the darkness. She froze.

When Logan saw that it was her, he smiled and beckoned, obviously thinking that what he'd heard was her approach.

Just as obviously, he assumed she was coming to seduce him. Logan had the original one-track mind. Just because he was her brother's second and believed a mating between their families was the ideal choice didn't mean that Wynter agreed. The last thing she cared about was Logan's ambitions. She was going to wait for her destined mate, following her brother's example. It might be a joke that they were both chaste, but Kirk's strategy made sense to Wynter.

She shook her head and saw Logan's eyes narrow at some minute sound. He pivoted and she knew he was going to shift shape, but he never had the chance.

It all happened so quickly.

There was a flash of silver light directly behind Logan, like a slit had been cut open in the air. A blond man stepped through the gap, as if he had opened the zipper on a tent flap. He was tall and broad, tanned golden, and built like a warrior. Wynter recognized that he was Fae.

She shouted a warning, and shifted shape, taking her Arctic wolf form.

Logan would have shifted to a timber wolf, but the Fae warrior's dagger flashed, slicing Logan from gullet to groin in one powerful stroke.

It was a strange weapon, one with a blade that looked like a silver flame. Wynter would have distrusted it even if she hadn't seen how lethal it was. Logan fell lifeless and bleeding to the floor and was kicked aside by the warrior.

The other wolf shifters burst from their rooms and a howl rose from several of them. The hair rose on Wynter's back as she leapt down the stairs. Most of her pack-mates had already shifted. They barked and snarled, led by her brother, Kirk, into the great room of the lodge. Wynter saw four more flashes of silver light, then the wolves were falling dead with stunning speed, those strange blades flashing on all sides.

The scent of blood filled her nostrils before she reached the fight. Kirk was already surrounded by Fae warriors. He was a big Arctic wolf who had never been defeated in battle before. He leapt at one of the intruders and sank his fangs into his opponent's arm. The warrior tossed his strange blade to his other hand, as if he didn't feel pain at all, then buried it to the hilt in Kirk's chest.

Wynter watched in horror as Kirk fell to the floor, blood flowing from his wound. The warrior bent and cut out Kirk's heart, smiling as he held it aloft. He took a bite out of it before Wynter's very eyes, then kicked Kirk's lifeless body aside.

The wolves fell on the intruders, but without Kirk to lead them or Logan to take his place, Wynter feared their attack was doomed to failure. She tried to take the lead herself, but a Fae warrior jabbed his blade at her. She twisted in the last moment and took a blow to the shoulder instead of her back, but it burned like nothing she'd ever experienced before. The pain made her stagger and fall.

By the time Wynter lifted her head, the warriors were stepping back through their openings between the realms. The rest of her pack was dead around her and the floor was wet with blood. Mates wept and shouted, and one threw whatever she could grab at the Fae. Lamps shattered but Wynter knew it wouldn't change a thing.

Her pack had been slaughtered, her brother was dead, and she knew this was the Dark Queen's plan to eliminate all shifters in action. Wynter saw four of the warriors disappear as her need for vengeance burned to life.

The first intruder to arrive was the last to depart. It had been less than two minutes since he'd arrived. He spared a cold glance over the carnage, as if counting the bodies, and Wynter instinctively closed her eyes. She played dead, letting him think he'd completed his task, and only opened her eyes when the silver light flashed one last time.

There was only the light of the moon then and the corpses of the werewolves she called both family and friend. They were all she knew and loved, and they were dead. Wynter checked, twice.

She was the last werewolf alive in the Alaska pack and that meant the honorable burial of her pack was her responsibility.

So was vengeance for their deaths.

The women who had been mates turned to her, the same lust for vengeance in their eyes, and Wynter knew she'd just become a leader of a different kind. The wound in her shoulder burned and she knew that no normal treatment would heal it.

When the burials were done, they would all to go to New York.

In her apartment, Sylvia woke up abruptly. She had a bad feeling and halfway wished she'd allowed the vampire Sebastian to stay, despite how irritating and enigmatic he could be. She sat up and looked around, wondering what had disturbed her sleep. The part of Maeve's book under her pillow glowed faintly red, as if it would protest its innocence.

Sylvia wasn't convinced.

She jumped when Sebastian suddenly appeared outside the windows on her terrace, his hands on the glass as if he'd force his way in. Had she summoned him with her thoughts? Then he stepped back. His eyes were bright and he glittered, a sign that he hadn't fed. His gaze fixed upon her and she retreated to the other side of the room, pressing her back against the wall.

His expression turned disparaging. "I won't feed on you," he muttered and she heard his words clearly despite the glass barrier. "I'll *never* feed on you." Sylvia wondered at his vehemence, but he flicked a lethal glance behind himself, then at the faint red glow by her pillow. The torn book seemed to be advertising its location. "Fucking magick."

"What's going on?" she asked.

"Can't you tell?"

"I know something's wrong."

"The Fae have attacked. Reliquary is a blood bath, so to speak. It won't be the only one."

The antique shop in Soho, Reliquary, was the haven of the vampires who followed Micah, including Sebastian whose alliance she often doubted. Sylvia guessed that Sebastian had left there in a hurry.

His lips tightened. "It's brutal." He shook his head. "There was no point in trying to help." She wondered whether he was trying to justify his choice then he glared at her again. "Yes. I chose to defend you over them. Don't shoot."

Sylvia couldn't deny that his decision pleased her. He glared at the door knob, a lock she knew he could pick or break, and she stepped across the room to open it and let him in. He swept into her apartment on a breath of cold air, moving with his usual grace and speed, then circled the apartment like a whirlwind. She wondered what he was looking for, but before she could ask, he stopped beside her pillow. He removed Maeve's book with his fingertips and studied it with obvious distaste.

There was a faint tinkle, like bells, and Sylvia saw more red light emanate from the volume. She only had half of the book, since it had been torn in their escape from Fae, but in Sebastian's grip, its remaining pages fluttered as if in a wind. There was no air moving in the apartment and Sylvia moved closer with suspicion. She could feel his agitation and distrust. Why did he hate magick so much? For all she knew, he'd told her before then made her forget his confession.

He was so annoying like that.

Pages separated themselves from the binding and took flight, twisting and turning as they rose in the air. Before they touched the ceiling, they disappeared, one at a time.

The book closed itself as one last page fluttered to the floor.

Even at a distance, Sylvia could see that it was the page documenting the Coven of Mercy, the thirteen vampires who had gathered in Manhattan. They had pledged to Micah's scheme to choose victims only from the sick and the infirm.

As Sylvia watched, lines appeared through the names of Adrian, Petronella, Oliver, Aloysius and Ignatius. It was as if an invisible hand with an invisible pen stroked them out. The magickal ink was red. A heartbeat later, the year appeared beside each name.

"Five," Sebastian whispered with quiet heat. "She accelerates the game."

Almost half the coven was gone.

"The other pages," Sylvia whispered.

"Yes, she's distributing the inventories," Sebastian said bitterly. "To taunt us all with her pending doom. This is the problem with her having her magick back again. I didn't like that dragon prince, but at least he gave her some competition. At least someone else could summon the magick." He paced the width of the room, simmering. "Now, we're screwed."

Sylvia ran a hand over the book cover, then tucked the loose page back inside. "Not quite," she said with quiet conviction. She met Sebastian's incredulous gaze. "Eithne said she was giving her magick to me. I should learn to use it."

"It's probably too late," Sebastian countered.

"We're still here. It's not too late." Sylvia picked up the book, aware that it seemed to weigh far more than it should. It was cold, too, as if she held a block of ice. "You could try to be a little more encouraging."

"Pessimism is my learned response to several millenia on this spinning rock," he countered, folding his arms across his chest to glare at her.

Sylvia hadn't realized he was so old. His expression persuaded her to refrain from comment on that.

"You must like it well enough," she said instead. "You chose immortality."

"Did I?" Sebastian smiled, looking more like his usual wicked self. "Or did it choose me?"

Sylvia had no reply for that.

Sebastian looked at the book. "Okay, wannabe witch. What are you going to do first?"

Sylvia knew a challenge when she heard one. "You could help," she challenged back.

"I know better than to mess with magick, but you suit yourself." He threw himself into a chair, lounging there even as his eyes glittered. He looked ready to pounce despite his posture and Sylvia was wary of him.

He was volatile because he was afraid, as afraid as she was, and she knew it. She turned the book in her hands, choosing her words. "The magick won't betray her. She has too much of it to command. It won't tell me how she can be defeated. But Eithne said that Regalian magick is sentient and, if the Dark Queen holds all the magick, that part of it might be less securely in her grasp." She looked up and met Sebastian's gaze, seeing unexpected admiration there. "I'm going to invite it to play and see what happens."

He gave a low whistle. "Not too daring."

"The time has come to take a risk."

"Stand back," Sebastian said grimly.

Sylvia ignored him as she concentrated and composed her first spell. She was vaguely aware that it started to snow outside the windows and that the wind was chilly, but she had more important things on her mind than the weather.

She saw red light illuminate at her fingertips and dared to hope for success.

Murray was locking up his restaurant and bar, Bones, stifling a yawn when a flash of light woke him up in a hurry. A portal to Fae opened on the dance floor, which had to make the short list of his worst nightmares. He didn't even have time to react. Someone or something was shoved through the portal, then it was closed, leaving the bar in darkness once again. How could that be? He'd had the wall faced in steel where the portal to Fae had been, and even buttressed it with a wizard's charm.

But the portal had opened in the middle of the dance floor. That meant it had been sliced open by a Fae weapon.

It also meant that there wasn't a safe place in all the world.

Murray made his way cautiously across the bar, then realized it was his bartender, Mel, unconscious on the floor. She'd been lost in Fae for over a month and relief flooded through him at the sight of her.

Unless, of course, she was dead.

Unless, her return was a trick.

"Mel?" Murray fell to his knees beside her and checked her pulse. She was alive, but she still had a red string on her wrist. Cursed but breathing. Murray would take it over the alternatives. He felt the air move around him, as if a maelstrom surrounded her, but focused on helping her. "Mel! Are you okay?"

"No," she murmured, her voice more husky than usual, then tried to sit up.

"Are you cursed?"

"No more than I was before," she said grimly, meeting his gaze.

He believed her. Mel had never lied to him and he didn't think she was starting now.

Murray helped her as best he could and finally got her to her feet. She was weak and she had some injuries, though he wasn't sure how serious any of them were. The greater issue was probably that it was Saturday night, late enough to be early Sunday morning. He knew she had to retreat to her sanctuary by the dawn for her weekly isolation.

It was her curse, and the red string on her wrist showed that it was still in force.

He got her into a seat at the bar, and poured her a shot of brandy. Mel knocked it back, then shook her head. She looked exhausted and had lost some weight, even though she'd always been tiny.

"It's good to be back," she said and managed to smile.

"I've never been so glad to see anyone in my life," Murray admitted, then came around the bar to give her a hug. He wasn't demonstrative, but he'd been so worried about her. "She let you go. I can't believe she let you go."

"You should be more skeptical, Murray," Mel said, her tone wry. "She has all her magick back, so anything's possible."

Murray understood. "She released you because you're doomed."

Mel nodded. "We all are. And she wants to watch. It's part of the game. One last spectacle." She put a crumpled sheet of paper on the bar and smoothed it out. "This is from her book. It's the werewolves, specifically those in the Alaska pack. Look, Murray. She's wiped them out, except for the alpha's sister, Wynter."

"All of them?" Murray couldn't believe it.

"All of them. Tonight." Mel shook her head. "And this is only one page. I didn't see it all, but it was bad."

It wasn't the most reassuring news she could have brought from Fae.

"It's Sunday," Murray told her and saw her eyes widen. He knew that it was easy to lose track of time in Fae. "I'll help you get home so you're there before dawn."

"Raymond's here," she protested, referring to the ghost of her dead husband.

"And since when has he been any help?" Murray demanded, knowing that Mel couldn't argue with that. "I'll call a cab, and we'll be at your place in a couple of minutes. Come on. I'll talk to you through the bathroom door, if you don't mind. We need to make a plan and it can't wait until Monday."

Alasdair, Hadrian and Thorolf had disappeared by the time Kristofer reached the main room of his house. Chandra stood at the window, rocking a dozing Raynor. Kristofer felt himself shimmer on the cusp of change but tried to hold back until he knew more. Quinn was staring out into the night and he could hear Sara urging the boys to go back to sleep. Kristofer's mate, Bree, was right behind him and he knew that any suggestion he might make about her staying back to remain safe would be ignored.

She might not be a Valkyrie anymore, but she'd never lose her fearlessness.

"Alasdair shouted that they were coming," Chandra explained. "Then he shifted shape and took off. He tried to warn us."

"Of what?" Bree asked from behind him.

"Who are *they*?" Kristofer asked.

"I don't know. He sounded frightened." Chandra frowned. "I wonder whether it was the Fae. It would stand to reason that he'd be sensitive to their presence after his experience."

Kristofer exchanged a grim glance with Bree. Alasdair had been tortured by Maeve, the Dark Queen of the Fae and his mind was a mess as a result. Rhys and his mate, Lila, appeared, looking as if they'd been sleeping soundly. Arach and Balthasar stepped onto the patio, appearing out of the darkness. The two of them had been bunking in the barn and there were strands of straw in Balthasar's man-bun.

"Should we go after them?" Arach asked. He was almost bouncing, ready to fight. Vivid blue light shimmered around him.

"Divide forces?" Balthasar suggested, also on the cusp of change.

"There are too many mates and kids," Quinn said. "Most of us should stay here." He inhaled deeply. "At least the dragonsmoke barrier is secure."

"That's not any defense against Fae warriors," Rhys noted just as a bolt of silver light flashed in the middle of the room.

Kristofer shifted immediately to defend Bree and his lair, becoming a dragon of peridot and gold that nearly filled the room. He bared his teeth at the flash, which elongated into a vertical slit. He braced himself for a Fae warrior to emerge through the portal, but the light blinked as a single limp figure was shoved through the gap. Then the portal between realms closed, as surely as if it had never been.

The man who lay unconscious on the floor moaned and shuddered.

"Theo!" Rhys exclaimed and fell to his knees beside their fallen comrade. Theo, a fellow *Pyr*, had been lost in Fae for over a month. He'd been cursed, too, and had attacked Arach when they both had been in that realm.

Theo was bleeding heavily and Lila, with her healing skills, was quick to join Rhys. Kristofer couldn't even see Theo's wounds for all the blood on his skin. There was a burn on his left wrist, as if a string had been tied too tightly there, and his fingers twitched convulsively. His skin was pale and Kristofer feared that he had been tortured by the Fae before release, like Alasdair.

"Dragon bait," Chandra warned and took a wary step back.

"She's right," Arach said, coming in from the patio "It could be a trap."

"But we can't *not* help him," Lila protested.

"He could be infected with something fatal to us," Quinn said.

"He could have been forcibly turned against the *Pyr*," Arach added. "I saw how potent the Dark queen's spells can be."

But there was no red light around Theo's fallen figure. He looked so broken that Kristofer couldn't ignore his need. "I think we have to help him," he said and Bree nodded agreement.

"His aura is heavily damaged, but its color is true," Lila said, dropping to her knees beside Theo. "I think he's badly injured but he's himself."

"Then why did she release him?" Chandra demanded, holding her son closer. "It *has* to be a trick."

Lila considered Theo's injuries. "He might have told her everything he knew."

"He might not be useful anymore," Bree agreed, her tone hard.

"He might be a spy, and not by choice," Chandra said, her suspicion undiminished. "I think we should be cautious."

"I'll take custody of him," Lila said. "With Rhys. We'll take him back to the city and Niall can Dreamwalk to help him, just the way he helped Alasdair." She looked up at Rhys. "He can't lie to Niall in his dreams, can he?"

Rhys shook his head. "No, he can't." He put his hand on her shoulder. "I think that's a good plan."

Bree shook her head. "I wonder what price he had to pay to gain his freedom." She clearly didn't expect a reply. Kristofer hoped Theo could tell them.

Thorolf and Hadrian returned then in a flurry of dragon wings: Hadrian carried an unconscious Alasdair. Alasdair was in his human form and murmuring incoherently.

"He just passed out," Thorolf said with disgust, after shifting shape. "Good thing we were there because he would have fallen right out of the sky. It would have been curtains."

"He dropped like a rock," Hadrian confirmed, setting his cousin down on the couch. His English accent was stronger, as it often was when he was agitated. He was close to Alasdair and even more worried about that *Pyr* than the others.

Thorolf stepped forward, evidently noticing the body on the floor for the first time. "Hey, is that Theo?"

"They threw him back," Chandra said. "I think he should be isolated, maybe even confined."

"Hard call," Thorolf said.

"You trust too easily," she countered and the air crackled between *Pyr* and mate. "He was delivered here for a reason. We should be careful until we figure out what it was."

Kristofer couldn't suppress a shiver, because he suspected she was right.

"We need to talk to Erik," Quinn said with authority. "Someone call him now."

"At this hour?" Kristofer asked.

Quinn shook his head. "If I know Erik as well as I think I do, he's already awake." A cell phone rang in the distance then and Sara appeared in the doorway, offering the ringing phone to Quinn. The Smith of the *Pyr* nodded as he checked the name of the caller. "Hey, Erik," he said, moving out to the patio to take the call.

"What's in his hand?" Bree asked, peering at Theo.

Kristofer pulled what looked like a page torn out of a book from Theo's limp grasp. He was startled by the shimmer of red light that emanated from it, then it was just a sheet of paper. "It's a list of the *Pyr*," he said.

"It must be the inventory from Maeve's book," Arach said, scanning the list then heaving a sigh of relief. "No recent losses. That's got to be a good thing."

But Kristofer wondered whether it was.

"What is it?" Bree asked, obviously noticing his expression.

"I won't trust anything that looks like good luck so long as Maeve is hunting the *Pyr*," he admitted. "What if she's just stacking the odds against us?"

"Then we need to armor up and be ready for the worst," Hadrian said with purpose, glancing after Quinn. "What about those gloves with the retractable steel talons that Quinn once made for Donovan?"

"If you're going into production, I'm first in line," Thorolf said and the other *Pyr* nodded agreement.

"Hey, what's with your cheek?" Kristofer asked Hadrian, noticing the blue-black mark there. It looked like the imprint of a kiss but was an unlikely color for lipstick.

Hadrian raised a hand to it, as if he'd been unaware of it. "It's cold again," he said, glancing at Lila.

"The kiss of death is back," she said with concern. "Let me see if I can make it recede again." She led Hadrian to one side and Balthasar followed. He'd apprenticed with Sloane, the Apothecary of the *Pyr*, so maybe he and Lila could help Hadrian together.

"I don't understand," Kristofer admitted to Rhys. "What does the kiss of death mean?"

Rhys was even more grim than usual. "Lila says it means Hadrian's marked for death."

"Like a curse?" Bree asked.

Rhys nodded. "Exactly like a curse, but apparently harder to break. She says its success is inevitable."

That wasn't the best news Kristofer had heard.

Maybe the numbers of the *Pyr* were being diminished in other ways, more cruel ways than simply being killed. Alasdair was suffering and so apparently was Theo. And Hadrian had an inescapable curse in the kiss of death.

Did Maeve intend to torment the *Pyr* before she eliminated them?

If so, could the *Pyr* undermine her plan?

CHAPTER ONE

Wednesday, December 4—Northumberland

adrian MacEwan should be dead.

No one had ever survived the kiss of death before, at least not for long. It was relentless, a ticking clock, an inevitable killer. What had changed? Rania had followed the formula, precisely as she had done twelve times before. But this time, it hadn't worked.

Was that the fault of the selkie healer? A good healer could counter many charms and undermine many toxins. She'd just never seen one succeed against the kiss of death.

Did dragon shifters have particular powers Rania didn't know about? She'd never hunted the *Pyr* before. Perhaps they had some additional resilience that she didn't know about. But then, why would Maeve have demanded that Rania choose one of the *Pyr* as her thirteenth and final victim? The Dark Queen understood the kiss of death better than anyone: it had been her gift to Rania, a tool to use in service of her will.

Had Rania herself made a mistake? That was the worst possibility. She didn't make errors and it was a bad time to start. She didn't want to betray Maeve's trust, or let her brothers down.

The unwelcome truth was that she felt different since meeting Hadrian. She'd been surprised that her chosen victim was so handsome, then startled by the flash of light he'd called a firestorm. Had she been sufficiently shaken to mess up? It was hard to believe. Maeve relied upon Rania's ruthless efficiency. The kiss of death required preparation and concentration, but it was almost second nature to her by this point in time.

Rania had reviewed the brief meeting with Hadrian a thousand times, seeking the solution to the riddle.

It was worrying that she'd even been tempted to give him a real kiss, never mind more. She hadn't even seen him at his best, but she'd never found a man more attractive. He'd been unconscious when she found him, hit on the back of the head. That shouldn't have made him intriguing. But there was no mistaking the fire that burned within him or the raw power of his nature. Even if she hadn't known he was *Pyr*, she would have sensed that there was more to this man than met the eye.

Something had flickered to life within her in that first moment. Something new. A spark of curiosity and of desire. And her ring, the ring she wore on a chain around her neck, had changed. The stone had ignited with an inner fire. She'd never seen it do that before. How had he done that?

Did he possess some kind of charismatic dragon magick?

Rania had been drawn to Hadrian, against her will. She'd wanted to slip her fingers into the unruly auburn waves of his hair, to caress the square line of his jaw, to touch the firm line of his lips. She'd wanted to seduce him, thoroughly, and that was so far from her usual inclinations that she wondered what was going on. Such attraction, after all, could compromise her effectiveness.

It already had.

She dreamed of Hadrian and daydreamed about him. She savored the memory of her first glimpse of this dragon shifter, and the admiration that had flooded through her. Hadrian was tall and broad, a warrior even in his human form. His eyes were green, but that single word didn't do them justice: they held a thousand warm hues of green from emerald to sea glass, even with some flicks of gold. There was humor in that gaze and intelligence, too, and the way his eyes had lit with admiration when he surveyed her had been an unexpected pleasure.

She'd only revealed her face to him, hiding the rest behind a veil of feathers, so it hadn't been lust that had lit his expression. The way he had smiled, just a little, had nearly stopped Rania from doing what had to be done.

That was what made him dangerous.

He could tempt her to hesitate.

"The firestorm," he'd called it when white light sparked between them and there had been awe in his deep voice. Like it was a marvel. Like *she* was a wonder. Rania hadn't ever felt appreciated like that. Maybe that was the secret. He had an accent, too, a British one, which seemed just about perfect for a hunky dragon shifter.

What did he look like in his dragon form? She wanted to see him in flight and when he fought. Curiosity was dangerous, but Rania couldn't resist the mystery of this dragon shifter who had dared to survive her kiss.

She'd studied since her failure, determined to make it right. Thanks to Melissa Smith's television specials on the *Pyr*, it was easy to find out more about the dragon shifters. She'd learned that the firestorm was the mating sign of his kind, the *Pyr*, the mark of one dragon shifter finding the woman who could bear his son.

It was a romantic notion, which meant Rania didn't believe in it one bit. It had to be a way to seduce women and create more dragon shifters. Maybe a kind of sex spell. She'd bet the firestorm sparked whenever one of them wanted it to.

She'd learned about beguiling, too, a kind of hypnosis practiced by the *Pyr*, and wondered if that was how Hadrian had made her pause before giving her lethal kiss. That delay might have been enough.

It wasn't a mistake she'd make twice.

Her ring, though, was a riddle she couldn't solve. It still shone with inner radiance, burning like a beacon, although she had no idea why. Had it changed forver? How? Why?

It was time to extinguish both lights forever and put an end to the distraction that was Hadrian MacEwan. The Fae spies had said he would return to his smithy in Northumberland this very day so Rania awaited him in his own lair.

Impatiently.

He would be with two other *Pyr*, the spies said. He'd left Manhattan with them: one who was injured from Maeve's exploration of his mind and one who was a dragon healer. There was a fearlessness in the decision to leave the other *Pyr* that Rania tried to keep from admiring—there had to be safety in numbers, after all, and the dragon shifters were doomed—but she told herself to be realistic. It might not be bravery. It could be a refusal to acknowledge that the attack the previous Saturday was the first of a sequence of forays that would leave the world devoid of Others.

Hadrian might be stupid.

He might be cocky and over-confident.

He wasn't necessarily courageous. Rania should give credit only when she knew it was due. She'd manifested inside his home, leaving the locks and any other protective mechanisms undisturbed. And then she waited.

It wasn't easy. After all, a blacksmith's studio was the last place Rania wanted to be, and even drawing close to one gave her the creeps. The only good thing about Hadrian's home was that it was located in the country, where there were fewer prying eyes to notice any change of routine. He'd converted an old mill to both studio and home, and a river ran merrily alongside it. Rania could hear the birds and the wind, too. She found the location of his home soothing, but told herself to remain on guard. She'd never yet adjusted to the modern world but she'd have plenty of time to worry about that later.

She was so close to completing her obligation. Just one dragon shifter stood in her way. Rania could taste triumph.

And immortality. She'd have plenty of time to follow her dreams once she became Fae.

It didn't take long to explore Hadrian's place thoroughly. It was simply furnished and comfortable. She concluded that he had simple tastes and pleasures, as well as a respect for tradition and history. He was tidy. He lived alone. He read books and did horrible blacksmith things in the adjacent workshop, which she refused to even enter.

She shuddered at just the smell of iron and ash. That scent alone should make him easy to kill. In his human guise, he was a man, and that meant women were his victims. A man and a blacksmith. This should have been easy.

His occupation was why she'd chosen Hadrian of all the *Pyr*. There was another blacksmith in their kind, the one they called the Smith, but he had young sons. Rania was protective of children, given her own history.

No one needed to know that she had a soft spot.

She paced and wished he'd hurry. It was already past noon. She should have asked the Fae spies for more detail. She had her plan and her strategy: she just needed her prey.

When Rania heard an approaching vehicle, she froze, listening, so utterly still that no living creature would sense her presence. When the engine was turned off, she hid, retreating to Hadrian's bedroom, and remained silent. Doors opened and closed; men spoke to each other.

Her heart raced and she tried to summon her usual mood of icy precision. She felt emotional and fluttery, uncertain, which wasn't a welcome change at all. She fingered the ring hung on a chain around her neck, soothed by its smooth surface.

It would all be over soon, she reminded herself. Maeve would cross out the name of another dragon shifter from her list and Rania, along with her brothers, would be free.

Hadrian was relieved to be home. Two firestorms in rapid succession had worn him out, never mind being trapped in Fae. He wanted to sleep in his own bed, return to the rhythm of his life and do some solid work that would make a difference in this battle against Maeve and her minions. Even if Lila's fears about the new mark on his cheek were valid, he'd accomplish something before he died: he'd see his fellow *Pyr* outfitted with new weapons.

Before leaving Kristofer's farm, he'd had a long consultation with Quinn, the Smith of the *Pyr* and his mentor, and they'd made a plan to produce all the steel-taloned gloves needed. No one among the dragon shifters believed Maeve had forgotten that the *Pyr* were on her list, too.

The *Pyr* had divided into groups to ensure their own defense and that of their mates and children: there was one group in Chicago with Erik, one group on Bardsey Island with Donovan and Marco, one group at Kristofer's farm in Vermont, a big group in Manhattan with Drake and Rhys, while Alasdair and Balthasar had come with Hadrian to England. Alasdair wanted to come home, too, and Balthasar had joined them to continue to monitor Alasdair's recovery.

The three *Pyr* had flown to London, then taken a regional jet to Newcastle. Hadrian's green Land Rover had been parked at the airport, while Alasdair's blue one was still at Hadrian's lair. Alasdair had driven down from Scotland and they'd traveled to America together over a month before. Their trucks could have been twins, both older and well-loved but completely reliable. Hadrian liked to joke that just like the two of them, Alasdair's Land Rover showed its mileage more.

It was after lunch by the time they approached the closest town to Hadrian's lair. They stopped for groceries and at the post office.

To Hadrian's satisfaction, the parcel had already arrived from Donovan. Over the years, he'd heard so much about Donovan's gloves. Though he'd seen them in action once or twice, Quinn's detailed description had made him want to examine them more closely.

He returned to the truck as Balthasar was loading groceries into the back and tossed the box with the gloves to Alasdair, regretting that he had to drive. Alasdair was checking messages on his phone, but he caught the box. Hadrian started the engine again as Balthasar got into the back then leaned forward between the seats.

"Is that them? Can I see them?" he asked. Alasdair passed him the box and finished up with his phone.

"Messages from Erik," he said with a shake of his head.

"News?" Hadrian asked.

"Advice," Alasdair said and they groaned in unison. It was a bit of a standing joke that the leader of the *Pyr* did tend to make a lot of suggestions—never mind commands. "Just be glad he's in Chicago and we're not."

"I wish I wasn't driving," Hadrian complained, his impatience so obvious that the other two *Pyr* chuckled. "I want to see those gloves."

"And you want to get to work," Balthasar noted.

"It's not that far to your place," Alasdair said.

There was a sound of tearing paper then Balthasar gave a low whistle. "These are amazing!" He put on one glove and held his hand forward over the gear box, wiggling his fingers.

Hadrian looked between the road and the glove repeatedly. It was a good thing they weren't on a busy road anymore. Each glove was made of fine leather, the long sharp talons attached to each fingertip. The steel continued from each finger across the back of the glove for strength, and the talons were hinged, like long fingers. They were also sharp, essentially five blades on each hand, and retractable. Balthasar flicked his fingers and the blades swung out, flashing dangerously.

"They *are* amazing," Alasdair said.

"You're killing me!" Hadrian complained and they all laughed.

"I might not give them up," Balthasar teased, then his tone turned thoughtful. "And Donovan carries them through the change?"

"That's what he said," Hadrian said. "He's able to augment his dragon talons with them."

"Incredible," Balthasar mused. "I totally need a pair."

"Me, too," Alasdair said, taking the other glove and tugging it on. "I can't be the only one who wants to slice Fae warriors to shreds." He slashed with his gloved hand and Hadrian heard the blades whistle through the air.

"Not at all," he agreed with heat. He was never going to forget how much his feet had hurt when he'd been compelled to dance endlessly. He doubted Alasdair would forget it either—plus Alasdair had endured Maeve rummaging in his thoughts.

"Are you going to take one apart?" Balthasar asked.

"I hope I don't have to," Hadrian said as he turned onto the smaller road that led into the hills around his lair. He was excited to get to work and didn't feel tired at all. "Quinn's instructions were pretty precise. I think I just have to study them closely."

"You two are competing, aren't you, to see who can make the most gloves the fastest?" Alasdair teased.

"Just a friendly competition," Hadrian agreed. "A comparison of methods."

"How about I make some dinner while you check them out?" Balthasar offered.

Hadrian smiled. "You can tell I want to dive in?"

"Call me psychic," Balthasar teased.

"Maybe you're projecting your own enthusiasm," Alasdair said.

"Probably. I want a pair of these and the sooner, the better." Balthasar slashed at the air again.

"Plus the sooner Hadrian starts making them, the sooner we'll all have another weapon," Alasdair said. "I'll help cook, too." He yawned. "Although I'll probably crash early tonight to try to get over the jetlag."

"Start tomorrow like you never left," Balthasar agreed. "It's the best way."

Hadrian hadn't admitted it to his fellows yet, but he was determined to do more than replicate the gloves: he wanted to improve upon them. It had been almost ten years since Quinn had made this pair for Donovan, after all, and Hadrian was inclined to use more modern resources. The Smith of the *Pyr* loved his wrought iron and artisan tools, but Hadrian respected the benefits of tradition melded to innovation. He knew he'd never convince Quinn to change his methods, and that wasn't his goal. In a way, he saw improving the design of these gloves as a challenge that would vindicate his view.

Plus, for Hadrian, the battle against the Fae was personal. He'd been imprisoned in that realm and compelled to dance until his feet bled. He'd been tricked by Kade, one of the *Pyr* who was under Maeve's spell, and even Alasdair had been forced to lie to Hadrian. He'd forgiven his cousin but not the Dark Queen behind it all. There was no telling when a Fae portal would open and a battle would start. Hadrian was done with spells and sorcery. He was ready to kick some Fae butt.

He also couldn't evade his sense that his own days were numbered. What Lila called a kiss of death felt like a block of ice in his cheek. It was impossible to ignore. He'd be sure the *Pyr* were ready if and when he died. That would be the best legacy.

Hadrian turned down his lane and his lair came into view. He parked the Land Rover beside Alasdair's and his cousin immediately got out to check his own vehicle—which was untouched, of course. Hadrian took a deep breath but there was no hint of Lynsay's presence.

He shouldn't have expected otherwise. There was no reason to be disappointed. He knew he'd done the right thing by breaking it off, but he would miss her. He wanted her to be happy, though, and knew he wasn't the one who could give her that.

Hadrian unlocked the door to the lair and Balthasar followed him with groceries. Hadrian claimed the gloves with purpose.

"I'm going to call Donovan and tell him the package arrived," Balthasar said. "And ask how he takes the gloves through the shift."

"I need a shower, then I'll get to work."

Alasdair trailed in with the last box of groceries, checking his phone with one hand.

The mill that had become Hadrian's home and studio was constructed in an L, which made the division between home and work easy. He'd built his studio in the larger arm of the L and his home in the other. At the junction was his office and a formidable barrier of dragonsmoke buttressing the entrance to his lair, hoard and home.

His lair had a large main room, with a high ceiling and exposed brick walls. The kitchen was at one end, immediately inside the door. There was a big fireplace on the opposite wall which divided the bedroom from the rest. Kristofer had done some amazing pointwork during a visit years before, building an arch in the wall to the right of the fireplace. It wasn't original but blended with the architectural details while still looking a bit modern.

The arch gave access to Hadrian's bedroom: there was a door between it and the bathroom beyond. Windows on the right of the great room and bedroom offered a view of the river that had originally provided power to the mill. That vista changed with the seasons and Hadrian never tired of it. There was a loft over the bedroom, a second bath for guests, and a room behind the office that could be used as a spare room.

Hadrian paused in the great room and took a deep breath, assessing. His dragonsmoke was undisturbed, although the protective barrier had faded a bit in his absence. It still gave a resonant ping, though, proof that it was intact. He'd have to fortify it before the end of the day. There was a bit of dust on everything, since he'd been gone more than a month.

If Lynsay had stopped by to collect her things, she would have done it right away. Her key was probably under the door mat. He wasn't going to dwell on the end of that relationship or even check for the key at this point. The dragonsmoke didn't stop a human intruder although that person might feel a slight chill when passing through it. Hadrian couldn't smell Lynsay's skin, though, and had to conclude she hadn't come by at all.

The odd thing was that Hadrian had the sense his lair wasn't empty. How could that be? He couldn't smell or hear anyone, much less see any signs of another presence. He shook his head, thinking that recent events had made him paranoid.

He left the box from Donovan on the kitchen counter, only giving the enclosed note the barest glance. He wanted to check out the gloves and they didn't disappoint. He tugged them on, snapping his fingers so the blades extended and catching his breath in admiration. He turned his hands, admiring the blades' flexibility and craftsmanship. Quinn had set a high bar even with his traditional methods. He was so detail-oriented.

Sunlight shone through the windows and glinted on the lethal blades. Donovan had explained to Hadrian that he didn't fold them away with his clothes: in his dragon form, they merged with his claws, lengthening them into swords.

Hadrian couldn't wait to see that. He moved into the center of the large living space, aware that Balthasar was talking to Donovan already. He summoned the shift and savored the brilliant shimmer of blue light that heralded his change between forms. It always made him feel invincible to shift shape. He thought of Donovan's advice during the transition and tried to follow it. The shift rolled through him, sharpening his senses and filling him with welcome sense of power.

As always, it was done in the blink of an eye. It felt great to be in his dragon form, his tail brushing against the kitchen counter, his wings almost reaching the high ceiling of the lair.

Hadrian wanted to roar with satisfaction when he saw that Donovan's strategy had worked. The steel blades were part of his front talons, and he slashed with one claw, watching them flash. Hadrian laughed and slashed again.

"Never mind," Balthasar said into his phone. "Looks like Hadrian has nailed it."

He'd intended to shift back to his human form, but his gaze fell on a patch of sunlight on the wooden floor. He saw a footstep in the dust. A small slender footstep, like that of a woman.

Bigger than Lynsay's footprint would be.

His senses were more keen in his dragon form and he inhaled slowly, checking his impression one more time.

There *was* an intruder in his lair.

A woman, a tall woman.

Impossible.

But he could smell her skin. It was faint, so faint that he'd missed it in his human form, but the scent was there.

"Who's having a firestorm?" Alasdair asked in old-speak, glancing around.

"Here?" Balthasar asked. *"Now?"*

"Absolutely," Alasdair said with authority.

That was when Hadrian saw the faint glow of white light at the end of his talon. He lifted his claw and it brightened as he reached toward the door to the bedroom. He was aware of both Alasdair and Balthasar watching him.

Hadrian felt the faint tickle of a cold flame and desire stirred within him.

It was different from the golden sparks of the firestorms he'd witnessed in the past, but it had the identical effect upon his body and mind. His thoughts turned to sensual pleasures and his body thrummed with desire.

It was the same light that had burned when he'd had the vision of that woman at Rhys' place, the one who had kissed his cheek. She'd said then that she'd been looking for him and he didn't think it was for a good reason. After all, she'd given him that kiss of death.

Hadrian had thought she was a dream, or that it was another fake firestorm, just like Kristofer's had been at first. He'd seen the red string on her wrist, the mark of Maeve's curse. He'd concluded that the *Pyr* were being targeted, starting with him.

But she was in his lair right now. The light revealed the truth.

She'd come after him, probably to finish what she'd started. Somehow she knew that Lila and Balthasar had managed to impede the power of that kiss.

"A fake firestorm," he corrected quietly in old-speak. *"Burning white instead of yellow."*

"A spell," Balthasar agreed.

"No," Alasdair said with authority. *"An ice dragon's firestorm. I remember that Notus' firestorm burned white."*

That reference to Hadrian's father was a surprise he didn't need. If his father's firestorm had burned white and cold, this might be genuine. But how could his destined mate be intent on killing him? It didn't make sense.

Either way, he wasn't going to be easy prey.

This time, she'd be the one who was surprised.

He shifted silently back to his human form, keeping the gloves on, then eased toward the bedroom. The light brightened, the cold light of a winter morning, and its demand for sexual satisfaction redoubled.

Hadrian reminded himself that the woman hiding in his bedroom had given him a kiss of death.

That wouldn't happen twice.

Hadrian moved so quietly that he might have been a predator. Rania was impressed despite herself. She felt the movement of the air as it stirred to let him pass, but only because she was listening so closely. She heard a rumble, like thunder, which made no sense, but refused to be distracted.

Her dragon was cool and collected, a hunter. That made them two of a kind.

No. They had no common ground. She corrected herself: he would be the victim and she was the predator. Only one of them would survive this encounter, and Rania knew who it would be.

The strange white glow that had lit on his return was brightening as he approached and it was distracting. It was more than a light. It sent a thrill through Rania and reminded her how attractive Hadrian was. It made her aware of how long she'd been alone, even though she knew a man's touch came with a price. It made her yearn in a way that was irrational and had nothing to do with completing her task. She tried to ignore it, but it reached right to her very core, lighting an unwelcome spark of desire.

And it brightened, becoming more insistent, as he drew closer.

Curse whoever was challenging Maeve's magick!

Curse whoever was compromising her concentration!

Curse *him*. Hadrian could have been ugly, short or gangly. He could have been unattractive or mean. He was a blacksmith, which should have made him repellent, but he was hot in oh-so-many unexpected ways.

Had she picked the wrong dragon?

Or was she losing her edge?

Was she caught in a greater battle, between Maeve and an ambitious competitor? The dragon prince was dead and she'd thought that fight was resolved.

Rania gripped her dagger, ready to strike. The kiss of death hadn't finished Hadrian, so she'd use a more traditional method. She narrowed her eyes and fixed her attention on her task, steeling herself against this *Pyr's* appeal. He had to die by her hand, as soon as possible.

She saw the blue shimmer of light that so often heralded a change between forms for a shifter, then saw it again. She was prepared for the man to turn the corner.

Rania felt him pause just before the threshold, assessing.

He knew she was there, then. The videos had noted that the *Pyr* had keen senses. She prickled with awareness of his proximity, that infuriating light as bright as starlight. She lifted the blade with purpose.

There was a shimmer of blue, then a dragon claw suddenly snatched at her.

The scales were a rich emerald gleam, as if they'd been carved from gems, and edged in silver. She was surprised by how beautiful they were and stared in awe.

She hesitated again. How could she injure such a heavily scaled creature, let alone kill him? The dagger she'd chosen suddenly looked small and ineffective, and she doubted her choice. Rania didn't like to hesitate, not when she was working.

She had to get it together. She gripped the hilt again, then changed to the other hand, thinking her dexterity might surprise him. Incredibly, she dropped the dagger at exactly the wrong time.

The weapon clattered to the floor, sliding out of reach.

Rania stared at it. If she went after it, he'd not only have a clear sight of her but her back would be turned to him. Without it, she had no way to take him down. Should she manifest elsewhere and try again later? She was paralyzed in indecision for a precious moment.

Her prey took advantage of that. Hadrian snatched at her without coming around the corner, that claw seizing her in a merciless grip and holding her against the wall. His reach was longer than she might have expected. He moved so quickly that she couldn't have evaded him. She saw the flash of steel talons attached to his nails and her heart skipped because they looked so sharp.

Rania instantly shifted shape herself, becoming a much smaller swan, and slipped from his grasp. She took flight, leaving him with a handful of white feathers, and sensed his surprise.

It wouldn't last long.

This was her chance.

Rania launched herself through the doorway and aimed for his eyes with her claws. The white light was blinding in its intensity and the surge of raw desire through her body was staggeringly real. The emerald and silver dragon roared, spewing dragonfire that singed her wingtips. He was magnificent and powerful, his torrent of flame hot and bright. She dodged it in the last minute, but still felt the wave of heat.

Something dissolved inside her, leaving her trembling, but Rania fought on.

Unlike Hadrian, she had room to move in the great room with its high ceiling. She dove for his eyes again but he batted her aside. She knocked over a floor lamp, which shattered, and the other two *Pyr* in the kitchen swore. They didn't engage, though she wasn't sure why.

She spun to attack once more, and this time, Hadrian was less gentle. She almost got his eyes before he seized her again and flung her toward the wall of windows. Rania shifted and turned so that her back broke the glass and she tumbled out the gap in human form. Before the shards had touched the earth, she shifted shape again and soared upward in her swan form, beating her wings hard.

She flew with all her strength, but it wasn't enough. Hadrian was immediately behind her, so much larger and more powerful in his dragon form that he was gaining on her steadily. The brilliant white glow revealed his proximity. She couldn't out-run him and her heart was already pounding.

Rania spared a glance back, unable to keep from admiring his majestic power, then pivoted and spiraled down toward him again. He spun with remarkable agility, avoiding her strike, and snatched her out of the air, trapping her between his claws.

Rania was surrounded by a cage of steel talons, each one deadly sharp. She squirmed and was nicked, her blood staining one blade red and then her own white feathers. She wasn't hurt but was definitely surprised. Meanshile, Hadrian was ascending, flying her to greater heights than she routinely flew in her swan form. In her plane, it was another issue, but this was exhilirating. The wind alternatively ruffled her hair and her feathers as she rotated between forms, trying to escape.

"Beautiful," he whispered in awe.

No, she wouldn't be swayed by a compliment.

"And deadly," she insisted, digging a claw beneath his talon hard enough to draw blood. He roared and tightened his grip upon her, those sharp metal claws alarmingly close.

She was going to disappear, but he froze and she hesitated again. Rania glanced up to see that he was staring at the red cord on her wrist. It followed her between forms, a sign of her bargain with Maeve.

"I thought I remembered that," he mused. He lifted her closer to his eyes and peered at her, even as he flew onward. "What does she have against you?"

It was obvious that he understood the meaning of the red string.

"Nothing. We have a deal, one I made voluntarily."

"I doubt that," he said with skepticism.

Rania shifted and flung herself at the talons, hoping that he'd release her instead of cutting her.

She was only half right. He twisted her around and expertly cut the tips from her longest feathers on one wing. Rania gasped in outrage as the ends of the white feathers spiraled down to the earth, glistening in the sunlight.

In a way, she had to admire his choice. He hadn't technically hurt her, but she wouldn't be able to fly. He definitely wasn't a stupid dragon.

"Now, tell me who you are and why you're hunting me," he commanded.

"Or what?" Rania challenged.

"Or I'll let you go." His eyes gleamed, as if he was certain he'd cornered her. If she'd only been a shifter, like him, his conclusion would be deserved. They were high above the ground, soaring through the sky, and her inability to fly was definitely a liability. He hadn't wondered yet how she'd gotten into his lair, but Rania doubted that oversight would last long.

She looked down, as if assessing the distance to the ground, but really she was choosing how much to reveal. How much could she learn before she left? He was sure he had her at a disadvantage and might confess some detail she could use against him later.

Far down below, his dark-haired *Pyr* friend with the man-bun was standing outside the lair, looking up. There was a shimmer of blue light around him but he didn't shift yet.

She heard a rumble, like a freight train or thunder but close by, and saw the other *Pyr* nod, as if agreeing with something. He went back into the lair, presumably returning to the other one.

That rumble must be the old-speak she'd read about in her research. She'd momentarily forgotten about that.

"Deciding that you need me after all?" Hadrian asked with confidence.

"How dare you cut my feathers?" Rania demanded. "I won't be able to fly."

He fixed her with a bright glare. "You gave me a kiss of death. You invaded my lair. You intend to kill me and are using a firestorm that's possibly fake to distract me. I don't think I'm the one who's daring too much." He soared high above the clouds and it was just as thrilling to fly in a dragon's grasp as any other way.

One word caught Rania's attention.

Possibly.

"If the firestorm's fake, it's not my doing," she argued, just to see what he would say.

"If it's real, then we're destined mates and you shouldn't be trying to kill me."

The white light shimmered and shone, its blinding brightness making it hard to think of anything other than getting naked with Hadrian. What kind of lover would he be? Quick and to the point? No, he'd take his time. Rania knew it. Were his thoughts turning in the same direction?

The firestorm was about a *Pyr* meeting his destined mate. If so, he might be more susceptible to her human form.

Rania shifted shape within his grasp and was rewarded by his start of surprise. He gave her a slow and appreciative survey, making her conclude that she was right. Unfortunately, she was distracted, too. That look made her warm. In fact, it made her tingle. It made her think of the big bed in his bedroom and what they could do there...

"I don't believe that story about the firestorm," she said. "I think it's a ruse and a lie, a trick to get sex whenever you want it."

He was obviously insulted. "I don't need a trick to get sex," he retorted and she could believe it. "The firestorm is the sign of a *Pyr* meeting his destined mate, the one woman who can bear his son." He said this with complete conviction.

Was he a romantic? She'd never have expected that.

"How many destined mates do you have? You dragon-shifters can live a long time."

"Only one," he insisted. "A treasure worth waiting for."

Rania wasn't going to be swayed by something so ridiculous. Believing in the firestorm put Hadrian at a disadvantage. If a destined mate was so rare, Rania guessed that he'd be reluctant to injure her, much less kill her, even in self-defense.

She could work with that.

He lifted her in front of his face, examining her closely. The air was cool, but Rania felt warm and protected in his grasp. There was something about that dragon perusal that made her feel as if he could guess all her secrets. She held his stare, defying him to do so.

"Why me?" he asked in a rumble. She felt the vibration of his voice, which seemed intimate. Seductive.

Rania bristled. "Why *not* you?"

Hadrian shook his head. The sunlight glittered on the emerald and silver of his scales, making him look like a jeweled treasure. "You have a reason." He did have a way of seeing past her glib answers.

It seemed harmless to tell him a bit more. "I have to kill one of the *Pyr*. I chose you."

He seemed to be intrigued. "Why?"

"Because you're a blacksmith, as well as a dragon shifter."

"But Quinn Tyrrell is the Smith of the *Pyr*."

"And he has kids. It's not going to ruin anyone's life when you die." Rania was surprised that she'd admitted so much, but something about this dragon's intensity made her talkative—or defensive about her choice.

His sudden smile surprised her even more. She hadn't thought dragons could smile, or that she'd find the sight charming. Being wrong on both counts didn't help her regain her focus.

"It'll ruin mine," he noted with amusement and she was almost surprised into a smile herself, because that was true.

Instead she scowled. "That would be the point."

He didn't argue it. He just flew higher, and she admired his powerful grace. His wings were so large that he was able to beat them slowly yet remain aloft. He made flight look effortless.

"You're an assassin for the Dark Queen, but you have a soft spot for children," he mused and Rania felt herself flush. "That seems inconsistent."

"I'm just not going to be the one to hurt them."

To her relief, he didn't immediately pursue that.

Rania continued. "And no one says my victims didn't deserve what they got."

He nodded slowly, considering this. "Why a *Pyr*?"

"I just follow the rules."

"What if you die in the attempt?"

Rania shrugged. "If I were you, I wouldn't count on getting lucky. I have a reputation."

He laughed. His voice dropped low and that white light seemed to burn even brighter. It certainly prompted a stronger reaction within Rania and she had a hard time keeping herself from stroking his claw.

Why did she want to touch him so badly?

"Maybe I feel lucky now," he mused.

This had to be beguiling. "Maybe you shouldn't."

"Maybe I want one last wish before you kill me."

"Maybe you're not that lucky."

Rania caught her breath as Hadrian pivoted smoothly and dove back toward the earth with incredible speed. Her hair whipped around her face as the earth loomed ever closer. She loved to fly but she never flew to such great heights in her swan form—and even in a plane, she preferred to be the one at the controls. A dive like this was a daring and thrilling move. It was an expression of confidence: he knew he could shift or stop at the last minute, even at such a speed.

She admired that. She clutched Hadrian's talon as he rapidly descended toward his house, letting him think she was more alarmed than she was. If he meant to alarm her into confessing more or agreeing to his request, she could respect the tactic.

He sped up. "So tell me: are you the pawn of the Dark Queen or are you in league with her?"

"Does it matter?" The earth was looming closer. No, he was aiming for the rocks in the river outside his studio.

"I think it does." He was too calm. Rania guessed he had planned a trick.

Well, she had one of her own.

"I don't have to tell," she replied.

"Maybe I can encourage you," he said, his tone daring. He opened his claws, smiled at her, then let her drop.

Rania shifted to her swan form, flailed ineffectively with her cut wing feathers, then shifted back to her human form again. She was falling fast and it was terrifying. Her heart raced, even though she had no intention of crashing into the earth.

She let Hadrian think she was in desperate straits, saw him surge forward to intervene in the last minute like a conquering hero, then played a trick of her own.

She wasn't going to owe him anything, even if it meant making her abilities clear.

Rania chose to retrieve her knife.

CHAPTER TWO

The swan maiden disappeared, right before Hadrian's eyes.

He blinked but he wasn't mistaken. She was gone. She'd switched between forms, changing from a swan to a woman then back again. Both were gorgeous. She'd fallen fast and just as he'd been about to snatch her out of the air—and earn her gratitude—then she'd vanished in the blink of an eye.

His plan had failed.

Worse, he had no idea where she'd gone. Hadrian couldn't see her. He couldn't smell her. He couldn't figure out how she could have hidden herself, but she was gone.

And she'd disappeared just when things had been getting interesting.

Maybe that was why she'd fled.

He swooped low over the river, then flew in a slow circle around his lair. There was no sign of his mate—beyond the half dozen white feather tips on the ground. He narrowed his eyes and used all of his senses, but it made no difference. She should have hit the ground hard. She should have been grateful for his last minute rescue. His ploy should have been a game-changer.

But he hadn't had the chance to save her.

Hadrian was annoyed. He liked plans. He liked executing them flawlessly. He liked using his powers for good, and winning the agreement of his reluctant mate to satisfy the firestorm would definitely be for the good.

But she had a plan of her own.

Why did she want to kill him? It almost sounded as if she was on Maeve's team, but that made no sense. She was a shifter, too, which meant she was included in the Dark Queen's inventory of Others to be exterminated. She didn't seem to be stupid. How could she have overlooked that?

He'd been surprised when she shifted shape the first time, when she'd become a beautiful and delicate swan. She was graceful and lovely, but there was a hard light in her eyes, one that followed her between forms. He'd known that she would finish him off without a heartbeat of remorse.

And then when she'd become a woman, she might have been his every fantasy come true. She was just as delicately made, her skin pale and her hair as fair as sunlight, but she was tall and strong. Her eyes were the glorious blue he recalled from their first encounter and her lips were full. But that fury in her expression had been undiminished.

There was no doubt that she'd happily cut out his liver and roast it for dinner.

How could his destined mate be an assassin determined to end his days?

Hadrian could have killed her in either form in self-defense. He might have done so if not for the combination of the firestorm's light and the red string on her wrist. She wasn't just his mate: she was in Maeve's thrall. He'd learned to respect the Dark Queen's powers. He knew that she could cast a spell to compel anyone to act against their own will—or arrange the situation so that making a deal was the only choice. He knew from personal experience that being bound to the Dark Queen's command was horrific and that her bargains never ended in anyone else's favor.

Killing him was probably what his mate had to do to gain her freedom. Hadrian couldn't blame her for that.

But he wasn't prepared to die just yet.

The white flame diminished to a glow, but it was still burning.

She hadn't gone far.

Of course not. Her quest wasn't completed.

Hadrian scanned his surroundings for a glimpse of her.

Nothing.

Well, nothing beyond what felt like a cold rock in his cheek. The place where she'd kissed him when they'd first met had become heavier and colder, like it had been reactivated by her presence. It was colder than anything he'd felt before and it seemed to spread frost through his muscles.

Hadrian forced himself to review what he knew. His mate could spontaneously disappear, which probably meant she could manifest wherever she wanted. He'd heard about *Slayers* who had been able to do that, but Rafferty was the only one of the *Pyr* with that ability. She was still close and he could follow the light of the firestorm to find her. He needed to have surprise on his side, though, to have a chance to negotiate. Surprise made her hesitate, and that's what had saved his butt so far.

If he could surprise her again, they might be able to find another way to break the curse together. If he could help her gain her freedom in another way, she might be glad to fulfill the firestorm.

In that instant, he remembered that she'd dropped her knife in his bedroom.

Hadrian raced toward his lair, dove through the broken window and shifted shape en route. Balthasar and Alasdair stared in astonishment as he ran across the main room in human form, but stood back, just as he'd requested earlier in old-speak.

The dagger was in the bedroom and the bedroom was the perfect place to close to his destined mate. He knew a few ways to surprise her there and smiled at the prospect.

The white light of the firestorm flared to greater brightness, feeding the burn of desire already thrumming in his veins, and Hadrian found himself feeling very persuasive.

The dagger was exactly where she'd dropped it.

Rania manifested in Hadrian's bedroom and reached for the blade, smiling with satisfaction. She was a bit superstitious about weapons and had chosen this one particularly for a dragon slaying.

Her fingertips had just brushed the hilt when white light flared behind her. Even that warning wasn't enough. She was attacked from behind before she could turn, and she knew who her assailant had to be. The dagger spun across the hardwood floor as Hadrian caught her up and flung her onto the bed. He trapped her beneath his weight, holding one wrist in each hand as she shifted shape over and over again. No matter whether she was swan or woman, he held fast. She could have manifested elsewhere, but she wasn't leaving without her knife.

"Let go of me!" she demanded, feeling an old fear at a most inconvenient time.

"Promise to stay and I will," he offered.

She studied him with skepticism. "Is that a joke?"

"Of course not. I want a chance to talk."

She stopped shifting, remaining in her human form, and he smiled. "Talk fast," she said and to her surprise, he did release her wrists.

Why would he trust her?

Hadrian braced himself over her, which didn't give her much of a reprieve from that piercing gaze. "For starters, you're my destined mate."

"I'm your destiny," Rania corrected hotly, but the gleam in his eyes wasn't fear.

He continued with an alluring confidence. "And that means we're stronger together."

"You can't know that. You don't know anything about me."

"But I do know that. The firestorm is always right." He smiled a little. "Even when it seems to be wrong."

"That makes no sense."

"Kristofer's firestorm was a spell, but when the spell was broken, he had a real firestorm with the same mate." He nodded, convinced of his own logic. "The firestorm never lies."

Rania was confused by his conviction, and by the firestorm. That white light sparked and sizzled around and between them, emitting a brilliant glow and making her think of better things they could be doing on the bed. She was hot and shivery at the same time, furious with him and wanting to wrap herself around him, too. She wriggled, feeling like her body was following his agenda instead of her own, and Hadrian's gaze darkened.

"What's your name?" he murmured.

She found his low voice more seductive than she wanted him to realize, so spoke sharply. "You don't need to know."

"But I *want* to know." He bent over her, inhaling deeply of her scent and she felt his chest rumble with a little growl of satisfaction. Her nipples beaded and she almost sighed with pleasure. "So perfect," he murmured, then touched his lips to the side of her throat. The almost-kiss made Rania's heart leap as she gasped in surprise. Something melted deep inside her and her blood simmered.

She'd never kissed a dragon shifter before.

Having the opportunity was more enticing that it should have been. He was her intended victim! Killing him was the key to her freedom. But Rania closed her eyes and enjoyed his touch, all the same.

Maybe it was just strategic to find out a little more.

Hadrian grazed her earlobe with his teeth and Rania felt her lips part as he kissed her ear. His caress was so gentle that she couldn't fight against him—and when he continued a trail of burning kisses along her throat, she could only enjoy. She closed her eyes, unable to think about anything other than smoking hot seduction.

Maybe just one taste.

Just to find out what it was like.

She turned her face toward him without intending to do any such thing and Hadrian kissed the corner of her mouth. His touch was so arousing that it made her forget everything—except wanting more.

"Tell me about the kiss of death," he invited.

Rania's eyes flew open but his mouth brushed over hers with captivating slowness. "I could give you another," she threatened, but knew she sounded breathless. It wasn't true anyway. She'd used up her last kiss of death.

That was the problem.

"Shouldn't one do the job?"

"Yes."

He grinned down at her, his eyes twinkling. He looked mischievous, cocky and a bit wicked, a combination that worked for Rania in a big way. "Then I don't have anything to worry about, do I? The damage is done." He touched his lips to hers again, coaxing her to participate in their embrace. "Tell me how it works," he invited. He was overconfident, but Rania admired warriors too much to be immune to that trait.

Playing along might be strategic. It might lull him into complacency.

That was all the rationalization Rania needed.

She parted her lips and stretched toward him, inviting more of a kiss. Hadrian didn't hesitate to slant his mouth over hers. His kiss was persuasive and powerful, demanding enough to drive every sane thought from her mind. She felt how he held himself back, and the combination of tenderness and strength was absolutely perfect. She opened her mouth to him intuitively, loving the feel of his arousal against her thighs. It was thrilling to know that she could excite a dragon shifter.

He broke their kiss, then surveyed her, his gaze hot. The mark of the kiss of death on his cheek was turning silver, as if molten sterling had been embedded in his cheek.

She'd never seen it do that before.

Rania remembered a bit late that he'd asked a question. "It waits for opportunity," she admitted, exhaling her words in a rush. Hadrian kissed her ear, then interlaced his fingers with hers. He'd noticed what she liked and was doing it more. She respected his technique—he was using her weakness against her, and she didn't want him to stop.

"What kind of opportunity?"

Rania parted her thighs, welcoming his weight against her. He was hard and she rolled her hips, her motion making them both inhale sharply. "An injury," she confessed, her voice so breathless that it didn't sound like her own. "If it should be a fatal one, the kiss accelerates its effect. If it should be a minor one, the kiss ensures it becomes fatal. A victim could die of a paper cut."

"Sounds fearsome," he murmured.

"It is." Rania opened her eyes and looked at him, pulling away slightly to study the silver mark with uncertainty. Why was it changing? "Why *are* you alive?"

He lifted a brow, which made him look reckless and sexy. "Strong constitution?"

"It's not enough."

"A healer's intervention?"

Rania shook her head. "It shouldn't be enough. It's not possible to heal a kiss of death. It's a killing spell."

Hadrian's eyes darkened with intent as he bent to brush his lips across hers again. It was a taste, a tease, and a temptation. Rania found herself reaching up to meet his touch.

This time, he closed his mouth over hers and kissed her thoroughly. This kiss was less gentle and more demanding, a kiss that seared her very soul. Rania was lost in sensation and didn't want to be found. The white light flooded through her as she surrendered to Hadrian's seductive touch. He hadn't been kidding when he'd said he didn't need a trick to get lucky. All he needed was his kiss. She moaned a little when he deepened his kiss, demanding more. The heat rose within her with insistence and she found herself wrapping one leg around his, trying to draw him even closer.

It had been far too long.

To her embarrassment, he was the one who broke their kiss. "But a selkie healer helped me," he murmured and it took Rania a moment to figure out what he was talking about. He watched her intently all the while.

"I doubt that the healer's nature matters," she admitted, studying his mouth again. "Maybe dragon shifters are immune." She was talking too much and she knew it but she couldn't stop.

Was she beguiled?

Hadrian shook his head. "No, I felt its effect. I still do."

"It's changing," she admitted, hearing her own uncertainty.

"Why?"

Rania shook her head, mystified. "I've never seen it do this before. I've never seen it be ineffective before."

He smiled and she could only stare. "Maybe it's because of the firestorm."

"You can't really believe that we're destined mates."

"What if I do? What if that's what makes me impossible to kill?"

Rania felt an uncharacteristic surge of despair. "No. That can't be it. I can't fail."

"Why not?" He was watching her closely, divining her secrets again. "Everyone fails sometimes."

"Not me. I can't." She wriggled against him, remembering her mission a little too late. "You don't know what's at stake..."

"Then tell me."

Rania glanced at her wrist and the red string, then found herself telling him the truth. "The deal is thirteen kills to set thirteen free."

"I expected one for one, but thirteen is a lot. Am I lucky thirteen?"

She nodded, then shook her head with a frown. "You're not lucky."

"I'll guess you're one of the thirteen who will be freed." He frowned slightly in concentration and rolled to his side, letting his hand slide down to her waist. She liked the weight of it there, and the way he absently drew circles against her skin with his thumb. "Who are the others?"

"My twelve brothers." She took a breath, aware of the way her nipples tightened. The white light was blinding and distracting, never mind how Hadrian's eyes glittered in awareness. It felt warm in the room, despite the cool fury of the firestorm.

"So you made a deal to set them free, and you're keeping your end of the bargain," he said, with a nod of approval. He withdrew slightly, as if he wanted to collect his thoughts, watching her closely. His thumb still circled, sending desire radiating through her. She braced herself but his next words surprised her, all the same. "I hope you're not thinking the Dark Queen is going to keep her promise."

Rania was insulted. "Of course, she will. We have a deal..."

"She'll change it." Hadrian interrupted her protest. "She doesn't care about keeping her word. She only cares about winning. She won't let you go that easily, or even your brothers."

"What do you know about it?"

"I know about the Dark Queen," he said grimly. "I know she lies and cheats to get her way."

Rania felt protective of Maeve. "You don't know that..."

"I do. I know that red string burns because I had one, too. And I was forced to dance until my feet bled." He slid a hand up to cup her breast, admiration lighting his expression as he watched its progress. He swallowed. She stared at his smile as he teased her nipple to a taut peak, rolling it between his finger and thumb, coaxing its response even through her clothes. "What's your name, swan-maiden?" he whispered, his voice husky. "You have to know that we're both on her list of intended victims."

"Speak for yourself," Rania said, pulling back a bit. She was alarmed that she was so susceptible to him and this firestorm.

He frowned. "What do you mean?"

"I don't have to tell you anything more. I've told you too much already."

Hadrian smiled crookedly at her and the sight was enough to make her stare. Had she ever seen a more attractive man? "It's like you *want* to talk," he murmured. Before she could argue, he flattened his hand and slid his palm down the length of her, the warm weight of his hand easing beneath the waistband of her tights. Rania knew his destination and couldn't bring herself to evade his caress. He met her gaze, waiting and watching, but she swallowed and stayed put.

Just one touch.

Then she'd finish him.

When Hadrian's fingertips slid into the warm wet heat of her, Rania knew she'd never felt anything better. She arched her back and gasped. He stole a kiss and she parted her legs, unwilling to deny herself the pleasure he offered. His fingers were gentle and strong, just like him, and he caressed her with a surety that brought her blood to a boil.

Just a little bit more. Just a little indulgence...

"You have told me a lot," he agreed in a whisper, his lips against her ear. Rania shivered with pleasure. "Maybe you need to confess your secrets."

"Or maybe I'm beguiled." The possibility was a reminder that made Rania pull away slightly.

Hadrian shook his head emphatically. "I'm not beguiling you."

"As if I would believe you."

"You should. It's true. There would be flames in my eyes if I was beguiling."

Rania looked. There were no flames. Was he telling the truth?

He nodded as if he'd guessed her thoughts. "I am. What if we make a deal?" he suggested, his gaze hot. "What if we satisfy the firestorm before you kill me? I'll make it worth your while."

Rania stared at him in astonishment. "You want me to have your son?"

Hadrian nodded, resolute. "You're making thirteen assassinations to free your brothers. Although I don't love your choice, I can respect your loyalty to your family. I think we have similar ideas about defending what's important."

"And what's important to you is the firestorm?"

"Right." He grinned at her. "It's a once-in-a-lifetime chance to have a son. How could I turn my back on that? It's a legacy."

"Nothing says you have to fulfill it."

"But I should. It's an obligation and an opportunity."

"It doesn't sound like much of an opportunity to me."

"But what if we made that deal? What if we surrendered to the firestorm, and then I made it easy for you to kill me?"

Rania couldn't believe it but Hadrian was serious.

"You'd let your assassin have your son?"

He chuckled. "I'd let my destined mate have my son."

Rania opened her mouth to argue but Hadrian captured her mouth with his, slowly and decisively, and she forgot whatever she was going to say. He was going to win his argument with sensation and she couldn't think of a reason to protest. She already guessed that it would be great. There was something deeply satisfying about his obvious desire. It made her aware of every pleasure she'd denied herself during these centuries in Maeve's service.

It made her consider his suggestion.

Even, potentially, at the price of bringing a *Pyr* son into the world.

"What do you know about the firestorm?" Hadrian whispered in her ear long moments later.

Rania was trying to catch her breath and gather her thoughts, without success on either front. "As much as I need to," she replied. "I'm not going to have a *Pyr* son."

Hadrian smiled with that dragon confidence that made her want to get naked with him. "I might convince you."

"Good luck," she replied, her heart leaping at the possibility.

"I like a challenge." His lashes swept down and he smiled, the combination making him look mysterious and potent. "Maybe you'll find me persuasive," he said so softly that his words were a rumble she felt against her chest.

Maybe she would.

He bent and kissed her ear again, his fingers working their magic against her. His breath gave her shivers. His touch made her gasp. Rania didn't know whether she'd be able to stop their embrace. She was pretty sure she didn't want to. Her leg was already locking around his, as if her body had a will of its own, and she was breathless as she stared into his eyes. They were so green. His mouth was so firm. He was taking his time, tormenting her with temptation, willing her to agree.

Rania could have disappeared.

She could have shifted shape.

But being the woman Hadrian was determined to seduce suited her just fine.

What if she made love to him—or let him make love to her? It might be kind to let him satisfy the firestorm as his last living act.

Although kindness had never been on her agenda before.

She was hesitating again, doubting her path, which wasn't like her at all. Maybe this firestorm was changing her somehow.

Maybe a certain dragon shifter was.

Hadrian brushed his mouth across hers again, a caress as gentle as the touch of butterfly wings, and Rania didn't want to think about anything anymore.

Strategically, sex might lead to a weak moment, one in which she could easily overwhelm this powerful dragon shifter.

Nothing said they had to complete the act. She just needed to catch him by surprise.

When Hadrian leaned closer, eyes gleaming, she reached to meet him halfway. She sighed with satisfaction when he slanted his mouth over hers, claiming her with his touch, then speared her fingers into his hair, drawing him closer.

This might be his last hour. She should make sure it was worth dying for.

Hadrian didn't trust his mate one bit—but he was enchanted by her. He was sure that she was welcoming his touch because she meant to trick him, but the insistent burn of the firestorm made it impossible to turn away from her. The firestorm fed his need for her and drove all coherent thought from his mind. When she welcomed him and kissed him back, there was nothing else in the world but his perfect destined mate.

Even though he didn't know her name.

Even though she was an assassin for the Fae, obligated to kill him. Hadrian chose to believe in the promise of the firestorm.

She was so sweet, her lips so soft, her enthusiasm so unexpected. She opened her mouth to him and touched her tongue to his, driving him wild. She was tentative, as if she was more accustomed to fighting than loving, but Hadrian was more than ready to guide her on this new path. Her hand was locked in his hair, drawing him closer in silent demand.

Okay, she was direct. That was best of all.

He heard a door close and knew that Alasdair and Balthasar had left the lair. He didn't actually care whether they overheard, but his mate might prefer the privacy.

Her confession, that she served Maeve's will to free her brothers, proved they had traits in common. Hadrian would have done anything for his fellow *Pyr*, and he had to admit that might include assassination if there was no other choice. He knew that when Maeve had compelled him to dance, he would have promised anything to end his own agony.

His mate was trapped in a bad situation. That didn't make her a bad person.

She was wearing black, like a burglar, tights and a hoodie, boots and a long-sleeved T-shirt that hugged her curves. He could feel her lithe strength when he ran his hands over her and he liked how responsive she was to his touch. That was another sign that this partnership was destined to be, and that the firestorm had chosen correctly for him.

And she was beautiful. It was easy to remember the glorious shine of her feathers, the grace she possessed in flight, how alluring she was in either form.

He braced himself over her, kissing her thoroughly as he undid the zipper of her sweatshirt. He pushed it off, tugging her shirt and bra after it, then bent to take one rosy nipple in his mouth. There was an old healed scar on her midriff, but he didn't want to talk about the past. She wore a ring on a chain around her neck, a ring big enough to have been a man's. The stone glowed, the way some opals or moonstones did. Hadrian didn't study it, since he had better things to do. He did wonder then whether she had another romantic commitment or a relationship that hadn't worked out.

Before he could ask, she caught his head in her hands and pulled him down for a scorching kiss, moaning with pleasure as if she couldn't do anything else. He was breathless by the time he lifted his head and could turn his attention to her nipple again. He wanted to give her pleasure. He wanted to convince her that the firestorm was right for both of them.

He was amazed by her splendor. She was so fair, her skin pale and smooth, each breast of exactly the right size to fill his palm. Her nipples were rosy and became redder as he tormented them. He teased that first nipple to a peak, then turned his attention to the other one, kissing and suckling until they were both taut and red and she was squirming. He could smell her need and that made his heart pound.

He ran his hands down her sides and pushed off her tights, taking her boots with them and casting it all to the floor. She was naked in his bed, her eyes vivid blue, a faint flush on her cheeks as the radiance of the firestorm crackled and snapped between them. She reached for him, but Hadrian ducked down and closed his mouth over her sweet heat. She gasped in surprise then arched back, opening her legs to him and falling back against the mattress. She was slick and wet, hot and luscious, and he fought to hold his own desire in check as he gave her pleasure.

He'd prove to her that he was worth keeping alive.

He tasted and teased her, driving her toward her release then retreating, ensuring that she was burning by the time he finally pushed her over the edge. She screamed and dug her nails into his back, thrashing in her release so that he grinned at her enthusiasm. Their gazes locked for an incendiary moment and he felt as if time stopped.

Then he saw the flash of her eyes as she tackled him, her move taking them both to the floor. She stripped off his shirt with impatience, then ran her hands over his bare chest. She smiled as she ran a fingertip around the silhouette of his dragon tattoo and her touch left a line of cold fire.

Her orgasm had shattered her shell, or maybe broken the ice that held her captive. Her gaze was on fire, her hair tousled, her lips red. Her cheeks were flushed and her hunger for his touch was undisguised. Hadrian had never seen anything or anyone as gloriously beautiful as his mate bent on seduction.

He was hers for the taking.

She surveyed him with satisfaction—as if she knew it—then bent and suckled his nipple, exactly as he had teased hers. She grazed it with her teeth when it was taut, making him burn for more. Hadrian was content to be at her mercy, savoring the sight of her as she turned her attention to the other nipple. Her hair had become loose and it fell around them like a golden curtain, or a net. Hadrain ran his hands through its silky length, content to be her catch.

Her smile was mischievous as she unbuckled his belt and pushed down his jeans. Hadrian couldn't resist the urge to lock his hands around her waist and draw her closer. He captured her lips with his and kissed her once again. White sparks flew as she closed her hand around his erection, and Hadrian found himself moaning as she tormented him with pleasure. She mimicked him perfectly, taking him almost to the summit then easing off, ensuring that desire made his heart thunder.

When he knew he couldn't hold back, he scooped her up and turned her around, settling her on top of him. She smiled as she walked her hands down his chest, then lowered herself over him. There was awe in her expression as she took the tip of him inside her and she moved so slowly that he thought anticipation might kill him. She was so hot and tight that Hadrian was barely able to take a breath. She moved with such deliberation, that the pleasure was exquisite.

He wanted it to last forever.

He knew he'd never manage that.

She exhaled slowly when he was buried completely inside her, closing her eyes. He wondered then how long it had been since she'd been with a man—she had to have done it before, didn't she? Then he caught a glimpse of her one hand moving quickly, away from his side. He wondered at that, then remembered.

The knife!

Hadrian rolled his mate to her back in the other direction, ensuring that the knife was out of reach. He saw her gaze flick toward it.

"Not yet," he murmured as if he hadn't noticed, rubbing against her so that she gasped.

When they kissed, she stretched one hand toward the knife again. Hadrian moved so that he apparently struck it by accident, sending it dancing across the floor. He pretended not to notice either the knife or her quick inhalation. He heard the blade hit the far wall and knew she couldn't reach it there.

Clever and determined. He liked her more with every passing moment.

He moved deeper inside her, catching her nape in his hand and kissed her again. The firestorm burned furiously, its light blindingly white, its power obliterating even his sense of danger.

There was just his mate, wrapped tightly around him; his mate, kissing him back; his mate whispering incoherently with pleasure. Just when he thought he couldn't bear any more, the firestorm increased his sense of union. Hadrian's heart matched its pace to hers; his breathing came at the same rate as hers. He looked into her eyes and felt the most powerful connection he'd experienced in his life.

He had to convince her to let him survive.

They had to find another way to save her brothers. He knew it could be done.

Her eyes widened in wonder, their gazes locked, and he was sure she felt the same potent force. She pulled him down and kissed him with sudden fervor, her silent demand taking them both higher and higher. He'd never felt anything more right and his heart thundered at the prospect of their future together.

The firestorm burned and crackled, sending white sparks in every direction, making his blood boil, and he knew they'd come in unison. He thrust and rubbed against her, heard her gasp, felt her pulse leap...

And then she was gone.

Hadrian was alone, clutching at air.

She'd vanished again.

He rolled to his back and roared with frustration.

He was alone, naked, and two seconds from the biggest climax of his life. He clenched a fist and pounded it against the floor.

So close.

She'd planned it that way.

Why?

Rania was losing her edge.

How had she come so close to making love with a dragon shifter? Was she losing her mind, too? Why would she even risk the possibility of conceiving a *Pyr* son? Maeve would probably count that as nulling out Hadrian's death—one more dragon shifter cancelled one less—and would insist that she fulfill another assignment.

She'd flung herself out of the lair and into the forest nearby, shifting shape so that she manifested there as a swan. She'd managed to seize her clothes on her departure, but not her dagger.

Rania felt flustered and chose the swan form on purpose. It gave her a moment to collect her thoughts. In swan form, her thinking was much more linear, so it seemed irrational that she'd forgotten her objective for even a moment. She groomed herself, smoothing her feathers into place with deliberate gestures. It was impossible to miss the cut wing feathers, which didn't help her to dismiss her thoughts of Hadrian.

The sooner this dragon shifter was dead, the better.

Rania sorted out her clothes, hidden beneath her feathers. She had to be able to shift smoothly and not end up in her tights in a tangle. That calmed her, too. It was imperative that she retrieve her knife, and not just to finish the assignment. It was part of her collection and specially selected for this assignment. It was sharp and lethal, a beautiful weapon that she could rely upon.

She wasn't going to start having doubts about the untimely demise of this dragon shifter. She'd chosen Hadrian, and there was no changing that now.

He was the one.

Rania realized that there was a car driving down the narrow lane that led to Hadrian's lair. She moved closer to watch, curious, still in her swan form. The car stopped at the last curve and she could see that a woman was driving it. The woman studied the vehicles in the driveway as Rania watched. There were two Land Rovers, a blue one and a green one. The blue one had been there when Rania had first arrived, so the green one must be Hadrian's. The woman's indecision was as clear as her longing, and Rania wondered who she was—and what she had to do with Hadrian and the *Pyr*.

The woman was pretty, with long red hair that she'd tied up in a ponytail. She frowned at the house, seemed to wipe away tears, then shook her head with frustration. Was she a girlfriend? An admirer? Rania wasn't sure, but she memorized the license plate for future reference.

The woman backed up the car and abruptly turned around, grinding the gears, then drove away from the lair so quickly that Rania had to jump back to be hidden in the shadows.

Once the woman was gone, Rania shifted back to her human form. The clipping of her feathers had followed her between forms: her fingernails on that hand looked as if they'd been trimmed shorter than the others. Rania wished she had a way to make the nails on both hands match.

Maybe she'd use Hadrian's clippers once she'd finished her assignment. She smiled at the image of herself, fixing her nails over the body of her victim. No, she'd go straight back to Fae to collect the reward she'd earned. There'd be no more time in the mortal realm than was absolutely necessary.

Rania turned up the collar of her coat, shivering a little at the cooler air. Her resolve grew. It would be evening soon and she wanted to ensure that Hadrian didn't live to see the dawn. This assignment would only get harder the longer it lasted, given the persuasive charm of this dragon shifter. As she walked toward his home, that white glow began to burn a little brighter and she steeled herself against the direction that it turned her thoughts.

She wasn't going to think about being cheated of a second massive orgasm.

She wasn't going to go back for more of that.

She'd wait until the *Pyr* went to sleep, then strike like a cobra in the night.

Hadrian would never know what had hit him—and he'd have no chance to persuade her to forget her oblication to Maeve.

By dawn, she'd be done.

CHAPTER THREE

hy had Hadrian's mate disappeared in that exact moment? Why would she sacrifice that pleasure?

Something else was more important.

Maybe she had doubts about the firestorm.

It only made sense that she might be uncertain about having his son. He'd lived his whole life waiting for the firestorm, but it was a big expectation to spring on someone within moments of meeting.

He recalled that ring on the chain around her neck and wondered if there might be another reason. Was she in love with another guy? Was that part of the reason she'd agreed to Maeve's bargain? Or had her heart been broken so badly that she never wanted to get involved with anyone again.

When it came to his mate, Hadrian had questions for his questions. He pushed his hands through his hair, then frowned at the realization that it was the second time she'd disappeared. She'd vanished into thin air when they'd been fighting, too. Plus, an ability to spontaneously manifest elsewhere would explain how she'd gotten into his lair without tripping any alarms in the first place. The dragonsmoke wouldn't have been an obstacle to her, but the plain old alarm system should have worked. Make that three times. Hadrian had to admit that he hadn't been thinking clearly since arriving home, thanks to the firestorm and the fact that his mate was trying to kill him.

He had to lift his game or she might succeed.

Alasdair was sure the firestorm was real, but maybe she was deliberately using it against him. She might take advantage of how distracting it was. After all, she had motivation. She was trying to save herself and her twelve brothers. Hadrian could understand that.

He had to be ready when she returned. He pushed to his feet and picked up his clothes. Hers were gone, which meant she'd made some fast moves. He was impressed.

Where had she gone? There was no glow from the firestorm, so she wasn't close. He supposed the possibilities were infinite—or close to it. She might even have gone to Fae. He had no idea.

When would she be back? Hadrian doubted he'd get a lot of warning when she did return. She'd probably manifest right beside him, a blade at his throat. His heart skipped. She was a hunter: she wouldn't take the chance of the firestorm's light announcing her approach.

But he had her knife. She'd definitely come back for her weapon.

She'd tried to retrieve it twice already.

He picked up the dagger and took it with him into the bathroom. If she wanted to reclaim this weapon, she'd have to fight him for it first.

He eyed his own reflection before turning on the shower, noticing how the kiss of death had changed. He turned his head and it caught the light. It looked like a piece of embedded jewelry, but its chill went right to his marrow.

Was the firestorm the reason it hadn't worked? Or was it just working slowly? Hadrian wished he knew.

His mate might wait until he was asleep to attack. That's what Hadrian would have done in her place. He'd have to be both lucky and fast to evade her then.

He had to find a way to improve his chances of survival.

What if he didn't survive? Under a hot stream of water in the shower, he forced himself to consider the worst case scenario, of dying soon, before satisfying the firestorm. What a waste that would be! But sadly, it wasn't out of the range of possibilities.

He wasn't going to wallow and he wouldn't feel sorry for himself. He would make a plan and execute it—no pun intended.

He'd make every moment count.

The first thing Hadrian had to do was start replicating those gloves. If nothing else, he'd leave a legacy that counted. He called to the guys in old-speak as he dressed so they'd know they wouldn't be interrupting anything when they returned to the house, then considered her dagger again.

Why this one?

Hadrian picked up the knife, testing the weight of it in his hand. It was a good weapon, well-balanced and beautifully made. It was ornate and unusual, and its characteristics might give him some insight into his mate.

"What's that?" Balthasar demanded when Hadrian strolled into the kitchen. He was already making pasta and Alasdair was stirring sauce. They were both trying to avoid showing their curiosity, but Hadrian thought his lair reeked of their unasked questions.

"The weapon my mate used to try to kill me," he said, setting it on the counter.

"This time," Alasdair added. "Last time, it was her kiss of death."

"Which apparently should have worked." Hadrian addressed Balthasar.

"That's probably Lila's doing," Balthasar said. "Anticipating two kinds of shifters helping each other would be a stretch."

Hadrian shook his head. "She said it shouldn't have made a difference. It's a wound no one can heal."

"Then why aren't you dead?" Balthasar asked. He got pasta bowls from the cupboard and the two *Pyr* served up a hot meal.

"I'm not sure that she even knows."

"Trust you to break the rules," Alasdair teased and they grinned at each other.

"It's an expectation I don't mind challenging," Hadrian said, his gaze drawn back to the dagger before he sat down. "Thanks, guys. This smells great."

"Hunger is the best sauce, as they say," Balthasar agreed easily.

"So?" Alasdair demanded as soon as Hadrian had taken a bite. "Did you satisfy the firestorm?"

"No."

"What?" his friends demanded in unison.

"She can vanish into thin air."

The other two *Pyr* exchanged a glance. "Is that a swan maiden thing?" Alasdair asked.

"Or just her thing?" Balthasar asked.

"I think it's her thing. She's an assassin for the Dark Queen, and has to take thirteen lives to free herself and her twelve brothers. I'm number thirteen."

"As if Maeve would keep any deal," Alasdair scoffed.

"I mentioned that to her. She seems to trust Maeve."

"But she's a swan maiden," Alasdair said. "That makes her a shifter and puts her on the list of Others that Maeve is planning to exterminate."

Hadrian shrugged. "She doesn't seem to think that applies to her. I wonder why."

"You won't be able to do much about it when she finds out she's wrong about the Dark Queen," Balthasar noted. "You'll be dead."

"Thanks for the vote of confidence," Hadrian said.

"You said you were number thirteen," Balthasar said. "When she kills you, she'll go to the Dark Queen and find out that there's a technicality and that the deal isn't done after all. You won't be able to defend your mate."

"I understood what you meant. I just think we might be able to free her brothers another way."

"Which means you need to change her mind." Balthasar shook his head at the low chances of that.

"Why you?" Alasdair asked.

"She had to pick one of the *Pyr*. She hates blacksmiths, so I won the lottery."

"Why?" Balthasar asked.

Hadrian shrugged again. "I don't know yet."

"You might never know," Balthasar noted.

"She could have picked Quinn," Alasdair said.

"She said she doesn't want to orphan his kids."

Balthasar laughed. "An assassin with a soft spot. That's interesting."

"It's an inconsistency, which *is* interesting," Hadrian said.

"Maybe it's because of the firestorm," Alasdair suggested. "It might be making her sentimental."

Hadrian snorted, unable to imagine that possibility. "No. I think it's about principle."

"Are we positive the firestorm is real?" Balthasar asked.

"I am," Alasdair said.

"Me, too," Hadrian agreed. "It doesn't seem to be part of her plan either. I sensed that she was surprised, too, and affected by it." Hadrian picked up her dagger as his friends ate, and examined it, trying to avoid any discussion of how close he'd come to satisfying the firestorm.

His tactic didn't work.

"But you *didn't* satisfy it," Alasdair said, insisting on clarity as he often did.

"You're not too nosy," Hadrian teased and they all laughed.

"We need to know if the spark of the firestorm will reveal her presence," Alasdair said.

"Like an early warning system," Balthasar agreed.

"I think she'll manifest quickly and strike," Hadrian said. "But I don't think she'll target you. Principles." He nodded, convinced of that.

"Are we going to be collateral damage?"

"I don't think so. But stay out of the way, just to be sure."

Balthasar snorted. "Don't go confusing her motivation with yours."

"I don't think we're that different."

Balthasar pointed his fork at Hadrian. "That's the firestorm talking."

"So, what about her knife?" Alasdair asked, indicating the weapon in Hadrian's hand.

"It's a ceremonial dagger," Hadrian said, showing his friends the curved blade. The hilt was an open oval, with a grip on one side and a dragon on the other. The dragon covered the back of his hand when he held the grip. "It's called a *bichuwa*," he said with appreciation. "I've never seen such an ornate one."

"Where's it from?" Balthasar asked.

"India," Hadrian said. "The name means 'the sting of a scorpion'. These ceremonial daggers always have a curved blade. Frequently they have an oval grip like this that wraps securely around the hand as a knuckle guard." He tested it, stabbing with the blade. "Good steel. Gold ornamentation. Very, *very* nice."

"You sound flattered that she picked a good weapon," Alasdair teased and Hadrian grinned.

"I am. It even has a dragon on the guard." He turned the blade. "That's the place for a protective demon. Hey, maybe that's why she couldn't kill me with it."

Alasdair rolled his eyes. "The ornamental dragon protected you? I don't think so."

"Like to like. Who knows?" Hadrian was still admiring the weapon. "It's ceremonial but it will definitely get the job done quickly. This blade is sharp."

His friends exchanged a glance and shook their heads in unison.

"I'd rather be slaughtered cleanly with a good blade than be hacked to death slowly with a dull one," Hadrian said.

"There is that," Balthasar agreed.

"No one wants their heart carved out with a spoon," Alasdair noted, and they smiled in unison at the movie reference.

Balthasar finished his pasta. "So, what's the plan?"

"Gloves," Hadrian said. "As many as possible and as soon as possible. Thanks for dinner. I'll probably work through the night."

"I can call someone about getting the window fixed," Alasdair offered.

A glow appeared then around Hadrian's hand and they simultaneously fell silent to stare.

"She's closer," Alasdair whispered, as if she might hear.

Hadrian wondered whether her senses were as keen as his own. "But not approaching anymore." The light wasn't getting brighter. "She's watching." The hair prickled on the back of his neck that she was stalking him. Would she give him enough time to arm his fellow *Pyr*? Would she satisfy the firestorm before she kept her pledge to Maeve?

Alasdair shuddered, then got up to clear the dishes.

"I'll be in the studio," Hadrian said, rising to his feet with purpose. He didn't want his fellow *Pyr* in the vicinity when his mate came for him, just in case.

"You think she won't come after you there?" Balthasar asked.

"I think she has strong feelings about blacksmiths, and every tiny bit I can shake her judgment is a good thing." He pursed his lips. "I think surprise throws her game a bit, and I'm not too proud to use it."

"We can defend you," Alasdair offered.

Hadrian shook his head. "Let her come. Let her try." At the sight of his companions' obvious doubts, he grinned. "You're forgetting that the firestorm is on my side."

Night fell slowly, beautifully, darkness claiming the sky in increments. Rania watched the stars come out high overhead. Would she miss them once she was Fae? Would she be able to return to this realm once her ability to manifest elsewhere was reclaimed by Maeve?

She shook her head, disgusted that she could be so whimsical, even for a moment. Stars were unimportant, compared to freedom.

Rania stood, arms folded around herself, and locked her gaze on Hadrian's lair again. She'd smelled their meal, which made her own stomach complain. When had she last eaten? She liked to fast a little before she struck a lethal blow, but this kill was taking too long.

A van had arrived with new panes of glass for the broken window after the *Pyr* had eaten and Hadrian's friends had come out to help the man carry them into the lair. It was hard to believe that his friends were both dragon shifters, as well, and she doubted that the handyman had any idea of their nature. He'd left as the sun was sinking, and the sound of his truck quickly faded from earshot. Creatures rustled in the fallen leaves of the forest, but otherwise, it was quiet.

She'd watched the silhouettes in the living quarters, then realized there were only two figures there. That was when she'd noticed there was a light in the studio.

An orange light.

Rania moved through the forest silently until she was alongside the studio. She was still a distance away, so the firestorm's light burned but not too brightly. She wished its flame was a little warmer, as she could have used the heat. At least there was no one around to notice its peculiar glow, a light in the forest where there shouldn't be one.

Through the windows of the studio, she saw Hadrian, silhouetted against the orange fire of his forge. He was working, sparks flying. He wore goggles, gloves and a leather apron, and seemed to be cutting something. She smelled the fire and the steel, the ash and the iron, and it should have fed her resolve.

It certainly made her shudder.

Yet she wasn't afraid of him. She admired his muscled strength as he worked, and thought about his seductive combination of power and tenderness. He could have killed her more than once on this day, but he hadn't even tried.

He'd given her pleasure instead. He'd tried to convince her to let him live just a little longer. That was different. The recollection of his touch warmed Rania a little. She retreated so that the glow of the firestorm was more faint—and more easily ignored—and watched the light of the forge through that window.

When it was extinguished, she'd make her move.

She walked a bit in the forest, to keep herself warm, and found a clearing not far from the lair. It was close enough that it had to be part of Hadrian's property, but it seemed secluded, even private. In the middle of the clearing were two pieces of metal. Rania eased closer for a better look. They were about two feet high, like markers. There was a heart at the top of each one, a heart on a post that went into the ground. They were slightly different and she had the sense that one was older than the other. Why were they there? What did they mark?

Was she standing on a *Pyr* grave?

That idea made Rania retreat from the clearing, a shiver running down her spine. She returned to the spot where she could see the light from the window of the studio.

Would she be able to find her knife in Hadrian's lair? Would she have time? It would be a shame to lose such a good specimen from her collection, but she had to keep her eye on the prize.

Her prey couldn't fall asleep soon enough.

Hadrian was aware of the burn of the firestorm, how it increased and decreased. He knew that his mate was vigilant but keeping her distance. She had to know that the light would warn him of her presence. As the hours passed, he suspected that his theory had been right: she would attack when he was out cold and unable to defend himself quickly.

The danger was that he might actually fall asleep. He'd been tired on arriving home and was becoming exhausted after the hours of work in his studio.

He was enjoying the challenge of the gloves, though. Hadrian knew that Quinn had created each blade for Donovan's gloves individually—in fact, the Smith had crafted each section of each talon before hinging them all together. The gloves were a testament to Quinn's skill as a craftsman, but Hadrian knew it would take the two of them precious months to replicate enough pairs of gloves for all the *Pyr* by Quinn's method.

Every moment counted, so Hadrian had turned to more industrial methods of knife-making. He routinely made knives for historical re-enactors by this method, as he could sell them more cheaply than a purely artisanal blade. He'd chosen stock steel from his inventory, picking an alloy that would be harder and hold its edge longer over one that was less likely to corrode. The battle against the Fae was now: he wasn't going to worry as much about rust compromising these gloves over time.

Hadrian had made a template for the blade on each finger, copying Quinn's work, then cut the profiles of the blades from the stock with his laser cutter. He'd been able to cut many in rapid succession this way. He'd made a series of jigs, one for each of the five blades, to cut the bevel with precision.

He'd then put the blades into a furnace to harden at more than sixteen hundred degrees Fahrenheit for several hours, working in batches. This took the steel to its maximum hardness, but also made it brittle. Once hardened, the blades were plunged into water to quench. He left them there until he'd hardened all of the blades he'd cut, then began to anneal them, which meant heating them at a lower temperature than the first time for several hours each in order to make the steel more durable. Again, they were cooled afterward. He checked them repeatedly, pleased with their color which revealed how well the tempering had been done.

For the next stage, he'd have to flatten and tension each blade individually, then finally they could be sharpened. He still had to cut and temper the other pieces to hinge the talons across the back of the glove, then assemble each glove, but the blades were the more challenging element. They had to be right, and Hadrian had done them first in case he had to start over. He was pleased with his progress and surprised by how much time had passed. The darkness was complete outside the studio. There was still another batch being annealed, but he was worn out. He photographed everything, stored the images in the cloud and sent the link to Quinn, hoping he might inspire the Smith to try something new.

Then Hadrian yawned, feeling exhausted to his marrow.

That was the moment of weakness his mate awaited.

What if he pretended to be asleep? If she struck immediately, he might have a chance to fight back. If he could lure her closer while he was awake, he might survive to surprise her again.

It was past midnight and Hadrian knew that both Alasdair and Balthasar were asleep already. He could hear the steady echo of their breathing in the lair. He considered the studio and made a few changes. He cleared more space, so he could shift if he needed to do so. He let the fire in the forge die down until the coals emitted just a faint glow. The forge had been hot for so long that it continued to radiate a welcome heat and would do so for a while.

He could feel the silence of the forest that surrounded his home and the faint trickle of the river. He was sure he could feel his mate watching, too.

He placed her knife on a table in front of the forge. It glinted there, the only thing on the table and the only thing reflecting the firelight, and Hadrian hoped it provided a distraction. It was a lure and he hoped she went for it.

Then he pulled up a chair that he loved and sank into it with a sigh. The Arts & Crafts armchair was made of oak, with broad armrests and leather upholstery on the seat and back. He liked the patina on the wood and how smooth it felt beneath his hands. There was a second one in his lair that was a rocking chair.

Hadrian leaned back and closed his eyes so that they were just slits. He was facing the table with the knife and felt the forge's heat wash over him. He slowed his pulse and his breathing, almost entering a meditative state, but still remaining alert and watchful. He'd been taught by Alasdair's father, Boreus, to do this. It was a means of conserving energy while guarding a prize. Boreus had called it 'banking the fire' and Hadrian had always been good at it. The idea was to become as still as possible but always be ready to strike.

The challenge when he was so tired was to keep from dozing off. Hadrian hoped his mate was decisive and arrived soon.

They were all asleep.

Rania listened and when she was certain that the *Pyr* were out cold, she manifested inside Hadrian's studio.

In the blink of an eye, she surveyed the entire space, verifying her assumptions. Hadrian was alone and asleep in a chair, facing the forge, his feet up on a table. His breathing was deep and regular, and there was no tension in his body at all. Rania was good at assessing such things and most creatures did a poor job of hiding or controlling their bodies' rhythms.

Convinced that Hadrian wasn't going to trick her this time, Rania relaxed slightly.

She guessed that he hadn't slept in a while to have crashed so hard. He hadn't even noticed that the white light of the firestorm burned brighter with her proximity. She glanced over his workshop, intending to choose a weapon from among his tools just for irony, and spotted her knife.

The *bichuwa* was on the table beside his feet. She stared at it, immediately distrusting that it was so readily available.

But Hadrian was a blacksmith. It would make sense for him to have an interest in weapons. Maybe he had been studying it before he dozed off. There was a pair of gloves on the anvil near the forge, and something shone beneath them. There must have been a blade there, but Rania reached for her own *bichuwa*.

She couldn't deny the temptation of following her original plan.

It was only after she took a step toward the dagger that she realized her mistake. She'd turned her back on Hadrian. In the instant that she could have corrected her pose, the shimmer of blue light warned her that he was shifting shape.

He'd never been asleep at all.

She snatched for the *bichuwa*, but a dragon claw roared past her and closed over it first. She spun to find Hadrian filling the studio in his glorious dragon form. His scales shone emerald and silver, and the firelight made him look like a mythical creature. He was watching her, tossing the blade from one claw to the other, like a magician tempting her to grab for it. The daring light in his eyes gave her a desperate urge to surprise him.

"Go on, disappear and try to get me later," he taunted, revealing his expectation.

"I'd rather finish this now," Rania replied. She seized the leather gloves, hoping to grab the blade that shone beneath them. Instead she discovered that there were four blades attached to the fingers. She had no chance to tug on the gloves, though, because Hadrian tackled her for them.

"No those!" he said.

They tussled over them, falling to the floor, until he was on top of her, his eyes flashing and tail lashing. She hooked her ankle beneath a chair and jerked it toward them so its weight fell on his back.

It wasn't enough to hurt him, but it surprised him so that she could shift shape and slither from his grasp.

Hadrian won the gloves, though.

He roared as she retreated, back in her human form, and his eyes flashed fire. He swung his tail, sliding it across the floor so that Rania had to jump to avoid being knocked off her feet. She tumbled in a cartwheel, shifted shape in mid-air and took flight. He tossed her blade in the air, taunting her again, and this time she took his dare.

She dove toward her knife and snatched at it in mid-air with her beak. Hadrian moved faster though, his dragon claw descending to grab the dagger before her very eyes. At the same time, his wing swept along behind her. He created a current that flung her toward the far end of the studio, the end where he stored raw steel. Rania resented her smaller size then, because she hated being defeated by brute force. The smell of the steel made her shudder, but it also built her resolve. She was flung through a cluster of cobwebs before regaining control of her flight, then pivoted and charged back toward him.

This time, she'd finish him.

There was a telltale shimmer of blue, and Hadrian stood before the forge in his human form. His arms were folded across his chest, and there was both a smile on his lips and a challenging glint in his green eyes.

There was no sign of her *bichuwa*.

Rania flew straight at him, but he didn't even flinch. He held her gaze, clearly expecting that she'd shift in the last instant. She did and landed before him on the balls of her feet, hating that she felt predictable.

He grinned. "Nice," he said with admiration.

Hadrian was officially irritating, interesting, and the sexiest male she'd ever met. He might also have been the best opponent she'd ever battled and the most wily target.

"Where is it?" she demanded as the firestorm blazed white between them. The last thing Rania needed to feel in this moment was desire, but lust burned through her veins to her toes anyway, making her yearn to caress him instead of kill him.

Maybe she could kiss him one last time.

She knew he'd make it worth her while.

"That was really smooth," Hadrian said, ducking the question.

"I don't care about your compliments," Rania replied, feeling cross as well as flattered—and aroused, too. He surveyed her with such obvious appreciation that her instinct was to preen.

"Why not those gloves?"

He smiled. "They're a tool against the Fae. I'm trying to replicate them, and need the originals as a model."

Rania was confused by a scheme that made no strategic sense to her. "But they only fit in your human form. Don't you fight better as a dragon?"

He laughed with that confidence. "We can take them through the shift, and augment our talons with steel blades."

That was amazing, but she averted her gaze so he couldn't see how impressed she was. "Where's the *bichuwa*?" she asked again.

"Safe," he said with a maddening smile, then turned to the forge. He turned his back on her with ridiculous and unjustified confidence, moving with a leisure that the situation didn't deserve. He stoked up the fire as she watched, and the light of the firestorm brightened as well. Rania could barely think straight with her impressions of Hadrian crowding her mind, and the need to touch him was almost overwhelming—never mind the wish that he would touch her again. It was impossible to keep from noting the flex of his muscles as he worked, or the audacity he had in turning his back upon her.

He was cocky. He knew she'd come to kill him and had to recognize that she didn't need her knife. She could kill him with her bare hands if she wanted to. There was a way to strike from behind, to snap the victim's neck, and leave him to a slow death.

Rania didn't do it, though, so maybe his confidence was justified.

She looked and yearned instead.

"I know you could kill me, right where I stand," Hadrian said easily, without looking back. "But I want to suggest that we make a deal."

"Why should I make a deal with you?"

"Because you want your knife back, of course." He cast her a glance and a smile that shook her to her toes. He nodded at the red string on her wrist. "I know she can compel anyone to act against their own will. I want to give you the benefit of the doubt."

It was more than she might have given him and Rania knew it. One question seemed harmless enough. "Why were you cursed?"

"Because I willingly entered Fae, with Alasdair and two other *Pyr*, Rhys and Kristofer. She took us captive and—" he grimaced "—Alasdair and I had to dance."

Rania felt a twinge of sympathy. She'd seen those victims forced to dance until it killed them. Their feet bled and they begged for mercy but the merry music never stopped.

Until they did, forever.

It was a punishment for a crime, though. They earned their sentence by charging into Fae uninvited. They were invaders. Maeve had to defend her domain and her people. The familiar justification flooded into her thoughts, even though it sounded a little less plausible when she knew the one who had earned the punishment.

Rania deliberately spoke with a harsh tone, refusing to feel sympathy for him or acknowledge any common ground. "You should be dead twice over then."

Hadrian's chuckle was unexpected. "Maybe I live a charmed life."

"You must."

He'd turned and was studying her, still smiling himself. The fire from the forge cast his powerful form in silhouette and the light of this firestorm illuminated his face. She saw a twinkle light in his eyes and wished they'd met under different circumstances.

That was crazy. There were no different circumstances, and there never would be.

"Are you going to tell me that the third time's the charm?" He seemed to be amused by the possibility, not as fearful as he should have been.

The studio seemed much too small. Rania was raging with desire again, remembering the feel of his hands on her skin and the sure touch of his caress. She was thinking of the way he'd pleasured her and the way he kissed and found herself wanting another taste.

Instead, she shook her head and put out her hand. "Give me my knife and we can find out."

Hadrian laughed. "Not a chance." His eyes narrowed as he surveyed her. "You haven't disappeared yet. Maybe you're changing your mind about killing me."

"Why would I do that?" Rania scoffed, knowing she should have cut him down already.

Would she be able to make the final strike? There was something intriguing about this dragon shifter, maybe the fact that he challenged her expectations and wasn't afraid of her.

She liked him. That was as startling as it was troubling.

"Maybe you like me too much to kill me," Hadrian suggested, as if he'd read her thoughts—again.

This time, Rania laughed although the sound was forced. "Maybe I just want my knife back."

"Why that one?"

"Once I choose a knife, I like to use it."

"Superstitious?"

"Following through on plans."

He nodded. "You picked it because of the dragon?"

"It seemed like a good augury."

"I've never seen such an ornate *bichuwa*."

She was surprised that he knew the name of it and by the admiration in his tone. "It was made in India in the seventeenth century. It's from Thanjavur." Once again, she was talking too much.

"Formerly Tanjore," he said. "I wondered." His quick glance was piercing. "You collect knives?"

Rania nodded.

"I guess you always need one."

"Not usually with the kiss of death, and not after tonight anyway."

He chuckled. "Who inherits your collection?"

"No one. I'm not going to die."

"Ever?" His gaze was piercing.

Rania shook her head.

"Is that a swan maiden thing or your thing?"

"It's a Fae thing."

He frowned and surveyed her, his gaze lingering on the lump of the ring beneath her shirt. "But you're not Fae. Are you?"

Rania had no intention of explaining the details of her deal to him. He'd just argue with her. She extended her hand.

"Let's make a deal instead," he said easily, leaning against the table. "Give me a day and a night to satisfy the firestorm, then I'll give your knife back. What do you say?"

"Sex doesn't take that long."

His grin was wicked. "Is that a challenge?"

Rania shook her head. "I want to finish this now."

"You didn't complete twelve assassinations overnight. What's another day?"

"Maybe fifteen minutes," she countered and he laughed.

"Not a chance. I've waited two hundred years for the firestorm. I intend to savor it."

Savor it. Rania's mouth went dry as she recalled how he'd savored her. "No," she said flatly, guessing that if Hadrian made love to her for hours, she'd never be able to finish him off.

Maybe that was what he was counting on.

Rania folded her arms across her chest to keep from reaching out to touch him. "Besides, there's probably a trick."

He shook his head slowly, looking leonine and reliable. She instinctively wanted to trust him—and agree with him. "No trick. The firestorm is satisfied with sex, plain and simple, and the mate conceives the *Pyr's* heir the first time they're intimate."

"What else?"

"Nothing else."

"No deal." She stretched out her hand for the knife.

Hadrian laughed. "So, you can kill me now? I don't think so. You'll have to pick another one." His eyes twinkled. "Maybe I'll start a collection of weapons you've been unable to use against me. We'll have to decide what happens after we get through your entire collection."

"You're not that lucky," she said. "No one is."

"Did you get the *bichuwa* from a collector?"

"I was the collector."

He tilted his head, studying her with a curiosity that seemed to echo her own. "What were you doing in Thanjavur?"

"What do you think?"

He held her gaze steadily for a long moment, then spoke softly. "Who did you kill there?"

"A djinn." Rania frowned at the memory. "It took a while to stalk him."

"Seeing that he could turn to a wisp of smoke."

Rania shook her head. "This isn't solving anything. You can give the knife to me or I can come back when you least expect me."

"True enough, but this is a great opportunity for me to learn more about southeast Asian metallurgy." Hadrian turned and walked away from her, as if she were no more dangerous than a mouse.

Where was the knife? She couldn't see it anywhere.

"You can't just take it!" she protested.

"Well, I'm not going to give it to you so you can kill me with it."

That wasn't an unreasonable argument. "But it's mine."

"And now it's mine. The djinn probably thought it was his, too."

Rania could have growled with frustration. She glared at him, but Hadrian just smiled again. "I like when your eyes flash like that. You look like you could take me out with your bare hands."

"I'm tempted."

"Go ahead and try," he said, his voice low and his gaze hard. They stared at each other for a potent moment, then his gaze slid over her as surely as a touch.

"How about it?" he murmured.

She knew he was referring to his offer. "Why would you give me the *bichuwa* just for satisfying the firestorm? That makes no sense."

"Because everyone deserves a last wish," he said. "Because a son is the greatest legacy a *Pyr* can leave."

"But you don't know that I'll be a good mother. You don't know that I'll raise your son the way you want." She flung out a hand. "You don't know anything about me!"

"Wrong," Hadrian said with conviction. "I know what's important. You're my destined mate."

"There's no such thing as destiny," she insisted. "And no such thing as romance. It's my task to kill you, no more and no less. That's the one thing you know about me and it's hardly the reason you should choose me to have your son."

He shook his head with conviction. "No. The firestorm chose you, and the firestorm is never wrong." He approached her and that white glow brightened. "I know that you've been trapped by the Dark Queen and that you're determined to free your brothers. That kind of commitment to the team and to family is something I live and breathe. I know we have that in common."

"But..." Rania took a step back, feeling the firestorm turn her thoughts in a predictable direction as Hadrian moved steadily closer. He didn't slow down or stop but kept taking one step after another, closing the distance between them. His eyes were very green and filled with intensity.

"I know that you think Maeve is going to keep her end of the bargain, which shows that you have a sense of honor. It's unthinkable to you that someone could break their promise, just as it once was to me."

"What changed?" Rania found her back against the wall.

"The Dark Queen lied." He stopped right in front of her. "She taught me distrust, just as she's going to teach you distrust."

"No. That's not going to happen."

His confidence was unshakable. "Yes, it is."

"You don't know that for sure." Rania's protest sounded desperate even to herself.

"Yes, I do."

"But you're still willing to let me kill you, in exchange for conceiving your son?"

"In exchange for a lot of pleasure, too. Don't forget that."

"You can't know that I'll take care of that son."

"But I do." His gaze locked with hers. "I know Maeve is going to do something unfair, something to cheat you of your due. You'll learn the truth about her, and eventually, you'll triumph over her and get the freedom you deserve. It'll be too late for me to help you or to celebrate with you, but that lesson will ensure that you take care of my son. You'll want to give him a legacy, because I warned you. You'll feel an obligation to me."

It sounded all too plausible. "You don't know that..."

"I do, because I would feel the same way. I think we're a lot the same." He reached for her and touched a fingertip to her cheek. "I think you're going to defend our son with every bit as much valor as you've used to fight for your brothers."

The raw admiration in his gaze made it impossible for Rania to look away from him.

But he was manipulating her!

She spun away from him, still looking for her knife. "You're making all of this up," she complained. "I trust Maeve! I know she'll stand by her terms."

"Why?" Hadrian asked, his voice hard. His hands closed over Rania's shoulders and she found herself leaning back against his strength as the firestorm crackled and burned, stealing her breath away. "What's in it for her?"

"Keeping her word. Justice."

Hadrian's lips were on the back of her neck and she felt his breath when he laughed. "Justice. That's rich. You're a shifter. You're on her list of species to be eliminated, just like I am."

Rania spun to face him. "That's why I have to finish the deal. She's going to give me a reprieve."

His eyes narrowed as he watched her, his confusion clear. "How so?"

"She's going to make me Fae. My brothers will be mortal men again and I'll be Fae. It's win-win."

"Not for me."

Rania forced herself to shrug. "Oh well."

Hadrian's hand moved quickly and he hooked a finger beneath the chain that hung around her neck. In a flash, he held the ring in his hand, his gaze boring into hers. "Does it always glow this brightly? I've heard of gems looking like they're lit with inner fire, but this one really does."

"No, it doesn't," she admitted reluctantly.

His gaze was mischievous. "Maybe it's as affected by the firestorm as both of us."

"No." She tried to tug it out of his hand but failed. She didn't want to break the chain so she gave it up.

"Who was he? Who *is* he? Are you still in love with him?"

"I don't owe you that story..."

"What kind of stone is it?"

Rania bit her tongue and kept silent.

That didn't silence Hadrian, but then, she hadn't expected otherwise. "And here I thought you were turning me down because of this guy, whoever he was. I thought you were holding out for love and romance."

"I'm turning you down because I don't want to have your son," Rania said, her voice rising slightly. "I'm turning you down because I don't believe in destined mates, and maybe you don't either. Maybe you're just trying to buy some time."

"Maybe I just think the firestorm shouldn't be denied," he countered, then leaned toward her, obviously intending to steal a kiss. Rania's thoughts were too jangled and her resolve too compromised to let that happen.

She wished to be home.

CHAPTER FOUR

one again.

And he'd been cheated of a kiss again.

Hadrian's mate had to be the most annoying woman he'd ever met—but she was also the most intriguing. He didn't know what to expect from her and that snared his attention completely.

After all, she admitted the most incredible things. She was a swan-maiden, which was alluring in itself, but how did she imagine Maeve was going to make her Fae? Could the Dark Queen really turn a mortal into an immortal? Hadrian shook his head, instinctively doubting the story. His mate clearly believed that she wasn't on Maeve's inventory of shifters who had to die—or that she wouldn't remain on it once her assignment was completed, once Hadrian was dead.

Hadrian had his doubts. He suspected the Dark Queen had been deliberately deceptive and that the so-called bargain could only end badly for his mate. If anything, that only made him feel more protective of her. How could he convince her of the truth, before he was toast? He admired her loyalty but wished it hadn't been misplaced.

And whose ring was this? The chain had snapped when she'd vanished and Hadrian still had the ring in his hand, the broken chain hanging from it. It was a man's ring, obviously, which made Hadrian wonder who had owned it. Father? Brother? Lover? Son? Friend? Each option prompted its own questions.

He'd thought at first that it was silver, but on closer examination, realized it was platinum. There was a single large stone in the setting. It could have been an opal or a moonstone, if not for that glow. He was sure a flame crackled in the heart of the stone, which he didn't think was possible. Was it magick?

He knew it was a particularly fine stone even though he wasn't a jeweler. He did have an affinity with the element of earth and the stone whispered to him of its own splendor, its size and clarity, its color and the commanding flicker of that inner light. It didn't confess what kind of stone it was, though. Where had she gotten it?

Why did she keep it? That was the important question. It didn't fit her fingers. Was she planning to return it? Or was it a memento?

Hadrian doubted his mate was sentimental, so this ring had to be about something else. Maybe it was a trophy from someone she'd killed. Her first assassination perhaps. Maybe it was from the man who had betrayed her or abandoned her, the one whose rejection or departure had made her prey to Maeve's plot. Was the original bearer alive or dead? Had it belonged to one of her cursed brothers? He could envision it as a family piece, with the feathers etched into the sides of it.

Hadrian wished he knew.

He doubted his mate would tell him. He put aside the broken chain and tried the ring himself. It fit the index finger on his left hand, and once he'd pushed it on, it fit so well that he couldn't pull it off. He supposed that meant it was safe there.

And if she wanted to retrieve it before she killed him, her efforts would definitely wake him up. That ring wasn't coming off easily.

Hadrian didn't want to consider that she might just slice off his finger. On the up side, though, that would wake him up, too.

How long would it be before she returned? He doubted it would be long. He guessed that she was someone who stuck to a task until it was done. He doubted he could stay awake much longer, but somehow he had to do it.

What did his mate's bargain with Maeve mean about his firestorm? Did Maeve's involvement mean that Alasdair could have been wrong? Hadrian hadn't known his parents at all, but he was curious to verify what Alasdair remembered about their firestorm.

He wanted to double-check that his own firestorm was real before he made any more choices.

Assuming that he actually had the chance to make them.

It was almost dawn. Maybe Alasdair was waking up.

He'd make some coffee in the kitchen and maybe encourage him to do so.

Rania landed hard in the middle of her own kitchen. The house was dark and cold, since she hadn't been there in a while. The back of her neck was sore and she raised a hand to discover that her necklace was gone. Hadrian must have held on to the ring which made the chain snap.

The loss shook her, as did the fact that she'd failed again. She hadn't just hesitated this time—she'd *talked* to him. She'd been curious. She'd been tempted and charmed. What had he done to her? Rania didn't care about anyone else. She was alone and always had been. Self-reliant. Indifferent to others.

But she wasn't indifferent to Hadrian MacEwan. Why not?

The bizarre thing was that she felt so different. She felt more than emotional and volatile, more than jangled and uncertain. Desire hummed through her body, insistent in its demand that she surrender to sensation. She'd never experienced such yearning before. Was it because of this firestorm? Was it really so powerful that it could change her nature?

She'd been treacherously close to agreeing to his wager. Why? Rania had no desire for children and there was no point in bringing another shifter into the world when Maeve was going to clear the planet of such abominations. The boy would have a short life, so short he might as well not be born at all.

But she'd been tempted to please Hadrian.

That was dangerous.

Funny how satisfying the firestorm didn't seem like such a foolish idea when Hadrian suggested it. Funny how he didn't seem like an abomination to her, even though she remembered Maeve's words about shifters. Far from it. Rania thought Hadrian was magnificent, in either form.

How could she be forgetting everything she knew to be true?

What was wrong with her?

Her eyes widened as she felt something moving beneath her skin. It started in her chest, then wriggled down her left arm. It was deep inside and felt both sharp and cold. Rania felt her arm, feeling the muscle flex as whatever it was edged down to her elbow.

She watched in horror as she felt its prickle in her lower arm, then was sure she could see a lump moving beneath the skin on the inside of her wrist. Rania moved toward the light as she felt something in her hand. She could see the ripple beneath the skin as it made steady progress toward the surface. She was both horrified and fascinated.

When one sharp point pricked through the skin, she was reminded of a sliver. A sliver could push its way to the surface over time, but this sliver moved too quickly. She wondered whether it had a mind of its own, then it popped onto her palm and stilled.

It was less than a half an inch long. It glowed red, like it was magick. It shimmered then, like starlight, and she bent closer to examine it.

A shard of glass? Where had that come from? Before her eyes, her skin healed so there was no longer a hole where the splinter had emerged. The sliver flashed silver, melted into a tiny puddle that evaporated. She turned her hand beneath the light but there was no sign that it had ever been.

It had happened so quickly that she doubted her own eyes. Had there been a sliver of ice, or had she imagined it? Her skin was perfectly smooth and there was no indication that anything had popped through it.

She felt lighter, too. More inclined to smile. More likely to care.

Rania wasn't going to think about Maeve's command of magick. She was definitely losing her edge if she was starting to hallucinate.

No, this was all Hadrian's fault. This was his so-called firestorm, bending her thoughts so that she didn't fulfill her obligation to Maeve.

Let him have the ring for now. Rania didn't really need it. She just preferred to keep it, since she'd had it all her life. She could retrieve it once he was dead.

How dare he suggest that Maeve wouldn't keep her word? They had a bargain and Maeve would do as she'd promised. Rania trusted the Dark Queen completely.

Hadrian was just trying to undermine her resolve, for obvious reasons.

It shouldn't have worked so well.

No doubt about it, this dragon shifter had a dangerous charm.

Rania went down into the secret room hidden beneath the main house, opening the panel to display her knife collection. The *bichuwa* had been the ideal choice, but she was ready to compromise.

She surveyed her collection and chose.

Sebastian was late.

Sylvia couldn't decide whether to continue waiting for him or not. She knew he had mixed feelings about the alliance between the Others, and that he was shaken—although he wouldn't admit it—by the death of other vampires in the coven of mercy. Had he left the city? Was he just sulking in his library? She had a feeling that he was annoyed with her, too. He hadn't liked her suggestion that she tempt the magick to play.

One thing she knew about Sebastian was that he hated magick.

Of course, they could have had a massive argument about her choice but Sylvia didn't remember because he'd removed her memory. They could have had a torrid affair that she didn't remember for the same reason. He could have confessed every single detail about his life and his motivation, then taken her recollection away. He really was infuriating in his insistence on remaining an enigma.

Was he really several thousand years old, or had that been a joke?

Sylvia had no idea what she knew or had known about him. As someone who loved to do research and remember it, this trait of Sebastian's drove her crazy.

Still, she liked him, in a strange attraction-of-opposites kind of way. He fascinated her. His touch excited her. Her reaction to him was more potent than any attractive she'd felt before—but potentially a lot more unhealthy. Was it the risk? Or was it her sense he that she could help him, with something? Maybe he was drawn to her for the same reason, and against his will.

Maybe the attraction was just as potentially threatening to him.

There was a thought.

Either way, they had a connection. An inexplicable and frustrating one, but a bond Sylvia couldn't deny.

Was he coming to meet her at all? Had that been a lie? Had he changed his mind?

Or was he in trouble? The possibility of Sebastian being in peril hadn't occurred to Sylvia before and she didn't like it at all. She thought of him as invincible—irksome but invincible—but there had been vampires killed at the coven just days before.

In daylight, Sebastian was vulnerable, whether she liked it or not.

What if something had happened to him? How would she ever know?

The book!

Sylvia was already wearing her coat and had what was left of Maeve's book in her purse. She pulled it out and turned to the page about vampires. Sebastian's name was still there—so he was alive but standing her up.

The sky was getting dark and the wind was blowing, as if a storm was coming. She looked out the window of her apartment over the street and saw Caleb leave, the wolf shifter sparing a glance back at the townhouse before briskly walking away. Sylvia pulled back from the window. He was headed uptown, in the direction of Bones. Did he know that she hadn't left for the meeting yet?

She went to her terrace, the one that overlooked the courtyard behind the house, since that was where Sebastian tended to appear. There was no sign of him. She even went out and looked over the rooftops, hoping to catch a glimpse of him. No luck.

She looked down into the garden, wondering again whether she should move into Eithne's apartment. The woman she'd believed was her aunt had died, leaving everything to her, but Sylvia hadn't cleaned out Eithne's belongings yet. She tended the garden in the courtyard, but hadn't been able to bring herself to change anything. She liked her apartment in the attic of the townhouse. If she moved down to Eithne's place, it would only make sense to rent out her own apartment to someone else. She just wasn't ready for more change, so she delayed over the move. It was probably inevitable and definitely was practical but Sylvia couldn't face it yet.

She missed Eithne. She'd been trying to figure out how to help the Others in their battle against Maeve, but every attempt she made at spellcasting had failed. The best she could do was produce a tiny red light, one that quickly fizzled out. She'd tried conjuring and she'd tried summoning the dead. She'd tried scrying and she'd tried fortune telling. She'd tried to cast protective spells and even had beckoned to the Fae, all without success. She'd taunted the magick and challenged it, daring it to play with her, but nothing. There was either some detail missing in Eithne's journals or Sylvia had no magickal abilities at all. She suspected she needed a tutor, but didn't know where to find one. A Google search wasn't going to turn up a contender.

It was depressing to be so useless.

She looked again for Sebastian, but there was still no sign of him. She had to leave immediately to have any chance of making the meeting on time. Sylvia grabbed a pair of gloves and pulled out her subway fare, tucking it inside her right glove, then went to the door.

She'd just put her hand on the knob when she saw a shimmer in the periphery of her vision. She turned slowly to look and found a man in the middle of her apartment, a man who hadn't been there before. He had a glow around him and seemed to be transparent—she could see through his figure to the table behind him. He had dark hair and the clearest blue eyes. She guessed he was about her age, maybe thirty or a little younger. He was dressed in ragged rough clothing. Was he poor or from another era? He smiled as he offered Sylvia something long and white.

She took it, amazed to see that it was a feather and it was real. It had to have come from a large bird, given its size, and it was radiantly white. It gleamed in her hand, so luminous that it could have come from another world. She looked back at him with wonder, uncertain what it meant.

His mouth moved and she heard a word echo in her thoughts, even though he made no audible sound.

Semyaza.

Sylvia pulled out her phone and made a note of it, just in case she forgot the word. It had to be important. It seemed familiar but not quite.

She looked up and his mouth moved again.

Sebastian.

Sylvia frowned at the echo in her thoughts. The man smiled. Then he waved and vanished, as if he'd never been there at all. He hadn't been her imagination, though, because she still had the white feather.

Semyaza and Sebastian.

Had he been giving her a clue about Sebastian's truth?

Sylvia decided to go to Reliquary and ask Sebastian herself, instead of attending the meeting at Bones. The Others argued so often that she doubted she'd miss much. She could stop in at the bar afterward. She hurried down the stairs, looking forward to seeing her vampire despite his likely mood.

Semyaza. That name sounded familiar, but Sylvia couldn't quite place it.

Sara was glad to be home. There was something about being back in Michigan in the house she and Quinn shared outside of Traverse City that made her feel safer. She'd enjoyed the visit to Kristofer's farm and that Quinn, the Smith of the *Pyr*, had been able to repair the scales of both Kristofer and Rhys, but she was always happiest when at home.

She could feel the icy tingle of Quinn's dragonsmoke barrier around the house, thanks to her psychic sensitivities. She welcomed its familiarity, as well as that of their five sons arguing good-naturedly over the rules of the game they were playing in the family room. Quinn was in his studio, replicating the gloves he'd made for Donovan years before. She'd cleaned up after dinner—a chicken from a local organic farm, roasted with all the trimmings, which had disappeared with amazing speed—with the help of the older boys.

After the boys were in bed, Sara made herself a cup of herbal tea and carried it into the study. She planned to choose a book blindly from one of the shelves, which was a favorite game of hers. She ran a bookstore in town, but here at the house, all of the books were her keepers. She liked to rediscover her old favorites randomly like this.

She scanned the shelves before making her choice. There was one book that hadn't been pushed in all the way. It stuck out a bit, reminding Sara of the way her Aunt Magda's ghost had chosen reading materials for her during her firestorm with Quinn. She smiled and sipped her tea. Sometimes she missed Magda's original store in Ann Arbor.

Sara took the hint and chose that book. It was a hardbound book without a dust jacket, bound in dark blue cloth. There was a title embossed on the spine in silver, a title she was certain hadn't been there a moment before.

The Swan Maiden.

Sara frowned. She knew she'd never read this story. Was it a favorite of Quinn's that he'd added to her collection? That seemed unlikely. She opened the book again, noticing a torn piece of paper that was obviously being used as a bookmark. Had that been there before? The hair prickled on the back of her neck and she wondered whether Magda's ghost was back.

There was something written on it and she held it to the light, curious.

> *The ice dragon summons frost and cold,*
> *His power is a force to behold.*
> *He can thaw the ice of a frozen heart*
> *To offer a lost soul a new start.*
> *His firestorm burns fierce and white*
> *Its radiance a beacon in the darkest night.*
> *But can it bring hope to that doomed soul?*
> *Or persuade his lost mate to become whole?*
> *If the dragon wins the swan maiden's trust*
> *It will be Fae not Others who are turned to dust.*
> *The future will be theirs, once allied*
> *If the assassin joins the dragon's side.*

A prophecy!

Quinn had said one of the *Pyr* was having a firestorm on their drive home. He'd admitted to feeling it ignite when Sara noticed he was driving more quickly. He'd said it was distant, but he'd still wanted to get them home sooner.

He hadn't mentioned it again, but she hadn't asked. She'd been hoping for a prophecy and here it was.

As usual, it didn't make a lot of sense to her right away. She'd show it to Quinn when he came in from his studio. She didn't want to interrupt his work, since it was urgent that he finish the gloves for his fellow *Pyr* as quickly as possible. She guessed that he'd work late and glanced down at the book again.

It looked like a fairy tale.

It had to be important, maybe relevant to the firestorm, since the prophecy had been within it.

She sat down, sipped her tea, and started to read.

Once upon a time, there was a king who dearly loved his wife. Their marriage had been arranged to further the fortunes of both families, but they had fallen in love immediately and, each day, their love grew only deeper. The king's realm was in the distant north, an empire of ice and wind and stone, but his beloved wife filled his palace with light, joy and warmth. The queen loved swans and the king admired her gentleness with them. She fed the birds as they migrated and he would often awaken and look out the palace window to see his wife, the wind in her hair, feeding wild swans by hand in the courtyard. During their courtship, he had changed his standard to that of a white swan in flight. Once she'd become his wife, he delighted in adding swans to every corner of the palace. The canopy over their bed was crested with a carved swan in flight. There were swans carved in stone and in wood, woven in tapestries and created in tiles on the floor. The queen was surrounded by swans and this gave her tremendous joy...

Herding cats had nothing on trying to build consensus amongst Others. Caleb, leader of the New York wolf shifters was nearly at his wits' end. The bar, Bones, where the Others met was closed for the night, but it was packed with furious shape shifters, each one determined to have his or her say. Pandemonium reigned, no matter what Caleb said or did.

He understood that the sudden slaughter of so many of their fellows had spooked even those shifters most determined to fight against Maeve—and those who had their doubts were ready to surrender.

Caleb had to wonder whether any of them had tried to make a deal with the Dark Queen already.

The *Pyr* were comparatively quiet, even though a large group of them were in attendance. Caleb had met Arach, Drake, Theo and Rhys before, and on this night, he'd also been introduced to Thorolf and Niall. Rhys' mate, Lila, was with them, as well, and Caleb could smell that she was expecting a child. More of her sister selkies had come with Nyssa, and at least two of them were pregnant as was Nyssa herself. The scent of hormones was a distraction Caleb didn't particularly need. The soft femininity of the selkies provoked his protectiveness and he hoped he didn't lose his temper as a result. At least the selkies and *Pyr* sat together, watching instead of arguing.

Caleb was becoming a fan of those who kept quiet and listened.

The bartender, Mel, was back, much to Murray's obvious relief, and bossing the owner of the bar as if she'd never been gone. Caleb knew he hadn't imagined the way she'd turned immediately when the *Pyr* arrived, or how her gaze had clung to Theo. That *Pyr* nodded once in her direction, a brief acknowledgement considering that they'd been trapped in Fae together, but she'd turned away so quickly that she spilled a beer. Caleb didn't like that Mel still had a red string on her wrist. It suggested to him that she might be drawn back into Fae again, and to his thinking, the fewer times anyone visited that realm, the better.

"Let's call this meeting to order!" Murray shouted, but the din only diminished a little. The dwarf got up to stand on the bar and shouted from there. "Order, already! Let's talk, not argue!"

"I need another beer," a bear-shifter said. "With a shooter."

"Make that two," another bear-shifter said beside him. "It's just wrong what happened to Ivan and Natasha. I never want to see anything like that again."

"I can't stop seeing it," the first bear-shifter agreed and they threw back their shooters in unison.

"Booze isn't going to help a single thing," said a woman from the doorway. Caleb winced in recognition of those cold tones and turned slowly, dreading who he would see.

Sure enough, it was Wynter Olson, the younger sister of Kirk, the alpha of the Alaskan wolf shifters who'd been slaughtered along with the rest of his pack the previous Saturday.

"Wynter Olson," he said, wishing it could have been anyone else, and she glared at him.

"Don't tell me that you thought I'd stay home and catch up on my knitting," she said, moving with purpose toward the bar. The crowd had fallen silent to stare at her. "You know I'm not interested in traditional gender roles, Caleb, and this is war."

Wynter was tall and slender, with black hair cut very short. Her eyes were a grey-blue, while her lashes were dark and long. Her skin was so fair that her lips looked red, even without make-up. Her movements were decisive and tinged with impatience, and she braced her hands on the bar to eye Mel. Animosity rolled off her in waves, just as it always had, and Caleb wished she had stayed home—whether she'd knit or not.

There was something about Wynter Olson that riled up males everywhere she went. Most hated her. Some wanted her. She challenged and defied them all and seemed to enjoy every moment of it.

"How many of you saw the battle up close and personal?" Wynter said as she walked into the bar, hips swinging. Caleb saw a veritable army of women behind her. They were wary but determined and most led small children by the hand.

The children were mostly boys.

Caleb inhaled deeply and recognized that the children were wolf shifters. These were the mates, then, the women whose wolf shifters had been killed. Judging by their expressions, they weren't in the frame of mind to forgive that easily—or to stand aside and let others take vengeance.

Just what they needed in this war: two dozen well-intentioned but vulnerable women, each one with at least one young child. Caleb rubbed his brow.

Wynter Olson was making even more trouble than could have been expected. She'd brought these women from Alaska to New York, and they weren't going to return home without a fight. He hoped at least some of them managed to return home at all.

Meanwhile, there was a rumble of assent to Wynter's question.

"I saw Kirk's murder," Wynter said. "I saw that Fae warrior cut out his heart and eat it. My alpha, my brother, my leader! I'm not going to stand by and let anything like this happen again! Are you?"

Fists were pounded on tables and Murray glanced to Caleb.

Caleb didn't like that the leadership of the meeting had been effectively stolen from himself and Murray. He raised his voice. "For those of you who don't know, Wynter Olson is the sole surviving wolf shifter of the Alaskan pack."

"I prefer to be called alpha of the Alaskan pack," Wynter countered, her voice hard.

Caleb was startled. "But you're the only wolf shifter left."

"Which means there's no one to remind me that I'm female and thus unqualified to be alpha," she replied with a snarl. "No other wolf shifter left standing means I win." She gestured to the women whose features were set with resolve. "And I have a pack already, the one you all insisted I didn't deserve to lead." The women gathered behind Wynter looked even more resolute than they had on arrival.

Whispers passed through the group gathered at the bar.

Caleb didn't know what to say, so he shared the news with the Others. "Twenty-three of our kind were lost in Alaska," he said. "And seven here in Manhattan."

"They weren't lost," Wynter said. "We didn't forget them in our shopping cart at Walmart." She gave Caleb a hard stare as her words elicited a few chuckles. "They were slaughtered in our lair by the Fae."

Caleb wondered whether Wynter meant to challenge him for authority over the New York wolf shifters, too. He glared at her and she took a step closer, shimmering slightly blue as their gazes locked.

"Fighting between ourselves is just what she wants," Mel said, appearing between them and holding up her hands. "I think we should take a closer look at Wynter's suggestion."

"What suggestion?" Caleb asked.

"It's shifters that the Dark Queen is hunting," Mel said. "And those with some skill with magick." She gestured to the women. "What about the mortals who have a stake in this battle, too? What about the mothers and mates? What about the allies you all have, the ones who aren't listed in the Dark Queen's inventory?"

"It's too dangerous," protested someone and an argument began again.

"While we're all safe?" Micah asked suddenly, appearing suddenly in the shadows. Several Others in his vicinity jumped in surprise. The other vampires in his coven hovered behind him, shadows against the darkness—but shadows with glittering eyes. "We lost five vampires in that attack," he said. "That never happens. We are the predators. It's only when we hunt each other that there's such carnage. No one is safe."

"I'm now the last medusa," the hostess of the bar said bitterly. "My cousin Hypatia is gone." Many Others murmured their sympathy and several touched her shoulder.

"Plus four bear-shifters," said the one who had ordered a beer. "It makes me sick to think of how our numbers have dwindled." He drained the beer, and then another shooter, pushing the glasses across the bar in a silent request for refills. His companion did the same.

"One selkie," Nyssa contributed.

"Three djinns," said one djinn, who was rotating between his human form and that of a wisp of smoke in his agitation. Another djinn waved a sheet of paper, one that must have come from Maeve's book.

"Another two demons," Rosanne said, also holding up a sheet of paper. "I found this in my trailer after the attack at the Circus of Wonders."

"Ivan, Natasha and their twin sons," the bar shifter said, shaking his head. His companion slapped a sheet of paper on the bar and Caleb could see that there were names crossed out of a list. The bear shifters ordered another round.

"Yet no dragons," Wynter said, her voice silencing the crowd once more. "How can that be?"

"We got lucky?" Niall suggested.

Wynter looked Theo up and down, her disdain clear. "They say you escaped Fae. How exactly did you manage that? What was the price you paid?"

"More than a month of captivity," Theo countered, his gaze sizzling. He rose to his feet and Caleb could see the shimmer of blue that heralded his shift. The last thing they needed was a dragon shifter fighting a wolf shifter at Bones.

"Not enough for the Dark Queen I know and despise," Wynter replied, apparently not as interested as Caleb in keeping the peace. "What else?"

"Nothing else, as far as I know," Theo said.

"As far as you know." Wynter shook her head then jabbed a finger in Theo's direction. "I think you made a deal," she accused. "You dragon shifters are late to this alliance and you have a reputation for wanting to play everything your own way. I think you made a deal and left us out of it, a deal that keeps the *Pyr* alive while the rest of us go down."

"That's not true," Theo said calmly, even as there were nods of assent in the bar.

"Even though you were captured with her daughter?" Wynter asked, turning to face Mel. Mel stood a little taller, her hostility at least equal to that of the wolf shifter.

"Don't expect me to defend my mother, or understand all of her choices," she said.

Mother?

Caleb felt as if he'd missed a cue. Mel was Maeve's daughter?

Murray caught sight of his surprise and nodded. He'd known then, but Caleb hadn't.

"You have a deal with her, too, then," Wynter accused.

Mel held up her hand, the one with the red string on her wrist. "If you count being cursed as a deal."

"But you're a shifter, too. Why hasn't she killed you? She must be cutting you some slack due to blood ties."

Mel paled but shook her head. "She's just not done playing with me yet," she said softly. "You could take a lesson from that."

"Maybe you should explain," Wynter challenged.

Mel sighed, then braced her hands on the bar. She nodded once, then spoke clearly, her voice carrying over the quiet bar. "You think she's targeting shifters and you're right, but there are three kinds of shifters and she's only after one. Maybe two. But the third kind could be allies."

Mel held up a finger. "First, there are all of you. You're shifters because it's your nature. The ability to change forms is part of what you are. You were born shifters and you will die shifters. Your children will be shifters. The majority of you can take two forms, one of which is that of a man or woman. Most of you can choose to shift, although some of you are compelled to do so under some circumstances."

"Full moons," Wynter said with a sigh.

Mel nodded. "Some of you have other powers, but the important thing is that you've always been a shifter and when you shift, you're still yourself."

"What other kind of shifter is there?" asked the bear-shifter.

Mel held up a second finger. "Sorcerers who learn the spell to shift shape. They can take multiple forms and they do it by choice. Their shift is determined by whim and is a mirror of their magickal powers. There aren't very many sorcerers of such power, and I suspect Maeve will target them, if only to try to claim their magick."

Wynter's expression had softened a little. "And the third kind?"

"Those who are cursed to shift, like me." There was a little stir in the company as Mel tapped the string on her wrist. "I was immortal but not a shifter, until I was cursed by the Dark Queen. I have no control over the shift. Mine happens in a specific way at a specific time." Caleb saw that Theo was listening to Mel with avid interest. "I can't stop it. I can't make it happen. It's imposed upon me." Mel's frustration was clear. "Most who are cursed to shift are stuck in that alternate form until the curse is broken. Sometimes they're silenced, too. It's a temporary thing, theoretically, but it can feel like it lasts forever." She fell silent for a moment, then nodded. "The thing is that anyone who is a shifter like me probably hates the Dark Queen and would make a good ally."

"And other than you, those shifters probably aren't on her list," Theo said.

Mel turned and smiled at him as she nodded. "Allies she won't hunt."

"They can still get taken out as collateral damage," Caleb said.

"But as our numbers dwindle, we can use all the help we can get," Mel said. "And like the mates who have followed Wynter, they'll be adding to our forces unexpectedly, at least to the Dark Queen. That can't be a bad thing."

It was the first positive idea they'd had in a while and the room erupted in chatter as various kinds made suggestions and lists of those cursed creatures and mortals that might prove to be good allies.

Wynter wasn't going to let it go easily, though. Caleb saw that as she spun to face the *Pyr* again. "Is it true that one of your kind warned you of the Fae attack last weekend?"

"Alasdair had a nightmare," Drake confirmed. "At the time, we didn't know what it meant."

"But now you have an early warning system," Wynter said. "Why did *he* have the nightmare? What's different about him?" She demanded this of Theo.

"He was trapped in Fae, as well, and also tortured by Maeve. She went through his thoughts and obviously left him sensitive to the presence of the Fae."

Wynter scoffed. "So, you got out of Fae by becoming her spy," she said to Theo. "And this Alasdair has the ability to hear them coming so he can warn the rest of you. Sounds like the *Pyr* have come out of this all right."

"Hardly," Theo retorted. Once again, he was shimmering blue around his perimeter and Caleb feared he'd shift shape to fight. Wynter looked as if she was ready to rumble as well, then something completely unexpected happened.

The door to the street opened and it seemed to admit the sun. Golden light flared in the darkened bar, a light so brilliant that it left everyone blinking.

"Sorry I'm late," one of the *Pyr* said as he strode into the bar. Caleb remembered that his name was Arach. He had dark hair and silvery eyes and moved with youthful purpose. He waved to his fellow *Pyr* and a stream of brilliant orange sparks launched from his hand.

The light flew across the bar, burning like a sparkler on the Fourth of July, and dropped toward Wynter. She stepped to one side, but the flame tracked her anyway. It landed on her lips with a sizzle that made her eyes widen, then extinguished. She rubbed her mouth and glared at Arach, clearly understanding the source of the spark.

A golden glow remained, burning between the two of them and driving the dampness out of the bar. Arach stared at Wynter with awe. She looked him up and down, then turned her back on him to continue her argument with Theo.

Obviously, she didn't realize that she was having a firestorm with a dragon shifter.

Or maybe she did. Caleb wondered whether she was feeling the mating sign of the wolf shifters. He'd never experienced it, but he'd seen the mark appear. It looked like a tattoo of a crescent moon, but it appeared suddenly and of its own volition. The location varied from wolf shifter to wolf shifter, and more than one had made a seductive game of tempting the mate to find it.

Caleb couldn't see any change in Wynter, but he thought things had just gotten very interesting. She would feel the mark burn, if she had it. What if she didn't? Could she be Arach's destined mate without him being hers? Caleb wasn't sure. Usually mates had no powers of their own.

But then, Maeve had turned everything and everyone upside down.

Murray was wiping glasses with gusto, his eyes round, looking like he needed to do something to keep busy. The *Pyr* were studying Wynter and only the wolf shifter mates, of all those beyond the *Pyr*, seemed to recognize what was happening. They looked between Arach and Wynter, smiling and whispering to each other.

"This means that to keep the faith with all of us, and prove that the *Pyr* haven't made a deal that leaves the rest of us out, you have to offer a hostage," Wynter said to Theo.

What? It was time for Caleb to intervene. This was his turf and they followed his rules. He'd let Wynter talk to deal with her grief but she was pushing too far.

Arach smiled and took a step closer to Wynter, too. She glanced back as the light flared to greater brilliance, burning yellow between them.

The rest of the Others seemed to finally understand. Maybe they were feeling the sexual demand of the firestorm too.

Caleb certainly was.

"Wynter, you're out of line," he said sternly. "This is an alliance..."

"And it's only going to work if we trust each other. When one group looks like they have an inside deal, we have to restore the faith of the Others in the alliance." She turned to those gathered in the bar, inviting their agreement. "Right?"

"Right!" they roared, toasting her with their drinks and raising their fists high.

"Looks like a done deal, Caleb," Wynter said, her eyes sparkling with triumph. If it hadn't been for the spark of the firestorm, he would have been tempted to wring her neck.

As it was, he figured Arach had won that honor.

"Don't worry," she said to Theo. "I'll take good care of you."

"Me?" Theo said then laughed. "You won't be my captor."

"You have to keep the faith," Wynter began to insist but Arach approached her quietly. When he dropped his hand on the back of her waist, a flurry of sparks shot from the point of contact.

"Take me," he said in a low rumble and Caleb heard a wealth of meaning in that invitation.

Wynter surveyed Arach again, her eyes narrowed, then Caleb watched her inhale slowly. "You're *Pyr*," she murmured and he smiled.

"And I'm all yours," Arach said.

"What's this light?" she demanded.

"A firestorm," Arach said. "It means you're my destined mate."

"I don't think so," Wynter protested as everyone in the bar watched with open interest.

"Well, since I'm your hostage, we'll have plenty of time to find out," Arach countered.

Wynter opened her mouth and closed it again, then glanced at Caleb as if she'd appeal to him. As far as he was concerned, she'd created her predicament herself, and he didn't mind one bit if the *Pyr* kept her busy while he regained leadership of the Others.

"You made the rules," he told her. "You get to live with the consequences."

Wynter's eyes narrowed, her gaze nearly lethal, then Arach took the final step between them. The firestorm's light flared to brilliant white and Wynter stared at him. Her lips parted, then she licked them. She shook her head, swore with gusto, then spun to face him. Without warning, she caught Arach's face in her hands and kissed him.

And the mates who had followed her from Alaska cheered.

CHAPTER FIVE

Alasdair had been sleeping so hard that Hadrian hadn't wanted to wake him up. Balthasar was out cold, too. Hadrian made a pot of coffee and poured himself a huge mug, then returned to his studio to examine the blades he'd left to cool. They'd come out better than he'd dared to hope. There was no telling when his mate would return, so he heated the forge again, drank more coffee, and got to work.

He could sleep when he was dead. Ha. Somehow that joke wasn't funny, given his current situation.

When would his mate return?

Hadrian soon forgot his exhaustion as he became absorbed in his task. He hammered each blade for the flattening and tensioning. It was good steady work, if a bit repetitive, but he was motivated to get these gloves done. It was satisfying to see his plan coming together, too. He finished the pot of coffee and made another, forcing himself to remain awake as morning progressed.

He knew the instant his mate arrived. The hairs prickled on the back of his neck. The air moved in an unusual way, just as he'd noticed when she'd vanished or appeared suddenly before. The firestorm flickered to life: he felt the glow of its icy fire and felt the flurry of white sparks collide with his back. It all happened at once.

He knew that it was now or never to make his play for survival. He'd already seen that she could be easily prompted to talk, and he had to think that the more she knew about him, the harder it would be to kill him. He'd work with what he had. Hadrian spun to find his destined mate a step away, a different blade raised in her hand. She was poised to strike, but then her gaze met his.

He saw the difference immediately. The expression in her eyes wasn't as hard as it had been. The line of her lips was softer, and she flicked a glance over him. She hesitated to make the strike.

She had doubts.

Was that because they'd been talking? Or had something changed in her?

Either way, Hadrian would welcome progress wherever he found it. He moved like lightning to close the distance between them, caught her around the waist and bent to kiss her in the same moment that he seized the dagger in her grasp. His mouth closed over hers and she sighed with satisfaction, then seemed to remember herself. She broke their kiss and snatched for the blade but it was too late.

Hadrian summoned the change since the most interesting things happened when his mate was surprised. She was visibly startled to find herself in the grasp of an emerald and silver dragon. Hadrian liked that she wasn't terrified. Her heart skipped once, then she surveyed him with curiosity.

Fearless. He admired that.

He loved how she ran her fingertips over his scales. It felt heavenly, the barest whisper of a caress lighting an urgency within him. He could get addicted to that pretty easily. Her touch and the shimmer of the firestorm sent shivers through him, making him want that kiss all over again. His heart pounded as he watched her eyes darken.

As if their thoughts were united.

Then she abruptly stepped away. Hadrian let her go, watching her lips tighten and her gaze lift to the blade.

"Give it back," she commanded, as if he would do any such thing.

He spun the blade, hooking a talon through the lace on the hilt, letting it catch the light.

"A Scottish dirk," he said with approval. "As sharp as the best ones are reputed to be. Nice ornamentation on the handle. I like the Celtic knot and the stone in the pommel. Is it amber?"

"Smoky quartz," she acknowledged, then glared at him. "Give it back."

Hadrian ignored her. "How old is this one?"

"Victorian," she admitted through gritted teeth. Her lips tightened into a thin line as she extended her hand in silent demand.

He laughed. "We both know that isn't going to happen. I like the collection I'm building, by the way." He twirled the knife and tucked it beneath his scales, well aware that she was watching him. It didn't matter. She'd never find the weapon on her own. Then he shifted shape again and had a thought. She liked challenges, too.

He lifted his hands, offering himself, and grinned at her. "Why don't you try to find it yourself?" he teased.

She propped her hands on her hips. "You're not making this easy," she complained.

"Why should I?" Hadrian countered. He leaned against the table beside her, watching the firestorm brighten between them. "I'm not in a hurry to die."

"I'm not going to make that deal with you," she insisted. "You're just delaying the inevitable."

"You talk a lot for a cold-hearted killer," he noted, studying her. "Are you lonely?"

She bristled visibly. "Why would I be lonely?"

"Maybe because you're alone. You work alone, maybe live alone. That would leave you with no one to talk to."

"How I live and work is irrelevant to you." She was fingering the partially finished blades, as if assessing how useful they might be to her. Hadrian suspected she could use one in a pinch and deliberately stepped away from his worktable. He guessed that she would follow him and, after a moment's pause, she did.

"You have my ring," she said and Hadrian lifted his hand to admire it. "You should return that to me, too."

"I'll trade it," he suggested.

"For what?"

"The story of it."

"The story?" She looked confused. "It's a ring. It's mine. End of story."

"Come on. That's not a story. Who did it belong to? How did you get it? Why do you keep it?" He wagged a finger at her. "If you want to learn about telling stories, you should listen to Alasdair. That dragon can spin a yarn, and illustrate it."

"I don't understand."

"I know. A little advice: if my cousin ever offers to tell you a story, seize the opportunity. Now, tell me about the ring."

"There's nothing to tell. I've always had it. It's always been on that chain around my neck, as long as I can remember."

"But you don't know anything about it?"

She shook her head.

"And you don't wonder?"

She frowned, her gaze locking on the ring. "I haven't. It just was. Now that you mention it, that does seem strange."

She was uncertain again, as if the rules were changing or the ground was shifting beneath her feet and she wasn't sure where to step next.

Hadrian would work with that.

"And it always shines like this?"

She shook her head, apparently mystified. "That's new."

"I have an idea," he said. "Why don't we ask your brothers what they think of my proposed deal to satisfy the firestorm? I mean, they have a stake in the result, too, and they might want your family line to continue."

"You can't talk to them. They're swans because they're cursed."

"I remember. Can't you talk to them in your swan form, or at least understand them?"

She blinked. "I don't know."

"You've never even tried!" he guessed. "Can't you find them?"

"I can go to anybody anywhere anytime," she said with confidence.

"But you never have." Hadrian shook his head. "In a thousand years, you never reached out to them." He could see her confusion. Had it been part of Maeve's curse that his mate should be oblivious to everyone but the Dark Queen? If so, he seemed to be breaking that edict. "I thought anybody alive would have more curiosity than that. Twelve kills in a thousand years must have left you with a lot of spare time."

"I had other things to do."

"But they're your brothers! Your only kin. Your family."

She frowned and looked across the studio, clearly shaken. "I'm helping them," she said, her tone tentative.

"That's good. When you fulfill the deal, the curse will theoretically be broken, right?"

Her eyes flashed. "It's *not* theoretical."

"And they'll be mortal men again, right?"

"Right." She was wary, as if he was unpredictable. But she was still listening. Hadrian would take it.

"And you'll be Fae."

"And immortal. Exactly." She nodded. "Assuming a certain dragon shifter ever stops talking."

Hadrian chuckled. Talking was keeping him alive. "Maybe your brothers deserve to hear that there's another option. Maybe they're less inclined to believe the Dark Queen than you are."

"The deal is the deal." She shook her head and took a step closer. "They'll stay cursed if I don't fulfill it. I can't believe they'd quibble over the details."

"But what if the firestorm is right about us being destined mates and belonging together? For the *Pyr*, a mate often has skills that complement his strengths and affinities, so they're stronger as a team than individually. What if our combined strengths could set your brothers free without you killing me?"

"You're just stalling for time," his mate said impatiently. "You're just trying to compromise my will to get the job done..."

He hadn't even thought it could be compromised, so having her admit as much was great. "Did you ask your brothers the first time?"

"No." She was startled. "Why would I?"

"You just decided for them?"

"I had the opportunity to free them. What was there to talk about?"

"They might have had other ideas. They might like being swans." He raised his hands, trying to think of something that would be better as a bird. "I'd miss flying if someone took it away from me. I'd want to be asked if it was worth surrendering that."

She nodded reluctant agreement. "But still, they're cursed. They must want to be free."

He folded his arms across his chest. "But don't you miss them?"

"I told you: I didn't even know I had brothers until the Dark Queen showed them to me."

He lifted the ring. "Then this doesn't belong to one of them?"

"I don't think so."

"You've always had it, you don't particularly care about it, yet the Dark Queen didn't take it, even though it's obviously valuable."

"It might not be. It might just look good." She shrugged. "She looked at it a couple of times, but she'd never touched it."

That made Hadrian wonder whether the ring was magickal in its own right. Why else would Maeve have avoided contact with it? Why else would it have started to glow? It was more important than his mate was letting on. Did she know more about it than she was sharing with him? "Maybe your brothers miss you. The portals between the mortal realm and Fae might close. You might not get to hang out together any more than you do now."

She shrugged. "I'm not going to worry about losing something I've never had." She frowned. "Give me one of my knives. Let's end this."

"No. I want to ask your brothers what they think of my offer. If they don't agree, then I'll give you whichever knife you want." He lifted his hands. "Come on. Twelve brothers cursed to be swans. I want to see that even if you never did."

She eyed him, her expression wary. Hadrian thought she looked dangerous and adorable, which he found a very alluring combination. "You are stubborn, aren't you?"

"I like being alive. I like you. I like the idea of spending more time with you. And I'd like to get my gloves done for my friends."

"You'd like to meet my brothers. And you'd like to satisfy the firestorm," she concluded, a hint of a smile curving her lips. "Trust me to pick a dragon with a long bucket list."

"It's not that long," Hadrian protested, taking a step closer to her. The firestorm shimmered and glowed between them and he heard her pulse increase. She licked her lips and he remembered the feel of her wrapped around him, the memory tightening everything within him.

He reached out a hand, uncertain whether she'd stay or not, and his fingertips brushed her cheek. He heard her sigh. He saw her soften. He saw her eyes close, those lashes fluttering as if she wanted to resist him but couldn't. He saw her lips part, as if their thoughts were united. He saw her lean closer and felt the firestorm brighten to incendiary heat...

Then just as his anticipation rose, his mate said "Uh oh" and vanished one more time.

Uh oh?

Where had she gone?

She hadn't said anything the other times.

He told himself that he was getting through to her, even though he'd really wanted that kiss. In this moment, it was hard to believe—but she hadn't killed him yet.

That was unassailable.

Being summoned by Maeve without warning couldn't be a good thing.

Did the Dark Queen know that Rania hadn't been able to kill Hadrian? If so, their interview wouldn't go well. She'd never had any dread about meeting Maeve before and found the change in her reaction unsettling.

How had Hadrian managed to affect her so much so quickly? Rania didn't even want to think about the power a *Pyr* might have when he beguiled anyone. She was finding Hadrian seductive and persuasive all on his own—well, with the firestorm on his side. With every passing moment and each new confidence exchanged, she had less desire to kill him.

How had she managed to do this twelve times before? She hadn't been lying to him—it had been easy.

Until now.

That was probably the point. He wanted to survive, and not just for the sake of the firestorm. It was just bad luck that she found him so attractive. It was probably a good thing that Maeve had summoned Rania when she had. Rania wasn't very confident that she would have been able to stop that kiss, and a kiss could easily lead to more. A child was the last thing she needed in her life, never mind a *Pyr* child.

She'd never thought about children before, never even considered the possibility. As she hurled toward Maeve, Rania wondered what Hadrian had looked like when young. He'd probably been cute. Precocious. Curious. Difficult to discipline, but so mischievous and adorable that it would be hard to care.

She was smiling when she arrived before Maeve, which proved not to be the best choice. Maeve was in her Dublin townhouse: Rania recognized it from other visits. It was in the mortal realm and elegantly decorated in black and white, with an impressive collection of antiques. Maeve appeared to be alone in her kitchen, standing at a granite counter, pouring a drink from a cocktail shaker. Given the olive, it was probably a martini. The Dark Queen was wearing a black dinner suit with feathers around the collar. They shone blue-black. Rania saw that it was evening by the light of the sky beyond the windows.

She would have expected it to be noon or so, roughly the same time as at Hadrian's place in Northumberland, but this wasn't the first occasion she'd witnessed Maeve bending time to suit herself.

"Enjoying ourselves, are we?" the Dark Queen demanded, her tone petulant. "Ignoring that there's a time element to this assignment?"

"It's been more complicated than I expected," Rania said, her manner deferential. "The kiss of death didn't work on him."

Maeve ate the olive. "Can't find a knife in your collection?"

Rania didn't admit that Hadrian had confiscated the ones she'd tried to use. "I haven't found the right moment yet."

"The right moment," Maeve echoed, as if she'd never heard anything so ridiculous, then sipped her drink with care. "I'm becoming disappointed, Rania."

"I promised, Maeve—"

"Excuse me? What did you call me?"

Rania blinked. "Maeve." She'd always called the Dark Queen by her name, but now Maeve shook her head.

"Only my nearest and dearest can call me by my name. It's intimate, you know."

"But..."

"But you thought you were intimate. And maybe you were." Maeve arched a brow. "I invite you to note the use of the past tense."

Rania felt things were changing too fast. Had Maeve discerned the change in her?

She'd seen others bow before Maeve and thought this might be a good time for her to do so. In the past, Maeve had laughed and invited her to stand again. "My queen, I only want to serve your will." She bowed low, then dropped to one knee.

Maeve just watched Rania, sipping her drink, and didn't invite her to stand.

"I fear, Rania, that you may be becoming unreliable," she said finally, her voice low with threat. "And that would be a terrible shame, when you've come so close to fulfilling your assignment and attaining your goal. It would break my heart to see you fail."

Rania had heard the question of whether Maeve even had a heart debated before, but knew it was dangerous territory for speculation. Besides, she trusted the Dark Queen. Why would she even think of that at a time like this?

When Maeve could read her thoughts? It was a bad moment to even consider a treasonous notion.

"I won't fail, my queen. I will finish the task."

"Not before you prove your allegiance to me."

Rania looked up in surprise.

"Tell me what you've learned."

Rania faltered, unable to guess what relevance there was to anything she'd learned. "He has a workshop in Northumberland..."

"No, no, no. I want to know how they intend to fight me."

Oh! "The dragon shifter and blacksmith I chose as my victim is making special gloves for his fellow *Pyr*."

"What kind of gloves?"

Rania tried to remember the details. "They have blades that flick out, like a switchblade at the end of each finger. They're made of steel—" Maeve hissed at the word "—and I think they can carry them through the shift to augment their dragon talons."

"Kill him now," Maeve said with heat. "Kill him before he finishes them."

"Yes, my queen."

Maeve drained her drink then glared at Rania, still on bent knee. "Are you still here?"

Rania was stung by the Dark Queen's tone, but she understood that Maeve was frustrated. It was her own fault, for failing to finish her assigned task.

It was time to make that right. She stood up and wished herself to her collection.

There was no way Hadrian would end up seizing it all, one weapon at a time. This time, she'd succeed.

Of course, Sebastian didn't answer Sylvia's knock on the door of Reliquary.

And the other vampires had probably gone to Bones already. Had he gone with them?

She pounded on the door again, then looked up at the window of his refuge. The curtain flicked. She was certain of it.

And that made her mad. "Ducking me!" she called out, not caring if she offended him. She would have said more, but in that instant, she realized why the word Semyaza sounded familiar to her.

It was the name of an angel.

A fallen angel.

And the man in the vision had brought her a *feather*.

Hadn't this whole battle started with a fallen angel stealing Maeve's book? And Sebastian had been the one to claim it, when the fallen angel died?

Sylvia knocked one last time at the door, glared at Sebastian's window, then headed for the library where she worked.

She was going to find out every single thing known about Semyaza.

And that might tell her more about one elusive, annoying vampire.

Hadrian whistled under his breath as he worked steadily on the gloves, making good progress. He had to use every possible moment. His phone chimed just as he reached a good point to take a break, and he checked the message.

It was from Quinn, thanking him for the images and notes. It was copied to Erik, the leader of the *Pyr*, which made Hadrian scroll down.

He caught his breath when he saw the prophecy that Sara had received. His firestorm was definitely real!

He righted his chair and sat down to read it.

> *The ice dragon summons frost and cold,*
> *His power is a force to behold.*
> *He can thaw the ice of a frozen heart*
> *To offer a lost shifter a new start.*
> *His firestorm burns fierce and white*
> *Its radiance a beacon in the darkest night.*
> *But can it bring hope to that doomed soul?*
> *Or persuade his lost mate to become whole?*
> *If the dragon wins the swan maiden's trust*
> *It will be Fae not Others who are turned to dust.*
> *The future will be theirs, once allied*
> *If the assassin joins the dragon's side.*

It all made sense. His mate had a red string on her wrist, so she was cursed by Maeve: that would make her a doomed soul. Was her heart frozen? Was that how she made her kills? That might just be a metaphor. She had warmed up a lot since they'd first met.

The big thing was that he'd been trying to convince her to give them a chance, and the prophecy indicated that he was on the right track: if he persuaded her to ally with him, they could change the tide of the battle against the Fae.

That was the best news Hadrian had heard in a while. He wanted to ask Alasdair more about his memories of Hadrian's father's firestorm, but had let his cousin sleep all day. It was time to rouse him. He turned down the fire in the forge and headed back into the lair.

It was time to eat something, too. He'd cook for the guys this time, and even the score.

Who knew—a good meal might even coax his mate to return.

Hadrian couldn't wait to see her again, no matter what she tried to do to him.

Someone had been in her home.

Rania manifested in the kitchen, just as before, but this time, the air smelled different. The door was slightly open and it was colder inside.

What kind of intruder left the door open?

A thief! Was he or she still in the house?

It was just sunset and the sky was streaked with orange. The shadows were long inside the house already.

Rania moved silently through the main floor, finding no signs of anyone. The house was still. She knew she wasn't wrong, though: someone had been there. She finally eased open the door to the stairs leading to what had originally been the cellar, and paused at the light gleaming from the lower floor.

She hadn't left it on.

Her collection, the only thing of value she possessed, was there.

Fortunately, there was only one way out of the lower level—unless the intruder was Fae or had similar powers to her own. That the kitchen door to the outside had been left ajar hinted otherwise. Rania took a kitchen knife and moved stealthily down the stairs, counting on the element of surprise.

There was a man standing in front of her collection, hands on his hips as he surveyed it. He was so motionless that he could have been a statue, but Rania could detect the faint sound of his breathing. She kept her collection in wall cabinets that she'd had custom-built, and she knew she'd left the doors closed and locked. They were flung open now, the light glinting off dozens of polished blades.

As far as she could see, the only missing weapons were the ones Hadrian had taken from her.

Who was this man? What was he doing in her home?

She took a silent step closer.

"Not the hobby I expected you to have," he said, his voice deep and rumbling. He'd heard her approach and she couldn't see that he was armed. He had to guess that she would be. Rania braced herself for a surprise.

He was tall and broad, built like a warrior, and his fair hair was tied back. It hung straight almost to his waist, a lot like her own hair except that Rania couldn't decide whether his was silver or gold.

He didn't stand like an old man, though. There was vitality in his posture, and she could see the muscles in his shoulders. He'd be a formidable opponent.

There was an undercurrent of amusement to his words, as if he smiled frequently, but when he glanced over his shoulder at her, Rania was startled by the sadness in his eyes. They were blue, clear blue, filled with shadows as if he'd wept enough for a dozen lifetimes. His brows were dark and striking.

His gaze flicked over her, lingering for a moment on the knife, then her neck. "Was it stolen from you?" he demanded, the very idea obviously offensive.

Rania didn't know what he meant. "What?"

"The ring. I can see a mark from the chain on your neck. Did someone steal it?" The idea seemed to insult him.

How had he even known she wore a ring on a chain?

"In a way," she said, not wanting to admit all of the truth. "I'll get it back." She'd retrieve it soon enough, but she felt his displeasure that she'd lost it at all.

"Are we talking about the same ring?" His tone hardened. "The ring on the chain your mother placed around your neck when you were born? The ring that is your legacy?"

Rania blinked. Her legacy? "It is?"

"Didn't you ever wonder? Didn't you ever ask?"

She hadn't and she knew it, although now, her choice seemed odd. Ever since that sliver had come out of her hand, Rania had felt different. Emotional. Unsettled. She was filled with questions, while previously, she'd felt no doubts at all.

He ran a hand over her hair. "Now, you'll never know," he said sadly, speaking so softly that he might have been addressing himself. He looked like he might weep.

"What are you doing in my house?" she demanded, trying to keep herself from feeling any sympathy for him. He was an intruder, after all.

He turned back to the collection of weapons, not answering her. Despite the fact that he was vulnerable, Rania found herself lowering the kitchen knife. She wanted some answers and she wasn't going to get them if she killed him.

She might not get them at all.

But she was sufficiently honest with herself to admit that wasn't the main reason she didn't strike him.

She was curious.

Again.

How did he know about the ring?

What else did he know?

"Why knives?" He sounded mystified. "Why not...dolls?"

"Dolls?" Rania scoffed. "Why *not* knives? I'm a warrior. They're the tools of my chosen trade. Why should I ignore my abilities? Just because I'm female?" She'd stepped up alongside him and met his gaze, knowing hers was filled with challenge.

He eyed her and slowly smiled. His eyes twinkled, which startled her. "My mistake," he said, bowing his head slightly. "Just because you look like your mother doesn't mean you share her nature."

He'd known her mother?

He studied her collection, his scrutiny so intense that she thought he coveted it.

She stepped past him and closed the cabinet doors again. She confronted him, then, staring him down. "Who are you and what do you want?"

"I wanted to meet you," he replied quietly, answering only her second question. He eyed her as if she was incomprehensible. "I wanted to know why you never wondered."

"Wondered about what?"

"The ring. Where you came from? Whose blood runs in your veins?"

"My parents are dead."

"Are they?"

Something about the softly-uttered question fed Rania's doubts. "Do you know where they are?"

"A thousand years," he mused. "And you never wondered. How can this be?"

Rania felt as if she'd failed a test, one she hadn't realized she was taking.

He turned and walked back toward the stairs. "Your house stinks of Fae." His tone was harsher than it had been. "How can you welcome their kind into your home?"

"I work for the Dark Queen," Rania admitted and his eyes flashed as he turned on her.

He pointed to the collection. "You kill for her."

Rania nodded. "I have."

"It *is* you, then. You're the one who is killing Others. I didn't want to believe it, but it's true. You even admit it yourself!"

"What does it matter to you what I choose to do? I don't even know you."

He flung out a hand. "You're one of us! Doesn't that matter to you?"

"Us?" Rania echoed in confusion.

He spun on his heel and headed for the stairs.

"Who are you?" she called, but he didn't stop. *Us.* Did he mean he was a shifter, too? "What are you?" His footsteps echoed on the stairs and she raced after him, only catching up when he had his hand on the kitchen door. "Why did you come here?"

He spun then to face her. "To see you," he admitted in a rush, his gaze roving over her as if she mystified him. "To try to understand."

"I don't understand," Rania admitted.

"You never wondered, not once," he repeated. "I would have known. You've lost the ring, lost your legacy and your touchstone, and I don't think you care." He shook his head. "You're a disappointment."

"I don't see how I'm any concern of yours..."

"You were conceived in love. You were your mother's last wish and the reason for her destruction. I had hoped that the poison of that place had not tainted you, that you were young enough, that you had escaped. I had hoped—" he raised a fist, then let it fall limply to his side. He frowned and cleared his throat. "I thought you would wonder and all would come right. I was wrong. If you can do this for the Dark Queen, then you never had a chance of becoming the woman I'd hoped you'd be." He looked her up and down and swallowed. His voice was husky when he continued and his eyes were filled with inexplicable tears. "She named you Rania. Your name was one of the last things she said. You resemble her so much, with the exception of your cold, cold heart. It must be made of ice for you to do what you've done." He smiled a little. "Hers had all the warmth of a midsummer day."

"How do you know about my mother?" Rania demanded, but her visitor had already left the house. "Stop! Tell me more! I'm wondering now." He didn't slow his pace at all. Rania ran after him, pleading for him to linger, but he raised his arms and blue light shimmered around him.

She knew in that instant that he was a shifter, too, but not what kind. She watched in awe as he leaped into the sky and became a large white swan in the blink of an eye. Her questions were silenced by the sight of such a magnificent and large bird. His feathers were radiantly white and, like Hadrian, he made flight look effortless. Rania could only stand and stare. His wingspan was enormous and each stroke was powerful. She watched him fly high, watched until he disappeared from sight, then she looked down at the kitchen knife, still in her hand.

Rania had the definite sense that something precious had slipped away from her.

How had he known about her mother?

Why hadn't she ever wondered about her parents?

What had that shard been in her hand? How long had it been inside her? And why had it emerged from her skin now?

It had something to do with Hadrian and his firestorm. He was changing her as surely as if he'd cast a spell upon her. He wanted to live, and he didn't care about the price, but Rania feared the implications. What would happen to her brothes if she failed Maeve? What would happen to her?

Maeve might kill her as she'd be one of the Others.

Rania pivoted and went back to her armory, then chose a special weapon for Hadrian's demise. She was looking forward to retrieving that ring.

And then, she'd have all the time in the world to *wonder*.

Once again, Hadrian felt his mate's return before he saw it.

It was early evening and the shadows in his studio were drawing long. He'd raided the provisions and cooked a beef stew for dinner, and the aroma had awakened Alasdair and Balthasar. They'd eaten together and he'd returned to his studio, intent on making every moment count. Alasdair had promised to tell the story of Notus and his firestorm, but after he composed his thoughts a bit.

The light of the firestorm flared suddenly, competing with the light from Hadrian's forge, and a wave of desire nearly took him to his knees. She was behind him and he didn't have to turn around to know she brandished a weapon.

"Why a blacksmith?" he asked and felt her pause. "You chose me because of my profession. Don't I have the right to know why that's important?" He glanced over his shoulder to find confusion clouding her gaze again. Then her eyes narrowed.

"You talk too much."

She brandished a *kesir*, a weapon he recognized easily by its distinctive wavy blade. Hadrian was flattered that she was pulling out the good stuff for him.

He laughed at her accusation. "It's been said before. Why a blacksmith?"

"The Fae hate steel."

"But you're not Fae."

She shook her head. "I was raised by them, though, by Maeve."

"Why did they raise you, anyway?"

"There was no one else to do it. I was lucky." This last she said with defiance, obviously guessing that he'd challenge her on it.

"Your parents?"

"Died." Her gaze slid away again and her frown deepened. "At least, that's what I was told." She flicked a look at him, and he saw that she was considering the ring that was now on his finger. Was it a family piece? "I'd like that back, please."

"You know what I'm going to say."

"Over your cold, dead body." She lifted a brow. "That can be arranged."

"So I hear. But your parents must be dead by now, even if they weren't in the first place. It's been a thousand years later—assuming at least one of them was mortal," Hadrian said. She nodded slowly, gaze locked on the ring.

She had doubts.

Interesting.

Why?

"How long do swan shifters live?"

"I don't know. I've only ever met one before and he didn't tell me."

"But they're mortal?"

She nodded.

"But you say there was no one to raise you except the Dark Queen." Hadrian put his hands on his hips to survey her and call her bluff. "I'm skeptical. There have been hundreds of thousands of orphaned children over the history of time, and I've never heard of another one being raised by the Fae. Is there some kind of charity program going on in that realm that the rest of us missed?"

She shook her head and her hair shone in the firestorm's light. "I was the only one."

"So, you're special. How? Why?"

She exhaled and glared at him. "It doesn't matter."

Hadrian thought it probably did. "Maybe because you were useful," he said and saw her eyes widen. "Why blacksmiths?" he asked again.

"You're relentless." There was humor in her tone, though, and a sparkle in her eye, as if she found him amusing.

"I'm motivated."

"You're stalling."

"I want to know about you. You're my destined mate, after all."

She spoke crisply then, closing the distance between them, the blade leading. It was a beautiful *kesir* and Hadrian openly ogled it. "I was shackled once. I'll never forget it or forgive it."

Hadrian met her gaze in astonishment. She'd spoken without inflection and her expression was impassive. He guessed this was important.

Really important.

He kept his tone casual. "Why didn't you just vanish?"

"I couldn't then. I was injured, and he pretended to help me, and then he trapped me." She spoke coolly, her gaze averted.

"What happened? I mean, how were you injured?"

She frowned a little. "It was my first assignment. A polar bear shifter. He was bigger and stronger than I'd expected."

"Impervious to the kiss of death?"

"I don't know. I didn't have that power then. He's the reason I got it, actually, to make me more effective in future. The second time we met, he wasn't nearly so lucky." She shook her head. "But the first time, we fought and he ripped my gut before I escaped from him. I only managed that because he couldn't fly." She touched her stomach. "I still have a scar."

Hadrian nodded because he'd noticed it.

"But I lost a lot of blood and ultimately passed out before reaching home. When I woke up, I was shackled by the ankle by some crazy loner on the tundra. He tended my injuries but intended to keep me captive forever. I remained in my swan form. He never knew I was a shifter." She met his gaze. "People keep swans, you know. Trim their wing feathers so they can't fly. Put metal bands on their ankles." She shuddered and dropped her gaze again.

"But you escaped?"

She smiled a little and raised her hands. "Obviously. He wasn't going to release me."

"What happened to him?"

"He died tragically some time after my escape." Her tone was hard and she held Hadrian's gaze steadily. "Maeve gave me both the kiss of death and the ability to manifest elsewhere by will, to ensure I was never injured or trapped like that again. She took care of me."

Hadrian was astonished by the story but had to keep her talking. "Because she's kind of your foster mother."

"No 'kind of' about it. She raised me."

Hadrian wondered why. "Do you remember your mother?"

"I never knew her. She died right after I was born."

"Your father?"

"I know Maeve," his mate insisted. "She provided for me. She's always been there."

"But what about the brothers you're trying to save?"

"I'm not *trying* to save them. I will save them. What about them?"

"Do you know their names?"

"Do I need to?"

"But once they're free, you'll get to know them?"

"Of course not. They'll be mortals and I'll be Fae." His mate shook her head then rounded the table, weapon at the ready. He wished he could get a good look at it. He'd never had the chance to examine one of the Indonesian blades closely, though he knew the wave shape of the blade was created by alternating laminations of iron and nickelous iron. "Let's get this done."

Hadrian wasn't quite as ready to finish his assassination. "You don't have family then?"

"I don't need one."

"And I'll guess you don't have friends."

"I don't need them either."

"No wonder you're so ready to talk," he teased, seeing that she was startled again. "You took this assassination job simply because Maeve asked you to," he guessed. "You would have done whatever she asked you to do."

"Why not? I owe her," his mate insisted. "There was no reason for me to decline."

"Except that you're killing people."

"Not people. Others. Shifters. Abominations and half-breeds." She repeated Maeve's accusations against shifters as if they were her own. She must have heard them hundreds of times. "And since she gave me the kiss of death, none of them have been particularly hard to exterminate." Her eyes narrowed. "Trust a dragon to challenge expectation."

"Abominations," Hadrian echoed. "But you're a shifter. That makes you one of the Others, just like me."

"Not for long," she replied. "I think that was why Maeve offered me the deal, so she could save me. It can't be easy to turn someone Fae and immortal." She fell silent for a moment and dropped her gaze. Her tone was wistful when she continued. "She must love me."

But she wasn't sure.

It was clear to Hadrian that Maeve had twisted the expectations of his mate, which was only possible because she'd spent all of her life—over a thousand years—isolated from anyone other than the Dark Queen. Whatever Maeve suggested to her would seem plausible. Her trust of her patroness was complete.

But it was also misplaced. Maeve was using her. The Dark Queen had turned his mate to her own purpose and Hadrian had no doubt that would continue.

The prophecy revealed that he was right to try to convince her otherwise. He had to succeed.

The future of the *Pyr* and the Others relied upon it.

CHAPTER SIX

"For what it's worth, I don't think it's even possible to turn someone Fae or immortal," Hadrian said, trying to keep the conversation flowing. "Let alone both."

"What are you implying?"

"Just that the Dark Queen is lying to you, the same way she lies to everyone else."

"She made a promise!"

"She makes promises all the time and breaks them. There's going to be some technicality that allows her to keep from delivering what you're owed." He shrugged. "It might just be that your nature is your nature, and that can't be changed."

His mate stared at him, frowning slightly. "You mean that you'll always be a dragon shifter, and no one can change that."

"How could they? It's my essence. Plus I'm mortal. A spell can restrict my ability to shift, maybe, but I am what I am. You're as mortal as I am. I don't think anyone with any amount of magick can change that."

"Maeve has all the magick. She has the gem of the hoard. She can do anything." It sounded as if she was repeating something she'd been told, maybe something she'd once believed, but Hadrian had to wonder whether his mate believed it now.

He really didn't want to think about Maeve possessing the gem of the hoard. He still felt that it was partly his fault that she'd managed to reclaim it.

Alasdair had tricked him, driven to do so by Maeve, but he should have guessed that something was up.

He stuck to their line of discussion. "Throughout time there are thousands of stories of the Fae taking children because they can't have their own, but in every tale I know, that child either dies or returns to the mortal realm. They don't become Fae, because it can't be done."

"You listen to too many stories."

"I think you don't listen to enough of them. Remember that she's had the gem of the hoard before."

His mate turned away from him, her expression impatient. "It doesn't matter what you think. You don't know everything about Maeve..."

"She offered what she thought you might want, but she has no intention of keeping the deal, much less paying up."

"You can't be sure of that..."

"I'm absolutely positive. And you should be wondering about it. Why does the firestorm think you're my mate?"

Her reply was quick and surprisingly mischievous. "Because you want to have sex with me."

Hadrian smiled. "The firestorm doesn't work like that, unfortunately, but I trust its choice. We should be partners. We could satisfy the firestorm, and create a son. You'd have a future then..."

"There is no future for Others," she said, interrupting him flatly. "Whether they're swan maidens or dragon shifters. All Others are doomed."

"Not if the Dark Queen is defeated."

"You won't have my help for that. I owe her everything."

"She's made you what you are," Hadrian acknowledged. "But what if that's a lot less than what you could be?"

His mate stared at him in surprise.

"Are you happy?" he asked. "Do you like what you do? Are you fulfilled? I'm thinking not. I'm thinking you're being manipulated by the Dark Queen to help her get what she wants. I'm skeptical that she cares whether you ever get what you want. She doesn't even want you to figure out what that is. I doubt she cares whether you live or die."

"You *are* stalling," she said.

"What *do* you want?" Hadrian asked. "What's the one thing you want more than anything in the world?"

"Why would you care?"

"Because you're my mate, and that means I'll do whatever is necessary to fulfill your dreams."

She shook her head. "That's a lie. You're not dying very easily and that's what will fulfill my assignment."

"Can you blame me?" he asked with a grin.

She laughed then and he was surprised again by how pretty she was. "No, actually, I can't. I respect that you want to live, and that you're willing to talk or fight, whatever it takes. It doesn't matter though. You're just delaying the inevitable."

"True," Hadrian said, not believing any such thing. "Look at this, though." He showed her the prophecy on his phone. She considered him, then came to stand beside him and read it.

"So now you're making up stories about us," she said, flicking an upward glance at him through her lashes. "Poems even."

"Not me."

"You have to know by now that I'm not much for romance."

"That's not what this is about. This is the prophecy associated with our firestorm. It means the firestorm is real and that you are my destined mate. It's a *Pyr* thing."

She read it again, more slowly this time, and he was glad that she was curious. "Where'd you get it?"

"From Sara, the Seer of the *Pyr*. She's the destined mate of Quinn."

"The Smith."

"She just sent it to me while you were gone."

"Where did she get it?"

Hadrian shrugged. "She just hears them. She's going to send me a book, too, one called *The Swan Maiden*."

"Too bad you won't have time to read it," his mate said, lifting the blade.

"Can I see the *kesir*?"

She gave him a pitying look. "You think I'll just hand it to you, after what you did with my other two knives? After you show me a poem that says I'm a lost soul and that you can save me? I don't need to be saved, Hadrian. I have a job to do and I need to get it done."

"So, that's a hard no on the *kesir*."

She rolled her eyes, exasperated with him but humoring him.

"It was worth a try," he said. "I've never had the chance to really look at one. Does it really have an essence of its own?"

She shook her head. "Close your eyes. It's time."

"How about one last kiss?"

"Another final wish? How many of those do you get?"

"As many as I can negotiate." He grinned again and once more she laughed.

"Relentless. Incorrigible. Stubborn." She walked around the end of the table, stalking him from the other side. It was probably a better angle for a strike. Her eyes gleamed with intent and the *kesir* blade caught the light of the firestorm. Hadrian held his ground, knowing that if the sight of his mate closing fast was the last thing he ever saw, it would be all right.

She stopped right in front of him, her gaze running over his face. The firestorm burned and crackled, its radiance so white that it was blinding. Its insistence made his toes curl and his breath catch—when he felt his heart match its pace to his, Hadrian couldn't complain about his situation. He looked at her mouth, so soft and red, and watched her lips part.

"Irresistible," she whispered, as if reluctant to make the concession. Then she swore under her breath and reached for him, sliding her free hand into his hair and pulling his head down. "Just one last time," she murmured and his heart skipped a beat.

This time, she kissed him and it wasn't a shy or tentative embrace. Her kiss was demanding and thrilling, as if she wanted to pick up right where they'd left off. Hadrian was more than ready to do that. He locked his hands around her waist and lifted her to the work table, then stepped between her thighs.

She wrapped her legs around him and he heard the *kesir* clatter to the wood table top. He claimed it and hid it away, never breaking their embrace. She didn't seem to notice. She was feasting upon him, demanding all he had to give, and Hadrian was going to make this last kiss worth remembering. Her fingers gripped his head, she opened her mouth to his embrace, and he could feel the heat of her even through their clothes.

When she started to roll her hips, he could barely stand it. He groaned and would have stripped them both naked to finish what they'd begun before, but in that very moment, Alasdair roared from the lair.

"They're coming! They're coming!"

Unfortunately, Hadrian knew exactly who his cousin meant. The firestorm—and his enticing mate—would have to wait.

Hadrian wasn't the only one who should get a last wish, in Rania's opinion.

And he wasn't the only one disappointed by the interruption.

She heard a roar like a freight train and guessed what it was. "Was that old-speak?" she asked, spinning to scan the studio. That the call was urgent was obvious by Hadrian's quick response.

"Yes. Alasdair is warning us that the Fae are coming."

Us?

Why would she be concerned that the Fae were coming? They were her allies.

Unless Maeve was checking up on her.

Hadrian was obviously looking for something in the studio, even as he shimmered blue on the cusp of change. He pushed through the tools on his work table, swearing under his breath.

The gloves. He was looking for the gloves. She'd been right about their importance.

He found them finally and tugged them on, their blades shining wickedly. Did he really need them to defend himself? After all, he could become a dragon.

And he did, right before her eyes, shifting shape in a brilliant shimmer of blue. The blades on the gloves followed him through the change and became steel extensions of his talons. Even though she'd expected as much, she was amazed to witness it

Then she reached back for her *kesir*, only to discover that it was gone.

"You!" she said and Hadrian's eyes glinted.

"Me. I'm building the best collection." That dragon smile was as surprising and attractive as the first time she'd seen it.

To her astonishment, he reached beneath his scales and retrieved the *bichuwa*, then tossed it toward her. Rania barely caught it, she was so surprised that he would surrender it.

"Stay safe," he said, sobering as he looked toward the door of the studio. He swore then looked back. Even in dragon form, his gaze was filled with concern. "You should use that disappearing act of yours to get out of here. They're not coming to party."

Rania was startled. No one was ever worried about her welfare, especially her intended victims. "I'm not afraid of the Fae."

"You should be."

She brandished the *bichuwa*. "You should be afraid of me."

"Looks like you're missing your chance," he noted as there was a cry from the main lair. Then he winked. "I'm getting the impression you like me better alive," he teased with that sexy confidence. The sound of fighting carried to her ears as he darted toward the door. "Go!" he commanded then joined the battle.

Alone in the studio, Rania looked down at the *bichuwa*, amazed that she held it. Hadrian had returned it so she could defend herself. She couldn't make sense of his choice, much less the surge of pleasure she felt in response.

If the Fae had come for his gloves, she didn't need to watch.

She wasn't sure she wanted to.

She wasn't going to help, not either side, when she felt so jumbled up.

Rania held fast to the *bichuwa*, then manifested in the forest, upstream of Hadrian's lair. She was breathing quickly and felt torn—this dragon shifter had the ability to confuse her and turn her expectations upside down. She'd confided in him so much.

Maybe she was lonely.

His decision to surrender the *bichuwa* was the kind of daring move that was perfectly typical of the dragon shifter she was coming to know. Did he just want her to survive for the sake of the firestorm? He couldn't seriously believe that she'd bear his son, could he? He was nothing if not optimistic.

How could he trust her not to take advantage of the opportunity? It was that confidence of his. He thought he was irresistible.

The thing was Rania did find this dragon shifter hard to resist.

She couldn't stay away from the battle. She had to know what was happening.

And it wasn't because she thought there might be an opportunity to strike Hadrian down in the confusion of the attack.

But Rania wasn't ready to admit that, even to herself.

Rania manifested closer to Hadrian's converted mill. She decided to approach from the river, since the windows were there and no one would expect company from that side. She took her human form again and gripped the *bichuwa*, thinking that her dark clothes were less visible than her white feathers.

She could hear the sounds of fighting and crept steadily closer to the big windows, moving from rock to rock in the stream. She heard a triumphant shout, then saw a flash of silver light. There was a blaze of dragonfire, then more silver lightning. Rania reached the window and peeked in, uncertain what to expect. Hadrian was in his human form in the main room of his lair, still wearing the gloves. The talons shone with menace and she saw that one was stained with blood. He was pumped and alert, almost bouncing on the balls of his feet and braced for attack.

The two other *Pyr* were there, too. The one who looked most like him, just a bit older and stockier, was beside him, both of them staring down at something on the floor. Hadrian had a line of blood on his cheek. His hair was disheveled but he looked uninjured other than his face.

There was also a dragon of citrine and gold, a sleek and sinuous dragon that nearly filled the space, flicking his tail and looking dangerous as smoke rose from his nostrils. His eyes glittered dangerously as he scanned the lair. He then shimmered blue, and she saw that in his alternate form, he was the *Pyr* with the man-bun. Which one was Alasdair? The one who had just shifted went to stand beside the others and looked down with them.

What was on the floor? She could see that the Fae were gone.

The light of the firestorm must have alerted Hadrian to her presence, because he looked up and sought her, then gave her a thumbs-up when their gazes met. He beckoned to her.

Rania manifested in the main room beside him, visibly startling the other two *Pyr*.

"I got two of them," Hadrian informed her with pride, then gestured to a shining puddle on the floor. It could have been liquid silver or mercury, because it was thicker than blood or water. Its diameter was already diminishing in size and there was a weapon in the middle of it.

Rania wasn't sure what to think of that. She felt jumbled up inside, her heart tugged with an unfamiliar mix of sympathy for the fallen warriors and an understanding of Hadrian's jubilation. Where were her alliances in this battle? They should be with the Fae, but she didn't like Hadrian being assaulted.

Not just because he was supposed to be her kill, either.

She'd never felt so much emotion or uncertainty before. It was as unsettling as the firestorm was seductive.

"They really attacked?" she asked, crouching down beside the puddle. She wasn't sure she'd ever seen a Fae die. Had he melted completely?

"Of course they attacked," the one with the man-bun said with impatience. "They've sworn to slaughter all shifters, at the Dark Queen's command. It's only a matter of time before we're all hunted down."

"Unless we do some hunting first," Hadrian said with resolve. Rania watched him crouch down to study the sword in the puddle. The silver liquid was disappearing quickly from around and over it. "How about one of these for your collection?" he murmured with a quick sidelong glance, apparently not expecting a reply.

Rania shouldn't have replied. She should have seized the opportunity of his inattention and taken the clean strike at his throat with the *bichuwa*.

She was close and her blow unobstructed. Hadrian was so interested in the blade that he wasn't even looking at her. The other two *Pyr* were similarly distracted.

But she was curious again. She didn't have a Fae blade in her collection. Maeve managed them very closely, since weapons were always in short supply in a realm with no ability to work metal. This particular one was a gorgeous intricately-carved blade, obviously the possession of a senior and elite warrior.

She wondered whether it was someone she knew. The truth was that she'd only met a few of the Fae: they avoided her because she was still one of the Others. That would all change when her wager with Maeve was complete. She refused to acknowledge a niggle of doubt that all would go as expected. Hadrian wanted her to doubt Maeve, because that was a better strategic choice for his own survival. It didn't mean he was right.

Why had the Fae attacked, though? Was it her fault for telling Maeve about the gloves? If they'd come for the gloves, though, they'd failed: Hadrian was still wearing the original pair and they hadn't even ventured into his studio.

Maybe they hadn't expected the *Pyr* to defend themselves so well.

Maybe surprise had been on the *Pyr* side.

"You got someone important," she said, instead of sharing the jumble of her thoughts.

"How do you know?" Hadrian asked.

"This blade is highly ornamented and must be rare." Rania indicated the Celtic knotwork on the hilt and the gem in the pommel. It looked like a star sapphire. There were inscriptions on the blade, too, although she couldn't read them. "The Dark Queen claims all of the weapons and awards them to her warriors for service and valor."

"The bigger the blade, the more important the fighter?" Hadrian asked.

"Pretty much," Rania agreed. "He must have been senior and trusted." She was thinking, as well, that Maeve would be very unhappy at the loss of a powerful warrior, never mind the loss of the blade. She glanced around, halfway expecting the Fae to slice between realms immediately to regain the sword.

"Are those charms?" the *Pyr* who looked most like Hadrian asked, pointing to the marks on the blade.

"Probably," Hadrian said, then glanced at Rania for confirmation.

She nodded agreement. "In most societies, weapons are inscribed with spells to protect the bearer and make his or her aim more true. The Fae are no different."

"Even though they can't do the work themselves," Hadrian noted.

"Didn't work this time," the *Pyr* with the man-bun said, obviously watching her.

"No." Rania stood and looked around, listening as she scanned the lair.

"You think they'll come after it," Hadrian guessed.

"It wouldn't surprise me," she admitted. "Because they don't forge weapons themselves, the Dark Queen doesn't like to lose a blade."

"Never mind the question of vengeance," the other *Pyr* said grimly.

"There is that."

"The other sword might have been more important." Hadrian pointed to a second puddle, which was rapidly evaporating. It was as if the essence of the fallen Fae had to return to their own realm. "The one who escaped back through the portal took that one's weapon with him." He frowned. "I barely got a glimpse of it."

"Me, neither," said the other two *Pyr* simultaneously.

"It's a good thing you weren't here," Hadrian said to Rania, his gaze filled with warmth, and she was surprised.

"You're right. Another one on their side might have influenced the result." She smiled at him and spun her *bichuwa*. "You might not have fared so well. Is that why you sent me away?"

"You know it wasn't," Hadrian replied with a smile.

His friends looked alarmed.

"Why such senior warriors?" Hadrian mused then flicked a glance her way, his gaze filled with questions. "Maybe they came for you."

Rania was startled. "The Dark Queen and I have a deal..."

"And it wouldn't be the first time she made sure she didn't have to deliver her end of the bargain," Hadrian said. "It's a pretty good way to avoid a debt. Just take out the recipient."

Rania took a step back. "You're wrong..."

"Believe what you need to." Hadrian straightened and turned to his friends. "Introductions are past due. This is Balthasar."

The dragon shifter with the man-bun inclined his head. His hair was dark and his eyes were blue. He was tall and more slender than the others, giving Rania the impression that he was young. She realized she had no way to guess the age of dragon shifters, or even any certainty of how long they lived. How old was Hadrian? He said he'd been waiting two hundred years for his firestorm. Did they wait their whole lives, or only after a certain period of time? She didn't know: Melissa Smith hadn't talked about that in the shows Rania had watched.

Maybe they waited for a firestorm after they fell in love the first time. Rania didn't know where that thought came from, much less the surge of jealousy that followed it, but she didn't like either.

She wasn't going to care for this dragon shifter who would be her last victim.

Enjoying his company and the view he offered, and even his kisses, wasn't nearly the same as actually caring. The rationalization sounded thin even to her own ears.

"And this is my cousin, Alasdair." The *Pyr* who looked like a slightly older and stockier version of Hadrian nodded. He had the same wavy auburn hair and green eyes. Rania wondered whether the two of them had scales of the same color in dragon form.

"And who do we have the pleasure of meeting?" Alasdair prompted.

Hadrian looked interested, too.

"My name doesn't matter," Rania said. "I won't be here long."

"Prickly," Alasdair said to Hadrian.

He chuckled. "But she grows on you." He gave her a warm smile. "I think the firestorm's right and we'll get along just fine."

"Don't kid yourself. You'll be dead and I'll be Fae."

"That's the persistent rumor," he said lightly, as if unconcerned.

"You okay, there?" Balthasar asked, indicating Hadrian's injured cheek.

"Just a scratch." He tugged off a glove and wiped the blood away, letting Balthasar peer at it.

"But from a Fae dagger. I'll put some of Sloane's salve on it." He strode away with purpose, then rummaged in a knapsack at the end of the kitchen counter.

"Sloane is the Apothecary of the *Pyr*," Hadrian told Rania. "Balthasar has apprenticed with him."

"I know maybe five per cent of what he knows," that *Pyr* said. "But his big secrets will only be surrendered to his son, Tynan, when he trains to become the next Apothecary of our kind."

It made sense to Rania that the healer's skills were passed along the family line so she just nodded.

It was interesting that the other *Pyr* were both handsome men who looked like they worked out a lot, and obviously, both were *Pyr*. Rania didn't find either of them as attractive as Hadrian, though.

Was that because of this persistent firestorm? It shone white, illuminating the lair as brightly as a beam of sunlight. Finally, she realized why one of the *Pyr's* names was familiar.

"Alasdair," she repeated, glancing at Hadrian. "Wasn't he one of the *Pyr* who entered Fae with you?"

Hadrian nodded and his tone turned teasing. "He's quite the dancer, my cousin."

"Very funny," Alasdair said, his tone more grim.

So, they'd both been cursed by Maeve. Well, if they'd entered the realm without permission, that was the price.

Rania looked at the Fae dagger again. The last of the pool of silver left by the Fae warrior was disappearing. The liquid clung to the inscriptions on the blade and the indentations in the hilt, then suddenly vanished completely. The blade's glow flickered, then started to dim. Was its fire cold or hot? What fueled it?

"I wonder about that light around the blade," she said. She remembered the intruder in her home and realized that once she started wondering, it was hard to stop.

"Me, too," Hadrian admitted. "And the blade itself. How does it generate the light? Is that why it can slice portals between realms, or is there more to that?"

"The light must be from a spell," Rania suggested. "Maybe magick, maybe conjured by the inscriptions."

"Maybe. Maybe it's something else. Magnesium burns white, for example." Hadrian bent and picked up the blade with care. "Cold," he said with satisfaction and tightened his grip on the hilt. The glow continued to dim steadily, like the blade was dying, too. The star sapphire in the pommel emitted a faint glow, as if a distant star was captured within it, but even that seemed to be fading.

"So, they light their blades?" Alasdair asked.

"With matches?" Balthasar said, his tone joking. "Like tiki torches?"

"Maybe. I'll have to analyze the composition of the blade. The weapon can't be steel, because the Fae can't touch steel."

"What if it's something else that makes the blade glow?" Rania asked, folding her arms across her chest. "You're thinking like a blacksmith, not like the Fae."

He grinned crookedly. "Guilty as charged. Call it a habit. What's your idea?"

Rania shrugged. "That it could be more like fireflies. There are so many of them in Fae, and often the Fae congregate in hollows where fireflies are found. How do they glow?"

"Bioluminescence," Alasdair supplied. "A chemical reaction. It's kind of the same: things glow when they burn oxygen. Magnesium burns white, as Hadrian said. Fireflies combine oxygen with calcium, adenosine triphosphate and luciferin in the presence of the enzyme luciferase."

"Whoa. How do you know that?" Balthasar asked.

"I looked it up once. I was curious one night. And it's a cold light, one that doesn't use a lot of energy or produce much heat." Alasdair smiled. "Not unlike the light of an ice dragon's firestorm."

"And just as effective when it comes to mating signals," Balthasar said, nudging Alasdair. The two were looking at the light of the firestorm, while Hadrian and Rania considered the Fae sword.

An ice dragon's firestorm. Hadrian had referred to being an ice dragon before, and so did that prophecy. What exactly did it mean?

"If that's so, why is the light fading?" Rania asked. "There's a lot of oxygen here."

Hadrian shrugged. "Maybe because there are no Fae. Maybe it's sensitive to their presence."

"Maybe they make it glow," Rania suggested. She leaned closer, noticing that something white was appearing on the edges of the blade. "What's that?"

"Hoarfrost," Hadrian replied, astonishment in his tone. Sure enough, fine crystals of ice were growing from the sharp edges of the sword and slowly covering it.

Rania was intrigued. "Is it freezing?" she asked and Hadrian shrugged, obviously as mystified as she was. "It's not cold in here, though."

"No, it's not." Hadrian frowned. "This sword is like you." He flicked a glance her way. "It gives me questions for my questions."

That didn't seem to trouble him and Rania found herself blushing a little.

"While you just give me trouble," she countered and he laughed.

He sobered as he peered at the blade again. "It's getting dimmer."

"It's almost like the light is changing to ice," she said, frowning.

"Then maybe we should act fast."

"Excuse me?"

"Maybe we should use the blade sooner rather than later."

Rania eyed Hadrian with suspicion. "How?"

"These blades open portals between the realms. What if we invite ourselves to Fae? We might have the element of surprise on our side."

Rania shook her head. "No shortage of verve," she murmured. Hadrian had a talent for challenging expectations, but this idea troubled her deeply.

"Count me out," Alasdair said and took a step back.

"You really don't learn, do you?" Rania asked. "You'll be invading the realm again. You'll be cursed again as a result."

"Ah, but you're going to kill me anyway," Hadrian said lightly. "I don't have much to lose. Maybe I should make these last moments count."

"I'd like to get on with completing my assignment if you're done stalling."

"I'm not. I might never be. After all, I still haven't convinced you about the merit of the firestorm."

Rania lifted the *bichuwa* and took a step closer, just as the glow surrounding the Fae blade winked out. All four of them stared.

"How did you do that?" Balthasar asked.

"I didn't. At least I don't think I did. Did you do it?"

Rania shook her head.

"So, it extinguished for some reason," Hadrian mused. "Too bad. It probably won't slice open portals anymore."

"Maybe that's a good thing," Alasdair said and Rania was inclined to agree.

"Maybe that's why," Balthasar suggested. "Maybe it guessed your plan and made sure you couldn't do it."

Hadrian and Rania looked at each other.

"Eithne said the Regalian magick was sentient. If that's what makes these blades light, it could have decided," Alasdair noted.

"Whoa," Hadrian said, picking up the blade with care. It was completely frosted over and was becoming transparent. "I'd love to take this into the studio and examine it more closely."

"You aren't going to make more of them," Balthasar protested.

"No. I want to know how to destroy them." Hadrian glanced at the *bichuwa*, then he met Rania's gaze. "What do you say? One last wish?"

"Another one?"

"Can't blame a guy for trying." He leaned closer to her, dropping his voice low. His eyes were sparkling and that smile got to Rania right where she lived. Never mind the steady glow of the firestorm and the effect it had on her thoughts. "How long have you been hunting on Maeve's behalf?" he challenged.

"A thousand years, give or take."

"Then what's another couple of hours?" Hadrian asked. "Let me check out the sword and see what I can learn from it."

"One track mind," Alasdair said, nodding at his cousin with obvious affection.

"I thought that track would be the firestorm," Balthasar murmured.

"Who says it isn't?" Alasdair replied.

"I shouldn't," Rania said, ignoring the two *Pyr*.

Hadrian wagged a finger at her, his eyes dancing. "But you're tempted. How long since you've surrendered to temptation?"

It was easy to remember the interlude in his bedroom and Rania felt herself blush a little. She wasn't used to blushing and the unwelcome heat in her cheeks made her feel flustered.

Hadrian turned toward his studio, the Fae blade in his grip. "It won't take long. I'll stay nice and still when it's time for you to kill me, so you can do it neatly. I promise."

"Fifteen minutes!" she said, trying to sound tough.

"Twenty!" he replied.

"You..."

Hadrian caught her up and spun her around, giving her an enthusiastic kiss that almost made her consider helping him leave another legacy.

"Go before you change my mind," she said, trying to sound stern, but he laughed.

"You know where to find me." He put her down, kissed her in the middle of the brilliant radiance of the firestorm's light, then strode toward his studio with purpose.

He was even whistling.

Cocky dragon.

Sexy dragon.

Rania watched him go, unable to drag her gaze away, then realized the other two *Pyr* were watching her.

Alasdair cleared his throat. "I know you have an obligation to fulfill to the Dark Queen," he said, his voice husky and his Scottish burr more pronounced than it had been. "I know you want to keep your word and that you want to see your brothers freed. I'm not going to argue with any of that."

"But you'd like me to spare Hadrian," Rania guessed, bracing herself against his inevitable appeal.

Alasdair shook his head. "There's another way for everyone to get what they want. You can have it all. You don't have to choose."

"The choice is made..." Rania began.

"Change it." Alasdair said. "Take me as your *Pyr* victim instead. Give me the kiss of death, spare Hadrian, and set your brothers free. Then you can satisfy the firestorm and stay together."

Rania was shocked and touched that Alasdair would make such an offer. She stared at him, unable to summon a word to her lips.

Because it was a lot more tempting a proposition than it should have been.

Too bad it was impossible.

Hadrian was glad that his mate had trusted him to examine the Fae blade before fulfilling her quest. He saw each incremental victory as a sign that her determination was weakening, and that she was appreciating the merit of the firestorm, too.

The sword had been tipped with hoarfrost when he'd brought it into the studio and gradually, it seemed to be turning to ice itself. He couldn't figure it out, but each time he touched it, the process seemed to accelerate.

Would it melt? Would it vanish completely, like the Fae warriors had?

Was it self-destructing because it was no longer in Fae, or because it was no longer in the possession of a Fae warrior?

He wished it hadn't changed. It would have been sweet to turn the tables on Maeve and surprise her in her own realm. The strategy might change everything. It might also have been a suicide mission, but Hadrian didn't give a lot of weight to that. He'd be dead soon, anyway, unless he could find a way for his mate to fulfill her quest and leave him alive.

The sword had given hope of that possibility, too, at least briefly.

What if he could satisfy the firestorm and leave a son to follow after him?

What if he could give his son an even bigger legacy, like a world without the Dark Queen hunting all shifters to oblivion?

He heard Alasdair gearing up to tell a story in the main room and smiled. He was going to get more than his twenty minutes, and he'd make it count.

He fired up the forge, wanting at least two pair of gloves done ASAP.

CHAPTER SEVEN

Rania was amazed that Alasdair would offer to sacrifice himself in exchange for his cousin. It was one thing to try to help family and friends, but dying for them was beyond her experience or expectation. She couldn't believe he'd volunteered for the kiss of death. "I can't do that," she began to protest.

But Alasdair wasn't dissuaded. "You just don't understand how important the firestorm is."

"It's about sex. And babies."

"No," Alasdair said with a shake of his head. "It's about partnership and destiny, about honor and becoming the best you can be. It's a dream and an objective, and it's not something to easily cast aside."

"All the *Pyr* work together to ensure that a firestorm is a success," Balthasar insisted.

"To ensure the survival of your kind," Rania said. "I understand that, but you have to see that there's no point. Others are going to be eliminated."

"But what if we aren't?" Balthasar asked. "What if the Dark Queen loses?"

Rania had never considered that to be a possibility. What if it was? "She has all the magick..." she began.

"But we have the firestorm," Alasdair said, interrupting her. "Let me tell you a story," he offered. "Let me tell you about the commitment of the firestorm, then maybe you'll understand why Hadrian should survive to enjoy his."

"Maybe you'll understand why the *Pyr* should survive," Balthasar added.

Rania understood what Hadrian had meant when he'd said that Alasdair was a good storyteller. She was already tempted to listen to him. She was curious again, even though she recognized that as dangerous. Would it hurt to learn more about the *Pyr* and their firestorm? She might end up the only person who knew or remembered.

She'd already given Hadrian permission to examine the Fae sword. A story would fill the time. He'd told her that she didn't listen to enough of them.

And he'd told her to seize any chance to hear Alasdair tell a story, too.

Maybe she'd been missing something.

Rania nodded agreement and Alasdair grinned.

"But I can't give you the kiss of death," she said, wanting to ensure he understood.

"I've no doubt you could still kill me." When she would have argued, he raised a hand and began to shimmer blue around his perimeter. He looked more vital and his eyes brightened, reflecting the light that indicated he was on the cusp of change.

"Is it a long story? Should I bring snacks?" Balthasar asked with enthusiasm.

"Why not?" Alasdair said as he moved into the middle of the great room.

"It's the middle of the night," Rania protested.

"Just about the right time to go to a movie in New York," Alasdair replied. "I'm still on Eastern time."

"This is a fog dragon thing," Balthasar assured Rania. "It rocks."

Then Alasdair shifted shape, becoming a dragon of hematite and silver. He wrapped his length around the perimeter of the main living space of Hadrian's lair, his tail tucking beneath his chin. His eyes glittered like mica as he narrowed them and breathed a cloud of fog. It hovered in the air in the middle of the room, becoming steadily whiter and larger as he continued to exhale.

Balthasar lowered the blinds on the big windows facing the river, as if they were going to watch a movie, then gestured for her to take a seat on the big leather sofa. Rania did, uncertain what would happen. It was meditative to watch Alasdair breathe his cloud of fog, but not exactly fascinating.

She certainly didn't understand why Balthasar made a big bowl of popcorn before joining her on the couch to watch. His anticipation was palpable and inexplicable.

'A fog dragon thing.' What did that mean?

She heard Hadrian hammering in the studio and found the steady rhythm of the sound reassuring. Of course, he was working on the gloves. With his keen hearing, he probably knew what Alasdair was doing and was making the most of every moment. She did admire that.

Maybe he'd even be able to hear the story.

A bit too late, she wished Hadrian hadn't taken the Fae sword with him. She wanted to see how it changed, too. She started to get up, but Balthasar put a hand on her arm. He pointed at the cloud, which had to be twenty feet across.

"Watch," he advised in an undertone.

Alasdair began to chant something, although Rania couldn't distinguish or understand the words. The rhythm of his voice was as soothing as a slow-running stream. She found herself relaxing despite her concerns and wondered whether this was a kind of beguiling. She leaned forward to see whether there were flames in Alasdair's eyes or not. There weren't, but to her amazement, images began to form in the cloud of steam.

That made her sit up and pay attention. It *was* like a movie.

"I remember Hadrian's father Notus well," Alasdair said softly. A dragon profile formed in the mist, then shifted into focus. Rania clearly saw a dragon of amber and gold turn a glittering gaze upon her. She knew it was an illusion of some kind, but the dragon looked solid and real. He had long red feathers and his eyes were a thousand shades of orange and red, as if his very being was aflame. He was stunningly beautiful and exactly how she'd always imagined dragons would look. There was something in his expression that reminded her of Hadrian, a certain audacity and confidence, a trait that maybe ran in families.

Alasdair continued. "He and my father, Boreus, were cousins and they were close in their youth. They mastered their *Pyr* skills together and fought together. They celebrated together and they challenged each other. It was said that they were often seen together, flying over the Highlands."

The dragon in the vision became smaller, as if a camera drew back to create a panoramic view. Rania saw the hills of Scotland, touched with the purple of heather, their rugged peaks wreathed in clouds. Above them flew a pair of dragons, sparring with each other playfully, spinning and diving, then locking claws to feign battle. One was the amber and gold one that had surveyed her, with magnificent feathers streaming from his tail and wingtips, while the other was amethyst and silver, a hundred shades of purple touched with starlight. His feathers were long and grey. Rania had never seen *Pyr* with such feathers before this and thought they were beautiful. They were as wild as the countryside beneath them and the sight of them in flight made her smile.

She liked that they had each other, equal companions. Cousins, not siblings, but they hadn't grown up alone and isolated from their kind. Her heart ached for something she'd never possessed.

"They were named for the Anemoi, the divinities of the winds in Greek mythology. Notus was named for the south wind, the hot, wet and changeable scirocco wind from Africa, the wind that brought storms, unsettled weather and change. Boreus was named for the north wind, a powerful cold force that brought both winter weather and fertility. Two other cousins were named Zephyr and Euros for the other Anemoi, the west wind and the east wind."

The two dragons were joined by another pair, all of them so slender that they seemed to have only just come of age. There were four older dragons with them, one breathing fire as the others watched. Rania realized it was a lesson as the four young *Pyr* followed his example with various levels of success. The second older dragon breathed smoke and again the young ones mimicked him. Rania watched as the fathers tutored their young.

She'd essentially been an only child, the sole mortal child in Fae. She'd always wanted this kind of camaraderie with a group of her own kind.

If she surrendered to the firestorm with Hadrian, would the *Pyr* gather to raise their son, even after Hadrian's death? It was a surprisingly reassuring idea.

"The names were a decision of four *Pyr* in homage to their legacy as the descendants of the Dragon Legion *Pyr*, Thaddeus, and his mate, Aura, who had been a nymph before their firestorm. Aura and Thad had two pairs of twins and it was their grandsons who made this pact."

The vision flickered, huts disappearing and vegetation changing with the seasons. Rania understood that time was passing. When the scene came into focus, the two dragons were together and they were larger. They looked more muscular and some of their scales had darkened. They were older, clearly. Rania wondered what had happened to the cousins and fathers, but perhaps that wasn't part of Alasdair's tale.

"When my father's firestorm sparked, it was Notus who defended his back while my father convinced his destined mate to accept him."

Rania smiled at the vision of a pretty young woman walking through the grass, laughing as she swung a pail of milk. The reason for her amusement followed behind her, a handsome man whose attention was fixed upon her. He was obviously using all of his charm in an attempt to persuade her of something, but she laughed at him. The light of the firestorm sparked between them, making them both oblivious to everything except each other. He caught her hand and she spun to face him with delight. She would have dropped the milk, but he caught it from her grasp and set it down, then kissed her sweetly. The way she leaned against him proved that she wasn't so resistant to his appeal after all and Rania could understand that. The attention of a dragon shifter in the presence of a firestorm made it almost impossible to refuse at least a kiss.

Rania listened, noting the steady hammering from the studio as Hadrian worked.

The firestorm's light flared to brilliance and even in a vision, it made Rania's heart skip. She scanned the scene, seeking clues as to the time and date, but couldn't be sure. The hut was roofed with thatch and could have been from any era. The maiden's dress was simple and modest, her hair long and auburn. Her feet were bare and the clouds bore down low, heavy with rain. A mist was falling and she recognized that it was still Scotland from the shape of the hills.

If these were his parents, how old was Alasdair?

There was a pasture behind the amorous couple where the cow was tethered. A man appeared behind the cow, startling it, his gaze fixed on the embracing couple. He had dark hair and dark eyes and there was an intensity about him that made Rania fear his intentions. He stalked the couple silently, unaware that yet another man followed him. She guessed that the second man was Notus, because he shared Hadrian's auburn hair and there was a similarity between the two around the eyes. Behind the second man, clouds gathered in the distance and Rania could see the wind blowing in the trees. It was as if a storm followed him.

The south wind, Notus, brought storms. Did the dragon shifter named Notus have the same powers?

Alasdair continued. "In those days, our kind were divided, into true *Pyr* and *Slayers*. *Slayers* had chosen not to defend humans as treasures of the earth any longer, seeing mankind as a pestilence to be exterminated. This was the result of dragons being hunted as trophies. For example, Sigmund, one of the Council of Seven, was killed by human hunters intent on gathering his blood as a curative. One of his three sons turned *Slayer* as a result of his father's death, a dragon shifter named Olaf. *Slayers* had blood that ran black instead of red, a sign that they had embraced the darkness over the light, but many of them were jealous of the firestorm. *Slayers* could not have a firestorm, and thus had no sons. Olaf was filled with bitterness and resentment, and believed he had been cheated in every way. When Boreus had his firestorm, Olaf was drawn to the spark and tried to steal Boreus' mate."

As Alasdair spoke, the dark-haired man bounded forward, shimmering blue and shifting shape in mid-air. He became a dragon of malachite and silver, a splendid creature of fierce power. He would have attacked the embracing couple, but the man following him moved like quicksilver. He also shimmered blue then changed to the amber and gold dragon with the feathers Rania had seen earlier.

He *was* Notus! Notus seized Olaf by the wings before the couple realized the threat and parted. Boreus pushed his mate behind himself and shimmered blue on the cusp of change as the green and amber dragons fought overhead. Boreus didn't change shape and Rania wondered why not. Shouldn't he be defending his mate? The maiden looked astonished as she watched the fight overhead and Boreus steadily backed her toward the hut.

Meanwhile, the pending storm arrived. The trees bent beneath the assault of the wind and dark clouds glowered overhead. Rain began to fall and she saw Boreus' mate shiver as the raindrops changed to ice and fell tinkling on the ground. Boreus cast a cloak over the maiden's shoulders and pulled her against his side, the firestorm glowing as she slipped an arm around his waist.

Would he truly defend her against the *Slayer*, or was he just sheltering her until the firestorm was satisfied? Rania instinctively distrusted the idea of romance.

"Olaf and Notus fought over Boreus' mate," Alasdair said. "While Boreus was compelled to stand and watch, because he had not yet confided the truth of his nature in her. Miranda was already so frightened that he feared his shift would overwhelm her with terror. There was a conviction amongst our kind that a mortal could not look upon the change without descending into madness, and Boreus was protective of his mate in every way."

The dragon battle, meanwhile, was ferocious. The pair grappled for supremacy, tumbling end over end through the air, breathing fire and slashing at each other. Olaf was bigger but Notus was more clever. Olaf struck Notus with his tail and Notus raked his claws across Olaf's belly, ripping open his guts. Rania watched as the *Slayer's* black blood flowed and saw steam rise where it hit the ground. The snow fell faster and thicker, and there was a thin coating of ice over everything. The dragons kept fighting, their fury melting the ice and filling the air with mist. Notus breathed fire at the wound and Olaf cried out in anguish, his bellow echoing over the hills. His eyes glinted and he dove after Notus, who soared high in the sky, drawing him away. He disappeared in the clouds that wreathed the summits of the hills, Olaf fast behind him.

Alasdair made a gesture with one claw and Rania saw the fight from a different view, as if she was hanging onto Olaf's tail. The dragons swept into a cloud and she felt as if she was flying himself. It was thrilling. The mist and the falling snow diminished visibility to almost nil, and she heard the tinkle of ice falling against the dragon scales. She felt Olaf's fury and his confusion, then Notus suddenly appeared ahead of him, those feathers glistening with drops of rainwater. Notus glanced back, apparently in fear, then lunged onward and disappeared into the clouds again.

Olaf gave a roar and raced in pursuit, only to slam into the side of the hill that had been veiled by the clouds. His head hit the rock hard and he slid down the face of the stone, unconscious. A trail of black blood from his temple followed his descent, sizzling on the surface of the stone. Notus swooped down and attacked the fallen *Slayer*. Rania winced as Notus cut away Olaf's genitals, then tossed them into the air and burned them with his dragonfire, deaf to Olaf's screams. The black blood flowed from Olaf's wound, staining the snow that was accumulating on the ground, and he shifted between forms before passing out as a dark-haired man. Notus surveyed him for a long moment, then took flight, disappearing into the swirl of snow. It was quiet then and Rania could only see the steady trickle of black blood into the snow.

So Notus had eliminated the *Slayer* who threatened his cousin's firestorm. He had risked death for his cousin, just as Alasdair offered to die in Hadrian's stead. The *Pyr*, clearly, had stronger bonds than Rania had realized.

No one would have offered his or her life in exchange for Rania's. The realization chilled her.

"Notus abandoned the *Slayer* to die," Alasdair said. "He believed that Olaf could not survive such an injury. But fury is a powerful force, and a thirst for revenge can provide a burning desire to survive."

Rania knew that well enough. She watched the snow fall, covering Olaf's fallen body as time passed. The *Slayer* stirred finally and sat up with a grimace, then brushed the snow from his shoulders. She saw Olaf's horror when he examined his own injury, then watched as the *Slayer* dragged his broken body toward what might have been a path or road. He managed to rise to his feet, bind his wound roughly with a length of cloth torn from his own garments, and cut a staff from a broken tree. He staggered onward, and eventually the opening of a cave came into view.

Rania guessed that Olaf had sensed the presence of the man there, the one who emerged from the darkness and surveyed him with concern. She shivered, remembering the trapper who had healed her injuries all those years ago when she'd hunted the polar bear shifter, and wondered whether this one had an agenda of his own as well.

"Olaf was lucky," Alasdair said. "He always had been, and on this occasion, his luck held. He reached the refuge of a hermit renowned for his healing abilities, and without revealing his nature, received care. His body healed, but his need for vengeance only grew stronger with each passing day. His fury was distilled into a dark and potent force, one he could not ignore."

The scene spun and it was clearly spring when Olaf left the cave. He looked healthy again. He embraced the hermit from the cave and walked away, continuing in human form until he was out of view. His eyes glittered when he glanced back, then he shimmered blue, shifting into his powerful dragon form and taking flight. He flew high over the hills, soaring through the clouds, then swooped down on the hermit's refuge. He returned from the opposite direction and roared on his approach. The hermit came out of the cave, wary but curious, and Olaf roasted him with dragonfire. The hermit screamed as he tried to retreat to the safety of the cave but Olaf was relentless. He landed outside the door, shoved his head as far as possible into the cave, and breathed dragonfire with such force that smoke came out the cracks in the stone.

"No one would ever know that Olaf had found sanctuary in this place, or that the hermit had healed him. No one would be able to challenge Notus' conviction that the *Slayer* was dead," Alasdair said.

Rania was shocked by Olaf's savagery even though it was strategic and defensive. Clearly, dragons weren't always the good guys.

Maybe her assignment from Maeve was justified.

"By the time Olaf abandoned the place where he had found refuge, it was burned and blackened, smoking with destruction. Nothing moved. Nothing uttered a sound.

Rania watched, fascinated, as Olaf took flight and disappeared into the blue."

"Olaf returned to his own lair, abandoning Boreus and his mate," Alasdair said. "Their firestorm was consummated and no longer of interest to him. He was determined to take vengeance upon Notus in retaliation for his injury. He waited for Notus to have his firestorm. He hid himself from both *Pyr* and *Slayers*, letting Notus believe he was dead." The vision showed a dragon sleeping in the dark shadows of a cave, his breathing so slow and steady that he might have been made of stone. Only the faint glimmer of his eyes and the occasional wisp of smoke revealed that he was alive. Rania was struck by the similarity to Hadrian the night before, when she'd appeared in his studio. Olaf appeared to be soundly asleep or even dead, but she could see the telltale glimmer of his eyes. He was awake and watching. "He banked the fires, as my father would have said, and he waited more than a hundred and fifty years."

The sudden spark of the firestorm made Rania jump, even though she'd expected it. The firestorm flared at a distance, but its powerful spark touched even the darkness of Olaf's lair. The glow was white, exactly the same as the light that burned between herself and Hadrian, and their firestorm felt stronger even with the illusion of the one long satisfied. In the vision, the sleeping Olaf lifted his head, inhaled deeply and smiled. The malice in his expression was a warning.

"When Notus had his firestorm, Olaf sensed the first spark. He was determined to strike at the heart of his opponent, stealing what was of greatest importance to Notus in retaliation for his own loss."

Rania saw Olaf emerge from his lair and take flight, a dark and fearsome silhouette against the sky. He flew hard and fast, his wings beating furiously, as he raced toward the firestorm. The *Slayer* landed in the fields outside a village in the darkness of the night, when the moon was new. There was a quick shimmer of blue as he took his human form. Rania realized there was already a man on the road, walking toward a small village.

She sat straighter, fearing Olaf's intent and his viciousness. He couldn't have succeeded, because Hadrian had been born of this firestorm, but the suspense made her heart pound. As she watched, Olaf stealthily followed the other man into the town, keeping to the shadows to disguise his presence.

Once again, there were dark clouds gathering in the distance, as if a storm was brewing. The wind whipped around the pair and they both pulled their cloaks closer, indicating that the wind was cold. The slate blue color of the clouds made Rania think they were snowclouds, just as the clouds had been when Boreus' mate had been attacked by Olaf and Notus had intervened.

The streets were quiet in the town, although music flowed from a tavern, along with the sound of laughter. The spark of the firestorm and the other man's path led Olaf to a comfortable house with a single light burning in a barred window. Olaf lingered in the shadows to watch as Notus, in his human form, spoke quietly to someone inside. The firestorm's light bathed him in silvery radiance, like the light of a full moon, adding to the faint light from the chamber. The wind danced around him and the first flakes of snow began to fall.

Alasdair cleared his throat. "Notus' mate was Argenta, the daughter of a wool merchant and a maiden who had a talent for spinning. Her older sister, Dora, had been able to spin straw into gold, and after her efforts added to her father's wealth, word of her skill had spread. She'd been married to a local prince, who kept her spinning all the day and night.

"Argenta, in contrast, could spin ice into silver, and her father didn't let that opportunity for gain pass either. She was locked in a chamber and compelled to spin day and night, while her father tried to keep the truth of her abilities secret. Rumors were already spreading in the town when her firestorm with Notus sparked."

Rania was struck by the difference between ideas of family. The *Pyr* defended each other and helped each other: this wool merchant used his daughters' skills for his own gain, with no care for their welfare or desires. She had to consider her relationship with the Dark Queen. Maeve had never asked what Rania wanted herself. She'd made suggestions and offered a deal, but even her gifts—like the kiss of death—were granted so that Rania could better serve the Dark Queen's will. No one had ever asked what she wanted, or helped her to achieve a goal of her own.

She bit her lip, wondering how much that mattered. It mattered to Hadrian and the *Pyr*. Should it matter to her?

The view moved closer, past Olaf and over Notus' shoulder. There was frost gathering on the edges of the window and snow dancing between Notus and the view of his mate. Rania saw the slender woman at the spinning wheel, her eyes alight as she listened to Notus courting her. She never slowed in her work, though she smiled at his attention.

The chamber was sparsely furnished, with only a bed, a pail and a small table. It looked more like a prison to Rania. There was a bucket of icicles beside the maiden and she took each one in turn, spinning it into a long strand of silver. She wore a heavy coat and gloves with the fingertips cut off, her face pale with the chill of the room. The silver was coiled on the floor, like gleaming wire, and rolled into chests stacked against the walls. Her hands moved deftly and Rania could sense her uncertainty of

Notus.

She couldn't blame her, either. He probably just wanted sex.

"Argenta hadn't been allowed to mingle in society since her gift had been revealed, for her father feared she might be stolen away. As a result, she was wary of men, particularly the handsome man who came to her window each night, intent upon charming her. Notus told her stories, though, and prompted her laughter, courting her affection. He made steady progress, and that was compounded by the firestorm, which turned Argenta's thoughts to love and romance. After two weeks of clandestine visits, she surrendered to his appeal."

Rania watched Argenta abandon her spinning. She glanced toward the door as if fearing a reprimand, then shyly came to the window. Her eyes glowed with happiness as she approached Notus and Rania wished she could hear the words they exchanged. Argenta's smile was quick and her blush was enchanting. She moved quickly then, putting her hand upon that of Notus on the sill and leaning against the bars for their first kiss. The firestorm flared to brilliant white and Rania heard Notus catch his breath at its power.

This would be the true measure of the firestorm. What would Notus do after it was satisfied? Would Argenta be abandoned once she carried his child?

This was the part where the myth would have to give way to the truth. Rania leaned forward to make sure she didn't miss a word.

Hadrian heard the rumble of Alasdair's voice from his lair and knew that his cousin was telling a story, using his gift as a fog dragon to show it at the same time. He smiled to himself, halfway wishing he was there to watch and listen.

He was surprised that his mate had agreed to listen, but maybe his cousin was more persuasive than he'd managed to be. Either way, he'd make use of every possible moment he had left.

Suddenly, the hair stood up on the back of Hadrian's neck. He was in the act of landing another blow on the last of the talons but his hammer never struck.

He was frozen, trapped in a single moment. He was motionless and couldn't do anything about it. The weight of the hammer made his muscles strain in his shoulder but he couldn't drop it, put it down, or lift it to a more comfortable position. Alasdair's voice had silenced, too, and the clock on the wall was no longer ticking.

The silver light in the periphery of his vision gave him a good idea why.

Someone grabbed his elbow and spun him around in place, like a mannequin in a store window. It was a Fae warrior, a big blond one who looked faintly familiar. He turned Hadrian so that the *Pyr* was facing one of his own worktables. Maeve sat on the table, legs crossed. She was wearing a black suit with feathers around the collar, and wore high-heeled shoes. One foot swung as she smiled at him. Her lipstick was the color of blood and her dark eyes were filled with fury, despite her smile.

"Apparently, it's true that if you want something done, you need to do it yourself."

He had a very bad feeling about this visit, but there was exactly nothing he could do about it. That made him feel even worse.

She picked up the Fae sword, balancing it on her hands. Her lips tightened as she glanced down at the blade. It had changed even more since Hadrian had last looked at it. The blade was completely clear, like it was made of ice, and the hilt had turned from silver to cloudy white. Water dripped from the tip of the blade, which had become much shorter, and Hadrian realized that the weapon was melting.

Was it because he'd killed the Fae warrior entrusted with it?

"This is your fault," she said accusingly, which didn't exactly answer his question. The Dark Queen grimaced and offered what was left of the sword to her warrior. "It'll ruin my skirt," she said and he took it, bowing low to her afterward. He placed the blade on a different table, then stood at attention between the Dark Queen and the melting weapon.

Maeve considered Hadrian and her eyes glinted with what might have been amusement. The apparent change in her mood did nothing to reassure him. "You should know that the Others are concerned that I don't seem to hunt the *Pyr*. They think there's something special about you dragon shifters, and some have concluded that you've made a bargain with me to ensure your own survival." She arched a brow. "The truth, of course, is much simpler. You fall lower on my list since you're not a native species, so to speak."

Hadrian didn't understand what that meant.

Maeve chuckled, as if she'd read his thoughts, and he remembered her reputation. He tried to keep his thoughts simple. "There were no dragon shifters on Earth," she informed him. "Not originally. No divinity created dragon shifters here either. You're all aliens who arrived out of the blue and mingled with the local inhabitants. You've been here a long time, but that doesn't make you native." Her voice hardened, even as

Hadrian wondered whether that was true. "You're still mutants and you still taint the planet with your presence, but you're foreigners. Immigrants. I'll get to you after the Others who originated here." She swung her foot a little more and smiled at him. "I didn't plan for the other shifters to turn against the *Pyr*, but it might work out quite well. The Others could do some of the work for me. There could be fewer of you to slaughter by the time my main quest is complete."

That wasn't the most reassuring thing she could have said. How could Hadrian save his fellow *Pyr*? The gloves were closer to completion but not done, and that annoyed him.

Maeve raised a hand and shook a finger at him. "You know, I didn't think much of it when Rania chose you as her *Pyr* victim. I gave her that assignment to worry you all a bit and it's a bonus that it's sowing some dissent amongst the Others. But she has an instinct, that one, and she chose very, very well."

Maeve slipped off the table and moved past the Fae warrior to look down at the weapon again. It was even smaller than it had been and the hilt was beginning to melt now. "You know I can't tolerate this. My warriors must be armed, and that means you must die now."

She would kill him before he could finish the gloves for the other *Pyr*.

She would kill him before he could have the same effect on the entire Fae armory. If Hadrian had been breathing, that realization would have made his breath catch. As it was, his thoughts spun. The Dark Queen had a vulnerability and he'd learned about it only when it was too late to do anything about it.

Maeve laughed. "Exactly," she said with approval. She snapped her fingers and a slit of silver light appeared. Someone stepped through the gap before it was closed. Hadrian was surprised to see that it was Kade, the *Pyr* who had betrayed him.

Hadrian had admitted Kade to Rhys' apartment when Kade had lied to him. Kade had then stolen the stylus Maeve had originally given to him, the one that let him enter Fae at will. He'd been forced to surrender it to the *Pyr*, but had tricked Hadrian to steal it back. Kade had then disappeared. Hadrian itched to teach the faithless dragon shifter a lesson, but he couldn't even blink.

Kade stared at Maeve with adoration. She ran a hand across his cheek, as if he was a pet poodle, and Hadrian realized that Kade was completely in the Dark Queen's thrall. Would that be enough to turn him against his fellow *Pyr*? Hadrian feared it might be, and once again hated that he was powerless.

Why hadn't Alasdair heard the Fae arrive? Did it have something to do with the clock stopping?

Were they outside of time?

Maeve reached up and touched her lips to Kade's mouth briefly, a move that made the dragon shifter tremble with desire. Hadrian saw the Fae warrior flinch, and wondered whether Maeve was aware of his jealousy.

"Destroy it all," Maeve whispered to Kade. She laughed and made a gesture, summoning a red halo of light. "In silence!"

Kade moved immediately to stoke up the fire in the forge and Hadrian knew what he was going to do. He would have appealed to Kade in old-speak, but he couldn't make a sound. He tried to call to Alasdair and Balthasar but he couldn't utter a word, in old-speak or aloud. He screamed in outrage in his thoughts but no sound emerged.

And as he struggled against the prison his body had become, Kade threw the newly-made blades into the crucible. They landed soundlessly and the fire jumped hungrily. The flames should have been roaring, but there was no sound. Kade pushed the crucible into the forge and Hadrian watched helplessly as his work was destroyed and the blades melted.

Kade then shattered the template for the laser cutter, an act that should have made a lot of noise, but one that also happened in silence. If that wasn't enough, Kade shifted shape, becoming a powerful dragon of amber and gold. Maeve's red glow seemed to pulse with malice as Kade smashed the laser machine, too, ensuring that no one could produce blades easily in the studio again.

Kade then breathed dragonfire with gusto, setting the studio alight. His ability to breathe fire had always been impressive, and Hadrian couldn't help wishing it had been a little less so. The tables and the walls began to burn, the bright light of the forge glowing in the middle of it all. There wasn't a single sound as the sparks jumped and the fire spread. Hadrian could only watch as his studio was destroyed.

He noticed then that the Fae sword had completely melted away, the last drop of the water sizzling as it evaporated. There was no sign that it had ever existed, except a faint shimmer of silver that vanished almost as soon as Hadrian noticed it.

Maeve stood beside the Fae warrior, watching with satisfaction as Kade shifted to his human form again and returned to her side. She pointed down and he knelt to kiss her shoe. Her eyes shone with triumph as she met Hadrian's gaze.

"No more," she said with quiet conviction. Again, she turned her wrist, as if summoning something to her. The red glow spun around the studio, then gathered in the palm of her hand, like an orb of fire. "No more from you," she said darkly. Her eyes lit as she cast the sphere of red light at Hadrian.

It struck him in the middle of the chest and flared to brilliance before it died away. Hadrian felt the cold in his fingertips and toes first, then watched as a layer of hoarfrost spread over his skin. His skin turned pale and white. He felt chilled first, then cold, then he couldn't feel anything at all. It was horrifying to only be able to watch the progress of Maeve's curse, to feel it traveling up his arms and legs, making steady progress from his extremities to his heart.

He panicked, knowing he was going to die, that his mate would never be able to fulfill her quest, that Maeve had tricked them both. He watched as the Dark Queen tucked one hand into Kade's elbow and the other into the arm of the Fae warrior. She surveyed the studio, then looked between her minions with satisfaction. She nodded and the Fae warrior sliced open the air with his dagger, leading her through a portal to the shimmering silver light of Fae. Kade followed like a devoted puppy and Maeve never looked back. The Fae warrior smirked at Hadrian as he closed the portal between the worlds.

And the fire raged on.

Hadrian felt himself begin to rotate between forms involuntarily and he knew he was dying. It nearly broke his heart for his last view to be the wanton destruction of his life's work. There were so many things he hadn't done, including the satisfaction of his own firestorm. He left no legacy: no talons to aid his fellow *Pyr*, no son, thanks to this Fae attack. He ached for his mate's lost chance to free her brothers and wondered how many more centuries she'd spend killing Others for Maeve.

He closed his eyes in his dragon form, knowing the next shift would be his last.

CHAPTER EIGHT

Rania felt an odd tick. For the merest second, it seemed as if everything had frozen, as if time had stopped, as if she was snared in the moment of watching Notus and Argenta embrace. Balthasar seemed to have stopped chewing popcorn. Alasdair was caught in the act of breathing fog and telling his story. There was no sound from the studio.

Then she blinked and all seemed to be normal again.

Hadrian hadn't warned her that the firestorm would make her lose her mind. She grabbed some popcorn and concentrated on Alasdair's story.

When the pair in the image broke their kiss, Argenta looked at Notus with awe and love. Rania knew the woman would agree to satisfy the firestorm. The firestorm and Notus were working their persuasive spell, but it was easier to wonder about the end result when she wasn't snared by its power herself.

She understood how Argenta felt all too clearly.

A key turned audibly in a lock and for a moment Rania wasn't certain whether it was in the vision or Hadrian's lair. Balthasar munched popcorn, untroubled as he watched, so she realized it was the vision.

Notus fled as a man who must have been Argenta's father opened the door to his daughter's room. A second man loomed behind him, and Rania saw that it was Olaf dressed as a rich nobleman. The father was obviously charmed with Olaf and Rania guessed what he would do before he put Argenta's hand in that of her new suitor.

"Olaf bought Argenta, paying her father a healthy price in exchange for her hand in marriage," Alasdair said. "The coin later proved to be counterfeit and there was never a wedding. By that time the father knew he had been tricked, Olaf was gone, leaving no sign of Argenta behind."

A malachite and silver dragon soared into the sky beyond the village, a maiden in his grasp, as the father discovered the coins were false. The father shouted in rage and ran from the house, even as Argenta called for help, so high above the clouds that no one in the village heard her cries. Rania next saw her secured in Olaf's lair, deep in the earth, and watched her drop her head to hands and weep.

"Olaf didn't claim the mate because he couldn't, thanks to the wound Notus had given him," Alasdair continued. "And their union wouldn't have resulted in a son, anyway, since he had turned *Slayer*. He didn't compel Argenta to spin because he didn't care about her powers or about silver—he had more than sufficient riches in his hoard. His sole objective was to deny Notus, and as Notus traveled far and wide, seeking some sign of his lost mate, the tale spread to the other *Pyr* and *Slayers*."

Notus looked for his mate? That surprised Rania. She'd expected him to move on, and to spark another firestorm with someone else.

That clearly wasn't how it worked.

Rania witnessed a gathering of *Pyr* and wondered who the other dragons were, and whether any of them were still alive. A majestic ebony and pewter dragon seemed to be in charge, although the gathering was a noisy one. Rania felt their outrage grow and saw their passion rise. She saw more than one breathe a plume of fire into the sky in frustration. Meanwhile, another group of dragons gathered close by, led by an elegant dragon of ruby red and brass. He had similar glorious feathers as Notus and Boreus, but his trailed red behind him. He was obviously eloquent and forceful, too.

Rania watched the two groups convene on a lonely mountain peak. They really made a splendid sight and she had to think that the world would be a little less marvelous once they were eliminated.

"Words were exchanged between Boris Vassily, the leader of the *Slayers*, and Erik Sorensson, leader of the *Pyr*, over the abduction of Notus' mate," Alasdair said. Rania understood that this red dragon was Boris and the pewter one was Erik. "Both were new to their leadership and not yet as skilled with diplomacy as they would become." Rania saw the dispute quickly become volatile, with dragons on both sides breathing plumes of fire and slashing their tails through the air. "Erik had lost his father, his mate and son to the influence of *Slayers* and was disinclined to tolerate their meddling in firestorms. Boris saw the conflict as an opportunity for the *Slayers* to change the rules and gain greater power. To interfere with a firestorm was an abomination in the *Pyr* view and soon *Pyr* and *Slayers* were bent upon battle. Their sole item of agreement was a mutual declaration of war. They would meet over the south Pacific, where few humans would witness their fight. The year was 1807."

Two hundred years before. Rania expected that dragons would fight hard, but she was unprepared for the vivid view of the conflict that Alasdair provided. She felt as if she was there, as if she could smell the fire and the blood, and she watched as numerous dragons fought and died. The battles were vicious and brutal. She saw two dragons spiral out of the distance and target each other, one malachite and silver, the other amber and gold with trailing feathers. They locked claws with such force as they collided that they spun in the air. She saw them taunting each other.

"The most anticipated fight was that between Notus and Olaf, since it had been the reason for the war in the first place," Alasdair said as the other *Pyr* and *Slayers* halted their battles and gathered closer to watch. "By the time Notus located Olaf, the *Slayer* had been injured."

Rania saw the slash in Olaf's side, the one that dripped black blood. She also noticed that Notus was missing a scale on his mailed chest, right over his heart. Notus struck Olaf hard with his tail then flung the *Slayer* from his grasp. Olaf made a sharp turn and came raging back, wings pounding the air as he raced toward Notus. He slashed with his talons and breathed fire with such ferocity that it was clear only one dragon shifter would leave the fight alive.

The battle was harsh and merciless. Notus was bleeding from many wounds when he finally tore Olaf's chest open with his teeth and spat the chunk into the sea. Olaf's flight faltered, a hint of the magnitude of his injury, but Notus caught him and held him captive.

"It was said that Notus offered Olaf the mercy of a quick death, if only he revealed Argenta's resting place," Alasdair said. "Instead, the *Slayer* laughed, telling Notus that his mate wasn't dead. She was so well hidden that Notus would never find her in all his days and nights, and Olaf would never confess her location. Notus argued that the firestorm would reveal her location if she was alive, but Olaf insisted that her location meant the firestorm was extinguished. Notus was skeptical but Olaf breathed fire in that moment, just when Notus was leaning close to catch every word, and the *Pyr's* face was disfigured forever by the fire. They fought again, even more savagely, and Notus tore off Olaf's wings, flinging him into the ocean far below. Olaf roared in pain and Notus slashed his gut open, ensuring that the *Slayer* was dead this time. He didn't even wait for Olaf to hit the surface of the ocean, but immediately left to seek his mate."

Rania watched the fight break up after Olaf's death. Erik and Boris reached detente, then the dragon shifters collected their dead and retreated.

The vision followed Notus, now scarred on his face, but driven to find his hidden mate. Once again, the dark storm clouds followed him, and snow fell often when he landed in a town or village. Rania saw his hopes rise and fall, as he returned to the village where Argenta had been born, as he visited Olaf's abandoned lair, as he sought her in every corner of the world.

The evidence of his devotion was powerful and it shook Rania's convictions. Notus had to have found Argenta, because Hadrian was here, but Rania wanted to see their reunion. She was impatient, wanting Alasdair to finish his story and reveal the final truth of the firestorm, but dragons, it seemed, did everything in their own time.

***

Sebastian was pacing in the library that was his refuge at Reliquary. He could tell that it was the middle of the night, even though there were black-out curtains on the windows. The air smelled different after the sun set. He hadn't opened the drapes for days, much less left his library, and he didn't want to. He distrusted the alliance with the Others and the slaughter of five vampires in the coven had made him feel his age.

Sylvia had come by and pounded on the door to the shop, then had thrown things at his windows. Micah had knocked on the door to the library, but Sebastian was done with all of them.

The heart of the matter was Sylvia. He was done with denying temptation, too. He wanted her. She wanted him. The only way he could possess her was to turn her, and he knew what a false promise that kind of immortality was. The destructive act of feeding would break her.

Her fragility was part of what attracted him to her, after all. It was countered perfectly by her growing confidence that she could do more than she believed possible. In one way, he wanted her to remain the same as she was, like a butterfly caught in glass, and in another, he wanted her to soar beyond whatever constraints either of them believed she faced.

Sylvia made him soft. Her company made him question what he knew to be true, about the world and about himself. Sebastian suspected that her influence might ultimately shatter the delicate balance that was his life, and he recognized that he already didn't care as much about his own survival—or his secrets—as he should.

Witches were trouble.

Sylvia was the worst kind of temptation.

And now, she tempted the Regalian magick to play. There was a recipe for disaster. Would he help her? Would he stand by and watch her invite chaos? Could he bear to see her destroyed?

Could he manage to stay away? That was the question and the test. Sebastian had always had willpower to spare. He'd always been decisive and he'd always been driven. Being caught between objectives and having conflicting urges was new.

He didn't like the change one bit.

So, he remained in his sanctuary, itself a potent reminder of how his possessions and achievements fell short of his ambitions. The library was only a pale shadow of the collection he'd lost, and in a way, having this poor substitute only made his loss feel greater. He took down a book, a first edition of Edgar Allen Poe, opened it, scanned the first page, and replaced it on the shelf with impatience.

Well, his original library wasn't exactly lost. It was inaccessible to him, which was close enough to being the same thing to make him irritable.

In a way, it would have been easier if it had burned to ashes. It would be gone then and while he might remember it fondly, he wouldn't be haunted by the possibility of reclaiming it.

The library was also a perfect metaphor for Sylvia. Or vice versa.

Sebastian snarled, as irked as he always was when he thought of his sanctuary or of Sylvia. He pivoted to pace the width of the room yet again and discovered that he was no longer alone.

The Dark Queen herself reposed in one of his oxblood leather club stairs, the one to the right of the large but cold fireplace. She was wearing a trim little black suit with feathers on the shoulders and her signature high heels, the ones with the Laboutin red soles. She was impeccably groomed, watchful, and astonishingly silent.

She yawned elaborately as he blinked. "So busy tonight," she purred. "But if you say there's no rest for the wicked, I'll have to hurt you."

So, she hadn't come with the plan of slaughtering him. That was curiously reassuring.

But then, he doubted that she did her own dirty work.

"Dolce & Gabbana?" he asked, gesturing to the suit.

She smiled and moved her shoulders so that the feathers rustled. They were inky black with blue highlights, colored like raven feathers but longer. "Good guess."

"Not a guess," he corrected. "I saw it in a shop window in Paris. Emu, aren't they?" She nodded and preened. He took a step back and surveyed her. "It suits you."

She smiled and ran a hand over the glossy feathers. "It seemed an apt choice."

Sebastian knew she wanted him to ask what she meant—he could tell by the way her eyes gleamed—so he didn't. He was in that kind of a mood. "Just stop by for a chat, or is there a reason for this unexpected pleasure?"

Maeve laughed. "Only you would call a visit of mine a pleasure."

"How sad." Sebastian pouted a little and she laughed again. "Am I supposed to feel sorry for you?" He dropped into the other club chair, more interested in her mission than he wanted her to know.

"No. But only you would have the audacity to lie to me."

"A direct consequence of having nothing left to lose."

Maeve shook her head, making those feathers sway again. "But that's not the same as having nothing to gain, is it?"

"I don't understand."

Maeve crossed her legs. "It's my understanding that there's only one thing you truly desire."

"Is there?" Sebastian deliberately kept his mind empty and neutral. He knew the Dark Queen's reputation for hearing the thoughts of others, of even rummaging through the minds of others in search of whatever she wished to know. He wouldn't even wonder whether she was referring to his lost library or to the enticing Sylvia.

Her smile broadened. "I've come to make the proverbial offer you can't refuse."

Sebastian was curious despite himself. "And what if I *do* refuse?"

"You won't." She rose smoothly to her feet and crossed the room to the glass-fronted bookshelves on the far side of the fireplace. That entire wall was shelved with books, as was the one adjacent to it, all of them safely behind glass. The opposite wall was all windows, but they were curtained against the light. The fireplace had bookshelves on either side and a rather splendid painting above it. With the thick oriental carpet underfoot, a glittering chandelier hanging from the ceiling, the club chairs and a leather couch, it was a cozy refuge. He liked the high ceiling and the ornate plaster molding, too. The room was timeless in his opinion, a refuge from modernity in all its hideous sloppiness and noise.

Maeve acted as if she was reading the titles of the books, but Sebastian guessed it was just a performance. "Nice collection," she said, casting a coy glance over her shoulder. "But I hear you had a better one."

"It doesn't really matter," Sebastian said, keeping all the heat out of his voice. "Not any more."

"Because that library is locked against you, with a Fae charm on the lock so you can't pick it, and Micah has the only key." Maeve strolled across the floor, stopping right in front of Sebastian. He could smell her perfume and the scent of her skin. It was the dry musk of a forest floor, the scent she couldn't disguise, the one that revealed her Fae nature. She widened her eyes slightly. "And you have to follow Micah's plan, just to have any hope of retrieving that key." She wrinkled her nose. "No matter how stupid the plan seems to be."

"There's no need to rub salt in the wound," Sebastian said lightly.

"It must burn, though," she murmured, feigning sympathy. Even though Sebastian knew it was an act, he couldn't stop listening to her words. "To be beholden to anyone would be anathema to one who insists on choosing his own path, who needs to make his own decisions. It would sting more to that individual than to any other being alive."

Sebastian frowned. "I assume you have a point."

Her smile flashed. "I can shatter that charm."

He met her gaze, snared by her assertion. She watched him knowingly, that smile playing over her lips. She had the perfect bait and she knew it.

Of course, Maeve could break a Fae spell. She controlled most if not all of the magick remaining in the world. Sebastian would have thought of it before, but he'd never imagined that Maeve would do anything for him.

Things had just become very intriguing.

"There must be a price," he said with care, trying to hide his interest. He was pretty sure he failed. That library meant everything to him—well, not quite everything, but it was the one thing he desired that he had a chance of having. He couldn't say the same for the alluring Sylvia—and Maeve knew it.

She held up a finger. "Just one little favor," she said, waving that finger playfully. "That's all I ask in exchange. One teensy favor in exchange for making it possible for you to claim your heart's desire."

Sebastian heard the distinctions and qualifiers. He wasn't clear of a trick, not yet. He folded his arms across his chest and stared her down. "Why?" he asked. "Why would you even make such an offer?"

Maeve spun and crossed the room, tapping her fingertips on every piece of furniture she passed. He sensed that she was weighing her options, assessing the value of telling him the truth, deciding whether it was worth it, seeking a plausible lie to surrender as a substitute.

The Dark Queen would play an excellent game of chess.

Maybe he should challenge her to one.

She pivoted when she reached the other side of the fireplace and he knew from the hard glitter of her gaze that she'd decided to tell him the truth. "Things are not proceeding according to plan," she admitted, much to his surprise.

"Please." Sebastian scoffed, hoping to prompt her into revealing more. "You command all the magick now that the dragon prince is dead. Any incompetence on your part isn't my problem to fix."

She inhaled sharply, those eyes flashing. "I do command all the magick. I have the gem of the hoard! There are no competitors left."

"Then what's the trouble?"

She frowned, then met his gaze. "The magick is making choices of its own."

That was new. But Eithne had said in her last confession that the magick she'd brought from Regalia was so highly advanced that it was sentient. Did Maeve know that? Sebastian wasn't sure.

"How interesting," he said mildly as if it was all news to him. "Would you share an example?" He went to the small bar he kept in a cabinet. He lifted out a crystal brandy snifter, holding up the glass toward Maeve in invitation. She nodded without hesitation. He took out a second and a wonderful bottle of Courvoisier that he'd been saving. He poured them each a generous measure and offered her a glass. She cradled it in her hand, warming the liquor, then sniffed approvingly of it. They toasted each other and sipped.

She stared into the glass for long moments, swirling its contents. Sebastian pretended to be content to wait. He should have been so, as an immortal, but he'd never managed to get over his impatience.

He struggled to keep from tapping his toe, silently willing Maeve to get on with it—and soon.

"I slipped a shard of ice into the heart of a child," she finally confessed, her voice soft. "Not a real shard of ice, of course: that would have been unnecessarily cruel. It was magick, a spell intended to freeze out all the empathy and compassion in her heart."

"Like the Snow Queen and the boy Kay."

Maeve glanced up and nodded. "But there is no Snow Queen. There never was."

"Of course. You inspired *all* the stories."

Her voice hardened. "Don't mock me, bloodsucker. I don't really need you."

Sebastian held up his hand in surrender. "My mistake. Tell me about the splinter."

"It was a plan to ensure the child grew up without emotions, that she became a creature of pure logic and precision, that she could be relied upon to do what others would not. She was a tithe to me, my possession and my slave, even though she was mortal. I had to control her natural impulses. I had to guarantee that she could be relied upon to follow my command."

"I'm going to guess you had a specific assignment for her?"

"To kill." Maeve swirled the contents of her glass, apparently forgetting that she was talking to a vampire who killed routinely. "She was to be my assassin of choice. It worked perfectly. She grew up, she followed my orders, she targeted victims with precision and never showed one sign of remorse. She was a killing machine, one with additional powers because of her heritage."

"That heritage being?"

"She was half mortal and half shifter. She could pass in mortal society as one of them, but had the ability to change form. I gave her the ability to spontaneously manifest elsewhere. There was no silver flash of light to betray her arrival, as there is when my warriors move between the realms. Once I gave her the kiss of death, she was the perfect assassin." Maeve fell silent, her lips tightening, and Sebastian noticed that she'd used the past tense.

"Was?" he echoed.

Maeve took a large gulp of the liquor, shocking Sebastian that she didn't savor its magnificence. She met his gaze, her own burning with fury. "The magick betrayed me."

"Fucking magick," he said, almost by habit.

"Exactly," she agreed with force. "The shard came loose from her heart. It worked its way to her palm, emerged and dissolved. It set her free and had absolutely no business ever doing so."

"Why would it do that?' Sebastian asked.

"I don't know," Maeve admitted with disgust. "I don't know and I don't actually care. I can't risk losing the tool of this assassin, which creates an opportunity for you." She took a deep breath and straightened, then held his gaze as she drained her glass. "One task in exchange for my breaking the Fae charm on the lock to your library."

"A limited time offer."

"I'll make it impossible for the charm to be renewed. The key Micah claimed from you won't work anymore. Only the original will do."

"I prefer to pick the lock."

She nodded. "That will work as well."

"For how long," Sebastian asked, sipping his drink in an attempt to disguise his interest.

"Forever," Maeve said with conviction.

There had to be a catch.

"What do you want me to do?"

Maeve conjured a small box from her sleeve. It looked like a jeweler's box for a ring. Not just any ring, either, a dinner ring set with diamonds or a large engagement ring. She offered it to Sebastian, who took it and opened it.

Instead of the anticipated ring, a wicked-looking sliver gleamed on the red velvet interior. It was sharp at both ends, about half an inch long, and appeared to be made of glass.

"Replace it," Maeve said, then smiled. "That's all. Just put the splinter back."

An assassin for the Fae wasn't exactly an innocent caught in a web of Maeve's design. She'd killed any number of victims. Sebastian didn't have any immediate scruples about accepting the wager.

Beyond distrusting Maeve.

"Why don't you do it yourself?" he asked, keeping his tone idle.

"She'll be wary of me or the Fae. She's in the middle of a *Pyr* firestorm and it's messing with her ideas. You know how dragons are, always challenging preconceptions."

"I do." Sebastian found himself inclined to accept the terms. "How will I find her?"

"I'll give you directions." Maeve shrugged and finished her drink. "Who knows? You might even enjoy it. I know how you enjoy setting all the pieces in motion."

There was that.

Alasdair continued his tale of Hadrian's parents. "Finally, Notus landed in the forest he knew best, in Northumberland. He intended to find shelter and sleep, for he was weary to his marrow and disheartened that he couldn't find Argenta. Instead he heard the sound of tears. He followed the sound to a humble cottage, which was almost in ruins. A man sat outside it beneath the light of the moon, weeping as if his heart had broken in two. The man roused himself at the sight of Notus and, taking him for a weary traveler, offered to share his last pot of porridge."

The cottage was small and in disrepair, although Rania thought there was another building behind it. The man had silver in his hair and in his beard, but he looked strong and hale. He also looked as disheartened as Notus.

"Notus had found the home of a blacksmith, who had been captured by the Fae to do service to them. He'd entered the hall under a mound and thought he had only been there a few days. Upon his release, he returned home to find that he'd been gone twenty-five years. His wife and children were gone. His larder was bare and his vegetable garden was overgrown. His hut was falling down. All he had were his tools, for he had been ordered to bring them to Fae, but he couldn't light a fire to work. Even the last of his firewood had been taken. He'd made the porridge with the last of the grain and water from the river, and it was both cold and gritty."

Rania felt sympathy for the blacksmith, and admired his generosity in sharing what little he had.

Then she thought about that: she was feeling kindness toward a *blacksmith*.

What was happening to her?

"It was a good site, though," Alasdair said. "Notus could see as much, with the river bending around it. The river itself was broad and seemed to sing as it passed over the stones beside the cottage. The forest was thick and he spied game within it; the sky overhead was clear and the wind was cool. The blacksmith said his people had been there since the beginning of time, and they laughed about that. Notus offered to stay and help the blacksmith to rebuild his life and the next morning, they worked together to re-thatch the roof. The blacksmith's name was Darian and they two became good friends."

Rania saw the two of them on the roof in the morning sunlight. A young boy came out of the forest to stare at them in silence, then ran back into the woods.

"Notus was there when word of Darian's return reached the closest village, when people came to look, when Darian's son, now a man, came to tell him of his wife's death." Rania blinked back her tears at the sight of the smith's reunion with his grown son and his grief at hearing of his wife's death. "The son brought metal for his father to work, bits and ends he'd foraged, for he had little coin himself. He had married the daughter of a farmer and worked their family's plot with her father and brother. When Darian bemoaned the lack of fuel after his son's departure, Notus chose to reveal himself."

Rania saw the two men talking, then the blacksmith's frown of surprise. Notus stood up and shimmered blue, then shifted shape.

"Darian wasn't as astonished as Notus might have expected, but then the blacksmith had been to Fae and seen many marvels. Notus breathed fire in his smithy, heating the forge so Darian could work. The blacksmith took the scraps his son had brought and turned them into marvels, inspired by the wonders he had seen. He made latches and knockers and cooking utensils; he made hooks and clasps for cloaks and marvels of every shape and size. Every item he made was distinctive, both beautiful and functional. On market day, he loaded up his work and went to town, leaving Notus to finish the repairs on the cottage. Darian returned jubilant that night, with a load more metal, a fat purse, and a chicken for their dinner. He told Notus that the items made with dragonfire fetched prices beyond compare, and the two settled into partnership together."

The vision spun, showing the passing of time and the cycle of the seasons. The hut gradually became a little finer, a little larger, and the blacksmith became a little plumper. Darian was singing at the forge when the vision settled, Notus breathing a splendid torrent of orange fire.

"Gradually, Darian began to tell Notus about Fae. He said it was filled with such wonders that even a dragon couldn't surprise him, and listed many of them. He told Notus that there was even a maiden there who could spin ice into strands of silver. Notus, shocked at this news of Argenta, shifted shape immediately and demanded to know how to get into Fae. He confided the truth in Darian, who then wanted to help his friend save his beloved. He told Notus all he knew of Fae, advised him to avoid all food and drink, then showed him the hill where he had entered that magickal realm. On the next full moon, they went to the mound, and both could hear the Fae music from within. The sound made Darian shudder with dread and he couldn't approach any closer."

Rania saw the hill and the light spilling from a door in its side, then she heard the wild merry music of Fae. Notus shook hands with Darian and walked toward the portal that shone with welcoming golden light. Rania knew he was making a mistake but it was impossible to warn him. She saw that Darian believed the same thing, and that his new friend would be lost forever.

"Notus entered the Dark Queen's realm willingly, in pursuit of Argenta, and though he tried to be stealthy, he was soon discovered. His true nature was discerned by Maeve and he was put to work, trapped in his dragon form to breathe fire for the forge of a maiden silversmith. This maiden was the daughter of a silversmith: she had volunteered to go to Fae in her father's stead when the Fae came for him, because her father was ill. Her name was Loreena and she was young, strong and lovely. She was compelled to work rivers of silver into jewelry for the Fae, into dagger hilts and even blades. Loreena had thought she would be only a night in Fae and, by her own accounting, it had been a year and a day. She feared this was only an increment of the truth, for she had heard tales of Fae before. She confided in Notus that she suspected everyone she knew in the mortal realm was dead. He tried to console her but could only breathe more fire for her work and hope that one day her debt to the Dark Queen would be paid."

"In time, Loreena told him of the source of the silver. She was commanded to work all of it into weapons, but suspected the supply would never be diminished. Each day, there was just as much of it as there had been the day before. This was because Olaf had traded Argenta to Maeve in exchange for a spell to see his hoard defended while he was at war. Since he'd died, the spell had been dissolved and the hoard stolen, but Argenta had remained captive in Fae, spinning silver endlessly."

Rania sat up straighter at this evidence of Maeve not keeping her pledge.

"Notus heard from Loreena how the maiden who spun the silver had come to believe that her father had been infinitely kinder than the Fae, for she was given no rest at all in the enchanted realm. Maeve's appetite for silver was voracious beyond anything she had known before. When Notus told Loreena his tale of his lost mate, who was Argenta, they schemed together to save her. They realized they could combine their efforts to free all three of them from captivity. They waited until the night of All Hallows, when the Fae were going to ride into the mortal realm on their wild ride, for the veil between realms was said to be thin on that night. Notus freed Argenta from her prison: Loreena knew the locks and locations of keys, as well as the maze of Fae, while only a dragon could fly them out of the realm in time. Notus flew hard, with the maidens in his grasp, and while he flew, Loreena told Argenta about Notus. The spark of the firestorm lit Notus' way and he reached the blacksmith's cottage at daybreak, exhausted. Darius recognized his old friend immediately, even though fifteen years had passed, and guessed that one maiden was Argenta. He took the trio in, fed them and let them sleep.

"None of them realized that Maeve, on discovering their escape, flung a curse after them, dooming Argenta, Notus and Loreena to die immediately after achieving their greatest joy."

Rania frowned at this cruel pronouncement. It seemed the *Pyr* had good reason to think that Maeve was unfair and unlikely to keep her word. She wondered whether they knew for certain that it was the Dark Queen's curse, or if there was part of the story being omitted.

"Argenta was thrilled that the dragon who had rescued her was the man she'd come to love while still in her father's home. Notus explained to her about the firestorm and the two pledged their troth to each other on the spring equinox, the day after their return from Fae. They wed beside the merry river as the last snow of the season fell around them." The scene changed and Rania thought that something about the bend of the river looked familiar—but then rivers in forests tended to be similar. Once again, the snow seemed to follow Notus, but the pair who pledged to each other had rosy cheeks and wide smiles. The firestorm's white light bathed all four of them in radiance and she saw Loreena wipe away a tear of joy.

"The pair satisfied the firestorm while Darian and Loreena went to market. The four of them lived happily in the cottage as Argenta's belly rounded and once again, the smith made good coin from work forged under dragonfire." Snow blew across the vision and swirled around the hut, which was cozy inside and lit by a roaring fire. "The wind was filled with the promise of winter when Argenta delivered her son, and Notus chose the name Hadrian for him. They were as much in love as ever and the arrival of their son made their happiness complete. The blacksmith wiped away a tear when he left them that night, then was surprised when the silversmith slipped her hand in his wizened one." Rania smiled as Loreena led Darian to her bed, smiling sweetly at him. "That night, they two made love for the first time, and pledged to each other."

Rania saw the pleasure that agreement gave both of them.

Alasdair frowned. "In the morning, though, Darian and Loreena found Argenta and Notus dead, struck down by Maeve's curse in the moment of their greatest joy. The two were curled around their infant son, their bodies forming the shape of a heart, their hands clasped atop the baby."

Rania gasped at the sight of the dragon shifter and his mate curved protectively around their infant son, who kicked his legs heartily despite his parents' stillness. She bit her lip, realizing that Hadrian had been alone, without parents or siblings, just as she had been.

"Darian buried them in a clearing in the forest that was tranquil beyond all others, ensuring that they remained in the shape of a heart together, their hands entwined. He created a marker of steel forged in dragonfire, a heart that he had thought too fine to be a knocker. He realized then that he'd been unwittingly saving it for this use."

Rania recognized the marker as the one she'd seen in the forest, and her heart thundered at the importance of that spot. It was a *Pyr* grave, but that of a *Pyr* with his mate. Hadrian's parents. She swallowed. There had been a second marker, there, though, as well, and she had a feeling whose grave it might mark.

"Darian pledged to raise their son as his own and asked Loreena to be his bride. She agreed and they were happy together, in their own way. They prospered and they never forgot the dragon and his mate, ensuring that the boy knew his heritage and legacy."

The vision spun again, seasons passing with dizzying speed.

"It was twelve years later when Darian had a dream. He awakened with a smile but no memory of the dream's details, save the word 'Boreus'. He conferred with Loreena but neither could make sense of it. Hadrian was tall and lanky by this time, on the cusp of manhood, and though the smith had watched, he had never yet seen any sign that the boy had inherited his father's nature. On that very day, a stranger approached the cabin. He looked somewhat like Notus, but older, and when he offered his hand, he introduced himself as Boreus, cousin of the boy's father, come to teach Hadrian what he needed to know. The younger man with him was his own son, Alasdair."

"You," Balthasar said.

Alasdair smiled.

Once again, Rania watched a dragon being tutored by other dragons. Alasdair was hematite and silver, but much more slender and agile in this vision. His father was amethyst and silver, a doughty opponent who moved with deliberation. He was both precise and encouraging in his instruction and Rania watched Hadrian master his skills.

"Darian and Loreena then had the honor of watching a *Pyr* instruct one of his own. They were as thrilled as Hadrian when he mastered the art of shifting shape, when he learned to fly, when he breathed fire for the first time. The cousins worked together day after day, until Boreus had been a fortnight at the blacksmith's home. He had come on the new moon, the first new moon of autumn, and by the full moon, he announced that he would return home. Hadrian chose to go with him, and though the blacksmith and his wife were saddened by this, for they loved the boy dearly, they knew it was right for him to be with his own kind."

The vision showed that cabin and clearing, the night sky overhead filled with stars. A yellow moon rose, hovering over the trees like a great lantern, then three of the people in the clearing shimmered blue. They shifted shape, one becoming a larger dragon of amethyst and silver, one becoming a slim dragon of hematite and silver, and the third becoming a slender dragon of emerald and silver. The three dragons bounded into the air and took flight as one—and if the youngest was a little slower in making the transition, the delay was barely noticeable. They circled the cabin as the couple below waved farewell, then turned and flew into the night. The trio were silhouetted against the moon for a long moment, then flew on, as swiftly as the night wind.

"And each year, on that same new moon, Hadrian returned to his foster father and mother. He stayed that same fortnight with them, helping them, breathing fire for their forge, taking them on dragon flights, until the day he arrived to find only silence. He found them still abed, for they hadn't awakened that morning, their bodies curled together and their hands entwined. Their posture was the same as that of his own parents, all those years before. What he didn't know was that Loreena had been ill and Darian had finally told her that he loved her with all his heart. The confession had been her greatest joy and she had died, after hearing it, thanks to Maeve's curse. Darian hadn't been able to imagine his life without her, and he had passed in his sleep, holding his beloved close to his heart. Hadrian buried them beside his parents and fashioned a marker for their grave, using the skills Darian had taught him and his own dragonfire. He made a heart of steel and fire, not unlike the one that was already there."

Rania recognized the second marker that she'd seen in the clearing. The vision changed quickly, the cottage becoming a mill and then the lair that she recognized as Hadrian's home.

"And then Hadrian claimed that hut as his home and his lair, for his people had lived there since the dawn of time, and they would remain there ever after."

A bright orb appeared in the middle of the vision. It became brighter and whiter until Rania had to close her eyes. When she opened them again, the vision had faded along with the light. Alasdair exhaled and the cloud of fog vanished, as if it had been dissipated in the wind.

There was a shimmer of blue light and Alasdair shifted shape, taking his human form once again. He appealed to Rania. "So, you see, my cousin has a legacy to defend, and the firestorm, once it sparks, has to be fulfilled. Take me instead. Fulfill your quota, free your brothers, and make a partnership with Hadrian."

"But..."

"Give me the kiss of death, Rania," Alasdair insisted as Balthasar looked on. "I volunteer to be the *Pyr* who dies. Just as our fathers defended each other's firestorms, I would defend Hadrian's."

"You don't understand," she told him. "I can't do that, not anymore."

But before she could explain, Balthasar tilted his head, listening. "There's no sound from the studio. Do you think Hadrian's okay?"

Alasdair straightened with alarm. "Do you smell smoke?"

CHAPTER NINE

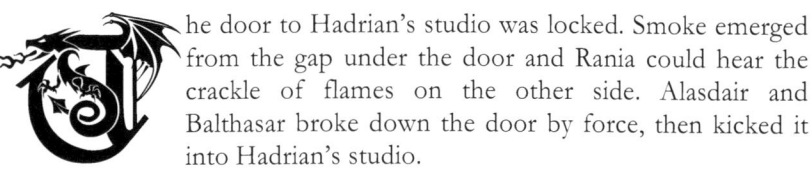

The door to Hadrian's studio was locked. Smoke emerged from the gap under the door and Rania could hear the crackle of flames on the other side. Alasdair and Balthasar broke down the door by force, then kicked it into Hadrian's studio.

They were greeted by a wall of flames. It was impossible to believe that anyone could survive such an inferno. Rania was amazed they hadn't heard the fire start. She stepped forward, even as Alasdair held her back, then pointed at a fallen figure before the forge. "There!" Hadrian could just be discerned through the smoke.

Balthasar had already run to get the hose from the garden and he turned it on the fire, slowly creating a path toward the glowing forge. Alasdair and Rania were right behind him, even though Alasdair wanted her to wait behind. She felt responsible for Hadrian's injury, whatever it was, and negligent for listening to a story instead of paying closer attention. Alasdair cleared away wood and burning debris, ensuring that they'd have a safe path back out of the studio. As they made their way closer, Rania saw that work tables had been tipped and smashed. How could they have missed the sound of this destruction? The *Pyr* had keen senses and she was observant. It made no sense, but she'd think about it later.

She saw the crucible in the forge, filled with molten metal, and turned to look for Hadrian's blades. There was no sign of them.

Was this her fault? Had there been no sound because the Fae had come to interfere with Hadrian's work, because of what she'd told

Maeve? Or had they come for vengeance? She couldn't see the Fae sword either.

They reached Hadrian just as the roof crackled overhead.

Balthasar shouted a warning and Alasdair shifted shape in a flash of pale blue light, taking his dragon form in a flash. He scooped up Hadrian's inert form and grabbed Rania too, then jumped toward the breaking roof. He shattered the joists with his back and sent burning rafters tumbling back into the studio as he soared into the sky. Balthasar abandoned the hose and shifted shape, as well, his citrine and gold form appearing through the hole in the roof immediately after Alasdair.

Alasdair landed in the river with a splash, letting the water run over his back where the fire had singed his scales. Balthasar shifted shape before he landed and immediately went to Hadrian.

Rania feared that she knew what he would find. She'd already noticed that there wasn't a glimmer of white light between herself and Hadrian. She could guess that the firestorm was extinguished because Hadrian was dead.

He also appeared to be frozen. He was in his human form, coated with a layer of ice. That also made no sense, given conditions in the studio. The Fae had definitely been at work. Hadrian's skin was pale and his eyes were closed, his features strangely impassive.

Rania was surprised to feel a mix of helplessness and grief welling up inside her, and found tears blurred her vision. She couldn't remember ever weeping over anything. She couldn't remember ever mourning the loss of anyone, but she wanted to wail that Hadrian was dead.

She'd been assigned to kill him and now she mourned him. Was it just because she'd never be able to strike the final blow? Rania knew that wasn't it.

As Balthasar tried to revive his friend, she realized that she could never have taken the life of this dragon shifter.

But it had happened anyway.

She admired Hadrian too much. She didn't want to think of a world without his crooked grin or his confident dares. She recalled Alasdair's story, of the *Pyr* cousins and how they had helped each other, how they had won the hearts of their destined mates and fulfilled the promise of their respective firestorms, and Rania realized that she wanted to believe that she and Hadrian were meant for each other.

She wished she'd had the chance to be with him in every way, and she even wished she had conceived his son. She wasn't sure how that could work out, not with Maeve hunting Others, but Hadrian's death made her question her loyalty to the Dark Queen.

His death felt wrong.

It was wrong.

And Maeve had commanded it.

Worse, Rania had been at least partly responsible. She should never have told Maeve about the gloves. Was it worth serving the Dark Queen if it meant a noble shifter like Hadrian had to die?

Balthasar had shifted shape again and was breathing a slow stream of dragonfire, gradually thawing the ice from Hadrian's body. Alasdair mimicked his actions, the two massive dragons bracing themselves against the running water of the stream. Their scales glistened and gleamed in the fading light of the day. Rania wondered whether Hadrian would melt away, but he didn't—he thawed.

He didn't wake up, though.

Once the ice was gone, she put her fingertips to his throat. There was no pulse. He was still cold. Balthasar changed back to his human form and tried to revive Hadrian, but Rania knew it was too late. She folded her arms across her chest, hating this new sensation of being ineffective.

She should have felt celebratory. Her thirteenth victim was dead. Her bargain with Maeve was fulfilled. Her brothers would be freed and she could begin her life anew.

But she was filled with regret instead. She wished she'd taken the chance to have Hadrian's son. She would have learned more about making love. She didn't doubt that the satisfaction of the firestorm would have been a great experience.

Maybe Maeve would have made her son immortal, too, just to please her.

Rania bit her lip. Maybe Maeve would have insisted on making a deal with that son, letting him earn his right to live.

Maybe it was better if Hadrian's son would never be.

She couldn't feel glad about that either.

Yet even that wasn't all of it.

She was going to miss Hadrian.

She was going to miss knowing that he was out there somewhere, being enthused about weapons and his skills, making things and solving puzzles, attracting ice and storms, and being loyal to his fellow *Pyr*.

His head fell to one side in that moment and she thought she could see a faint shadow on his cheek where she'd given him the kiss of death. It hadn't been what killed him, though: it hadn't worked. The mark was blue now, as if it had been frozen and kept from doing its worst.

Rania frowned. The kiss of death always faded from view after the victim died. It left no sign of its existence. It was a Fae thing.

Why was Hadrian's visible now?

Why hadn't he died of it earlier?

She followed the *Pyr* as they carried Hadrian back into his lair, her thoughts spinning. She was remembering Alasdair's story and also the prophecy sent to Hadrian. Somewhere there was a solution to the riddle, if she could just figure it out.

> *The ice dragon summons frost and cold,*
> *His power is a force to behold.*
> *He can thaw the ice of a frozen heart*
> *To offer a lost shifter a new start.*
> *His firestorm burns fierce and white*
> *Its radiance a beacon in the darkest night.*
> *But can it bring hope to that doomed soul?*
> *Or persuade his lost mate to become whole?*
> *If the dragon wins the swan maiden's trust*
> *It will be Fae not Others who are turned to dust.*
> *The future will be theirs, once allied*
> *If the assassin joins the dragon's side.*

His being an ice dragon had to change the result of spells like the kiss of death. But how? Why? Rania frowned as she tried to solve the riddle.

The fire department had arrived and were hosing down the studio. There was a gathering of curious onlookers in the driveway and Alasdair went out to speak to them while Balthasar still tried to tend Hadrian.

Rania would have followed him, but she never had the chance.

Rafferty had arrived at Bardsey Island with Melissa and their adopted daughter Isabelle. Donovan, the Warrior of the *Pyr*, had greeted his former mentor with enthusiasm. His mate Alex was with him, and their boys, too: Nick and Isabelle immediately disappeared together, as they always did. Marco and Jac were also there with their sons—it took a noisy dinner and a long evening to catch up with everyone's news.

The ancient *Pyr* who Rafferty had rescued were doing well, to his thinking, dressed more like modern people but still speaking an ancient variation of Welsh to each other. Another one had joined them, one with a mysterious smile who looked younger. Rafferty heard the story of the hitchhiker and guessed that this was the elusive Uther.

When he asked, that *Pyr* just smiled.

The entire house was asleep, including the recent arrivals, when Rafferty awakened with a jolt. He laid there, listening, uncertain what had disturbed him. Melissa was sleeping deeply beside him and the house was quiet.

Then he saw a flicker of blue light outside the windows.

He rose and went to look. The sun was just rising. The rubble left by the mound where Marco had slumbered safely for centuries were gilded with rosy morning light. He remembered old battles and smiled that Marco had found such joy with Jacqueline. He looked more closely, realizing that there was a stag behind the mound, standing so still that he'd missed the creature. It was looking directly at him.

No, it was looking at something behind him.

Rafferty turned, jumping a little to find the ghost of his grandfather, Pwyll, in the shadows. *"You must help,"* he said in old-speak and in Welsh, then gave Rafferty instructions.

Rafferty nodded understanding when he'd heard it all, then looked back out the window, unable to stop himself.

The stag was gone. He wondered whether it had ever been there, because he was certain there were no deer on the island. Then Uther stood up behind the mound and strolled toward the house, whistling softly, as if he'd been out for a walk in the moonlight.

Rafferty wondered, but then Pwyll tapped his shoulder and he knew it was time. He close his eyes, summoned his salamander form, then hurled himself through space and time to give the assistance Pwyll had requested.

Of all the *Pyr*, Rafferty was the most inclined to guide a firestorm to its successful conclusion. That would never change.

There was a brilliant shimmer of silver light beside Rania as she left Hadrian's lair. A slit opened from the ceiling to the floor, then a Fae warrior reached through the gap between realms and seized her.

She struggled against her captor, but he was larger than her and stronger. She saw Balthasar leap at the intruder in her defense and was surprised that the *Pyr* considered her to be one of them. It must be because Hadrian believed she was his destined mate, but Rania was amazed that Balthasar could overlook her role as Hadrian's assassin.

The *Pyr* really did have each other's backs and Rania admired that.

It also made her feel solitary and lonely.

The portal was quickly closed against Balthasar, though, and she was alone with her captor. Rania shifted shape and tried to escape. But the Fae warrior held fast and she found herself in Fae.

It wasn't just anywhere in Fae. She was at Maeve's court and had a bad feeling about that. She was flung down in front of Maeve, the warrior's treatment of her so rough that she wondered why she was in disfavor. Maeve sat on her throne before her court and watched, not saying a word in Rania's defense.

Things had gone very wrong. Rania was more than a little worried about the outcome of this interview, even though she'd always trusted the Dark Queen. Had Hadrian been right about Maeve's intentions, after all?

No, Rania wouldn't believe it.

All the courtiers were dressed in red and silver finery and merry music played for a dance. Rania got to her feet and glanced around, well aware that she was the focus of attention.

What was going on? Why had she been summoned?

She bowed low. "My queen," she said with reverence.

"Indeed." Maeve's smile was hungry. "I wanted to commend you on an excellent choice of victim," she said, her tone gloating. A servant brought her a goblet brimming with a golden liquid. Rania guessed it was mead. Maeve toasted her and sipped. "Here's to a brilliant elimination. I'm curious to see who you choose next."

Next? Rania's heart chilled. Had Hadrian been right? Was Maeve breaking her word?

She had to know.

"I chose the *Pyr* Hadrian as my thirteenth victim," Rania reminded the Dark Queen. "He's dead, so our wager is complete." She held up her wrist, displaying the red string that was still knotted there. "This should be gone."

"Not quite yet." Maeve laughed at Rania's obvious surprise. "You didn't kill Hadrian MacEwan. I did. As a result, his death doesn't count as your victory."

"I gave him the kiss of death," Rania insisted.

"But it didn't kill him. I did." Maeve's gaze hardened. "You lose. Choose another victim."

Rania feared that she should have expected this. She should have believed Hadrian and anticipated that the Dark Queen would wriggle out of keeping her end of the bargain on a technicality.

She felt foolish for trusting Maeve to keep the spirit of their deal.

And even more foolish for not taking Hadrian's warning. He'd been right, not just about Maeve but about Rania learning the truth when she didn't have a dragon shifter to defend her anymore.

It was interesting that she was so certain Hadrian would have defended her.

"That isn't our agreement," Rania said, keeping her tone polite but firm. "I've made thirteen assassinations for you. You should free me and my brothers..."

"You've made *twelve* assassinations," the Dark Queen corrected, then drained her chalice of mead. "Choose another victim, and make it quick. This has already gone on too long."

"You acknowledge twelve kills," Rania said, trying to negotiate. "You could free my brothers now, as a gesture of goodwill."

Maeve laughed again. "I don't have to do anything for goodwill," she snarled. "You're in my thrall until you fulfill our bargain."

"I can't give another kiss of death. I only had the ability to give thirteen."

"Oops." Maeve widened her eyes in mock alarm. "Then you'll have to make your kills the old-fashioned way." She was clearly unsympathetic to Rania's plight. Rania had the definite sense that the Dark Queen had planned their bargain to end this way.

She'd said 'kills', plural. The next assassination wasn't going to end it either. Rania was trapped forever.

She should have listened to Hadrian!

"Choose your next victim," Maeve commanded.

"And you'll beat me to the kill, once again," Rania accused, forgetting herself in her anger. "You'll prolong this deal forever!"

Maeve smiled and held out her chalice so a minion could refill it. "What if I do? It's useful to have a pet assassin."

Rania folded her arms across her chest. "But there's no point. If you're never going to release me, there's nothing to be gained by serving you."

Maeve gave her a smile that chilled her to her marrow. "Isn't there?" she murmured as she leaned forward, eyes gleaming. "I suggest you get to work or we'll start dining on swan every night."

There was a clatter of chains and a familiar cry filled the court. Rania spun to see a golden cage on a cart being rolled to the middle of the court. Three swans were locked inside it, most of them flapping and calling. Rania's heart sank with the conviction that they were her brothers. Were her other nine brothers free or already dead? The Fae laughed and poked at the birds as the cage passed, more than one pulling a feather as a souvenir.

"You have no right!" Rania cried, turning on Maeve. "They should be free! I kept my promise!"

"Not quite yet," the Dark Queen insisted and sipped her mead. She lounged on her throne, smug in her triumph. "Which of the *Pyr* will you eliminate next?"

Rania was trapped. She knew it, but she didn't like it. If there was a way out, she didn't know what it was—and she couldn't risk the survival of her brothers while she plotted against Maeve. Could she even find her remaining brothers before the Dark Queen did.

Her heart sank with the realization that she probably would have to kill a *Pyr* to complete her wager with Maeve.

Alasdair had volunteered.

She couldn't name him, though. Not only did she need to keep Maeve from cheating her of the kill, she had to talk to Alasdair again and make an agreement. Maybe then she could make sure that Maeve didn't cheat her.

Maybe not.

"I have to assess which dragon shifter offers the best opportunity," she said, dropping her gaze as if in deference. The truth was that she didn't want Maeve to notice her defiance.

"There's another blacksmith," the Dark Queen noted. "I know you dislike them."

"He might expect me," Rania said, doubting that was true. "I have to do my research."

"Don't dally too long," Maeve said. "Tomorrow night, we dine on swan." The court cheered and a number of Fae poked at the swans trapped in the cage. Rania knew her brothers were agitated and she didn't blame them. She'd worked all these centuries to secure their freedom, and Maeve had changed the deal.

It was exactly as Hadrian had warned her.

And he was dead, unable to witness that his prediction had come true.

She looked at her brothers, remembering Hadrian's questions about them, and wondered why she hadn't ever sought them out. Why hadn't she talked to them or made a connection? She'd always been alone, but she'd also repeatedly chosen to be alone.

What if this was her chance to choose differently?

What the world needed was more of Hadrian and his lineage. Rania suddenly had a ghost of an idea about the kiss of death but she couldn't think about it while she stood before the Dark Queen. Her actions had to come as a surprise.

"As you command, my queen," she said, bowing before Maeve's throne as rebellion burned hotter in her heart.

Then she wished to be with Hadrian and vanished from the Fae court.

It was darker than dark.

Hadrian couldn't see anything in any direction. He couldn't feel anything around him or sense the presence of any other being. It was strange. Even in his human form, he was always aware of the pulse of another creature at a distance or the faint sound of movement. Now there was nothing. He couldn't tell whether it was cold or hot either. He stood on something firm, but had no idea whether it was just a single spot or continued, like ground, underfoot. If he took a step, would he fall into a void?

He was in his human form and tried to shift, but couldn't. There wasn't even a shimmer of blue light, let alone the familiar sense of the tidal wave of transformation sweeping through him.

Was he dead? If he wasn't *Pyr* anymore, Hadrian wasn't sure he wanted to be alive.

Even the familiar tinge of cold that was always at the periphery of his awareness was gone. He could always feel that the ice and snow were there, just awaiting his summons. No longer.

Hadrian could move, at least. He brushed his right hand over his left wrist and was relieved that he couldn't feel a string there. He'd take the good news where he could find it.

He wasn't relieved that his fingers seemed to slide right through his arm, as if he'd become insubstantial.

Or a ghost.

He didn't hear his heart beating or feel his lungs filling with air. He couldn't exactly feel whatever was beneath his feet but when he stamped a foot, he heard a faint sound of impact.

He didn't feel it, though.

Being dead was a definite possibility, given what he remembered of Maeve's visit. He couldn't smell smoke or iron, and knew he wasn't in his lair or studio anymore. There was no light of the firestorm, so either Rania was gone or the firestorm had been extinguished, unsatisfied.

An opportunity lost forever.

He pivoted in place, trying to peer into the distance, but it was all black.

He wasn't going to just stand in one place for eternity, though.

Hadrian took a step. He was reassured that whatever supported him seemed to continue, so he took another. Then he took a third step and, convinced that he was on some level surface, he began to walk, gradually increasing his speed.

He didn't know how long he walked or how far—he was starting to wish he'd counted his footsteps—when a faint glimmer of light appeared in the distance. He stopped, wondering whether his eyes were deceiving him, but the light remained there. It was golden and moving, like a shifting cloud. He had no idea what it was.

Since he had exactly nothing left to lose, Hadrian walked toward the light.

As he drew nearer, he realized that he was seeing a cluster of individual golden lights, each one on the move. It reminded him of a picture he'd seen of an atom, with electrons orbiting its nucleus, each cutting its own path, snared in a web of attraction. Another dozen steps and he saw that the lights circled a woman. She was sitting cross-legged on the ground and seemed to be reading a book, although he doubted there was enough light for that. Her hair was grey and hung down her back in a silken river.

The lights were fireflies, not just surrounding her but winking on and off as they did so. She looked up and smiled at him, as if she'd been expecting him, but Hadrian didn't recognize her. She was wearing a dress that looked medieval to him. There was embroidery on the neckline and along the hem, but the garment was worn and a bit stained. Her hair was loose and blond, her eyes sad but clear blue.

"Hadrian," she said as if they were old friends and patted the ground beside herself. "I thought you'd be along soon."

Hadrian sat down beside her. In the light of the fireflies, he could see that he was dressed in his T-shirt and jeans, as he had been in his studio. His skin looked normal in color, just as hers did.

"Do I know you?" he asked, uncertain whether he'd be able to make a sound before he did.

She smiled sadly. "You know my daughter, Rania."

Rania. That was his mate's name. Though he was glad to finally know it, her name was just another thing Hadrian had learned too late.

"Where are we?"

"The realm of the dead," the woman said with a complacent nod.

"It's not so bad," she continued, patting the back of his hand. "No pain. No fears. No dread about any event, mostly because you can't do much about anything anymore." She pursed her lips. "At least, that would be the case if you stayed."

"I have a choice?" Hadrian felt a spark of hope.

"No, but others do." She stared at his hand, her gaze fixed on the ring that had been on the necklace around Rania's neck. It seemed as if she couldn't tear her gaze away. "Have you seen him?" she whispered, raising her gaze to his with hope.

"I don't know whose ring this is," Hadrian admitted. "It was on a chain around Rania's neck. I was holding it when she manifested elsewhere and the chain snapped." He couldn't seem to keep himself from confiding the whole story, which reminded him of Rania's apparent need to talk when they'd first met. "It's kind of stuck on my finger. I thought she might come back for it, and I'd feel it if she tried to take it."

Her mother nodded, her gaze drawn to the ring again. She brushed it with her fingertips, reverently, then spoke before he could ask a question. "You know why the Dark Queen wanted to kill you, don't you?"

"Because I extinguished the Fae sword? Or because I killed a Fae warrior with my steel talons?"

Rania's mother smiled. "You're forgetting your legacy."

"What about it? I'm an ice dragon, but all that means is that snow and ice are attracted to me. Storms, too."

She was shaking her head slowly. "That's not all it means, not to you."

"I don't understand."

"You're your father's son, but you're also your mother's son." She gave him an intent look, willing him to work it out.

Hadrian frowned. "I never knew either of them. They died the day I was born."

"You should have paid more attention to Alasdair's tales."

It was startling that this stranger knew so much about him, and even more strange that she was giving him similar advice to what he'd given Rania. "Argenta, my mother, could spin ice into silver."

She nodded. "And your foster mother, Loreena, worked that silver into the most prized Fae weapons when they were both captive in Fae. When exposed to the light of the moon by Maeve, the moonlight filled those weapons with a fiery cold glow and fierce power."

"And I extinguished one."

"Two," she corrected, holding up a finger. "And worse—you melted them."

"Do you know how? Or why?"

"The fact that those blades were wrought in Fae by mortals meant they could slice portals between the realms. They had some of each realm in them."

Hadrian nodded understanding.

"But they were forged of silver spun out of ice, which answers the summons of an ice dragon like you. You turned that sword back into ice, just by touching it, by beckoning to the ice without even knowing that you did as much. And then it melted." Rania's mother shook her head. "Imagine what would happen to the Fae's armory if you paid it a visit."

Hadrian nodded. "I thought of that. It might all melt."

She nodded mildly. "She thought of it first."

"Why are you telling me this?"

"Because I'm dead. There are no consequences any more for sharing a truth that others would prefer to keep secret or deny." She reached out and touched his hand, her fingertips close to that ring. "And I think you have the ability to bring joy to my daughter, as I never did."

Hadrian wished he could console her, but he didn't know what she'd done or not done. He stood up, filled with purpose. "How do I get back to Fae?" he asked.

"I don't know. It's not in my power to give life to anyone." She sounded a lot more philosophical about that than Hadrian felt. She gestured with a fingertip, making a little spinning motion in the air, and the fireflies zoomed toward her. They circled the tip of her finger so closely and flew so quickly that Hadrian could only see a globe of golden light. Was it an illusion that there seemed to be a sphere within the orb of light?

He looked closer and thought he saw a spider in the act of killing a wasp. "The gem of the hoard!" he whispered, recognizing it. As soon as he spoke, the fireflies dispersed and the illusion was gone. He looked at his companion in confusion but she smiled.

"Just think what else you could freeze, if you were free of this place," she mused. Her eyes were filled with a challenge and that expression reminded Hadrian of his mate.

"I have to get back."

"If you can." She reached out for the ring again and her voice caught. "If you see him, ask him to dream of me. In that realm, we might meet again."

Hadrian nodded agreement.

She stood up then, her expression serene. She brushed off her skirt, then tipped her head back to smile at the fireflies. They surrounded her more tightly, flying in close circles as she raised her hands. So many fireflies buzzed around her hands that Hadrian could only see a blur of golden light. Their glow became brighter, as if they became more numerous, then slowly, ever so slowly, the cloud of insects began to lower toward the ground.

He thought he'd see her hands as the glowing cluster of fireflies descended, but he didn't. It was as if the insects—or their golden light—consumed her. They flew more frantically when they obscured the view of her feet, then they suddenly spiraled upward, creating a blinking trail of light in the darkness.

Rania's mother was gone.

Hadrian turned in place as the line of fireflies trailed into the distance. They weren't bright enough to illuminate anything, but he was disappointed when their lights winked out, one at a time.

He was surrounded by darkness again and this time, it felt cold.

His situation was frustrating. It was unfair that he could have made the difference in the battle against Maeve, but that he hadn't known it until it was too late to actually do anything. He hated not having influenced the outcome. He hated the possibility that his fellow *Pyr* would be eliminated because he'd failed them. The talons he'd made were destroyed. His firestorm wasn't satisfied. Rania's quest was incomplete and her brothers were still cursed. She would probably be in thrall to Maeve forever.

It was way too soon for him to die.

Hadrian started to walk, because that had to be better than just sitting and feeling sorry for himself. Regret weighed him down, but he kept walking. He couldn't help but think of all the things he could have done differently and how he'd seize opportunity, if he could just have another chance.

He thought he was imagining the faint glow of white light when it appeared in the distance. He considered that it might be a lure or a trap, that Maeve might not have exhausted her store of tricks. But he walked toward it anyway, unable to deny the spark of hope that the sight gave him.

Then he felt the coldness in his cheek again, the chill that had haunted him since Rania had given him the kiss of death. The place where she had first touched her lips to his cheek burned a little, exactly the way frozen fingertips do when first exposed to warmth again. It stung as it hadn't in a long while, sensation returning to the spot with a vengeance. And he could feel his cheek. Something was changing! The light brightened ahead of him even as the pain in his cheek sharpened.

Hadrian felt heat slide through his veins and desire coil deep inside himself. In that moment, he knew that he was seeing the light of his firestorm and that Rania was trying to save him.

The least he could do was meet her halfway.

He started to run toward the light.

He ignored the pain in his cheek as it throbbed with insistence. Even if she was just reviving him to assassinate him again, Hadrian didn't care.

This was the chance he wanted and needed.

He would make it count.

Rania manifested on her knees beside Hadrian. He was in his bedroom on the bed, and she wasn't sure how much time had passed. The blinds were closed and the room was in shadows. He was cold to the touch and so still that her heart clenched. His death was her fault—and for no point at all. The firestorm didn't spark between them, even when she reached out to touch him, and she feared she'd been in Fae too long.

What if she was too late?

Balthasar was sitting on the other side of the bed. At her appearance, he jumped in shock. "I hate when you do that."

"You'll like it better this time," she said, tracing the shadow of the kiss of death with her fingertip. Could she reverse it?

The younger *Pyr* eyed her. "Tell me about that kiss of death. Is that what got him?"

"No." Rania shook her head. "At least I don't think so. Giving the kiss is a condemnation. The recipient will always die and it never takes long."

Balthasar frowned and gestured to his fallen friend.

"It should have worked ages ago, if it was going to work at all."

Interest brightened the other *Pyr's* gaze. "But it didn't. Why not?"

"I thought maybe because the selkie healed him, but maybe it was his own nature as an ice dragon."

"I don't understand."

Rania was becoming excited: the more she thought about her idea, the more sense it made. It would help to talk it through with Balthasar. "When I grant the kiss of death, I have to prepare first. I have to gather up all the ill will that I can find. I have to distill it and focus it, until there's enough. Then I pour all that evil into the kiss. It's not just any kiss. I can only give it when I've done the preparations."

"You inject the victim with malice, essentially." Balthasar had his arms folded across his chest, his disapproval clear.

Rania nodded. "The kiss of death is like a ticking clock, counting down to oblivion. It's only a matter of time before it finds a place to fester and multiply. It might take advantage of an existing injury or weakness. It might have to wait for one. But the kiss of death amplifies *any* injury, even a seemingly innocuous one, and makes it fatal." She met his gaze. "I told Hadrian it could make someone die of a paper cut, because that's the truth."

"Nasty," Balthasar said.

"Effective," Rania corrected, then pointed at Hadrian. "But it didn't work. That's the first time ever."

"So? He's dead now all the same."

"I wonder."

"How many times have you done this, anyway?"

"This was the thirteenth time. Maeve gave me the ability to bestow the kiss of death thirteen times."

"So, you're done."

Rania nodded. "But I wonder whether it's done." Balthasar shook his head, obviously not understanding, but she leaned toward Hadrian. She gathered her thoughts and made space within herself for the malice she'd poured into Hadrian.

"What are you doing?" Balthasar demanded.

"I'm going to try to take it back." She touched her lips to Hadrian's cheek, fitting her kiss exactly to the mark she'd left there weeks before. Instead of exuding malice into him, she drew it back into herself. She sucked it into herself, pulling it from every sinew of his body, willing it to abandon him as a victim.

She felt Balthasar watching, his eyes wide. His gaze danced over her and she wondered how much of the transaction he could see.

What should she do with the toxin once she had it? Should she give the kiss to Alasdair, fulfilling his promise? She'd been so intent on saving Hadrian that she hadn't thought of the subsequent details. And she didn't particularly want to kill Alasdair, either.

The important thing was to save Hadrian.

For long precious moments, Rania thought her efforts might be futile—but then, the firestorm lit again. Her heart leaped at the white glow of light and the little flurry of sparks between her lips and Hadrian's cheek. She heard Balthasar's hoot of triumph, but continued to concentrate on her task. Frost formed around her mouth and she felt a chill move into her mouth, but she kept drawing the power of the kiss of death from him. There were icicles on her tongue and her mouth was numb, but Rania kept gathering that malice.

The firestorm burned brighter with every passing moment. She stole a peek to find color returning to Hadrian's skin and continued to draw the toxin from him. She found herself running her hand over Hadrian's chest, caressing him as she undid the damage, and his heart pounded beneath her fingertips. She kept drawing out more, feeling his skin warm, her sense of victory growing when his hand closed over hers in a reassuring grip.

She felt Hadrian take a breath. She heard his groan. He shivered and stirred to life again, his skin warming beneath her lips. When there was no more toxin to withdraw from him, Rania straightened, holding her breath. She saw Hadrian open his eyes. He ran a hand over his hair, scanned his surroundings, then his gaze locked with hers. He smiled and she felt warm to her toes. His green eyes were glowing with affection that Rania knew she didn't deserve. He held her gaze as he lifted her hand to his mouth and pressed a kiss against her palm.

"You really want to use that *bichuwa*," he teased and Rania almost laughed.

She held her breath, though, wondering what to do with the toxin of the kiss of death. She didn't want to give it to Alasdair or Balthasar. She didn't want to disperse it, to spread its poison everywhere.

A flicker of movement caught her gaze and she saw a salamander dart across the floor. It wasn't a normal salamander, because its skin like jewels. It could have been made of opals edged with gold, which made her wonder whether some of the *Pyr* could take other forms.

The salamander darted over Hadrian and leapt toward Rania. She caught it instinctively and it looked her right in the eye. It seemed to wink, then coiled its tail around her wrist.

"Stay with me!"

Rania heard the words in her own thoughts, spoken in a man's commanding voice. She chose to trust her instincts and follow his suggestion. She nodded and the salamander shimmered blue. He then vanished right before her eyes and Rania did her best to keep up.

"What was that?" Alasdair demanded as he charged back to Balthasar's side. After the emergency crews had put out the fire and left, he and Balthasar had taken Hadrian into his own room. Alasdair had driven into town for pizza because neither of the *Pyr* felt like cooking.

He'd felt the spark of the firestorm suddenly and had come as quickly as possible. He found Balthasar staring down at Hadrian, who was drifting off to sleep.

But he was alive. Alasdair nearly wept with relief when he reached the side of the bed. Hadrian's hand was warm and Alasdair shook it, even as Hadrian smiled.

"Rania saved me," Hadrian murmured, his eyes drifting closed. "She really is my destined mate." He smiled a little. "It really is love." Then he fell asleep, his breathing slow and steady.

Alasdair looked at Balthasar, knowing his question was obvious.

"She came back," that *Pyr* said, his tone thoughtful. "She thought she could reverse the kiss of death and she did it."

"But why? I thought she had to kill Hadrian to save her brothers?"

"I'm going to guess that Maeve broke her word."

Alasdair nodded agreement. "Rania?"

Balthasar shrugged. "That's what he's calling her now. Maybe she finally told him her name." He shrugged.

"Then where did she go?"

"With the salamander."

Alasdair turned to Balthasar in confusion. "The what?"

"Didn't you hear the old-speak? It said *'stay with me'* in old-speak."

"Then it was *Pyr*."

Balthasar nodded. "Sloane said that some of the *Slayers* who had drunk the Elixir had the ability to take a third form, that of a salamander. Rafferty is the only *Pyr* who can do it."

"Was the salamander opal and gold?"

"Yes, it was."

"Then it had to have been him. I wonder how he knew to come here," Alasdair mused.

"I wonder where they went," Balthasar said. "I'd like to know where all that nasty malice ended up."

"If it was Rafferty who guided her away, then we don't have to worry about it anymore," Alasdair said with conviction. "Is Hadrian really okay?"

"Sleeping normally. It's incredible." Balthasar smiled as he tucked Hadrian under a duvet and left him to sleep. "I'm going to guess that he'll be hungry when he wakes up. Do I smell pizza?"

"You do." Alasdair waved a parcel that Balthasar hadn't noticed.

"Plus there's a package for Hadrian from Sara. Do you think we should open it?"

"Absolutely. Hadrian said she was going to send a book. Where's that prophecy? Didn't he write it down? Maybe we can figure some of this out for him."

"Sounds like a plan."

CHAPTER TEN

Sebastian wasn't a fan of airline travel. While it had the advantage of speed, it had so many other drawbacks that he avoided it as much as possible. The schedule was inflexible, for starters, which created challenges in ensuring that he wasn't exposed to sunlight. Going to Europe was about as easy as that could be, since many flights left in the evening and arrived early in the morning. He booked business class, to minimize his check-in time, and disliked that he had to hope for the best.

After that, there was the crush of the airline terminal to survive, the inconvenience of security checks to tolerate, and interminable delays to endure. He hated the crowds and the lines and the scent of mortal flesh on all sides. He hated being trapped in a metal tube with several hundred mortal strangers even more.

He pulled up the hood on his sweatshirt, put on his eyeshades and tugged a blanket over himself, as sure a combination of signals that he didn't want to be disturbed as he could provide. Of course, the businessman next to him wanted to drink and chat. Sebastian seethed all the way across the Atlantic, fantasizing about the days of the big ocean liners. That had been traveling in style, with all the amenities and the option of retreating to a stateroom at any time. Staff on all sides. Every request fulfilled. He'd even been able to feast on sorry specimens in third class, if he'd been careful.

The contrast was striking.

Of course, he became thirsty. It was inescapable with humanity pressed upon him on all sides. He'd feasted after Maeve's visit, knowing it would only stave off his hunger for a few hours. In Manhattan, he could go days without feasting, but airline travel undermined his resolve. It was as if he stood before a buffet of temptation.

Except the morsel he truly desired wasn't there.

It was probably good for him—or at least for Sylvia—for him to accept Maeve's commission. He amused himself by trying to remember all the titles in his locked library, the order of them on the shelves, the times and places of acquisition. He teased himself with the thrill of regaining his greatest treasure and told himself that the prospect seemed flat because he was grumpy.

After Maeve's visit and that quick snack in an alley, he'd caught a flight to Heathrow, which had arrived at dawn. He lingered all day in a hotel, blinds drawn, chafing to be on his way. Fortunately, darkness fell early in the UK in December. Sebastian bought a heavy coat and a hat he could pull down to hide his face in case his eyes began to glitter. It was perfectly reasonable to wear gloves and a scarf, and both hid the pallor of his skin. He booked an express train to York, then a local train to the train station closest to Hadrian's lair. By eleven that night, he had taken refuge in the pub closest to his destination, stymied as to how to complete the last stage of his journey.

And burning with thirst.

And irritable.

The small box Maeve had entrusted to him seemed heavy in his pocket, as if it became heavier the closer he came to his goal. Fucking magick. It was completely untrustworthy, which made him wonder whether he could rely upon Maeve to keep her word. That was a question to ponder.

Later.

He could walk to Hadrian's lair, but he couldn't keep himself from yearning for the days when mortals had kept horses and carriages. He did like to arrive in style.

There was little chance of that in this backwater. Why couldn't the *Pyr* live in cities, preferably cities with limousines—and dark alleys where countless multitudes could vanish, unnoticed? This obsession with wilderness was tedious, although he could understand their desire for privacy.

He entered the pub, surveyed the few inhabitants, noticed the beautiful redhead behind the bar without interest, then headed for the table in the darkest corner.

"There are better tables," she called to him, but Sebastian shook his head.

"I like it dark." He sat in the booth without removing his coat, hat or gloves.

She followed him and he was surprised when she laughed. "So, it's like that, is it? Can't say as I blame you. I've been in a bit of a funk myself lately. Something to eat? The special tonight was steak and kidney pie, and there's still a bit left."

The prospect of cooked meat disgusted him. "No, thank you." He could get by with steak tartare in a pinch, but this didn't look like the kind of place to order raw meat with confidence.

"A drink, then?" she asked with a smile.

"You don't have what I want."

"You can't know that unless you ask." Her tone was mild and that irked him.

Anything would have irked Sebastian in this moment. He wanted to be with Sylvia, which could only lead to trouble, so he'd put an ocean between them, not told her he was leaving, and felt like an asshole as a result. He'd always been self-centered but it never bothered him.

Until now.

Until Sylvia.

The redhead was still waiting. He flicked a hostile glance her way. "What I would like is a glass of Château Latour Bordeaux Red Pauillac from 1929." She winced. "Failing that, I'd like to find a cab that will drive me to this address." He conjured the paper with Hadrian's address from his pocket and put it on the table.

She looked down, frowned and paled. "You know Hadrian MacEwan?"

"I've come to see him." Sebastian paused, assessing and took the chance. "Or actually, his mate."

The redhead inhaled sharply and became taller. "He has a girlfriend already, does he? Wants some time alone. Doesn't see that we have a future. No, there's no one else." She rolled her eyes, took off her apron and flung it in the direction of the bar. "Come on. I'll give you a ride. I wouldn't mind giving Hadrian a piece of my mind myself."

"Aren't you working?"

"I own the place." She pivoted and raised her voice. "Eddie, go home to Tilda already!" she shouted at the last patron, an older man sitting at the bar. "I'll not pour you another. That one's on the house if you leave now." Eddie thanked her profusely as he slid from his stool and tugged on his coat, obviously thinking that she might change her mind if he didn't accept her offer quickly. She turned back to Sebastian and offered her hand. "I'm Lynsay Barnes. My car's not fancy, but it'll get us there."

It wasn't the most reassuring claim she could have made, but Sebastian was sufficiently curious to accept her offer.

Riding in her car had to be better than walking.

Once upon a time, there was a king who dearly loved his wife. Their marriage had been arranged to further the fortunes of both families, but they had fallen in love immediately and, each day, their love grew only deeper. The king's realm was in the distant north, an empire of ice and wind and stone, but his beloved wife filled his palace with light, joy and warmth. The queen loved swans and the king admired her gentleness with them. She fed the birds as they migrated and he would often awaken and look out the palace window to see his wife, the wind in her hair, feeding wild swans by hand in the courtyard. During their courtship, he had changed his standard to that of a white swan in flight. Once she'd become his wife, he delighted in adding swans to every corner of the palace. The canopy over their bed was crested with a carved swan in flight. There were swans carved in stone and in wood, woven in tapestries and created in tiles on the floor. The queen was surrounded by swans and this gave her tremendous joy.

In time, the happy couple conceived a child but the queen died in the delivery of the daughter. The king was devastated. He cherished the child, at first because she was the fruit of his union with his beloved, and later because of her own nature. The princess was beautiful, inside and out, as gracious and generous a lady as her mother had been, clever, lovely and gentle as well. As she grew older, the king dreaded the day he would be compelled to surrender his daughter's hand in marriage, for he would miss her company so much. He and his daughter agreed that she would wed for love and that she would choose her own spouse. The daughter, who loved her father as dearly as he loved her and lacked for nothing in life, didn't rush to make that choice. They were happy, each in their own way, and disinclined to make a change.

In that area, there was a family of swan shifters who were considered royal. A terrible plague had come upon the swan shifters and the eldest son of the swan-king was the last of his kind. He visited the king's palace to see the wonders he'd heard described, hoping to diminish his loneliness. While he admired the many depictions of swans, it was the king's daughter who stole his heart away. With one glimpse, he was smitten—but when he presented his proposal to the king, the king forbade the swan-prince to even speak to the princess. The king feared the mingling of their kinds and wished his daughter to wed a man, not a changeling. The swan-prince was disappointed, but true to his promise to the king, he neither spoke to the princess nor remained at the palace. He left and wandered, hoping to find another woman he could love somewhere in the world, but the memory of the princess burned bright in his heart.

There was a brigand on the king's borders, though, one who grew increasingly bold with every passing year. This warrior was a thief and a killer, treacherous to his marrow, and disinterested in anything beyond his own desires. The first time he saw the king's palace, he wanted it for his own. The first time he rode close to the king's palace and glimpsed that man's lovely daughter, he swore that she would belong to him. He sent word to the king of his demand, but the king declined even to speak with him.

This brigand was not a man to be put aside. He began to raid the villages on the borders of the kingdom, leaving only destruction and death in his wake. Each time he attacked, he sent his request to the king and, each time, the king refused to hear of such a marriage for his beloved daughter. The brigand used his stolen riches to hire mercenaries and his army swelled in numbers and power. He was a pestilence upon the king's realm, slaughtering and stealing so that eventually there was only the palace left. The brigand made his demand again and was rebuffed for the last time. He besieged the castle, killing all who opposed him and forcibly seizing the princess. The king tried to defend her, but the brigand cut down the king before her very eyes. He then claimed the castle and kingdom, and married the princess by force. He consummated their match before all in attendance, then locked her into the king's chambers, where only he could visit her. He went to her every night without fail, claiming her until she begged for mercy.

He told her that the price of mercy was a son.

The princess prayed that she would conceive the son of the monster who held her captive. She sent messages from her window to every wise woman she knew, asking for their council in the rapid conception of a son and heir. She endured her husband's attentions, hoping that the ordeal would not last long.

Within two moons, she knew she was with child.

The mercenary, to her relief, considered the matter resolved. He left her locked in the chamber, forbade all to visit her, and vowed she would be released with the safe delivery of his son and heir. For nine months, the lady lived alone, had no maid to tend her and no friend with whom to converse. For nine months, her meals were surrendered to her through a hole cut in the door, a hole too small for her to use for escape. For nine months, she endured the restraints put upon her by her husband, knowing he pillaged the holdings of their neighbors, piled his ill-gotten gains in what had been her father's treasury, and indulged his gluttony each night in her father's hall. Her hatred of him distilled until it was as brittle and hard as an icicle, or a diamond forged in the core of the earth. And then, on midwinter's eve, she delivered his son.

The boy was tall and strong, a robust babe who yelled with vigor when he entered the world. The brigand came to look upon his son and heir, but instead of pronouncing himself pleased, he demanded another.

"Life is full of uncertainty," he informed his lady wife, even as he took the boy *from her breast.* "You will grant another son unto me with all haste."

The lady cried out when her son was taken away from her, but the brigand decreed that the babe would have a wet nurse—so that his wife would be able to conceive more quickly again. She was not to see the child at all until she was pregnant again.

The lady thought she could not have despised her husband more but on that dark morning, she learned she had additional capacity for hate. Again she prayed and again she strove to do his will, and again—in three moons' time—she conceived a child. Just as before, the brigand vowed she would remain locked in the royal chamber alone until the child was born and hale.

He lied about allowing her to see her oldest son, for he did not bring the boy or let any other bring him. The lady's heart began to harden yet more.

Once again, the lady endured her solitude. Once again, her hatred of her husband grew. Once again, on midwinter eve, the lady delivered of a healthy son. If anything, he was stronger and larger than the first boy. She was certain she would have a reprieve and had just put the babe to her breast, thinking of what she would do first when she left the confines of her chamber, when her husband arrived. As before, he took the child from her. As before, he demanded another son. As before, the lady was left locked within the chamber, her son was given to a wet nurse, and she was compelled to endure the attentions of her cruel husband each night until she conceived.

And so the tale repeated nine more times. Each midwinter night, the lady delivered of a healthy son and her sentence was renewed again. Her hope steadily dwindled until it died. Her husband never noticed that the spark died in her eyes, that her hair lost its luster, that she no longer had any ability to smile.

When the lady was round with her twelfth child, her hatred of her husband had grown to the point that she no longer cared about her survival. It was no life, to her thinking, to be confined to one room. She had no one to love, for her sons were lost to her and her husband was a man she could never love.

It was in that year that her husband began to train his sons in the courtyard beneath the queen's window. If he meant to impress her with their prowess, his choice did the very opposite: the lady despaired to see that her sons mirrored their father in every way. She hated that she had been the means of eleven more brigands coming into the world to pillage and slaughter. She sickened then, that autumn, and did not care whether she lost the child. So ill was she that even her husband noticed, and he tried to rouse her by complaining that her illness might affect the child in her womb. The lady did not respond.

On midwinter night, she delivered of a boy once more. This boy was smaller and more slender, but his kick and cry were just as robust as those of his brothers. If anything, she loved him more because of his size, and she tenderly put him to her breast, wishing she could nurse him for more than a moment. The brigand came to see his son and was less pleased than before. He thought the boy weak and unworthy. He *decided his wife's womb had exhausted its bounty.*

"I want a daughter," his wife said, rebellion in her eyes, and he recognized that she was prepared to fight him. The brigand didn't care what his wife desired. He had younger and more beautiful women to bed, and he had twelve sons.

"Nurse this one then," he said with scorn. "Make your daughter out of him. I make sons out of the other eleven."

"I will leave this chamber," she said when he had turned away.

"So another can bed you? I think not, lady wife. Here you have been for thirteen years, and here you will remain until your dying day." With that, he left and locked the door against them both.

"Asshole," Balthasar said when Alasdair stopped for breath. He considered the pizza, then took another slice, leaving three for Hadrian as they'd agreed.

"I wonder what this has to do with anything," Alasdair said, glancing at the cover of the book again. "Sara must have thought it important to send it overnight."

"Then we'll get to it," Balthasar said.

"Is there anything to eat?" Hadrian demanded from the doorway of the bedroom. His hair was rumpled, but Alasdair grinned at him all the same.

"We saved you some pizza," he said, then stared at the ring on Hadrian's hand. He'd noticed it earlier and had meant to ask. The single stone set in it glowed with that pearly radiance and it seemed to be even brighter than before. "Where'd you get that?"

"From my mate. She wore it on a chain around her neck."

"Where's it from?"

Hadrian shrugged. "She said she'd always had it, but the glow was new."

Alasdair frowned, wondering.

"Keep reading," Balthasar advised and Alasdair did, because his instinct was exactly the same.

Rania didn't know where she was. She stood in a cool breeze and turned in place, wondering where she'd ended up. Had she managed to stay with the salamander? It seemed to be twilight, wherever she was, but there were no stars overhead. It wasn't overcast either, and she couldn't see the moon. Was she in Fae? She couldn't hear any music or see the red glow of magick anywhere. She looked.

She realized then that she was in the middle of a stone circle, thirteen tall stones emanating a steady chill around her. At her feet, in the middle of the circle, there was a cairn. A hole, darker than dark, led into the ground.

That glittering salamander appeared suddenly from the opening and perched on the crest of the highest rock in the cairn. He was watching her, his eyes and scales sparkling as his tail flicked. She was glad she'd managed to follow him through the realms and wondered why he had brought her to this place.

If she'd thought he might tell her, she was to be disappointed.

Suddenly, the salamander darted across the ground, heading for the rocks on the perimeter of the circle. Rania followed him, not wanting to lose track of him now. He circled the base of the largest stone, the one that towered over her, pointing to the sky. On the outer side of the stone, the salamander stopped beside a dandelion in full seed, the flower head round and white. The weed was growing at the base of the stone, its roots lodged in the narrow crevice between the stone and the ground. The salamander coiled around the flower stem so that it swayed slightly, then gave her an intent look. When he bared his teeth, Rania guessed what he was going to do and what he wanted from her. She bent down and held the stem while the salamander bit into it.

Rania lifted the dandelion flower, straightening slowly so she wouldn't disturb the perfect sphere of white seeds. Why did he want her to have this?

The salamander watched, his manner expectant. What should she do with the dandelion? She thought then of children blowing the seeds and making a wish. She pursed her lips as if to blow, wondering, and the salamander nodded vigorously.

Rania understood that she should exhale the toxin of the kiss of death to blow the seeds. Maybe that was a way of making a wish. Maybe that was one way of dispersing it. She nodded, and he scurried to one side, still watching.

What should she wish for? That was easy: Rania wanted her brothers to be freed. She wanted Hadrian to live. She wanted to be rid of Maeve's curse herself. She wanted the Others to be safe from the Dark Queen's wrath. She wanted a second chance to get it right, to have the chance to trust Hadrian, to satisfy the firestorm and even to have Hadrian's son. Her wishes had wishes, it seemed.

She began to blow, surrendering all the malice and poison that she'd pulled out of Hadrian. The seeds took flight, one at a time, floating into the distance. For a long time, it didn't seem that the flower had any fewer of them. Maybe there were enough seeds for all of Rania's wishes to come true. She blew and blew and wished until there was no more toxin inside of her.

With her final breath, the last seed took flight.

She was left holding only the stalk of the flower, the seeds floating higher and higher as they drifted away from her. When she glanced down, her companion beckoned to her. She followed as the salamander pursued the stream of dandelion seeds, each on its own herbal parachute. There was a long ribbon of them stretching into the distance, dancing on that gentle breeze.

When they caught up to the end of the trail of them, Rania saw that each seed had changed: instead of a brown seed on each white tuft, it looked like there was a drop of ruby-red blood. No, not a drop. A tiny shard, like a sliver of red glass. She shivered at the sight, but her companion nodded approval, as if she had done particularly well.

The seeds swirled higher and she wondered where they would go, then what would happen when they arrived. The salamander was satisfied, though. He led her back toward the stone circle, purpose in his movement. Once they stood beside the dark abyss in the central cairn, he bowed his head to her, those scales glinting a little, then shimmered blue. The salamander vanished in a flash.

Rania didn't know where he'd gone, but was in agreement with his choice. She'd dispensed with the poison behind the kiss of death, and she knew exactly where she wanted to be. She didn't want to linger in this place, whether it was Fae or not.

She closed her eyes and willed herself to Hadrian's side.

She had a second chance and she was going to make it count.

For the first time that she could remember, Rania felt a thrill of anticipation.

Rania didn't see that the transformed seeds drifted until the mound of a hill rose in the distance. Merry music became discernible then grew louder as the seeds floated nearer. There was a party beneath the hill, a party at the Fae court, attended by hundreds of glittering Fae dressed in silver and red. Their wings arched high, their laughter echoed loudly, their mead flowed in quantity.

The seeds blew right through the open portal to the Fae court, almost as if they were dancing in time to the music. The seeds wafted high once they were through the portal, then they swooped low, caught in the currents of air in the court. The faceted red crystals of the transformed seeds caught the light and sparkled.

The first one fell on the exposed shoulder of a Fae dancer. Red light flared brightly from the point of impact for a fraction of a second, then a tiny port wine stain appeared on the skin of the Fae. It could have been a mole or a freckle, except for its color. The recipient barely noticed it, brushing one hand across the point of contact and continuing with the dance.

Thousands of seeds slowly descended upon the revelers. Most of the Fae didn't seem to take notice of them. Others reached for them, as if they were toys to be gathered. A few opened their mouths to them, as children do with snowflakes. Each seed touched bare skin, each one giving a little pulse of light as it turned into a purple freckle and vanished.

All the while, the merry dance continued as if it would endure to the end of time.

Not fancy.

There was an understatement.

Maeve had a lot to answer for, to Sebastian's thinking. Lynsay's car was small and cramped. It was cold and less than comfortable.

Worse, his companion was a talker. Why did mortals insist on filling the air with their babble and their confidences? He'd never been chatty, even before he'd been turned, and he resented her conversation.

It interfered with his brooding.

He felt the thirst begin to gnaw within him as they drove away from the pub. Lynsay was the most convenient candidate to satisfy his need, but she was robustly healthy and she was doing him a favor. Choosing her as his victim felt wrong, and that made Sebastian irritable.

Was it Sylvia's influence at root or Micah's?

Either way, he needed to find better company.

Actually, he wouldn't need company at all after this quest of Maeve's was completed. He could lock himself into his beloved library and only emerge to feed as necessary. The solitude would be bliss.

"How do you know Hadrian MacEwan?" Lynsay asked.

"I don't," Sebastian acknowledged.

"But you're looking for him."

"I was entrusted with a package to deliver to him, by hand."

"Oh! Something for his business?"

"You could say that." Sebastian deliberately turned to look out the window, hoping that would end the conversation. He could smell her body lotion, a light feminine scent, but he was keenly aware of the aroma of her flesh beneath it, the pulse of blood, and the heat of her body. He could smell the warm rich blood that coursed through her veins, so close. He couldn't even glance at the length of her throat, pale against her velvet scarf but just as smooth and soft. His teeth would sink in easily, without resistance, and she'd gasp. She might cry out but not for long, and no one would hear her. Not here. He could feast to his heart's content and arrive at the dragon's lair, sated, with his thoughts clear.

He clenched one fist and fixed his gaze on the passing scenery without really seeing it.

"Do you believe in true love?" Lynsay asked abruptly. "Or in there being one perfect partner out there for everyone?" She was concentrating on the road, so she missed Sebastian's poisonous sidelong glance.

"No," he said flatly. "It's romantic drivel."

She smiled. "That's what I think, too. The idea that there's one person out there who's your perfect mate just seems a little far-fetched. It also makes dating into a kind of a treasure hunt." She laughed under her breath. "And as the kid who never ever found the prize, that idea doesn't appeal to me. Who wants to be a loser at love?"

Sebastian allowed himself a small grunt, which could have been interpreted as agreement or encouragement. Lynsay was turning onto a smaller lane so this ordeal couldn't last much longer. The road became a bit bumpier and there was no other traffic. The thirst raged and he clenched the other fist in his bid for control.

Not much farther.

Lynsay nodded, clearly unaware of the threat beside her. "But when the person you love believes in all that stuff, things can get complicated."

"How so?" Sebastian asked, for the sake of distraction as much as anything else.

"Well, I guess only if you fall short. It's the worst thing in the world to be told that you're not the One."

"Surely not the very worst thing," Sebastian muttered. "You could be attacked and left for dead at the side of a quiet country road, for example."

To his surprise, she laughed at what could have been taken as a warning. Why were mortals so foolish with their trust? "Okay, you're right. Not the worst thing, but it's bad. You're in love and he's apparently not, even though you thought everything was going so well."

"How can you be sure of that?" Sebastian turned to watch her, hearing the yearning in her voice. He felt a strange commonality with this mortal, one that wasn't entirely welcome.

"Because he dumped me. He said I wasn't the one. He said he preferred to wait." She geared down and her voice dropped low. "As if I wasn't good enough."

Sebastian frowned. He looked out the window at nothing and reminded himself that her business wasn't his business. Her broken heart certainly wasn't his problem. But he knew the *Pyr* and their code of honor and he could connect the dots.

"You love Hadrian MacEwan," he guessed.

"Oh, God, yes," she said with such feeling that even Sebastian's weary heart clenched.

It really *wasn't* his problem.

He was the last individual in the world to become an agony aunt or give advice on matters of the heart. He had no empathy and didn't care.

But he felt her ache and oddly enough, it found a resonance within him.

Sebastian meant to sigh, but instead, he found himself talking. "Maybe he thought he wasn't good enough," he said, then wondered where that suggestion had come from. It had nothing to do with his relationship with Sylvia, certainly. Sebastian had no illusions that he was less than magnificent himself. He kept his gaze fixed on what passed for a road ahead of the car, well aware that Lynsay was studying him.

"You think so?"

"It's always possible. Some men are idealists. Some think that love should bring more than sexual satisfaction and contentment, that it should be a pairing of opposites, or a partnership of complementary strengths. Some think that a union should be more than the sum of the parts, that it should exult each partner, making each better and stronger than before."

He sounded like a propagandist for the *Pyr* and their wretched firestorm, which annoyed him. On the other hand, he understood why Hadrian had acted as he had. He'd heard the argument before. The irony was that Hadrian might actually have loved Lynsay, but the spark of the firestorm and appearance of his destined mate would have compelled him to turn away from her anyway. Had he anticipated it? Or had he simply thought it easier to break up sooner rather than later?

Sebastian was glad he didn't believe in destined love or, really, in love at all. It had to be worse than magick for making trouble where none was wanted.

The car was silent, the atmosphere charged. Sebastian glanced over to find Lynsay frowning in thought. "I can respect that," she said finally. She turned to face him so suddenly that Sebastian was surprised and their gazes caught. "Buy why wouldn't he try to change?"

"Change?" Sebastian was incredulous. "Do you truly imagine that anyone is capable of real change?"

"Yes," she said with heat. "Yes, I do. Anyone can ditch a habit or be more noble in their goals or try harder. They just have to want to do it badly enough." Her lips set as she parked in front of what looked like an old mill. "And you know, if he thought he wasn't good enough, but he didn't have the stones to try to do better, then he's right. We're better off apart." She turned off the engine with a decisive flick of her wrist.

There were two Land Rovers parked there already. One side of the building had burned and had done so recently: Sebastian could still smell the smoke. On the remaining side, there were lights behind the windows, indicating that the fire had been contained. Lynsay peered into the darkness. "They said he was back, and also that there had been a fire in his studio. I didn't realize it was completely gone. That's a shame. But Hadrian will rebuild. Nothing stops him when he pursues a goal." Her gaze lingered on the shadowed ruins as she apparently realized the implication of what she'd just said. She looked at Sebastian, new understanding in her eyes. "Which pretty much says it all, doesn't it?"

Sebastian knew he should get out of the car. He knew he shouldn't involve himself or offer a suggestion. But her disappointment was palpable and he felt like he should encourage her somehow.

There had been a time when Sebastian would have surrendered to his need and put Lynsay out of her misery in the simplest way possible. That was one solution.

Instead, he actually smiled at her.

"All good things come to he—or she—who waits," he said.

"But is it true?"

"I hope so."

She laughed and her eyes lit. "How long have you waited?"

"Much longer than you." She surveyed him, obviously trying to guess his age. "Trust me on that."

"All right, I will. Because you're right. I just have to let it go and move on." Her eyes widened. "I'll keep waiting for the good stuff."

"Keep your eyes open," Sebastian found himself advising. "It might be in the most unlikely of places."

"My father used to say that, but then, he was a poet." She looked at the door to Hadrian's lair again, then restarted the car. "I'm not going to go in," she said with admirable resolve. "Are you going to need a ride back? You could call me."

"You've already done more than enough," Sebastian said, shaking her proffered hand. He ignored the surge of the thirst at the glimpse of that pale wrist. "I'll solve it."

"Stop in for a pint before you leave town."

"Perhaps I will. Thank you, Lynsay, and good luck."

"I don't even know your name."

"You don't need to. Goodnight." Sebastian got out of the car, raising a hand as Lynsay turned the car around and drove away. He stood in the shadows, watching the tail lights of her car fade from view, fingering Maeve's box in his pocket.

If he thought he wasn't good enough, but he didn't have the stones to try to do better, then he's right. We're better off apart.

Sebastian heard the echo of Lynsay's ferocity in his thoughts. Was she right about the ability to change? He'd never even tried to change, not for anyone or anything.

What if that was the secret?

CHAPTER ELEVEN

The pizza, even cool, tasted better than anything Hadrian had eaten in a long time. Balthasar and Alasdair brought him up to date on the story so far, then Alasdair continued to read.

It couldn't be a coincidence that there were swans in this story and that his mate was a swan shifter. He'd wanted to know everything about her even before she'd saved him from death so he listened closely.

If the brigand king thought to leave his wife and youngest son in misery, he erred in his judgment. Relieved of the prospect of her husband's presence, the lady blossomed anew. She began to smile and the sparkle returned to her eyes. She indulged her youngest son, who she named Trymman in her father's memory. She taught him to read and to write, and told him the tales of her family and her people, sharing with him all the lore she had ever known.

The brigand turned all his energies to training his eleven sons in warfare, and in bedding his new mistress, the village witch, with enthusiasm. That woman dared him to get her with child, hinting that his vigor was insufficient—in truth, she took a potion to prevent any conception and wished only to have the brigand's attention and favor. She suspected that if he turned her out of his bed for any reason, she would lose her influence over him. Power, once tasted, is impossible for some to relinquish: in that, the witch and the mercenary were similar.

Seven years had passed when Trymman noticed his mother weeping on the first day of spring. The castle should have been filled with spring sunlight, the calls of birds and the first blooms on the trees. People should have been singing and thinking of new loves, but there was a pall upon the land. The winter had been hard. The crops the previous year had been taken by pestilence. The brigand king's temper was foul and blood had flowed on the floor of the hall more than once. There was a sense of pending doom, as if a tide turned against them all, and the son thought his mother wept for fear.

"No, my love," she said, wiping her tears. "I weep because I never bore a daughter and that was always my fondest wish. It was once said to me that if I should have a daughter, she would be blessed beyond all others." Trymman protested that she still might bear another child, but his mother shook her head. "My womb shrivels, my son. By winter, I will not be able to conceive again." She sighed and smiled for him, framing his face in her hands and kissing his brow. "But I am foolish and greedy in this yearning, for I have the gift of you to light my days."

Trymman was troubled to see his mother unhappy, for he loved her dearly. Indeed, he had no other soul to love. He wanted his mother to have her desire and be happy, though there was little enough he could do. Unbeknownst to the queen, the swan-prince still admired her. He had often visited the palace and village in his human form but disguised his royal status, simply to look upon her. He was troubled that the brigand king was creating eleven more villains like himself. He was more troubled that the lady he loved and admired was a captive in her own chamber. When he heard the queen weep one night, the swan-prince vowed to see her happy, if it was the last thing he did. He bribed a maid and learned the truth of the queen's desire. Once he knew he could give her joy, he couldn't stay away any longer.

Trymman thought he dreamed when he saw the beautiful swan fly through the window of the chamber at sunset one night and land gracefully in the middle of his mother's chamber. The bird was massive and its feathers shone with a radiance that made Trymman want to touch them. The bird turned to look at him, as if it would talk, then there was a shimmer of blue. When the light faded, a man stood before him and the swan was nowhere to be seen.

The man was tall and handsome, with blond hair that hung past his shoulders and eyes of vivid blue. He was dressed simply but in garments of good quality, and there was a silver ring on his finger with a large clear stone set in it. That stone shone with an inner fire that fascinated the boy. The stranger's smile was kindly and Trymman wasn't afraid of him at all. The man touched his finger to his lips, requesting the boy's silence and complicity. At the boy's nod of agreement—for he had learned the merit of secrecy from the cradle—the man crouched down and beckoned. Trymman leaned close as the man whispered that he should run to the kitchens and eat his fill, that there were stairs to the right that no one used any longer.

Before Trymman could argue that the door was secured, the man glanced toward it and the boy heard the tumblers in the lock. He crossed the room to discover that he was free to leave the chamber. He looked back in astonishment at the man, still crouched down where he had stood. The man smiled and gestured to him to go. Trymman gladly followed his bidding, for he had always yearned for the adventure of exploring the palace. He glanced back from the threshold to see the man approaching his mother's bed. The stranger's expression was tender as he looked down at the sleeping queen, and Trymman knew all would be well. Then the door closed, seeming with a will of its own, and Trymman heard the lock turn again.

By the time he had avoided the cook, raided the larder, eaten his spoils, explored the palace, fetched more from the kitchen for his mother and returned to the chamber, the moon was high in the sky. To his disappointment the stranger was gone and the chamber door was standing ajar again. When Trymman entered the room, the door swung closed behind him, then audibly locked.

But he had been on an adventure and he had brought back as much food as he had been able to carry. His mother slept with a smile upon her lips, a smile of such tranquility and beauty that Trymman could only wonder what had happened in his absence.

Neither of them knew that the stranger also visited the witch and the brigand. He looked upon them while they slept in her hut, then poured out the tonic the witch drank each day to ensure that she didn't conceive. The stranger put plain water in the bottle instead and replaced it, as if it had never been disturbed.

The stranger came three times, at regular intervals, though Trymman and his mother never spoke of him in his absence. On his third visit, he gave the queen the ring that was on his finger, a silver ring graced with that large gleaming stone. The swan prince's ring was too large for his lady's hand, but she wore it on a chain around her neck and often closed her fist around it as she slept. By midwinter, the queen's belly rounded and she wept with joy when she told her youngest son that he was going to have another sibling. She bade him keep it secret from the brigand king, for he had not visited her bed in years and he would know it was not his child.

The brigand king's attention was occupied, though. He shouted with pleasure when he told his men that he had bested the witch's dare and gotten a child upon her—the stores of ale were deeply diminished that night in the hall as the men celebrated with the brigand king. The witch, however, was less pleased. Not only did she fear that the brigand's attention would stray from her and she would lose influence, but she knew she would have to pay a debt she had never anticipated would come due. The tonic she drank to keep from conceiving had been created by a great Fae sorceress, Maeve. The price for the tonic was that the witch would have to surrender any child she conceived to Maeve. She had thought this wager a jest, since the tonic would ensure that she didn't bear a child, but now she fretted about the fate of the babe in her womb. She knew enough of Maeve to doubt that the Fae sorceress had any kind plan for the child. She had given her word, though, and she knew that Maeve would collect. Her fears affected her pregnancy, for her stomach twisted and turned, she slept little and she ate poorly.

On midsummer's day, wife and whore labored in unison, though none outside the queen's chamber knew of her condition. The queen delivered of the daughter she had always desired, a girl of radiant beauty with a rare light in her eyes. Her hair was as fair as the moonlight, her eyes were as blue as a robin's egg, and she was both delicate and lovely. Her mother and the youngest brother looked upon her with awe.

"How shall we hide her?" Trymman whispered and his mother had no answer.

"Her name is Rania," she said instead. She took the chain with the ring and placed it around the child's tiny neck, for it was her legacy from her father."

"Rania," Hadrian said, looking at the ring again. "My mate's name is Rania."

He really had met her mother.

And this ring had belonged to her father. Why hadn't she known him, or her mother? Could the answer be in this book? He indicated that Alasdair should continue.

"The witch, too, delivered of a daughter, much to the displeasure of the brigand king. The child was dark, her features twisted in a scowl, and he feared the future when he looked upon his spawn. It could be no good portent that such a disfigured child was of his seed, but he had ensured that the witch laid with no other man. It was in his moment of doubt that he heard a second babe cry.

The sound came, against all reason, from his wife's chamber.

The brigand king strode to the queen's room and unlocked the door, fury upon his brow. He found the queen with a new babe at her breast and ripped the child from her, casting it aside as he bent his anger upon her. Trymman, forgotten for the moment by his father, caught his infant sister and hid in the shadows, holding her close and keeping her quiet. The brigand king shouted, calling his wife a whore and a slattern, and vowed he would ensure her chastity forevermore.

He drew his dagger and he killed her in her own bed, before the horrified gaze of their youngest son.

Trymman fled his father's rage, knowing that his sister might share their mother's fate. He took advantage of the open door and the brigand king's inattention. He used the forgotten stairs that the stranger had shown him and slipped through the palace unseen. He heard his brothers mustering and feared of their intentions. They ran up the main stairs to their mother's chamber, boots pounding on the stone, the sound of their rage filling the castle. Little did Trymman know that they, too, had come to hate their father: four of them were of age but their father surrendered nothing to them. He kept all in thrall and that created bitterness in the hearts of those who should have loved him best.

Trymman fled into the village, holding his sister close, uncertain where he might find help. From the celebration in the streets and the tavern, he learned that his father had a new daughter by the witch. He followed the revelers to the witch's hut, in time to see her hurry into the street.

There was a hue and cry from the castle above, then the voice of Trymman's oldest brother, Edred, rang out. "The brigand, our father and king, is dead for his crime of murdering our mother! I declare myself king in his stead!"

"Long live King Edred!" cried the other ten brothers in triumph and Trymman saw the flash of their swords at the high window.

"He will not prosper from this deed," the witch muttered. "No son kills his own father and lives to celebrate as much." She raced toward the castle, her own child abandoned in her dismay. She raised her hands, summoning a curse as she hastened to the queen's chambers.

Trymman wanted only to save his sister. On impulse, he exchanged her with the wizened and dark infant sleeping in the witch's hut. He wrapped the witch's daughter in the robe from the queen's chamber, tucking it over her face, and left his sister in the rough furs of the cradle in the witch's hut, her father's ring on that fine chain around her neck. He saw the light in the stone die and feared the portent of that.

When the witch saw her lover dead in the queen's chamber and knew her influence was gone forever, she invoked a curse of ferocious power. She bestowed it on the eleven brothers, for they were responsible for her loss, and they were powerless to escape her wrath.

Far below, Trymman heard the trumpeting of one swan and then that of another. He watched in wonder as eleven swans flew out of the window of the highest tower of the castle, soaring high in the sky. They called as they flew and he understood that they were his brothers, enchanted forever. The witch had cursed them to become swans, to live as wild birds instead of the sons of kings, as the price of their offense against their father.

The sight was Trymman's undoing, for as he stared in disbelief, the witch returned home and spied him. She guessed his identity and his burden, mostly from the once-rich robe wrapped around the baby, and snatched the infant from him. She cursed this twelfth son as well, and Trymman could only watch in horror as he also was transformed into a swan. He watched in despair as his arms grew into wings, as his stature shrank, as feathers appeared all over his body. He opened his mouth to shout in protest, but only a houp-houp call came from his beak. He soared into the sky, trumpeting in frustration, trying to catch up with his brothers.

The witch then killed the infant in her fury, shattering the child's skull on the ground with brutal force. It was too late when the witch looked into the robe and realized she had killed her own daughter.

She guessed then what the boy might have done and ran toward her own hut, intending to kill the queen's child, too.

But the cradle was empty and the babe had vanished. Maeve had come to collect her due of the witch. Left with nothing but the malice in her heart, the witch tried to cast a spell against Maeve. That was when she discovered that all the magick she had ever possessed was gone, as well, seized by Maeve along with her child."

"Taken as a tithe by Maeve," Balthasar mused. "That explains a lot."

"It does," Hadrian agreed. He would have said more but he felt the glow of the firestorm.

Rania was back!

Lynsay thought about her conversation with the dark stranger as she drove back to town and the pub. The hour was late and it was really dark on the lane that led to Hadrian's studio. Maybe she was better off without seeing Hadrian. She'd recognized his truck and that of his cousin at the house. He'd been gone more than a month and hadn't even sent her a text on his return. His studio had burned down, but he hadn't contacted her for consolation or help from her.

The break was obviously permanent to him. What if she did let it go and move on? What if there was a better relationship ahead for her, and that pining after Hadrian was an obstacle to her own happiness?

The more she thought about it, the more it seemed like the right choice.

Something white suddenly flashed ahead of the car and Lynsay swerved hard to one side. She swore as the car spun and she felt her rear tire slide into the muck at the side of the road. She knew without getting out to look that she'd be walking the rest of the way home. No one would come out to give her a tow at this hour.

The car was sideways on the lane, the headlights shining into the woods on the other side of the road. To her astonishment, there was a swan there. The bird blinked in the light but didn't fly away. Was it dazzled by the light?

Lynsay got out of the car as slowly and as quietly as she could. The swan held its ground. It was also watching her, and if a bird could have had an expression, this one's would have been wary.

"I won't hurt you," she said quietly, lifting her hands. Was it wild? It had to be, since there were no more tame ones up at the big house anymore. It hopped a little, heading toward the woods and flapped its wing. Was it hurt?

Lynsay moved closer, taking her time, and the bird just watched her.

It was much bigger than she'd realized swans were, and when she crouched beside it, they were almost eye to eye. Funny how it seemed to understand her intention, like it was a person and not a wild creature. She reached out slowly and lifted the wing that had flapped. She felt the swan quiver, but it didn't pull away.

She caught her breath when she saw the gash in its side and the red smear of blood on its white feathers.

"Who would do such a thing?" she whispered in horror. She took off her scarf and tried to staunch the bleeding, amazed that the swan let her touch it. It must be dazed from the injury. The wound seemed to be scabbing up, so it must have been hurt for a while. There was blood on the ground: she could see the dark stain of it but had no idea how to guess the quantity.

She bit her lip and looked around, well aware that she had no transportation now. How could she help?

The big house. Lynsay recalled that Abigail, the housekeeper, had tended the swans while there had been any living on the pond. She would have a better chance of knowing what to do than Lynsay did.

The fork in the road just ahead led to the big house. It couldn't take her twenty minutes to walk there, even carrying a swan. Abigail had often complained to her that she didn't sleep until the wee hours of the morning, so Lynsay wouldn't be disturbing her. And Lynsay had walked these woods all her life: she felt perfectly safe doing it alone at night.

Her mind made up, Lynsay turned off the car and locked it, then returned to the swan. It seemed to be waiting for her.

"I can take you up to the big house," she explained, knowing it was silly to expect it to understand. Maybe the sound of her voice would be soothing. "There used to be swans living on the pond there so Abigail will know how to help you."

The swan ruffled its feathers, apparently waiting.

Lynsay crouched down in front of it and lifted it into her arms. For all its size, it wasn't that heavy, and its feathers were wonderfully soft. The swan laid its wings on her arms, such a gesture of trust that Lynsay was amazed. When she stood up, it twined its neck around hers. Lynsay felt the warm soft feathers where her scarf had been and saw the swan lay its beak on her chest, right over her heart. It sighed then, as if it felt safe. She smiled as she started to walk, carrying her burden with care.

The swan was right to trust her. She would take care of it as best she could.

Hadrian felt the firestorm and in the instant before Rania appeared, his heart thundered with anticipation. He'd returned her *bichuwa* to her so she could defend herself, knowing the risk, but instead of taking the opportunity to pay her debt to Maeve, she'd saved him. She'd taken back the kiss of death and it had to be because she knew the firestorm was right. She was his destined mate, his partner and his complement.

They were going to be an amazing team.

She manifested on the other side of his kitchen counter, the firestorm lit to brighter radiance, and he grinned. "Rania," he whispered, savoring the sight of her, and her eyes widened.

"How do you know my name?" she asked with suspicion.

Balthasar shook his head and went to get a beer. "I'll never get used to that," he muttered and Alasdair chuckled.

Hadrian didn't worry about his fellow *Pyr*. He concentrated on Rania. "Your mother told me, in the realm of the dead." He frowned as he wondered at his own words. "How did I get from there to here? Did you do it?"

"I took back the kiss of death. I hadn't even known it was possible, but I guessed and it worked."

"It sounded plausible," Balthasar said but Rania and Hadrian ignored him. "Any gift can be retrieved, and it makes sense that a curse could be undone by the creator..."

"Shut up," Alasdair muttered. "Let's go outside."

"In the middle of the night?"

Alasdair gave Balthasar a hard look. "Yes. I need some fresh air." He jerked his head toward Hadrian and Rania and Balthasar sighed. He put back his unopened beer and the two *Pyr* left.

Hadrian thought it was about time.

Rania moved to stand beside him and he felt taut with need. Her eyes were shining and she smiled slightly as she reached up to run her fingertips over his cheek. Her touch made him simmer and shiver at the same time. "The mark is gone now."

"Why did you do it?" he asked. "My death should have fulfilled your bargain."

She frowned, her gaze clinging to his. "But it was wrong," she said with quiet heat. "You were in the realm of the dead because Maeve killed you. She wanted to cheat me and keep me in her service. You were right: I think that was her plan all along."

"So you brought me back to do the dirty work yourself?" Hadrian didn't really think that but he had to ask.

Rania, to his relief, shook her head. "I like you being alive."

"That's all?"

She opened her mouth and closed it again. "I like how you all work together, how you support each other. I've always been alone." Her hand stayed on his shoulder, the white sparks of the firestorm dancing between them. She moved her hand, playing with them, driving Hadrian crazy. "Alasdair offered to sacrifice himself instead," she said, then raised her gaze to his. He saw her awe. "I can't even imagine anyone doing that for me."

"I would," he said immediately.

"Because I'm your mate?"

He nodded, watching the full import of that dawn upon her. She'd never had anyone love her, but he was going to teach her that she shouldn't expect anything less. She was already learning rapidly.

He had to tease her then. "So, you came back to take Alasdair instead of me?"

"No!" Her frown deepened. "I don't want to kill anybody, not for any reason, not anymore."

"You've changed."

"Yes. I don't know how and I don't know why..."

"I do. It was the firestorm. It cauterizes and it heals. It creates possibilities and offers a promise."

She considered this, her gaze still fixed on the sparks beneath her fingers. "The other thing is that it was my fault that she came after you." She looked up. "I told her about the gloves, before I knew I shouldn't trust her."

"She appeared in my studio with one of her warriors and Kade, too." Hadrian frowned, half-remembering something important. It was elusive, though, and he couldn't quite grasp the memory. "They destroyed the blades, too, and set the studio on fire. I was powerless, frozen, and could only watch. It was awful."

"I can imagine." She shivered in sympathy, as much a fan of controlling her fate as he was.

"Kade helped her instead of me," Hadrian said with bitterness.

"I thought he was *Pyr*."

"I think he's loyal to her now. Who knows what his price was? I don't think I want to."

Rania nodded and swallowed. "You said my mother told you my

name." Hadrian nodded. "What was she like?"

He smiled down at her, dropping one hand to her waist and pulling her closer. The firestorm raged between them, and he caught his breath as his heart matched its pace to hers. "Like you. Feminine but strong. Her hair was more silver, but she had blue eyes like you. She was concerned for you."

"Why?"

"She wants you to be happy." He lifted his hand so the ring glinted in the light. "She said this was your father's."

"Really?"

"Really. She misses him." He nodded. "I think they were very much in love. They're mentioned in the book. He gave her the ring when she got pregnant with a daughter, his daughter."

"But they're not together," she mused, her fingertip sliding around the stone set in the ring. "I wonder why." She was obviously thinking for a long moment and Hadrian was content to watch her and savor the firestorm. Then she glanced up. "What book?"

"The book Sara sent." He retrieved it and handed it to her. "We were reading it. We got up to here."

"It's hardly the time to lose myself in a book," she said, chiding him.

"I think you'll find it interesting. Go on. Read it."

Her skepticism was clear, but she did as he suggested and sat down at the counter. He watched her, recognizing the moment that she realized she was reading her own family history. Her attention became sharper as she turned the pages and he moved to stand beside her. He inhaled at the sizzle of the firestorm, knowing he was going to miss it.

Rania stopped at the page they had read last, and glanced up at him. "This is about me."

Hadrian nodded.

"She set a trap for me all along."

He nodded again. "And you were just a kid. Totally out of line."

"You were right," Rania acknowledged, closing the book. "You warned me about Maeve and you were right, but I didn't believe you. She tricked me in the end, claiming that she'd killed you so that didn't count as the fulfillment of my obligation." She took a deep breath. "She's captured my brothers and intends to roast them for the court, one at a time, unless I choose and kill another *Pyr*." She made a face. "I really don't want to kill Alasdair."

Hadrian smiled. "I know he volunteered, but you're right. He shouldn't die."

"Because Maeve will twist the deal again and he'll die for nothing," Rania said. "Maybe Kade?" She met Hadrian's gaze again.

He shook his head. "No *Pyr* deaths."

"It wouldn't be for the team," she said. "I understand." She frowned. "But then I'm trapped forever."

"No." Hadrian shook his head, remembering what had eluded him. "I thought she came to kill me to get even for the loss of her warriors, but that wasn't it."

"She came to destroy your gloves."

"Not just that. She came because I melted the Fae blades."

Rania watched him. "They froze first, then melted. Was that because they weren't in Fae?"

"It was because my mother spun the ice into silver and my foster mother forged the silver into blades for the Fae."

Rania's eyes lit with sudden understanding. "And you're the one who can undo it all, just with your presence. *The ice dragon summons frost and cold...*"

He grinned at her. "I'm thinking we should go to Fae. I could destroy their entire armory and maybe even more." He was thinking of the gem of the hoard, but didn't even want to say that out loud.

"How long would it take?"

"I don't know. We'd need a distraction."

She shook her head. "But you were trapped there before. It wouldn't be safe. If she catches you again, you'll never escape."

The fact that Rania was concerned about his welfare reinforced Hadrian's convictions that they belonged together. "That's why we need a plan." He nodded at her. "We're destined mates, Rania, and that makes us a team. We'll solve this together. You know the court and you can get us right to the armory. You know the pitfalls and how we can avoid them. We can break the curse over you and save your brothers, too."

She frowned a little, the light of the firestorm caressing her features. "You don't think this firestorm is going to give us away?"

"Not if we satisfy it."

She jumped off the counter then and paced the room. He could almost hear her thinking—and her excitement. They were onto something! "I had the malice of the kiss of death and didn't know what to do with it," she admitted. "I didn't want to give it to anyone, but this salamander appeared and told me to follow it. I thought maybe it was in old-speak." She looked up at him and Hadrian smiled.

"That would have been Rafferty. He's the only one of the *Pyr* who can become a salamander and manifest elsewhere. Was he opal and gold?"

Rania nodded.

"Where did he lead you?"

"I'm not sure. It might have been Fae." She shrugged. "I exhaled it all there, as he suggested. There was a dandelion flower and he told me to blow the seeds."

"So the malice joined with the wind. Maybe that dispersed it, the reverse of how you gathered it."

"Maybe."

Hadrian folded his arms across his chest and smiled at her. "You know what that means, don't you?"

Rania shook her head, mystified.

"Rafferty helped you. You're already part of the *Pyr* team."

"Why would he do that?"

"Because he likes to see a firestorm satisfied. And you followed his instructions. You trusted him."

"It's true," she said, nodding slowly. "You trusted me by giving me back my *bichuwa*. Balthasar tried to save me, so he must trust me, too. And Alasdair told me that amazing story, and Rafferty helped me get rid of the malice."

"And Sara sent the book."

Hadrian watched Rania smile. "It made it all so much easier. I like being part of a team." She said this last as if it was a surprise, but then she'd always been alone.

"You just don't want to stain that *bichuwa*," he teased, liking how she laughed again.

"Turns out I have a thing for dragon shifters," she confessed, eyes dancing.

"All dragon shifters?" he asked, pretending to be insulted.

She laughed once more and poked him in the chest with her fingertip. "This dragon shifter."

"Want to do something about that?" Hadrian invited.

"Maybe I do," she said softly. "But maybe it's not just up to me." She surveyed him, a challenging gleam in her eyes. "You said I never asked my brothers what they thought before."

"Right." Hadrian didn't know where she was going with this.

"Then let's do it now. Hold on, dragon shifter, and think fast."

It was a playful warning but one Hadrian didn't have time to figure out. Rania reached for him, shimmering on the cusp of change. Hadrian caught her hand and she laughed. He understood her joy in her abilities and knew they had that in common.

Then everything spun around them. He felt nauseated and dizzy, but he held tightly to her hand. It was the only thing he could see. Even her slight form was lost in swirling mist and light.

Suddenly the spinning stopped, as if they'd been kicked out of a cyclone. There was clear blue sky above them and a slight warm breeze. Far below were green hills and a body of blue water shone in the distance. He saw all that in the blink of an eye, then his mate shifted to her swan form and he lost his grip on her silky feathers.

He was falling fast toward the earth, his shout caught in his throat. *Think fast.* Hadrian summoned the change and shifted shape, beating his wings hard as he flew in pursuit of his mate.

She'd joined a flock of white swans which were flying in a V, as if that distant lake was their destination. He realized it was early in the day wherever they were as the sky was rosy in one direction. He reached the flock of swans and matched his pace to theirs, intrigued that he could distinguish Rania from the others.

There were eight swans, nine including Rania. The others were larger birds and he sensed that they were male. She was smaller and more delicately built, plus there was a luminous shine to her feathers.

All of the swans were pure white, with yellow beaks tipped in black. The wind whistled through their wings as they flew, and Hadrian found it a soothing sound. He knew they were watching him, and he hoped his gleaming dragon scales met with approval. They were graceful and beautiful, and more elegant than dragons.

As they approached the lake, the lead swan made a low call that sounded like *houp-houp* to Hadrian and he guessed that the flock were being given directions. That lead swan led the flock to descend, and they followed so elegantly that their flight might have been choreographed. They landed on an island in the middle of the lake. There was no sign of humanity.

There were rushes surrounding the island and he heard the croak of frogs. The air was damp and the ground flecked with dew. The swans landed, then immediately turned to confront Hadrian. He understood that he was an outsider. Rania landed and shifted shape, the other swans forming a barrier between her and Hadrian. Hadrian shifted shape, sensing that a negotiation would be better than a fight.

The glow of the firestorm shone white between himself and Rania, competing with the light of the morning sun. The swans looked between them and at the light, and he had the sense they discussed it all.

"Where are we?" he asked.

Rania looked around, the wind lifting her hair. "Halfway to the Ukraine."

The swan that had been in the lead came toward Hadrian, head down and wings spread as he hissed in defense of Rania. The swan was almost as tall as Hadrian and much wider with his wings up.

Hadrian suddenly realized who they had to be. "Your brothers," he guessed and Rania smiled.

"Yes, the ones who aren't captive in Fae. I thought we should find out what they know." She nodded. "I like to learn as much as possible when planning an attack."

It was a good strategy.

"Edred?" Hadrian guessed. The swan hissed then snapped. Hadrian took a step back. "I hope he's better looking in his other form." Edred didn't look amused.

Rania didn't smile either. "They can't shift, remember. They're cursed to be swans."

"And when the curse is broken, they'll be mortal men again?"

Rania nodded.

Edred came closer, eyes glinting, and hissed at Hadrian again, punctuating that with a snap of his beak. "How about you do the talking?" Hadrian suggested to Rania and she laughed.

Then she raised her hands, shimmered blue, shifted shape, and all he could do was watch. He didn't feel powerless, though. He felt like they were each working with their strengths to solve their situation together, and he liked that a lot.

He was winning the trust of the swan maiden, just as the prophecy said, and he liked the implication of that even better.

"With a swan, you want to peel away the skin carefully," the head cook of the Fae informed his assistant. They were trudging toward the cage where the Dark Queen had trapped her victims, and he was planning the feast that would result. It was twilight, because it was always twilight in Fae, and there were no stars overhead. There never were. Behind them, the court was carousing as usual, the music lilting and the mead flowing. He wanted to get this job done and head back to the party. "Then you save it until after the bird is roasted to perfection. Finally, you wrap the roasted bird in its feathers again for the presentation to the queen."

"Why?"

The cook shook his head. No matter how long Tink served him, that Fae just didn't learn much of anything. Tink was strong and bigger than most, he was willing to work long and hard, but the cook didn't think he'd ever met a creature so dumb. "Because it looks better. It's fancy."

Tink frowned and scratched his ear. There was a purple mark there, like a bruise—except the Fae didn't get bruises. A wine stain maybe. But what was it doing on his ear? "But you can't eat feathers. No one can."

"No one wants to," the cook explained, seeing that Tink was still confused. "Think of it like wrapping on a gift."

"I like gifts," Tink confided.

"Everyone does, even the Dark Queen. Especially the Dark Queen. And this way, she can unwrap her dinner, like a surprise."

Tink's brow furrowed. "But it's not a surprise. Underneath the swan skin, there will be a swan." He blinked in confusion. He scratched that ear a bit more and to the cook's surprise, the ear became entirely purple.

"What's wrong with your ear?" he demanded.

It was a normal ear for a Fae, a bit less pointed than the most attractive ones, but perfectly serviceable. The color, though, was distinctly odd. If anything, Fae skin tended toward brown hues or the greens of the forest, maybe the silvery grey of tree bark—but never purple.

"My ear?" Tink echoed and scratched it again. "It's itchy." His claim made no sense.

It made even less sense that the ear fell right off.

They stopped together and stared down at it on the heath, both watching as the ear shriveled and curled. It looked like a dried leaf before it crumbled to dust and disappeared. The cook hadn't smelled that scent of forest floor in a long time and he looked around, wondering what was happening to the magick.

Everything looked normal, at least at a glance, except that one of Tink's ears was gone. He beckoned to his assistant with impatience and hurried toward the cage. "We need to keep the heads, too," he instructed. "In order to make the illusion complete."

"If you want a swan to look like a swan, why not leave it be a swan?" Tink asked, scratching the other ear. It was turning purple, too, and the cook had a strange feeling that time was passing too quickly.

He felt a twinge of panic. Time passed slowly in Fae, if at all.

He gripped the cord he'd brought to strangle the birds and hurried on. "So, we don't want to damage the plumage," he said to Tink, who looked at him blankly. "Since we need the feathers for later." He shook his head with impatience. "Just hold them carefully but firmly."

They drew closer to the cage. The three swans began to hiss. They stuck their heads through the wooden bars and snapped at the cook and Tink, obviously having an idea of what was in store for them.

"You go ahead," the cook said cheerfully. "I'll wait with the rope."

Tink gave him a look that was surprisingly shrewd. "I'm the assistant. I'll keep the rope." He then scratched his other ear so thoroughly that the cook could see the purple stain spread across his skin like a flood.

"You'll do what I tell you," the cook said. "And stop scratching your ear!"

"It's not my ear I'm scratching. It's the purple freckle."

"It's not a freckle. Your whole ear is purple."

"So is your cheek," Tink retorted and the cook realized that he was feeling a considerable itch. He reached up to give his cheek a little rub as Tink put a hand over his remaining ear and rubbed vigorously. That ear fell off, too, shriveling up just like the first one.

Tink cried out in alarm as purple spots appeared on his arms and legs. He spun in place, swatting at them and complaining, but his voice rose high, then was silenced. The cook found a garter snake in front of himself, and no sign of Tink. It was particularly large garter snake and seemed to be as startled as the cook. It darted across the heath and disappeared, leaving the cook looking for his assistant.

"Tink!" he shouted, rubbing his cheek all the while. "Get your lazy self back here! There's work to be d—" He finished his sentence with a strange croak and found himself crouched on all fours on the ground. He surveyed himself, amazed to find that he'd become a leopard frog, albeit one with purple spots that gleamed silver before they turned dark.

A swan snapped at him, that beak brushing against his back. He realized he could easily become lunch. The cook hopped away as quickly as he could, unable to explain his situation.

Much less change himself back.

CHAPTER TWELVE

The story in Hadrian's book was incredible to Rania, like a fairy tale—but one that had happened to her. Although she'd never heard any of it, it felt familiar in a way she couldn't explain. It had the resonance of truth.

Just like the firestorm.

Just like Hadrian's trust of his fellow *Pyr*. He was never alone, even though he'd been orphaned, because he was surrounded by a team of fellow shifters who would even sacrifice themselves for his survival. She felt turned upside-down and inside-out, all of her preconceptions challenged, and yet, she felt alive for the first time ever.

The firestorm had brought her an awakening and a second chance, an opportunity to make amends for what she'd done in the past and to shape a better future. Rania didn't want to let that slip away.

She'd never sought out her brothers. She'd never met them or been curious about them at all, and it had felt right to bring Hadrian to meet them. She liked the idea of having a family, just as he had his cousin, Alasdair. She'd flung them through space on impulse, but it was a whim that felt right.

She loved how Hadrian accepted her dares and met her challenges. She loved that he never took her for granted and seemed to welcome adventure. That daredevil glint in his eyes made her heart skip and she hoped she had the opportunity to prompt it over and over again.

She eyed the ring on his hand, the one that she'd had all her life, the one that the story claimed was her father's gift to her mother. She liked the look of it on Hadrian's hand, which was why she hadn't asked for it back. It looked right to her there.

Had that been her father in her home in Iceland?

Were there more swan shifters? The book said that her father had been the last of his kind, before her conception. Did he have other children? Did she have siblings who were shifters?

If there were, they'd be on Maeve's list of shifters to eliminate. Rania realized the Dark Queen didn't intend that she'd survive, either, unless she continued to serve as an assassin. She'd been betrayed and deceived by the only one she trusted, because that had been the plan. The realization made her angry and she recognized that she'd never felt such passion before. There was joy and there was anger, there was desire, and she wanted to experience all the feelings on the spectrum.

With Hadrian.

There had only been three of her brothers in the cage in Fae. As soon as she had the idea of finding out more from the rest, she'd known it was the right answer. Asking them about Hadrian felt instinctively right, too. Even if she didn't know her brothers, maybe they had her best interests at heart, too. Maybe they had ideas about family that were similar to Hadrian's. They'd stuck together all these years, after all.

They might also have some knowledge of Maeve's plan to share.

Rania couldn't help but notice how the swans divided her from Hadrian, their postures protective and defensive. They had to know who she was and, even though she was a stranger to them, the blood bond was strong enough that they'd protect her. That was encouraging.

She shifted shape as Hadrian watched with such obvious admiration that she felt warm to her toes. To her relief, once in her swan form, Edred's hissing made sense to her. The others gathered closer, still keeping a barrier between her and Hadrian, and she wanted to laugh that they were all talking at once. They were excited to see her! They welcomed her. Her heart glowed with what she hadn't even realized she'd been missing.

Edred was the most emphatic and Rania listened to him closely when he told her about the capture of their brothers. Rania felt like she was in the midst of a large and noisy family, and a surprisingly affectionate one. Her brothers admitted how they'd been worried about her since they'd been cursed.

"We tried to watch over you," Edred said. "Our annual migration takes us to Iceland for the summers and we have circled your home."

Rania was astonished. She knew that there were swans that arrived each spring near her home, though the locals commented that they didn't nest like the other migrating swans did.

Of course not: they had no mates.

"You stopped in the yard a few years ago," she said, remembering the incident. "I didn't know it was you."

"No," Edred said sadly. "We saw that, which was why we left."

Rania felt that she had failed them, and vowed silently to do better.

Edred then explained that four of the brothers had been captured by Fae warriors armed with shining weapons, but Rania knew there had only been three in the cage in Fae.

They discussed this but each was adamant and the conclusion was inevitable: one brother was missing.

Edred admitted that their youngest brother, Trymman, had been injured in the Fae attack. No one wanted to mention the possibility of his death but Rania knew they were all thinking about it. One of the brothers noted that Trymman had a tendency to wander away but had always shown up again.

Then Edred asked about the strange light of the firestorm. Rania explained and her brothers walked around the *Pyr*, looking him up and down. They were surprisingly regal and not a little judgmental.

Hadrian met her gaze and raised his brows. "Do I pass?" he asked, obviously understanding what was happening and so confident in the result that Rania was amused. She flapped a wing at him and he laughed, a wonderful rich sound that lifted her heart.

"It should be an exchange," Edred said. "In a union, it's better if each party benefits."

"Invading Fae will be dangerous," Cnut, the second oldest brother agreed. "If you each give, you should each get."

"Being partners will improve your chances of success, too," Edred continued.

"You think I should satisfy this firestorm, in exchange for his help in freeing our brothers."

Edred and the other swans bowed their heads in agreement. "It's only fair, and if you're his destined mate as he claims, then it's right, too." He tilted his head. "What do you think?"

"I think I could love him," Rania admitted, only knowing it was true as she said it. "He's strong and kind, and his heart is noble. I like him and I trust him." She swallowed at the power of her realization. "I want to make the world a safer place for both of us and our respective kinds."

"You're ambitious, little sister, to take on the Dark Queen," Edred said. "But we agree with you. Sometimes, the hard choice is the only one that's right. We'll help you however we can." He stepped back and trumpeted a cry, flapping his wings as the barrier between Rania and Hadrian was removed. She thought of him striking down his father over his mother's murder and knew he understood about hard choices for justice.

"Is that a yes?" Hadrian asked, looking as dangerous as a dragon shifter should.

Rania nodded, then Cnut whispered to her. "You are a swan, little sister. Although we're only cursed to live as swans, we all know how they formalize their bonds."

"Swans mate for life," Edred said. "Their bond is as permanent as human marriage should be. It's a commitment and one that should be celebrated here and now, with your family as witness."

"Dance for us," Cnut admitted and Rania knew they expected the courtship dance that swans performed before mating.

She shifted shape and went to take Hadrian's hand. First he had to meet her brothers. "This is Edred, my oldest brother."

"And the one who struck the fatal blow," Hadrian said, then his tone turned resolute. "I like that he exacted justice for your mother's death." He nodded at Edred and the pair seemed to understand each other.

Rania gestured to the birds on either side of Edred, first the left one, then the right. "That's Cnut and Oswy, the second and third sons."

Each swan bowed his head as he was named and Hadrian bowed in return. Rania felt like they were at a formal party, or a ball, where each attendee was announced and honored.

"Betlic, Athelstan, Sherard, Willan, and Gimm," Rania said, gesturing to each swan in turn. "It's Modig, Isen, Deman, and Trymman who were captured by Maeve."

Hadrian nodded understanding after he had bowed to each swan.

"But I only saw three," she whispered, seeing the concern appear in his gaze as she confided in him. "I'm hoping Trymman is there. He was injured in the attack and is missing." Hadrian's lips thinned. "They said he vanishes sometimes but always returns."

Hadrian squeezed her hand. "Then we'll hope for the best until we know otherwise."

Rania held tightly to his hand as she turned back to Edred and raised her voice slightly. "My brothers, this is Hadrian, the *Pyr* dragon shifter who says he's my destined mate."

"I am your destined mate and you're mine," Hadrian said. He lifted their linked hands, showing the white light that burned between the two of them. Its radiant glow made Rania keenly aware of the strength in Hadrian's grip upon her hand. She thought of the combination of power and tenderness when he'd touched her and couldn't wait to feel his hands upon her again. Would that desire fade with the firestorm's light? She had a feeling it wouldn't. "As shown by the light of the firestorm, Rania is the one who can bear my son and the woman I would honor above all others." He shook his head and his tone turned teasing. "Even if I only know her first name."

Edred turned on Rania and pecked in her direction, his disapproval obvious.

"It's Rania Hingston," she admitted.

Hadrian smiled at her. "One day, I'll know all your secrets," he joked, those eyes glinting with mischief. Rania's heart skipped as he turned to Edred again and sobered. "I want you to understand that I'm one of the *Pyr* who believes in making a permanent commitment to his mate. Satisfying the firestorm isn't just about physical union. I will defend your sister to my dying day."

There was a rustle of feathers among the company of swans. "They like the idea of that," she told Hadrian. "They want us to formalize the agreement."

"How?" He was clearly puzzled.

"You'll see." She shifted shape before Hadrian could ask for more detail and her brothers surrounded her, trumpeting and making that *houp-houp* sound. Their feathers shone in the light of the firestorm, gleaming with the luster of pearls. Edred made a loud trumpeting call, like a herald announcing the arrival of a king. Rania felt celebratory herself. The swans formed a wall of lustrous white feathers, then backed away, letting Rania approach Hadrian while they formed a circle around the couple.

Edred trumpeted again, and Rania raised her wings. She'd never done this dance before but she knew the steps, right in the essence of her being. She felt as if this was a moment she'd awaited all of her life. She reached high, knowing this would be the only time she would perform the courtship dance and wanting to do it right. She followed her instincts, trusting them, knowing the choice was right. She stretched her neck skyward and gave the same trumpeting call as Edred, then bent toward Hadrian, as if she was bowing to him. She spun in place then, fluttering her wings.

The moves reminded her of formal dances in Regency courts and she wondered whether humans had been inspired by swans.

She repeated the sequence three times, then she waited, heart fluttering, as she faced Hadrian.

Hadrian grinned crookedly and she knew he understood. He shifted shape in a brilliant shimmer of blue, obviously proud of his dragon form. There was no reason why he shouldn't be. He was magnificent, his scales emerald and silver, his body filled with raw power. Her brothers had to move back to give him space and her heart thundered that he would be her mate, forever.

Despite his size, Hadrian danced gracefully and lightly, an athlete in command of his body and one who knew it well. He spread his wings high and wide, casting a shadow over the island, then flapped them so that they stirred a wind. He stretched his neck high and bared his teeth in a dragon smile as the sunlight glinted on his scales. Rania knew her brothers had to see that Hadrian was sufficiently powerful to defend his mate. She could defend herself, but she respected this ancient masculine tradition. Instead of Edred's trumpeting call, Hadrian blew a plume of dragonfire into the air, then spun in place and bowed toward her.

He performed the sequence three times, and then he waited.

The fourth time, they danced together in perfect unison. The sun was rising higher and becoming warmer but its light was no competition for the silvery glow of the firestorm. The firestorm glistened and gleamed between them, shooting sparks as they approached each other, filling Rania with a simmering need to satisfy its promise. They finished the sequence by circling around each other, in a promenade, their wingtips touching as they watched each other.

Then Rania stretched out toward Hadrian and bent her beak downward. Her neck made the shape of half of a heart. Hadrian mirrored her pose, touching his brow to hers, to complete the heart and she felt a wondrous sense of completion. Despite the differences in size between them, she felt the ripple of approval through the flock of her brothers. Edred gave a trumpeting call again and her other brothers joined him this time, a sound as merry as the pealing of church bells after a wedding service.

Rania shifted shape along with Hadrian and stood facing him as their gazes locked. She reached out to touch his shoulder, making the firestorm spark white-hot, and they caught their breath as one when Hadrian caught her close. "Two halves of a heart unified into one," he said. "I like that."

"It feels right."

"It is right," he declared. "Now I get to kiss the bride?" His voice dropped to a wicked whisper that made her pulse leap.

"More than that. Now, we mate," she said. "We extinguish the firestorm's light, so it can't reveal us when we invade Fae."

"That's not the only reason to satisfy the firestorm," Hadrian said with a smile.

"No. We need to create a son, then defend the future for him."

"I like how you think." Hadrian lowered his voice. "Not here, though, right?"

"Not here." She lifted a brow in warning of what she was going to do.

Her dragon took the challenge.

Hadrian held tight, just in time, then he hooted in triumph as she cast them back to his lair.

In the blink of an eye, Hadrian and Rania landed on his bed, tangled around each other. The firestorm crackled and burned, sizzling at a fever pitch, urging Hadrian to fulfill its promise. Best of all, his mate was more than onboard with the plan, given the enthusiasm of her kiss. Rania had her arms around Hadrian's neck and locked her lips over his, kissing him with a passion that echoed his own.

This was more like it.

Hadrian rolled Rania to her back. He ran his hands over her, liking that she arched her back to meet his touch. They were picking up where they'd left off days before and this time, the firestorm would be satisfied. It was the middle of the night, a time he should have been sleeping, but the firestorm's heat drove all other concerns from his mind.

There was only Rania, soft and sweet. Rania with her sparkling blue eyes and long fair hair, Rania with hunger in her kiss. The firestorm crackled and snapped between them, burning white hot and flooding him with need. He was hard and ready, his thoughts filled with the memory of her around him, tight and sweet and hot. He both wanted to rush and yearned to make it last, but he suspected it would be quick this time.

Rania seemed to share his sense of urgency. She rolled him to his back and straddled him, pinning his wrists to the bed over his head as she kissed him. Her kiss was so hot and demanding that he wondered whether she'd eat him alive. She was feasting on his mouth, rubbing herself against him, making him crazy with desire. Hadrian didn't care what she did. He was content to be with her however she wanted it to be.

She slid down the length of him, releasing his wrists and unfastening his jeans with quick fingers. Her hands were on his skin then, caressing him so that he groaned aloud. He closed his eyes as she took him into her mouth and speared his fingers into her hair, losing his hands in its silken softness. He loved that she wasn't shy and appreciated that she was as committed to pleasure as he was.

Rania tormented him, driving him to the summit, then stopping just before he found his release. Hadrian was almost incoherent when she flicked her tongue against him and halfway thought he'd come in the air.

He growled and rolled her over, knowing that wasn't good enough. She laughed when he grabbed her waist and he realized she was ticklish. Her laughter lifted his heart. She looked young and carefree, happy as he'd never seen her, and Hadrian couldn't resist. He tickled her until she was breathless and managed to slip off her tights and T-shirt in the progress. He took her belt, with the holster holding the *bichuwa*, and put it on the nightstand, surprised to find mischief in her smile when he met her gaze again.

"I promise not to go for it," she teased and he laughed, then kissed her again.

He paused, the weight of his hand on her waist, while he eyed her scar. He'd seen the scar before but studied it more closely now. The large wound had healed a long time before, but there was still a mark on her skin. This had come from that polar bear and Hadrian was amazed that she'd survived the injury. He bent and touched his lips reverently to the end of the scar, loving that she was so strong, wishing he could have been there to help her.

She pushed her fingers into his hair. "You would have kicked his butt," she said, her tone light.

"Both of them," he vowed, meeting her gaze so she could see his resolve. She swallowed as if surprised by the heat of his reaction and he kissed the scar again. He moved down the length of her, sliding his hands down her legs, then noticed something he hadn't seen before. There was a mark on her ankle, as if it had been injured as well. He looked up at her, a question in his eyes.

"I was shackled as a swan," she said, her voice husky. "The only way to get the key and use it was to shift."

Hadrian understood though the truth made his chest tighten in sympathy. The shackle hadn't changed size when she did. "The pain must have been excruciating," he said, running a fingertip over the dent in her skin. "I'm surprised the bone didn't break."

"It did," she admitted. "But I ran on it anyway until I could get out of there and take flight."

Hadrian was awed by her resolve. She was so strong, so resilient, so fearless.

His mate.

He touched his lips to her ankle, then slid his hands up the inside of her thighs. The firestorm glimmered and shone, and he closed his eyes against its brilliance, closing his mouth over her. He was determined to bring her complete pleasure so he teased her until she was breathing raggedly, her hands locked in his hair. He already knew some moves she liked and he used them all, then tried some new ones. Rania twisted beneath him. Her legs were locked around him and she was writhing against the sheets when he finally pushed her over the edge. He smiled as she came and came and came.

She tackled him immediately and they rolled to the floor together as he wiped his mouth. Then she was kissing him again, demanding more, demanding all he had to give. If she vanished on him this time, Hadrian wasn't sure he'd be survive it.

She lifted her head and looked down at him. "You're overdressed," she accused, her eyes sparkling and her hair tangled. She plucked at the hem of his T-shirt and he tugged it over his head, casting it aside. She ran her hands over his shoulders and chest, tracing the outline of his dragon tattoo as she had once before, her eyes darkening.

"Will he be a dragon shifter or a swan shifter?" she whispered.

"Or both?" Hadrian asked, then shrugged. "He'll be one kick-ass warrior, either way."

She smiled. "Yes," she agreed. "We'll teach him together."

That sounded like a deal to Hadrian. The firestorm's light was a radiant white, as if they were trapped in a snowstorm together, or lost in the halo of her feathers. He wasn't cold, though—his blood was simmering and he burned with need.

Rania lowered herself over him again, her hair surrounding them like a golden veil. Once again, she took him in slow increments, their gazes locked as they drove each other to the pinnacle. She bent then and framed his face in her hands, bending to kiss first one corner of his mouth and then the other. Her caress was as gentle as the touch of a feather, though it sent a surge of need through him.

"I love you," she whispered and Hadrian knew that she wasn't going to vanish on him again.

He grinned at her. "I love you, too," he confessed, losing himself in her eyes. They balanced on the cusp of release, enthralled with each other. The firestorm crackled and burned, the sparks danced between them, and when he felt their hearts synchronize, Hadrian closed his eyes in ecstasy.

Rania moved, and the stars exploded, and there was nothing but his mate in Hadrian's universe.

The firestorm was satisfied, but that didn't mean they wouldn't do it again and again.

"You should have kept reading," a man drawled as Hadrian left the bedroom at first light.

Hadrian shimmered on the cusp of change immediately, the brilliant shimmer of blue lighting the early morning air, and was glad Rania was behind him. He knew he shouldn't be surprised that she was poised to fight, too. No doubt she'd already pulled her *bichuwa*.

She was going to be one fierce mother to their son.

He was shocked to recognize the vampire, Sebastian, lounging on his couch. "What are you going here?" he demanded.

Sebastian sat up. He had the book in his hand, the book that Sara had sent. "There's not much left. You should read it." He rolled his eyes. "I suppose you thought the firestorm was more important."

Hadrian bit his tongue to keep from asking the vampire how he knew how much they'd read. Sebastian had probably been hanging around the night before, unbeknownst to the *Pyr*. He could only barely discern the vampire's scent, and that was only because he was concentrating. Sebastian must not have feasted recently, because then he'd smell of blood.

Come to think of it, the vampire did look glittery and insubstantial.

"How did you get in?" Hadrian asked.

"Please." Sebastian's expression was pained. "Don't even glorify those trinkets by calling them locks." He stood up and stretched, looking like a wild and unpredictable predator. Hadrian didn't trust him one bit. Sebastian spared a glance at the windows and grimaced. Hadrian realized the sun was rising. "I don't suppose you have black-out blinds anywhere in this place?"

"In the loft," Hadrian said. He crossed the room and plucked the book from the vampire's hands, then quickly found the spot where they'd left off. Rania followed him, wearing one of his shirts and not much else, her feet bare and her hair loose. He wished the vampire hadn't been there, because another round would have been great. Even though the firestorm was extinguished, he was still keenly aware of her and wanted her all over again.

He could hear Alasdair stirring in the loft and Balthasar in the spare room behind the office. He began to read aloud, as Rania started to make coffee.

"The witch could only watch as her spells came undone throughout the village and people turned against her. She fled the village and into the wilderness, pursued by the villagers and in despair. She had lost her lover and her child, as well as her wager with Maeve and her magick. In the darkness of the night, she fell into a ravine and broke her leg, then was eaten by wolves when she could not escape them.

The swan-prince returned to the palace, hoping to see his daughter and his beloved, but he arrived too late. He found only the queen dead in her chamber, the villain who had been her spouse dead beside her. There was no sign of the small boy he had met previously, of the ring he had given the queen, or of the lady's newly born child. Those who remained in the palace were in the midst of fleeing the place and he could learn nothing of the child's fate.

He made one last wish, for he had a small measure of magick himself. He wished that when his child wondered about him or about his queen, he would know of it. He vowed then to find and reveal himself to his child, drawn by that query. To be sure, though, he wasn't even sure the child lived. Despondent at the death of his beloved, he left the palace to mourn his loss in solitude."

Rania spun to look at him, her lips parted in surprise. Obviously that part meant something to her, but she flicked a glance at the vampire—who was listening avidly—and turned back to the coffee pot.

Hadrian understood that she'd tell him later.

He kept reading.

"The palace fell into disrepair after that, for there was no one to govern it, either justly or unjustly. The people abandoned the place, for there was no food and no coin to be had. The neighboring lands had been pillaged and robbed, so those survivors scattered wide in search of new homes. The palace steadily crumbled over the years, becoming a pile of broken stone, forgotten in the wilderness. Only the wild creatures took shelter there, including a dozen wild swans that returned each year on Midwinter's Day. They flew in a circle around what remained of the high tower, trumpeting their sad song, then left again.

The child, Rania, was raised in Fae, which was a curious situation indeed. There are no children in Fae, for the Fae are immortal. They neither age nor grow: they simply are. For a while, they found the child to be a marvel, but ultimately their interest dimmed and young Rania spent her time alone."

Alasdair and Balthasar entered the main room then, each clearly surprised to find Sebastian lounging on the couch. They exchanged glances then joined Rania in the kitchen. Balthasar put the last slice of pizza in the microwave, while Alasdair began to fry bacon.

"The Fae are also not known for their empathy: each is essentially selfish, concerned only with his or her own pleasure. They certainly can be cruel. Rania, as a result, had no one to teach her to care, and no one particularly to care for. This might have been bad enough, but Maeve had a plan for the child's future and ensured it would come to fruition. She distrusted the influence of the child's mortality. She had slipped a shard of ice into the palm of the infant as soon as she had seized her from the witch's hut. Being a magickal spell of its own kind, that shard of ice worked its way ever deeper into Rania until it reached her heart. Once there, it froze her heart solid, making her incapable of sympathy for any other being."

Hadrian paused for a moment, reading that passage again in silence. Rania's solitude and her ability to even keep Maeve's bargain was the result of a kind of spell. She'd been trapped by Maeve from infancy and had never had a chance of choosing otherwise. He looked up to find her watching him, her eyes wide with surprise.

The Dark Queen had manipulated her, and here was the proof.

"Do continue," Sebastian urged in a bored tone.

"The shard of ice had done its damage by the time Rania came into her ability to change shape. She was clumsy with these transitions at first, for there was no one to tutor her in the endless twilight of Fae, but she persisted and mastered her powers in time. Once she had become an adult, adept with her skills, and cold of heart, Maeve put the rest of her plan into action. Rania knew little of Maeve's true nature, for the Dark Queen had been the one most likely to show her kindness. She knew she owed Maeve a debt for raising her, too. Rania trusted Maeve, just as the Dark Queen had planned.

Maeve told Rania the tale of her brothers' enchantment, showing them to her in a vision, then offered Rania the opportunity to free them. There was enough emotion left in Rania's heart that she felt an obligation to her own kin, a desire to please Maeve, and a need for some family of her own. She took Maeve's bargain, agreeing to make thirteen assassinations for the Dark Queen in exchange for the freedom of herself and her brothers.

She had made twelve kills when she felt the spark of the firestorm, when the kiss of the ice dragon drew Maeve's splinter of ice out of her heart."

Hadrian fell silent and the three *Pyr* looked at Rania. "Is it true?" Balthasar asked.

"I think so," she said. "The parts I know are true, so the rest must be as well."

"A splinter of ice in your heart?" Alasdair said, grimacing.

"She tricked you," Hadrian said to Rania.

"Even more than I'd realized." Her heart was in her eyes. "I saw the splinter of ice," she told him, putting out her hand and tapping her palm with her fingertip. "I didn't know what it was. It came out of my palm after we first met, after we..." She blushed as Hadrian grinned in recollection of what they'd been doing. "And then everything felt different." She shrugged. "It was as if I could feel for the first time ever."

"Not like that," Sebastian said. "It *was* that. But you're missing the most salient detail."

They all turned to look at him, mystified.

He raised his hands in exasperation. "You were the wrong child. You weren't the promised tithe." Rania and Hadrian gasped simultaneously. "Maeve adores technicalities, especially when she can break a deal because of one. I would dearly love to witness the moment that she realizes she's in your debt, for putting that splinter in your heart and compelling you to act against your will, with no justifiable cause on her part."

"I didn't enter Fae willingly," Rania said slowly.

"You were seized, and enchanted," Hadrian said. "Against your will."

"Who would volunteer for such a fate? No, she was wrong." Sebastian shook his head as he mused. "What would she owe you for such injustice?"

"You were in her thrall for a thousand years," Hadrian said.

"Twelve assassinations," Rania said.

"Not to mention a splinter of ice in your heart," Alasdair reminded them.

"I'm thinking the breaking of the curse on your brothers would be a good start," Hadrian said.

Rania lifted her wrist to display the red cord. "And the disappearance of this."

"You dream too small," Sebastian said, strolling toward the counter. Rania poured him a cup of coffee which he sipped tentatively. "Columbian," he said and sipped again. "Better than I expected."

It was clear that the vampire's expectations were low, but Hadrian didn't care. "You have a better idea?" he asked, suspecting that the vampire was waiting for the question.

"The complete annihilation of her kingdom," Sebastian said with surprising bitterness. He looked up and his eyes shone with fury. "And the scattering of her miserable magick. I would see her helpless, for once and for all."

"It probably won't last," Alasdair noted. "She'll summon the magick again."

"But the interval would be sweet while it lasted," Sebastian said. "Perhaps even long enough for the Others to create a viable plan for their own survival."

Hadrian and Rania exchanged a glance. "Can you get us into Fae today?" he asked her. "Without the Dark Queen knowing it?"

Rania nodded but Sebastian cleared his throat. "Your petty ambitions will be the end of me," he murmured. "I would suggest that you consider the merit of making a more cohesive plan." He gave Rania a scathing look. "I expect dragons to lunge in without a scheme, relying on brute force to get the job done, but had hoped for more from you. After all, you're an *assassin*. You're supposed to be stealthy and organized."

"We'd have a better chance of success with a distraction," Rania said. "That way, they can draw her ire while we destroy the armory and free my brothers." She frowned. "But who would enter the Fae realm willingly?"

"Not me," Alasdair said flatly.

"And how would anyone else get in?" she continued. "I can't move an army: just taking you will max me out."

"There's a Fae court under a mound near here somewhere," Alasdair said. "Your father used that portal to save your mother."

"Centuries ago," Balthasar said. "It's probably under a shopping mall now."

"The more important issue is who would distract the Fae," Rania said. "If we can figure that out, we might see how to get them in."

"You must know that there are many in Manhattan who would avenge themselves upon the Dark Queen for recent deaths," Sebastian said.

"Others," Alasdair said. "After those surprise attacks."

"More than Others," Sebastian reminded them. "The mates of the wolf shifters slaughtered in Alaska are keen to defend their children and have retribution for their losses." He shook his head. "I would not want to face the wrath of those mortal women."

"But they're in Manhattan," Hadrian protested. "And they still have to get into Fae. It's not going to work. Rania and I will have to stage a sneak attack and hope for the best."

Sebastian pinched the bridge of his nose.

"Murray sealed the portal at Bones," Balthasar reminded them.

"I wish those Fae swords hadn't melted away," Hadrian said with frustration. "We could have sliced ourselves a portal between realms."

Sebastian smiled slightly and sipped his coffee, apparently reassured.

Hadrian and Rania exchanged a glance.

"Do you know where we can get a Fae sword?" she asked Sebastian.

"As a matter of fact, I do."

"Where?" Hadrian asked. It was annoying that every detail had to be drawn out of the vampire.

"I happen to have a Fae sword," Sebastian replied. "And I don't actually need it."

The other four exchanged glances.

"I'm going to guess that you have a price," Hadrian guessed.

"I do." Sebastian put down his mug on the counter. "But it's a wager I must make with Micah. If we come to terms, he can deliver the sword to Bones in time."

"In time?" Alasdair asked.

"You should wait until the full moon to attack," Sebastian said, his tone pedantic. "Everyone knows that's the time to enter Fae, and that will be on Thursday, just four days from now." He sighed and shook his head.

"We'll have time to coordinate our attack," Balthasar said.

"I wonder how Quinn is doing with those talons," Alasdair said, pulling out his phone. "If the *Pyr* are armed, it will be better."

"It takes time for you to melt the weapons," Rania said to Hadrian. "Maybe you should enter Fae sooner to get started."

Hadrian recalled her mother's advice and wondered whether he could destroy the gem of the hoard, as well. That would really make a difference to Maeve's power, but he didn't even want to mention it aloud in the vampire's presence. Could Sebastian really be trusted?

"A multi-prong attack," Alasdair said, grabbing a piece of paper. "We need a plan."

Hadrian had turned to study the vampire. "Why *are* you here?" he asked. "It seems unlikely that you just stopped by to help."

Sebastian laughed. "A little out of character, you might say."

"I would," Hadrian agreed. "I think anyone would. You're being helpful and that makes me wonder what you really want."

"Perfectly understandable," the vampire acknowledged. "Allow me to explain." He produced a small cube and Hadrian realized it was a jeweler's ring box. He tossed it to Hadrian who caught it but didn't immediately look inside. He wasn't sure he should. "I'd take care of that now, if I were you. When she finds out that I chose not to keep my end of the deal, things may get ugly." He nodded at the box. "You don't want that to fall into the wrong hands."

Hadrian opened the box and stared at the glittering sliver of ice. It was another splinter, probably with identical powers to the one that had melted from Rania's heart. "The Dark Queen wants her assassin back," he guessed and the vampire inclined his head. "She sent you to deliver this." Sebastian nodded again, even as Hadrian indicated to Rania that she should back away. "Why are you breaking the deal?"

"Let's just say I prefer an alternative solution," Sebastian said. He nodded once, then pushed aside the coffee mug, his lips drawing to a resolute line. When he looked up again, his gaze burned. "Sometimes, something—or someone—has to change."

He put a strange emphasis on the last word, but Hadrian didn't want to know the vampire's secrets. He had a lot to do and an invasion of Fae to plan, with his destined mate by his side.

First things first. He closed his hand over the box, feeling the splinter begin to melt.

CHAPTER THIRTEEN

emyaza.

Sylvia went through all the online resources she could find, and accessed the academic archives, too. She checked obscure print books in the library collection, doctoral theses, research and new translations. She chased down every lead, compiling information, sources and cross-indexing as she worked. She loved every minute of the hunt, even though it took her a while.

Semyaza was said to be the leader of the fallen angels who had descended to Earth to couple with mortal women. Two hundred angels of the heavenly host had accompanied him—they hadn't just mated with women, they'd taught mortals a wide array of skills and shared hidden knowledge.

His name meant 'he who sees the name,' meaning the name of God.

In the Book of Enoch, Semyaza was the leader who doubted that the renegade angels, despite their desire to seduce mortal women, really would foreswear the celestial realm. Those rebels were called the Watchers—or the Grigori—and they swore an oath together to descend to earth and satisfy their lust.

Their sons were called giants, or the Nephilim, and proved to be a destructive generation. The Watchers themselves indulged in every pleasure and crime, and became a plague on human society.

They did, however, teach men sorcery, metallurgy, weaponry, medicine, seductive ornamentation and the use of cosmetics, and more. This incurred the wrath of God, who sent his angels to compel the

Watchers to battle each other and their sons, then bound the survivors in a valley for seventy generations. God then sent the flood to cleanse the lands of their corruption.

Sylvia wondered whether that was the whole story or not.

Variations of Semyaza's name, depending on the source, included Semyaz, Sahjaza, Semjaza, Shamazya, Semiaza, Shamchazai, Shamhazai, Shamiazaz, Azza, Ouza, and Amezyarak.

One source said Semyaza was tempted by the maiden Ishtahar to reveal the explicit name of God.

Another declared that he remains suspended between Heaven and Earth as punishment for his transgressions. He is said to be constantly falling, with one eye shut and the other open, aware of his plight but unable to affect it. He now hangs, head down, and is the constellation of Orion.

The Book of Enoch said that Azazel had taught men the arts of metallurgy, while Semyaza had taught them of enchantments and root-cuttings.

Enchantments were magick.

Sylvia knew that magick and medicine were two sides of the same coin in many societies. She considered her note, then turned the long white feather in the light. She thought about Mel calling Sebastian the Watcher, about him being present when the fallen angel emerged from Fae with Maeve's book, waiting for that quest to be completed. She recalled his comment about several thousand years on this spinning rock, then had to acknowledge his interest in mortal women, given her own experiences with him.

He said he hated magick.

Hate was so often the flip side of love. Sylvia had to wonder whether Sebastian was the tutor she needed to master her inherited skills. If he'd been the first instructor in the dark arts, he was the original source.

How had he become a vampire? Sylvia smiled, guessing that there had been a woman involved. What was in his library? She had to believe he had some great books, if he was willing to do anything to regain access to them. She understood that need, very well.

She sat alone in her basement office, studied the feather, and wondered just what it would take to find out Sebastian's story. She wanted to know the truth. She was sure it would have a price.

But Sylvia Fontaine was ready for both risk and adventure.

She'd go to Reliquary and if she couldn't find Sebastian himself, she'd talk to Micah. Someone had to have some idea where she could find the vampire who had captivated her so completely.

The *Pyr* conferred and Rania watched their plan come together. Sebastian had gone to the spare room behind the office, presumably to sleep for the day. Rania was glad the vampire was gone. She didn't trust him any more than she thought Hadrian did.

Alasdair had set up a virtual meeting, with all of the *Pyr* logging in. It was amazing to Rania to realize that there were so many dragon shifters, and inspiring to see how determined they were to work together.

Hadrian wanted to get into the treasury soon and Rania knew she could deliver him there. Donovan's gloves had been destroyed in the fire, but Quinn was finishing up his first batch of the new ones. He surprised them all with the confession that he'd been inspired by Hadrian's methods to change things up. He was going to send two pair overnight to Alasdair and Balthasar, then the rest to New York as soon as possible. He thought he could finish enough pair by Thursday for the participating *Pyr*. Theo said he'd talk to Murray about arranging an emergency meeting at Bones to talk to the Others about joining the invasion of Fae. The details of what to do once they were in Fae were being hotly debated.

Rania was wondering how Hadrian would avoid detection in the Fae armory, when he took Alasdair's notepad and began to write. When he was done, he spun it around for Rania to read his note.

Your mother suggested that I could destroy the gem of the hoard by freezing it.

Rania blinked. Of course, he could. And that would eliminate Maeve's hold over the magick, which would give them all a fighting chance. She met his gaze, letting him see her excitement and he grinned.

It made sense that they weren't having this conversation aloud. There should be no chance of Sebastian overhearing and potentially reporting it back to Maeve.

She took the pen from his hand and wrote.

Sebastian was supposed to deliver that splinter of ice:
Maeve is going to believe I'm on her side. We can use that.

Hadrian read her note and nodded. She took the pen back and wrote a bullet list.

1. I'll take you into the Fae armory so you can start melting weapons. How can you avoid detection?

Hadrian took the pen.

I'll bank the fires. Can you take me in dragon form?

Rania winced and shrugged. That was a lot of mass to move. He nodded in understanding and wrote again.

Then I'll shift once my pulse is low; you can take me there and I'll shift back. You'll only need to be there for the blink of an eye.

Rania nodded and took back the pen.

2. I'll go to Maeve's court, as if I'm bringing a Pyr *victim to kill in front of her to fulfill our deal, but in the end, we'll turn the tables on her. I'll need a volunteer.*

Hadrian nodded.

3. That battle will provide a distraction for someone—also a volunteer—to steal the gem of the hoard and get it to you in the armory.

4. Meanwhile, the Others will invade Fae, using Sebastian's sword to open a portal between realms, and make as much trouble as they can while we free my brothers and escape.

Hadrian gave her a thumbs-up. He wrote *Thursday Night* beside the fourth item, *ASAP* beside the first one, then lifted his hand, inviting her suggestions on the timing of the other steps.

Rania tapped the word *volunteer* in item number two and met his gaze.

He indicated Balthasar and Alasdair, then shrugged, implying that one of them would step up. That would be one detail resolved. Rania circled *someone* in item number three and offered Hadrian the pen. She thought he might make the same answer, that either his cousin or his friend would volunteer for the first role and the other would be the thief.

Hadrian tapped it for a minute, then wrote.

A djinn.

Their gazes met and held. A djinn was a perfect choice. They could be terrific thieves and spies, given their ability to disappear into mist without warning. They were elusive and silent.

But they had to hate Rania. No djinn was going to be in a hurry to save Rania from the Dark Queen's clutches. She pointed at the *bichuwa*, the holster back on her hip, and Hadrian sighed.

He took the pen.

You could apologize and ask for help at Bones.
That might convince the Others to join us.

Rania exhaled and took a step back. She frowned at the very idea. She'd never spoken to her victims until Hadrian, and had never faced the consequences of her actions. She certainly wasn't in a hurry to meet anyone who hated her, but she met Hadrian's gaze and found understanding there. He nodded gently.

Maybe she *could* explain.

Maybe they'd help for the sake of the greater good.

Maybe her apology would make the difference.

She took the pen, hesitated, then wrote something she'd never expected to confess.

I'm afraid.

Hadrian smiled with that alluring confidence and reclaimed the pen, his fingers brushing over hers.

It's only sensible. But I'll have your back.

He winked at her, as cocky as ever, and Rania found herself smiling. Maybe she could do it. It certainly was worth a try. She nodded and Hadrian caught her close, rewarding her with a kiss that had the *Pyr* protesting that they weren't paying attention.

But they were.

And they had to find a djinn to help.

Hadrian was so proud of Rania that he thought he might burst. It couldn't be easy to face the crowd at Bones, given her past, but she took them both to New York in a flash. Once the decision was made, she didn't hesitate or try to avoid a hard task. He respected that she was so unflinching.

It was late in Manhattan and the sky was dark overhead. Hadrian couldn't see the stars because of the ambient light of the city. He was surprised, as always, by the noise level. He could hear cars honking on the closest avenue and the sound of traffic, buses rumbled and hissed, the subway growled deep beneath her feet, making the concrete vibrate. There were voices in the distance and the persistent throb of dance music. A door slammed and dogs barked, something clanged in an alley and a cat howled at a distance.

The door to Bones was steel and not the most welcoming entrance Hadrian had ever seen. Rania regarded it with obvious trepidation and he dropped his hand to the back of her waist. "We should go in," he said and she smiled up at him, her uncertainty clear. He would have done this for her, if it had been possible, but she had to make the appeal.

"Are the Others there already?" she asked, obviously confident that his keen senses would reveal the truth to him.

Hadrian nodded. "All of them. It's time."

"And the other *Pyr*?"

"Some of them. He narrowed his eyes and knew he shimmered blue a bit as he assessed the situation. "Drake, Theo, Arach, Rhys, Niall. Hey, Sloane is here, too." He smiled at her. "The Apothecary of the *Pyr*," he explained.

"I hate groveling," she muttered and Hadrian chuckled.

"Then don't. Just apologize." Hadrian put his arm around her and leaned closer. "Everyone makes mistakes. And a lot of those here have been cursed on enchanted against their will. What's going to count is your sincerity."

"I am sincere."

"I know. And they will, too."

She exhaled, obviously uncertain. "If you say so."

"Trust me."

That prompted her smile. "I do."

Hadrian gripped the handle and opened the door. A waft of scent and smoke assaulted them both. He smelled roasted meat and barbeque sauce, fat in a deep fryer, the press of human bodies, cigarette smoke and beer.

A woman dressed in black turned to face them and blocked their passage. Her eyes were cold. She looked between them but didn't move. "We're closed."

"I'm Hadrian MacEwan and this is Rania Hingston. We requested an audience at the meeting of the Others." Hadrian stepped into the bar and let the door close behind them.

The woman's eyes narrowed.

Rania held up her wrist to display Maeve's red cord. "It's time to break free."

"No one's going to help you here," the hostess said with hostility.

"We'll see about that." Hadrian led Rania right past the medusa hostess.

He felt everyone in the bar survey their progress, and heard the whispers of speculation. He was aware that he shimmered blue, on the cusp of change, ready to defend his mate.

"Trust a dragon to bring a Fae assassin into our midst," muttered a heavy-set guy and there were nods from the group.

"Dragons always have to run the show," agreed another.

"Dragons are unafraid to mix it up," countered Theo. He was standing on the far side of the bar, with the rest of the *Pyr* in attendance. Hadrian headed toward them but Rania stopped beside the bar.

"I've got this," she murmured to him and he felt a surge of pride. "Go to the *Pyr*."

He looked into her eyes for a moment, wishing her all the luck in the world, then nodded and strode to sit with his fellow dragon shifters. They clapped him on the back, moving to include him but making sure they all had space to shift in case his mate needed their help.

Hadrian had a feeling she wouldn't.

The bar was crowded with Others of all kinds. Hadrian couldn't even identify all of them. He'd heard about Wynter Olson, the leader of the mates of the Alaskan wolf shifters and readily identified her both by her proximity to Arach and the golden glow of the firestorm between them. He wished his buddy luck with that. There were bear shifters, and he recognized Caleb, the alpha of the Manhattan wolf shifters, as well as a number of Others from the Circus of Wonders. Mel was at the bar with Murray, pulling beers and pouring shooters. He was aware of the red string on Mel's wrist and the way Theo avidly watched her. Sylvia was sitting at the bar alone and kept glancing over her shoulder. Hadrian wondered whether she even knew that Sebastian had left town. There were noticeable absences, too, a hint of the damage Maeve had caused.

That had to count in Rania's favor.

She turned in place, surveying the crowd and probably choosing her words. Conversation ceased gradually as she just stood there, an icy beauty with cool eyes.

When they were silent, she spoke.

"I'm Rania Hingston, the swan-maiden assassin cursed by the Dark Queen to do her will. I've come to suggest an alliance and to ask for some help."

Murray pointed to the red cord on her wrist. "You're still in her power. I don't like you being here at all."

Rania gestured to Mel. "She has a red cord, too."

"Let her talk," Mel said and Murray nodded with obvious reluctance.

Rania took a deep breath. "I have served the Dark Queen for over a thousand years. I was her assassin, but not by my own choice. I was my mother's thirteenth child, although I was orphaned as an infant. My twelve older brothers were turned into swans against their will and flew away once our parents were dead. I knew nothing of this until I had grown up in Fae, reliant upon the Dark Queen herself. She might have been my mother. She acted as if she was. She offered me a wager one day: that if I assassinated thirteen victims for her, she would free my brothers from their curse and release me from her service. I didn't know that she'd already turned my heart to ice, so I was unable to feel empathy or compassion. Still, my first attempted kill went badly and I nearly died myself. As a result, she gave me the ability to grant the kiss of death thirteen times and the ability to spontaneously manifest elsewhere. She made me a stealthy killer because that suited her purposes."

There was a whisper in the ranks of the Others, and Hadrian knew they were aware of that weapon.

Rania continued. "I used twelve of those kisses, as many of you know, but the thirteenth didn't proceed as planned. The Dark Queen demanded one of the *Pyr*, and I chose Hadrian, only to have a firestorm spark between us. That firestorm thawed the ice that had encased my heart, but it didn't matter: I'd already given him that final kiss."

"He's not dead," Caleb noted when Rania paused.

"Not nearly," Hadrian said, standing up. That caused a number of agitated whispers.

"That was where the plan went wrong. Hadrian fought off the kiss of death, which meant I had to attack him instead. He's not very easy to kill." There was a reluctant chuckle at that. She turned to look at him, her eyes glowing. "That trait and the firestorm meant I got to know him. His power as an ice dragon meant that the sliver of ice in my heart melted and I began to heal. By the time the Dark Queen broke her bargain with me, tricking me into eternal service by killing Hadrian herself, I knew I'd never be free of her."

"You could stop doing her will."

"I could, but she threatened to roast and eat my brothers if I don't comply. She holds three of them captive now and I hope they're all still alive."

There was a gasp of horror at this.

Rania shook her head. "Instead, I want to change the rules. I want to invade Fae and break my brothers free. I want to turn the tables on the Dark Queen, allied with Hadrian, and I need your help to do that."

A protest rose immediately, but Rania held up her hand for silence. She addressed Caleb. "You're right that dragons change the rules. You should know that Hadrian, because he's an ice dragon, not only had the power to thaw my heart but he can melt and destroy the Fae blades that allow them to move between realms." She paused, then continued. "He even melted the replacement splinter of ice that Maeve sent for me. She thinks it's in my heart."

A murmur of excitement passed through the room, and Hadrian knew he wasn't the only one who believed this could contribute to their success.

"But any Other who enters Fae could be killed," Murray protested. "We all know we're on her list."

"But what about those who are allied with us who aren't Others?" the bartender asked. She gestured to the group of women seated with Arach and Wynter Olson. "What about mates?"

A woman in that group, one with long dark hair and two young sons, stood up. "We would need to know the risks," she said and her companions nodded. "We would need to know the plan, and we would need to know that we could trust whoever led us." She gestured to Rania and spoke coldly. "I saw your kiss of death once. It was effective, I'll give you that."

"It is the Dark Queen's tool and it is relentless," Rania acknowledged. "It worked twelve times, but not the thirteenth, and now no one has the power to give it again except the Dark Queen herself."

There was chatter at that, then Murray called for order. "So, what's the plan?" he demanded. "And what do you want us to do?"

The vampires appeared then, stepping out of the shadows as if they'd always been there. Hadrian knew they hadn't been. Micah led them, carrying something shrouded in a dark cloth. He placed it on the bar and retreated. Hadrian guessed it was Sebastian's Fae sword and kept his distance. He didn't want it to melt before they used it. Sylvia watched intently as if she knew what it was, as well, and a faint silver glow came through the cloth.

"You want to know the plan. It's fairly simple." Rania nodded briskly. "Hadrian is going to invade the armory and melt the Fae stock of weapons. I'm going to pretend to still be on the Dark Queen's side, and take a volunteer from the *Pyr* to her, supposedly to be slaughtered in front of her. Actually, we'll be creating a distraction, both for Hadrian and for another volunteer who will steal the gem of the hoard."

Pandemonium erupted then, protests coming from all sides about the strength of the Fae defenses of their treasury, the extent of Maeve's malice and the potential price of willingly entering the realm of Fae. There were comments about the untrustworthiness of a known assassin and accusations of manipulation. Rania stood in silence, her head high, and listened. When the furor died a bit, she produced the *bichuwa* and set it on the bar.

Silence ensued.

"Djinns make the best thieves," she said quietly, then pivoted to look at the two tables they occupied. At least four djinns turned immediately to smoke to avoid being chosen. "We are talking about taking down the Dark Queen forever."

The tension in the bar could have been cut with a knife. Rania had thrown down one of her challenges and Hadrian hoped someone would take it. He was aware of all the sidelong glances and the uncertainty, then a dark-haired woman stepped forward. She seemed to walk out of a ribbon of smoke, becoming more substantial with every step she took. Her eyes were dark and her gaze was hard. She was slender, moving with the stealth and elegance of a great cat. She stopped in front of Rania and put out her hand.

"My uncle," she said.

"Yes." Rania spun the blade so that the hilt was toward the djinn and bowed her head. "I'm sorry."

"You thought you had no choice," the djinn said. "I think maybe you didn't, not the way the odds were stacked against you, and even if it was a choice, there is honor in defending your own." She took the blade, smiling down at it as it caught the light. "He had this made."

"It's beautiful, lethal and beautiful."

The djinn moved like lightning, catching Rania around the shoulders and spinning her so that the tip of the blade was at her throat. Hadrian stood up but Rania's eyes flashed and he recognized that she wouldn't fight back.

Was she surrendering her life or did she know that the djinn wouldn't strike the final blow? He wasn't sure but he eased back, trying to quell the telltale blue shimmer of light that surrounded him.

The djinn addressed the Others, still holding Rania captive. "I was the wise woman of my kind. They came to me for counsel and for healing, for advice, for my glimpses into the future and for my wisdom. The Dark Queen stole that from me when she seized all the magick, trapping mine in the gem of the hoard along with her own. My uncle was devastated by the loss and his vigor failed, because he had lost hope in the future. I blame the Dark Queen for that as much as for the final stroke of the kiss of death. His death disheartened us even more, and I would take that back." She flung Rania aside and held the *bichuwa* high, so that the curved blade glinted in the light. "I am Yasmina, and I would be wise woman of the djinn again. I would retrieve our legacy, so wrongfully taken from us, and I will ally with this swan-maiden to see justice served for once and for all." She raised her voice to a roar. "Are you with me?"

And the Others roared agreement.

Rania ran toward Hadrian, her eyes alight with pleasure and he caught her up, swinging her around in triumph. "Take me there now," he urged. "I need to get started, then you can come back for Yasmina."

She framed his face in her hands and looked deeply into his eyes, her own filled with unshed tears. "We will win," she said with heat. "We will win, for our son."

"We will win because you apologized," he told her with pride, his heart bursting that this warrior maiden was his destined mate. "It takes strength to admit a mistake."

"I had to learn to do it, from you," Rania said with a smile.

The firestorm couldn't have chosen better for him. He loved her with every fiber of his being, and knew their partnership had been meant to be.

Rania laughed, then the *Pyr* and the Others shouted approval as she kissed Hadrian thoroughly.

He didn't even notice the vampires or Sylvia leave.

Mel watched as Hadrian breathed slowly and deeply in the middle of the dance floor at Bones. He'd shifted to his dragon form and Rania sat beside him, watching in silence as he banked the fires. He was much better at it than any dragon shifter Mel had seen before and she was impressed by how quickly his pulse and breathing slowed. When she thought he couldn't go deeper into what had to be a trance, he did, until it seemed that he wasn't breathing at all.

She looked at Theo, only to find him watching intently, as if he could learn by example. When she looked back, Hadrian had shifted to his human form. He was so still that he could have been dead, but Rania seized his wrist, nodded once to the *Pyr,* then they both vanished into thin air.

Murray gave a low whistle and turned back to pull a beer.

It was Raymond who gave her a poke and pointed at the dance floor. "Unless I am mistaken, the dragon will have need of his armor," the ghost whispered.

Sure enough, an emerald and silver scale was resting there.

"It's not just a firestorm," Mel told the Others, indicating Hadrian's lost scale. "Hadrian loves her."

"That tells us all we need to know," Drake said, claiming the scale from the floor. "The firestorm always chooses right for the *Pyr.*"

Yasmina nodded agreement. "She won't betray us. I could see the honor in her heart."

"It's just the Dark Queen and her minions you have to worry about then," Murray said wryly. "Oh, and the magick."

"Don't forget that the Regalian magick makes its own rules," Caleb added, then drained his drink and got up to leave.

As much as Mel hated to admit it, they were right. There was plenty of challenge to go around. "I'll follow Wynter and Arach," she said on impulse. "Who else is with us?"

Rania manifested in the Fae armory and put Hadrian down gently in the middle of the collection of weapons. She could see them glowing in the darkness around the perimeter of the locked room, which fortunately was of considerable size. It had to be to house Maeve's collection. There weren't any guards within the chamber, so she guessed they were stationed outside.

Perfect.

Hadrian shimmered blue, summoning the shift without leaving his relaxed state. Rania wanted to linger to make sure he was okay, but the longer she stayed in Fae, the greater the chance that she would be discovered.

The success of the entire plan depended upon each of them trusting the other completely.

She closed her eyes against the bright blue shimmer of his shift and admired his dragon form for a moment, those emerald scales glinting in the glow of the Fae blades. His claw moved and she saw the wavy blade of her *kesir* catch the light. She bent to retrieve it, knowing that Hadrian was giving it to her. He still had the dirk beneath his scales. She kissed his cheek and hoped he would be safe.

Rania willed herself back to his lair to collect Alasdair, who had volunteered to be her supposed victim in Fae.

When she got back to Hadrian's lair, she learned that Sebastian had vanished. Balthasar had his doubts about the vampire's intentions, but there was nothing to be done at this point. They had no chance of stopping him if he meant to betray them.

They had to carry on with the plan and hope for the best.

"Incompetence," Maeve said, seething as she strode toward the cage where the swans were captive. Bryant knew to keep his distance when she was in this foul mood. Someone would pay the price and the trick to survival was to ensure he wasn't the one.

The swans watched her, all three of them, their gazes steady and unblinking.

"I've yet to have a bite of roast swan," she continued, her tone scathing as she glanced back at Bryant. "And now you tell me that you haven't managed to capture the other brothers. I might need to find a new favorite."

"I'm here for you, my queen," Kade said, hurrying along beside her. When she stumbled over the heath in her heels, he caught one of her elbows and lifted her, even as Bryant did the same on the other side.

She only thanked Kade.

Bryant didn't like that the dragon shifter was around all the time, or that he was always close beside the Dark Queen. The truth was that Bryant didn't want to leave Fae himself long enough to hunt down the other swan brothers. They were irrelevant when his position in Maeve's court was potentially in peril.

He didn't like having competition. Maeve had always taken lovers, but this one seemed to have wormed his way into her affections with speed. There was no telling where this infatuation would end. It wasn't like the other one, the *Slayer* who had been the last of his kind. And Bryant couldn't figure out the attraction. Kade wasn't that good looking. He couldn't provide any insight into the activities of his fellows, not anymore. From Bryant's view, Kade was useless, but Maeve seemed determined to keep him as a pet.

They reached the cage with the three swans within it, and the birds hissed at them in agitation. There was no sign of any cooks or assistants.

"I've sent three teams," Maeve complained. "Where could they have gone?"

"The swans are all still here," Kade noted, as if to prove that he could count to three.

"Just because they aren't thieves doesn't mean they haven't betrayed me." Maeve turned to Bryant. "Find them!"

He couldn't see a single thing as far as the horizon in any direction. Nothing moved. There was only the radiant glow from the Fae court under the closest mound and the endless heath. "Where should I start, my queen?" he asked, trying to keep his tone respectful.

"If they were attacked, there could be signs of battle," Kade provided.

"I would know if anyone had attacked Fae," Bryant said, his tone withering.

"If they died..."

"They did not die," Bryant said with impatience. "Because we are all Fae except you. We don't die. We don't have bones. We don't leave remains to disintegrate. We aren't born and we don't die, and You. Aren't. Like. Us."

He was about to say that Kade didn't belong, but Maeve spun suddenly and looked back toward the Fae court, her eyes narrowed. "Did you see that?"

Bryant shook his head.

"I felt something," Kade said, predictably. Whether he'd felt anything or not, he always agreed with Maeve.

Bryant glared at him.

"Such a sensitive boy," she cooed, patting Kade's shoulder. She was distracted though, her manner intense as she stared back at the court. "I saw a light," she said. "You'll have to go back immediately." She took Kade's arm and waved at Bryant. "We'll stay here and find those cooks. I want a swan dinner and I want it soon."

His mission was a ruse and Bryant knew it. There had been no light. Maeve just wanted to be alone with Kade.

"And if I don't find a disturbance, my queen?"

"Then set the table for dinner. Tonight we feast!" she said, then laughed. Kade laughed with her, the two of them enjoying themselves enormously as they made their way toward the caged swans, their arms entwined and their heads bent together. "And do something about that blemish on your face, Bryant. It's most unattractive."

What blemish? Bryant pulled his sword and looked at his own reflection in the blade. There was a mark on his forehead, one that hadn't been there before. It was purple, which he couldn't explain.

Did Maeve find it unattractive? Was that the issue? If so, he had to find a way to get rid of it. He'd send someone else to check on the light, then try to get rid of the mark. There had to be an upside to having the right to delegate.

Bryant glanced at the entangled couple as his resentment built, then pivoted to return to the court.

The supposed glimpse of light was obviously a ploy. Still, he'd follow orders in the hope of an eventual return to favor. He had to get rid of that blemish. A dragon shifter couldn't keep her satisfied forever.

Could he?

Hadrian kept his fires banked low with an effort. He was impatient to see their plan succeed and wanted to learn as much as possible to help Rania. He wanted to begin the slaughter of the Fae, triumph, and escape the Fae realm. Then their life together would really begin. Lying in the darkness, breathing as slowly as he could, didn't feel like he was doing enough.

But it was the right choice. This was the part that only he could contribute. He could feel the hoarfrost forming on the Fae blades stored all around him. The armory was getting colder as he drew out the ice, reverting the silver blades to the ice his mother had spun. He dreamed of the past and he dreamed of the future, letting his thoughts drift as his pulse slowed even more.

He didn't know how much time had passed when he heard the footstep outside the armory.

It was stealthy. Cautious.

Someone knew he was there.

Hadrian forced himself to continue breathing slowly and opened his eyes the barest slit. He heard the lock turn and saw the door to the armory open a tiny increment. The silver light of Fae illuminated the gap, then silhouetted the visitor as the door was opened wider.

His unexpected company slipped inside, closing the door behind himself. His presence was impossible to ignore and Hadrian reviewed the glimpse of his silhouette. He was tall but a bit leaner than the one who had been with Maeve at his studio. Had this warrior come to get a weapon? No, there was one in the scabbard on his belt, one that still glowed with its full power.

He possessed the key to the armory. That meant that either he was trusted by the Dark Queen, or he was a traitor.

Maybe the Dark Queen had sensed Hadrian's presence and sent a trusted servant to discover the truth.

Maybe this warrior meant to betray Maeve for some reason and had stolen the key, intending to arm himself and whoever followed him.

Either way, this visitor could never leave the armory.

Hadrian opened his eyes the merest slit and watched. The armory had no light source except for the Fae blades that glowed faintly where they were stored around its perimeter. Their light had dimmed since Hadrian's arrival and soon would be extinguished. He watched the warrior shiver, then move with purpose to claim a large sword with an elaborate hilt.

He whispered the blade's name beneath his breath, like an invocation, then swore softly. Hadrian could see that the blade was covered with frost and that it was considerably shorter than it had been on his arrival. The warrior lifted it before himself to examine it more closely and its meager light illuminated his confused expression. He glanced toward Hadrian, apparently mystified, then turned around to replace the blade.

He might have chosen another, but Hadrian shifted shape and pulled Rania's *kesir* from beneath his scales. He struck the Fae warrior down with a clean single stroke before the intruder could even put a hand on the hilt of his own sword.

He spun around, his mouth open in astonishment, then dissolved into a silver puddle that gleamed on the pounded dirt floor of the armory.

Hadrian waited, listening, but he didn't hear any signs of pursuit. He lifted the sword from the rapidly-diminishing puddle and added it to the collection in the armory. He exhaled on the blade to encourage the frost to form, then wiped Rania's blade and hid it again. He shifted back to his dragon form and coiled on the floor of the treasury, willing his pulse to slow as he watched the only door.

There might be others, but he'd be ready.

CHAPTER FOURTEEN

"You win, Fae bait," Wynter said to Arach in the challenging tone he was getting used to hearing. "You get to slice the portal open."

They were in Central Park on Thursday night, as scheduled. The Fae sword glowed with its sinister silver light in Arach's grip. The firestorm burned golden between himself and Wynter but he'd known without asking that the chance of satisfying it before this attack on Fae had been non-existent.

It was hard to believe that the firestorm had chosen such an infuriating, contrary, defiant woman as his destined mate. Arach had decided that his firestorm had to be a spell.

The sooner they extinguished the Dark Queen's power, the better. He couldn't take much more of this persistent desire.

He'd chosen the North Woods in the hope that they'd be unobserved. That was a long shot, given that they were accompanied by twenty determined women who were widowed wolf mates—the rest of the group from Alaska were guarding the kids—Caleb and six other wolf shifters from New York, five dragon shifters, two pregnant but resolute mates, Murray, Mel, the medusa hostess from Bones whose name he could never remember and most of the remaining members of the Circus of Wonders.

Of the *Pyr*, Kristofer, Rhys, Thorolf and Theo were right behind Arach. Bree and Lila were with them, too. The *Pyr* each had a new pair of gloves from Quinn. Bree had her Valkyrie sword and Lila carried a trident. Each one in the invading party had armed his or herself with a weapon—or two—of choice and each was grim. They were a veritable army and Arach suspected that even here, the gathering or the open portal might be spotted by some curious human.

The sword was cold and heavy in his grip. He wasn't entirely sure how to wield it, much less whether it would respond to the will of someone who wasn't Fae. He and Wynter had debated the merit of testing it in advance, but ultimately had agreed that doing so might reveal their scheme to Maeve.

At least they agreed on something.

A distant clock struck six.

It was now or never.

"Good luck to all of you," Arach said to the silent company gathered behind him in the shadows. "Remember: don't drink or eat anything. Don't be fooled and don't make any deals. Whatever you do, don't start dancing. I hope to see you all afterward."

He sensed their nods and felt them brace themselves for the worst. More than one gripped a weapon more tightly. Arach lifted the blade and tried to forget how he'd been cursed by Maeve just for entering her realm uninvited.

"Do it, dragon dude," Wynter whispered and he grimaced that she never called him by his name. "Do it *now*."

Arach willed the weapon to open a portal for him, sliced downward with one savage gesture and hoped. He and Wynter gasped in unison as a silver sliver of light opened between the realms. Arach could see the endless heath of Fae and the twilit sky, the one devoid of clouds and stars. In the distance, there was a mound, a golden light shining from a portal near its base. Lilting music carried over the heath, beckoning them closer. Arach shivered deep inside, unable to forget his last visit to the Fae court, and opened the portal wider. Wynter, of course, pushed past him to enter the hidden realm first, which didn't surprise him in the least.

He followed her, then stood guard as the intruders silently surged through the gap. No sooner had Arach closed the portal between the realms than the Fae attacked.

"Ready?" Rania asked Alasdair.

That *Pyr* shrugged. "As ready as I'll ever be. Let's do it."

The group from New York City should be entering Fae and Rania hated that she had no way to verify that they were in position. It was terrifying to embark on such an important quest and be reliant upon others to ensure success. On the other hand, they needed every talon, claw, and blade. Rania had to trust that Hadrian had melted the Fae armory, and that he'd remained undetected for three whole days. Who even knew how long that might seem in Fae? She hadn't slept at all since leaving him there. She'd been surprised that Alasdair had changed his mind about entering Fae, but he'd insisted that he wasn't going to miss out on a battle to the finish with the Dark Queen.

They'd decided that instead of pretending to kill him in front of Maeve, which could go badly wrong, she'd bring his apparent corpse to the court. He'd bank the fires so that his pulse couldn't be detected and would play dead.

It still felt risky to Rania.

Balthasar had left earlier in the evening, hoping to locate the old mound where Hadrian's father had entered the Fae realm. His reasoning that they should attack from as many points as possible was hard to dispute, but Rania felt that they were too scattered. She had two knives from her own collection, including the *kesir* that Hadrian had returned to her, and an old favorite, a fifteenth-century *katar*. The push dagger was small and easy to hide. She feared her entire collection wouldn't be enough—not if Maeve starting casting spells.

"You're sure?" she asked Alasdair again.

He grinned and that made him resemble Hadrian enough to make Rania's heart tug. "Let's go. Sooner started, sooner finished, as my father liked to say."

Rania took a deep breath, gripped his hand, and flung them into Fae.

At least she thought she'd taken them to Fae. When the maelstrom of light stilled, she didn't recognize their location at all. It was dark, darker than Rania remembered Fae to be. She realized that it wasn't twilight anymore, even though it had always been twilight in Fae in her experience. There were still no stars overhead, though, and no clouds, and the heath spread from beneath their feet into the distance.

Alasdair lifted a finger and pointed to the glow of light emanating from beneath a hill nearby. That music flowed from the hall, along with the sound of laughter and singing. As always, the eternal party was in full swing.

She'd deliberately not taken them right into the court, wanting to have a sense of what was going on before revealing themselves. Except for the sky being darker, everything was as expected. She and Alasdair exchanged a glance and he shifted shape in a shimmer of brilliant blue. She sat beside him and listened as his breathing slowed.

When it seemed he wasn't breathing at all, he shifted back to human form, just as Hadrian had done. He could have been a corpse on the heath. Rania closed her eyes, gripped his hand and wished them to Maeve.

Yasmina had stayed low in Fae after Rania delivered her there. It had taken her some time to get into the treasury—even though she could assume her smoke form and slide beneath the door, the chamber had been heavily guarded. Leaving with the prize in her human form, and doing so unobserved, had been the challenge.

She could have struck down a guard if she'd moved quickly and surprised him, but Yasmina was a healer through and through. She couldn't bring herself to end even a Fae life. She knew the stakes and she told herself to get over it, but each time she raised the blade, she let it slide to her side again.

She listened at a lot of keyholes, gathering what tidings she could, and soon realized that there was a plague of some kind in Fae. They whispered of it, fear in their hushed voices, and she saw the purple blemishes that stained their skin. She saw the marks spread and had never seen the like of them. As a healer, she was intrigued.

Time had to be slipping away, though. It was hard to keep track in Fae, but Yasmina knew that Rania would be challenging the Dark Queen at the arranged time. She had to get the gem of the hoard to Hadrian in the armory before that.

The sky grew steadily darker, as if deepest night was falling.

When Yasmina saw the caged swans being hauled to the court, she knew she had to act.

The guard before the treasury was one she'd learned was the least energetic. Maybe it was because of the purple stain spreading down his arms. It was on his neck, too, and he seemed to find it itchy. He rubbed his brow and sighed, then one of his fingertips fell off.

Yasmina and the guard watched it shrivel, then turn to a brown leaf and blow away. He chased it, snatching it up from the ground and trying to fit it back on his hand. Instead, it crumbled to dust.

He looked around and spotted her. His mouth opened to raise the alarm. Yasmina lifted her uncle's *bichuwa*, but the guard suddenly shrank into himself. He transformed into a field mouse before her very eyes, one that had a faintly purple tinge to its fur. He looked to be as surprised as she was. Then his fur changed to plain brown and he scurried away, disappearing into the growth on the heath.

The brass key to the treasury lay on the ground where he had dropped it. Yasmina seized it and entered the treasury to claim the prize.

The old Fae mound wasn't under a shopping mall after all.

It was in the middle of a cemetery. Balthasar couldn't believe it.

The church beside the cemetery had to be two hundred years old and was both tiny and a bit rundown. Several of the windows had been broken and were boarded over. It looked abandoned. The door was locked and also padlocked. He parked in front of the gate and turned off the engine.

Silence.

Balthasar had taken Hadrian's Land Rover and just followed his whim, and ended up in this place, wherever it was. He wasn't sure he was even on the map anymore. He hadn't passed another car on the winding road for at least half an hour before reaching the churchyard. The road ended at this place and he had the definite sense that he'd arrived.

Balthasar got out of the truck and looked around. There were no houses in the vicinity. He hadn't been anywhere so desolate in a long time and had a serious case of the jitters. The moon was full and high in the sky, so bright that it was like a searchlight. The iron gate to the cemetery hung askew and the trees were old and crooked. That had to be a hawthorne in the very center of the cluster of worn gravestones, so crooked and huge that it had to be older than the church.

A golden light shone from beneath its roots. That sight made his heart stop, then race.

As he moved closer, Balthasar saw that there was a gap between the roots, like the entry to a cave. And he heard the music, that infectious merry fiddle music that could set the most reluctant toes to tapping.

He'd found a portal to Fae and he was going to enter it.

The alarm on his watch buzzed. It was midnight. It was time.

Balthasar took a deep breath and walked toward the golden light, knowing what he had to do. Just before he reached the hawthorne, he heard the calls of birds above him. He stopped and looked up, wondering what kind of bird would be in flight so late at night. Maybe he was stalling, but he looked anyway.

Eight trumpeter swans descended out of the starry night in perfect unison. They landed in a circle around him in the deserted cemetery. One came toward him and inclined its head as if in greeting.

"Edred?" Balthasar guessed.

The swan gave a *houp-houp* sound.

They were Rania's brothers. Balthasar smiled, glad that he wouldn't be completely alone.

He gestured to the tunnel opening. "I think this is it."

Edred stretched out his neck as if sniffing the air that emanated from beneath the hawthorne. Then he straightened and nodded, looking Balthasar right in the eye.

"After you?" Balthasar suggested and the swan quacked, like he was laughing.

Balthasar grinned and led the way. Rania's brothers clustered behind him when he stepped into Fae, moving between realms beneath the roots of the ancient tree.

They gathered together on the heath, which stretched as far as the eye could see in every direction. There were no stars overhead, even though the sky was clear. It was really dark but Balthasar could see both a mound with light emanating from a doorway and a cage silhouetted in the distance. The light from the mound was what he had seen shining beneath the roots. It was a beacon, and he hoped it wouldn't lead them to disaster.

The brothers rustled their feathers in agitation as the cage was pulled toward the mound. There was something white inside, which fluttered.

"Let's bust them free first," he whispered. "We've got surprise on our side." Edred nodded and Balthasar shifted shape. He flew toward the cage, his citrine and gold scales glinting, and eight swans flying right behind him in a vee.

The problem with battling the Fae was that they came in every shape and size.

Thorolf fried an ogre, then slapped six small Fae dead against his scales. The last group were riding beetles, their wings flying as fast as the beetles, and had descended upon the invaders like a swarm of locusts. The dead ones dripped from his hide like drops of pewter and gleamed on the heath before they disappeared. The ogre made a bigger puddle than that.

There were bogies and brownies, pixies and phoukas, spriggans and sprites. Some were winged and some had tails; some wore hats and some had spiked boots. Some had thorns and some had sharp teeth. Their variety was almost infinite, but they were all bent on destruction. They stabbed and they bit, they lanced and they sliced, they stung and they gnawed.

Thorolf felt as if he was being attacked on every side. He slapped and sliced and squished every being he could. He cracked heads like nuts and snapped weapons like twigs. He breathed fire when his allies were out of harm's way, and he scooped up the wolf mates who stumbled. He'd never multi-tasked so effectively in his life, and once he got his rhythm, he had the time of his life.

Kicking butt and taking names was part of the joy of being a dragon shifter after all.

Bree was swinging her Valkyrie sword with gusto, slicing Fae to bits and sending that silver liquid flying in all directions. Kristofer had her back, breathing fire and slashing with his talons. When she was cornered, he snatched her up and flew her high above the throng. Lila jabbed with the trident of the selkies, switching off with Nyssa at intervals. Rhys defended both of them from behind, exhaling a masterful plume of dragonfire that fried a swatch across the heath that made Thorolf want to stand up and cheer.

Mel was riding Theo's back as he flew over the battle repeatedly, breathing dragonfire on the Fae attackers on the ground, then chasing more of them through the air. Murray was flattening all comers with the hammer he'd brought, and looked to be knee-deep in silver liquid. There were eight wolves snarling and snapping on the heath below Thorolf, rounding up Fae, biting them and tearing into their flesh. The white Arctic wolf was Wynter, he knew, because he'd seen her shift, but Caleb and the others in his pack were fearsome grey timber wolves with cold eyes and impressive fangs. Thorolf wouldn't have wanted to face down any one of them.

The crew from Bones fought in a loose ring around Murray: the medusa hostess was holding her own. Arach fought with them, alternating between his dragon form, and using the Fae sword in his human form. Bear-shifters tore at the Fae; djinns eluded them in smoke form, then reappeared to surprise them from behind; there was an entire company of demons with Rosanna from the circus, all glowing red as they spiked Fae with their pitchforks.

The hobgoblins came out of the heath and charged the attackers, scattering the wolf mates—which was probably what they'd intended. Thorolf roared and dove into the fray to gather them all back together again. Others joined him and the hobgoblins were soon reduced to shimmering puddles of silver.

A cheer rose from the invading company when the surviving Fae turned and fled.

Arach shouted and pointed the glowing Fae sword at the distant court. "Let's take this battle to Maeve!" he roared.

The company shouted agreement. Thorolf swooped low and the wolf mates climbed on his tail and his back. Several even managed to reach the top of his wings. Thorolf picked up more in his claws, and the other Pyr did the same, carrying their forces to the new battlefield.

This was as good as it got, in Thorolf's view.

Yasmina had the gem of the hoard and was hurrying toward the armory when she saw a Fae warrior heading in the same direction. There was purpose in his stride and she felt a premonition of dread. She tucked her prize amongst a cluster of rocks to hide it, then shifted to a wisp of smoke to follow him.

It was the tall warrior she'd seen at Maeve's side, although he had a purple mark on his forehead that she didn't remember. Yasmina floated behind him, glad of the darkness to hide her smoke form. He crept close to the door of the armory, and paused there to listen, his eyes narrowed with suspicion.

"Liam?" he asked, but she could tell he didn't expect a reply. "Hurry up, Liam. The Dark Queen is waiting on us."

There was no sound from within the armory. The Fae warrior straightened, stared at the door for a long moment, then marched away. Yasmina knew she didn't imagine that he was making sure his steps were audible. He pulled out a key and drew his sword, then darted back to the armory and unlocked the door.

There was a roar and the brilliant glow of dragonfire. The Fae warrior lunged into the armory, pulling the door behind himself, and Yasmina heard sounds of battle. Weight crashed against the walls. Something shattered. Someone grunted and fell to the earth.

And then there was silence.

Quick as a wink, Yasmina slid through the lock of the armory and was horrified to see Hadrian in his human form on the ground, blood running from a wound on his chest. The Fae warrior stood over him, his expression fierce, then swore as the blade on his sword became tipped with hoarfrost. He stepped away from Hadrian, circling the armory with increasing speed as he examined the melting weapons.

Then he turned to survey the fallen *Pyr* with mingled horror and awe.

"You did this," he whispered as Hadrian groaned. He kicked Hadrian who rolled to his back as if close to death. "I don't know how it was possible, you will pay the price for this travesty. The Dark Queen will want to exact her own revenge." He kicked Hadrian again, but the *Pyr* went completely still.

Yasmina didn't think Hadrian was even breathing anymore and she feared their quest had claimed its first victim. The Fae warrior swore again and kicked Hadrian again, with no response.

"You were supposed to be dead already," the Fae warrior complained. "Your corpse should have been burned to cinders in that fire." He bent down and listened for Hadrian's breath, then opened one of the *Pyr's* eyes to peer into it. He stood up then, his disgust clear. "You will not escape the price of this," he vowed. "If you can be roused, my queen will do it." He nodded. "And then you will pay."

Hadrian didn't move.

The Fae warrior sheathed his weapon with a vicious gesture then hefted Hadrian over his shoulder, grunting beneath the weight of the other man. Then he left the armory, carrying the dead *Pyr* toward the court.

Yasmina feared that Rania might lose heart when she saw that her mate had been killed. She wondered whether the plan should proceed, then hoped that she might somehow have a chance to heal Hadrian. She hurried to retrieve the hidden gem of the hoard, and when she picked it up, she glanced toward the departing warrior.

And she saw the green glimmer of Hadrian's eyes.

He was alive!

He had to be feigning the extent of his injuries in order to be taken to Maeve. Yasmina gripped the gem of the hoard and hurried in pursuit of the Fae warrior, slipping from shadow to shadow as she tried to keep up.

This was a confrontation she didn't want to miss.

Rania manifested before Maeve with her prize and Alasdair fell hard against the ground. His scales looked shimmery and vital, even though he was supposedly dead, and she feared that their ruse would be discovered too soon. She was glad when he shifted one last time to his human form and remained motionless beside her. She bowed low before Maeve, trying to disguise her doubts and what would be seen as her treachery.

She didn't want her thoughts to be read.

"That took you long enough," Maeve said, rising from her throne.

Kade, the dark-haired and dark-eyed dragon shifter who had betrayed his kind, hurried to her side. She stroked his cheek and kissed him, letting everyone see the affection between them.

He approached one of his own kind, apparently dead, but he was indifferent. Did he know that Alasdair was banking the fires, or had Maeve put a splinter of ice in his heart, too?

Rania felt herself tense as the Dark Queen drew near. The court gathered closer, chattering and speculating. She strove to keep her own expression bland.

"An easy kill?" Maeve asked.

"Never, my queen. The *Pyr* are most resilient." Rania eyed Kade, who returned her survey steadily.

Maeve stood beside Alasdair. "I can smell that he's *Pyr* but why isn't he a dragon?"

"They rotate between forms when in distress, my queen, then remain in their human form once dead."

"Really? The last two who died in my court were dragon corpses."

"But they weren't actually dead, my queen," a Fae warrior said, striding into the court. He was carrying a man on his back and to Rania's dismay, it was Hadrian he flung to the ground. Her dragon shifter wasn't moving any more than Alasdair was.

Was he dead or had he banked his fires? Rania wished she knew.

"Bringing presents, Bryant?" Maeve asked. She bent and peered at Hadrian. "But that's the dead one."

The Fae warrior, obviously Bryant, nudged Hadrian with his foot. "He wasn't as dead as you thought he was, my queen. I found him in the armory, melting the weapons."

Maeve inhaled sharply and spun to face Rania. "Is this your doing? Did you revive him so that you could kill him yourself?"

"Does it matter?" Rania asked, indicating Alasdair. "Here is my thirteenth kill and the *Pyr* you requested. I would ask you to free my brothers."

Maeve looked between the two *Pyr*, then eyed Bryant. "Melting the weapons?" she echoed and he nodded. "How much progress had he made?"

"We are unarmed, my lady."

A whisper passed through the court at that, a fluttering of wings and a hissing of speculation. Maeve came toward Rania, her gaze dark with intent. Rania felt the Fae queen's will bend upon her and winced as Maeve began to probe in her mind. She tried to close her thoughts against the intrusion, squeezing her eyes shut as she fought off Maeve's advances.

There was a shout and a brilliant shimmer of blue light. Hadrian had shifted shape to his dragon form. He roared and breathed a torrent of dragonfire over the Fae, compelling them to retreat. Bryant lunged at him, sword drawn, but Hadrian shifted back to human form. Rania's dirk flashed in his hand. Bryant fell on him and the blade nicked Bryant's shoulder. The Fae warrior moved quickly, thrusting the remnant of his Fae sword at Hadrian. Hadrian dodged the blow and Bryant slashed at his feet, moving so quickly that Hadrian fell to one knee. He shimmered blue, taking his dragon form, but Maeve cast a wave of red magick at him before he could defend himself.

Hadrian was frozen in place, trapped and powerless. His mouth was open, poised to breathe fire, and he was crouched low against the ground. His tail was raised, caught mid-swing, and his wings were raised high.

Alasdair had already started to shimmer blue and was changing to defend his cousin. Maeve flung a fistful of magick at him and he might have turned to stone, right in the act of snapping his great dragon teeth at Bryant.

"Do continue," Maeve invited Bryant.

He bowed to his queen, then raised the last dripping stub of his sword to drive it into Hadrian's throat. He lingered over the task, savoring his victory a bit more than a noble warrior should, to Rania's thinking.

"No!" she cried, lunging forward.

Maeve spun to confront her. "Traitor!" she cried and froze Rania in place.

In the same moment, a Fae dagger sliced through the air, seeming to fly in slow motion. It was a masterful throw, and the blade turned end over end, flashing silver as it sped toward its target. Maeve turned from Rania and cried out as she spotted it but it was too late. The blade caught Bryant between the shoulder blades, burying itself so deeply that the tip emerged from his chest. He stared down as the silver liquid began to flow, his expression astonished, then he crumbled. He became a puddle before he hit the ground.

There was a shout as the company from New York descended on the Fae court and chaos erupted on all sides. Wolf mates attacked Fae and Fae fought back. Wolf shifters barked and howled, driving the Fae into a tighter cluster, and dragons flew overhead, burning the gathered Fae with volleys of dragonfire. A company of swans flew into the fray, honking and flapping, snapping at the Fae with their beaks, accompanied by a citrine and gold dragon. Rania wanted to cheer.

But Maeve braced her feet against the ground and called an ancient summons. The ground shook and the lightning cracked overhead. A wind whipped around the court, snatching away the sound of music and tearing at clothing, wings and hair. She stood in her heels and called, her command imperious, and the magick answered her, rising from the heath around her in a wave of glowing red. It flowed skyward, engulfing everything and everyone—and every being it surrounded became motionless. When it rose over their heads, the court was so silent and still that the hair stood up on the back of Rania's neck.

Except for Maeve. She turned and walked toward Rania, her gaze cold. "I know you didn't come unarmed, traitor," she said with hostility. "Show me what you have."

Rania couldn't deny her. It was as if her body answered Maeve's will and not her own. She found herself displaying both the *kesir* with its waved blade and the *katar*.

Maeve didn't touch them. "Steel," she hissed.

Maybe that would help, since the Fae couldn't wield them... Rania got no further in her thinking before Maeve beckoned to Kade.

He strode to her side immediately, bending his head attentively toward her. "Yes, my queen."

"We must see an endeavor completed," she said to him. "You and I must do it together. I've already ensured that you won't be interrupted."

"Yes, my queen."

"I want you to choose a knife, then use it to ensure that he—" she pointed to Alasdair "—dies and that he—" she indicated Hadrian "—stays dead this time." She turned and framed Kade's face in her hands while he stared at her in adoration. "Then I will ensure that you're rewarded beyond your wildest dreams."

Kade smiled. His eyes lit. Rania had no doubt that he would do exactly as bidden. "What about the swan maiden?" he asked.

Maeve smiled at Rania and the sight was chilling. "She's just learned to feel, Kade. It would be unfair to take that away, just when she's about to have so very much to mourn." She walked back to her throne, hips swinging. "It's a shame about Bryant, but then, he hadn't been himself lately." She sat down and gestured to Kade. "Slice them open, gullet to groin," she commanded. "I want to see some blood."

There was a sliver of ice in Kade's heart. Hadrian could feel it. He called to it, hoping he could melt it, just as he'd melted the other two, hoping he could save Alasdair, Rania and himself from Maeve's wrath.

If only the splinter responded to him in time.

They were toast.

Alasdair figured the effort had been valiant, but Maeve had out-magicked them. They couldn't exactly fight back, defend themselves, or defeat her when they'd all practically become statues.

It stunk, but there was nothing any of them could do about it.

Kade approached Rania and examined her two blades. After some deliberation, he chose the *katar*, the short push-dagger. Alasdair was glad in a way that both of Rania's weapons were fiercely sharp.

"But you took the wrong child," a woman cried when Kade turned around.

A slender dark-haired woman manifested suddenly in the midst of the Fae court, seemingly appearing out of nothing at all. Alasdair had never seen such a beauty in his life. She lifted her chin, her dark eyes bright with defiance, her dark hair flowing as if she stood in a slight breeze. She confronted Maeve with an audacity he admired, a golden orb cradled in her hands. It was the gem of the hoard, Alasdair guessed, because Maeve leaned forward in outrage.

"Where did you get that?" Maeve demanded. "How dare you touch it!"

"I took it, just as you took the magick within it. I am Yasmina, wise woman of the djinns," the new arrival said and Alasdair understood how she'd suddenly appeared. She'd been a wisp of smoke before. "You stole my magick, Maeve, and snared it in this orb. I demand its return."

"You can't have it," Maeve said. "It's mine."

Yasmina shook her head. "No longer. You have made your last theft."

"I'm no thief!"

"You're a thief many times over. You stole my magick. You stole the magick of others. You stole many lives. But most importantly, at this moment, you stole the life of Rania when you took her from the cradle. You owe her recompense, because she was the wrong child."

"Wrong child?" Maeve demanded, rising to her feet in indignation. "What a lot of nonsense. She was a tithe owed to me, and I used her as I saw fit. It was my right!"

Dragon's Mate

"Rania wasn't the witch's daughter," Yasmina said. "She was the queen's daughter, and the daughter of the swan-prince."

"Ulrik has nothing to do with this," the Dark Queen retorted. "He's the last of his kind and I'll take him out next..."

But Rania was a swan-shifter. If this Ulrik was another swan shifter, then he couldn't be the last of his kind.

And if Maeve knew that Rania was a swan-maiden, then she had to have realized that Rania wasn't the witch's daughter, after all.

"*You knew*," Hadrian charged in old-speak and Alasdair realized they'd made the same conclusion. Sadly, no one else could understand the communication of the *Pyr*.

"You knew," Kade echoed aloud, turning to the queen. His expression was one of surprise and even a little disappointment. He turned the blade in his hand. "You knew," he said again.

Maeve took a step back.

"It didn't matter who she was," the Dark Queen protested. "She was mine. I took her as a tithe and I used her as I saw fit."

"And for that, you owe Rania compensation," Yasmina informed Maeve, then lifted the gem of the hoard.

"No!" Maeve protested.

"Yes," Yasmina said with resolve. "I've already chosen the only gift that will suffice. This must be shattered to make amends to everyone."

"No!" Maeve cried and Kade turned on Yasmina. Alasdair feared he'd have to watch her be slaughtered, but she crouched down then vanished, becoming a wisp of dark smoke. Kade slashed at her but his blade passed through nothing at all.

He realized then that Yasmina had rolled the gem of the hoard toward Hadrian. It glinted gold as it rolled, casting a red glow, until it disappeared beneath Hadrian's chest.

"You can't do this!" Maeve protested, shoving at Hadrian's side without effect.

She pointed at Kade but he took a step back, his gaze clouded with doubts as if he was awakening from a dream. She summoned the magick again, gathering the red cloud to her and pointed at Hadrian.

He shifted shape in a shimmer of blue, taking his human form. He stood before her then, the amber sphere cradled in his hands. Maeve tried to rip it free from his grip but failed. Alasdair could hear Hadrian singing to the orb in old-speak, his chant sending a resonance through the ground. The sphere was soon covered with white frost, so that the spider and the wasp snared within it couldn't be discerned. It cast a white glow instead of a red one and Maeve screamed in frustration.

Meanwhile, Maeve's spell slipped. She was gathering magick in the hope of foiling Hadrian. As they were released, the Fae roused themselves to attack. They stopped to scratch their skin and their scalps, that purple stain spreading across their skins with remarkable speed.

There was an earthshattering crack as the gem of the hoard split into two halves. Maeve cried out in anguish, even as they crumbled into chunks of ice and melted away. Alasdair saw the wasp take flight, freed from the tomb of resin, carrying the spider in its grasp. The wasp flew high, illuminated by a faint red glow.

Alasdair had no time to think about that marvel, because dust began to fall on all sides. It was a storm of shimmering iridescent snowflakes, dark as ash on one side and glimmering a million colors on the other. The dust fell from above them, revealing that the sky was only an illusion. He felt as if he was on the set of a play and the curtains were being drawn back, the backdrops folded up, the set being pushed aside and destroyed. The borders and boundaries, the very fabric of Fae and its inhabitants, were disintegrating all around him.

The Fae court was fading. There was no other way to describe it. The brilliant red he was accustomed to seeing on the Fae was now burgundy, if not brown. The silver that shone in their hair and on their wings was now as dull as tree bark aged by the wind and weather to grey. Their skin was marked by purple stains, and they seemed misshapen to him, as they hadn't before. They reminded him more vehemently of the forest than of the starlight he had previously thought they favored.

They were no longer beautiful and bewitching.

Maeve's throne seemed to be made of old trees now, instead of carved silver as it previously had appeared. Her lipstick was no longer brilliant red, but was the deep brown of chestnuts. Her hair was no longer black, but had become dark brown, streaked with a thousand shades of lighter brown and even gold. Her skin had become more golden and Alasdair thought she looked like the old woman of fairy tales, the one who lived in the woods with her familiar and mixed potions for those bold enough to visit her hut. Her hand, braced on the arm of her throne, was speckled and tanned.

Small red lights flew in and around everyone, like fireflies gathering— but these burned red, little spheres of glowing magick. They multiplied with every passing moment, as if the shredding of the realm created more of them—or freed them once again. Alasdair closed his eyes against the relentless shower of shimmering particles and shook his head.

When he looked again, he saw that the Fae themselves were changing. That purple stain was changing them, not just the color of their skin. They shrank and shifted, changing to birds and bugs and beetles. Each one was briefly touched with purple, which abruptly faded into the browns and duns of the forest floor. Instead of singing and making music, they squeaked and fluttered and slithered. As the dust fell on all sides, the transformed Fae darted into the shadows of the forest that was revealed to be all around them.

Meanwhile, the wasp flew higher and higher, and as it progressed, all those red fireflies of magick gathered behind it. It was a current of crimson dots, an army of tiny specks streaming upward. It seemed that a fiery comet flew out of the realm of Fae, soaring into the sky until it punched through the dissolving veil to the mortal world above and beyond.

The sky cracked and the dust fell with greater intensity. The ground was dissolving, too, the Fae court itself crumbling on all sides. Maeve's cry turned to a hoarse croak as she became a lizard. She jumped and snapped after the spiraling red comet as if she would eat it, but there was no chance of that.

Alasdair knew then that the magick was abandoning Maeve and returning to Regalia, and that Fae was no longer a separate realm from the world of mortals. The barrier between the worlds was being shredded and only the magick specific to the Earth remained. The dust fell in enormous quantities, more than enough to suffocate them if they didn't escape.

And as the tide of magick flowed upward, those snared in Maeve's last spell were released.

Hadrian snatched up Rania.

"I can't manifest elsewhere anymore," she said. She held out her wrist, showing that there was a burn mark where the red string of Maeve's curse had been.

Hadrian laughed and swung her around. "Then we'll fly!" he said, taking flight to follow the red comet. "We're free!"

"My brothers!" she protested.

"We set them free," Balthasar said, appearing out of the dust. "Let's get out of here!"

It was chaos in what had been the Fae court. Alasdair lost track of most of their company as they made an exodus to their own world. The *Pyr* from New York had snatched up wolf mates and Others, carrying everyone back toward the realm they knew best. Wolf mates hung on to dragon claws and tails, and great leathery wings beat against the air. Theo carried Mel, while Kristofer carried Bree and Rhys had Lila. Balthasar shifted shape and snatched up Murray, all of them creating a convoy to the mortal realm. The dust fell endlessly on all sides and Alasdair couldn't catch a glimpse of Yasmina at all. In her smoke form, she could be lost!

"But Yasmina!" he protested. "We can't leave her behind."

"You're not," murmured the djinn, her voice soft. "I'm in your ear." She laughed a little. "It's much more comfortable than a bottle."

"You're not lost," he said in relief, even as he took flight after Rania and Hadrian.

"Let me see what I can do about helping your mind heal while you get us out of here," she said with a confidence that made him smile. "That's only fair. Don't worry: I'm tough to lose, Alasdair MacEwan."

He cupped his claw over his ear, just to be sure.

CHAPTER FIFTEEN

Nick Shea awakened in the middle of the night without knowing why. He was getting a bit bored with their unexpected family vacation on Bardsey Island, but at least Isabelle was there. There was something fascinating about Rafferty's adopted daughter. She wasn't like any of the girls Nick knew at school. Was it because of her accent? He thought there was something more. She got this look sometimes, as if she knew something special, a secret or a mystery. Nick couldn't figure it out.

Maybe when he finally got his dragon shifter powers, the truth would be clear. He couldn't wait for that.

The house was quiet and there was no sound of traffic at all. No fire engines ever. No internet connection or cellphone service. It was like they'd gone off the end of the world. Nick wondered again when they'd be going home to Minneapolis.

His brothers were sound asleep in the room they were sharing, but he had the sense that someone was awake. Maybe it was one of those weird old guys, the ones he couldn't understand. He eased out of bed and crept down the hall in his flannel pj's. The wooden floor was cold underfoot but he wasn't going back for his socks.

Not when he saw Isabelle at the bottom of the stairs. Her fair hair caught the moonlight and she glanced back when the top step squeaked under his foot. She held a finger to her lips and Nick nodded, then continued down the stairs to her side.

She must have been awakened by the same thing.

He felt excited when he reached her side, as if they were a team.

Isabelle was two years older than him and a bit taller, even though Nick was the tallest boy in his class. She pointed to the back door, which was slightly ajar, and he nodded agreement.

They stepped out into the night as one and he caught his breath at the coldness of the air. He could smell the sea and the full moon cast a brilliant light. It could have been the middle of the day instead of the middle of the night. Even so, he could see zillions of stars overhead. It was so dark here, at the end of the world.

Isabelle, though, was staring into the distance. He followed her gaze and saw the old weird guys behind the mound, the one that Rafferty said had once been a cave for the Sleeper. It was hard to believe that anyone could have slept for a thousand years or so, but Marco had that mysterious smile, the one that made Nick believe. And the weird old guys were supposed to have been enchanted for that long, too. That's why no one could understand them.

Isabelle pointed and Nick nodded. They crept toward the old guys, who were in a circle. The dew was cold on his feet, but Nick didn't care. As he and Isabelle came closer, he could hear that the ancient *Pyr* were chanting. That hitchhiker guy was with them, the one he'd seen around, and he seemed to be leading the chant. Nick and Isabelle crouched behind the rubble of the cavern to watch and listen.

Nick couldn't understand the words. Isabelle shook her head that she couldn't either. But they both stared when red light began to swirl before the hitchhiker. He laughed lightly and moved his hands as if he was gathering it into a ball. His chant became louder and the other guys were louder, too. The red light swirled and danced, like a thousand individual lights gathered into a cloud. He spun it in his hands and the light became brighter and brighter. Nick realized that the red dots of light were multiplying.

The guy moved into the middle of the circle as the sphere became bigger and brighter. His arms were spread wide as he kept gathering it and building it. The chant was making the earth vibrate beneath their feet and Nick felt Isabelle's hand close over his. They clutched hands as the light doubled and redoubled again, the red light illuminating the faces of the entire group.

The chant became more insistent and grew in volume. The other guys got to their feet and began to dance in a circle, stamping their feet in time with the chant. The sphere grew bigger and brighter, as if the leader was drawing the power from somewhere else. The chant rose to a crescendo and then the leader shouted with joy.

He shimmered blue, then shifted shape, becoming a dark dragon. Nick and Isabelle gasped as one, even though they'd seen the *Pyr* shift all their lives, and the dragon laughed as he snapped at the glowing orb of red light.

He ate it.

The light was extinguished as his mouth closed over it, then he began to shift shape rapidly. He became a stag, a rabbit, a snake, an eagle, a salamander, then a dragon again. He changed shapes so quickly that Nick didn't want to blink in case he missed one. The leader cycled through his forms with dizzying speed, then the fourth time that he was a dragon, he leapt into the sky. He seemed to be lit from within, glowing red from the tips of his teeth, the ends of his talons and the tip of his tail. Each scale was outlined in brilliant red light.

When he jumped into the sky, the others shifted shape and followed him, an entire company of dragons soaring into the night sky. They flew straight toward the moon as Nick and Isabelle watched, transfixed. High in the sky but silhouetted against the full moon, they flew in a tight circle, seven dark dragons in a ring.

One, who had to be that leader, breathed fire from the middle of their circle, as if he was howling at the moon. Instead of dragonfire, though, Nick saw a plume of glowing red shoot from his mouth. He wished he had a telescope as the light launched itself into the distance, like a shuttle being launched from the earth. The red light spread like a plume beneath the shimmer of the northern lights, and he guessed that those tiny lights were scattering.

When they merged into the northern lights, becoming lost in the moving curtain of lime green, he understood that they were leaving.

Isabelle pointed at the circle of dragons, drawing his attention back to them. They flew in tight formation again, the leader joining the circle of his companions. Each took the tail of his neighbor into his mouth and they flew with greater and greater speed, spinning into a whirlwind so that their individual figures blurred. They went faster and faster, and there was a flash of blue-green light before they vanished completely.

It is done.

The old-speak echoed in Nick's thoughts, though he didn't recognize the voice or the source. He looked around, but the weird old guys were gone. They'd vanished without a trace. Isabelle shivered and they headed back to the house together.

She was the one who looked into the room off the kitchen that the old guys had shared. It was empty, so empty that they might never have been there.

"Their quest was completed," Isabelle whispered.

Nick nodded. The weird old guys were the seven thieves who had set out centuries before to save the world from Blazion and his magick. With the magick's return to Regalia, their mission was complete. Nick felt both sad that they were gone and glad that they'd triumphed. He and Isabelle both returned to bed and fell asleep immediately.

In the morning, the adults seemed to have forgotten that the weird old guys had ever been there.

By lunchtime, even Nick and Isabelle had forgotten about the ancient *Pyr* and what they had witnessed, though they both would feel a twinge of recollection whenever they saw the full moon.

Thorolf landed hard against the ground. It was wet with fresh snow and the air was cold enough to wake him right up. He was surrounded by the wolf mates he'd been carrying, many of whom were scarred or nicked. He did a quick count to make sure he'd brought everyone through with him.

Then a man cleared his throat. It was a portentous sound and a familiar one. Thorolf was on his feet in a flash.

He winced as a flashlight beam was shone over him, into his face then down the length of him. He felt rumpled and suspicious, especially when he realized it was two police officers who had found him.

"I suppose you have an explanation for being in the park with your friends at this hour," one said. He lowered the light and Thorolf saw that the older policeman was speaking to him, the younger one standing back. He was well aware of the way their scrutiny lingered on his jeans, his dreadlocks and his many tattoos. He ran a hand over his hair and straightened, smiling a little and trying to look innocent.

It wasn't his best trick and he knew it.

Neither was beguiling, but there was no question that it was the best possible solution.

"Well, you see, officer, there was this party," he began, keeping his tone deferential as he lit the flames in his eyes.

The younger cop laughed under his breath. "Some party," he murmured.

"So, there was this party," the older officer echoed, inviting Thorolf to continue, and he dared to hope that he had a chance of pulling this off.

Hadrian burst through the dust under a million stars in a midnight sky. It was so cold and clear that the wind nearly stole Hadrian's breath away. He soared high into the sky, Rania safely in his grasp, and only belatedly realized where they were.

"Callanish," he murmured, then flew low over the standing stones. He circled them, eyed the gaping maw in the earth in the middle of the circle where they had erupted, then pivoted and flew high again. The sky was alight with shimmers of lime green as the northern lights wavered and flowed, seemingly so close that he could touch them yet also far away.

"My brothers," Rania whispered in anguish and Hadrian realized they were completely alone. The sky was empty in all directions and the ground was still beneath them. He flew over the spot repeatedly and would have gone back into the earth, but Rania shook her head.

"And the *Pyr*, too. The Others from Bones. I hope everyone got out okay."

"Me, too. Let's go home and check on them."

"Back to my smithy?"

Rania smiled, her fair hair flowing over her shoulders. "No. That way." She pointed west. "My home." Her smile broadened. "I'm *wondering*."

Hadrian chuckled and turned in a broad circle, taking his directions from his mate. He flew low over the north Atlantic, enjoying their time together and his sense of triumph. He was surprised when she directed him toward Iceland, then realized her choice was perfectly right.

Her home was even more right. It was an ancient cottage, built of stone and settled low against the earth. There was sod growing on the roof so it was hard to discern from above, and she said it was half-buried in the earth. It was the stone circle surrounding it that he spotted first, its shape distinctive even beneath a layer of snow.

The inner circle was a good sixty feet across, and the ring of stone that surrounded it was eight feet wide and eight feet tall. It was all fitted stone and resonant with the songs of the earth. Hadrian felt immediately at home. There was one break in the barrier, and that opening aligned with the cottage set right in the middle of the inner circle. He could see the ocean crashing against the rocky shore in one direction, icebergs in the sea far beyond it, and a wisp of smoke rising from a volcano in the other direction.

"Fire and ice," he said to Rania as he set her down and she laughed.

"Just like you." She stepped back and watched as he shifted shape, exhaling with relief when he was in his human form again. Rania cast her arms around his neck and kissed him, then tugged him into her home.

"Someone's here," she said softly on the threshold.

Hadrian found himself shimmering on the cusp of change before he realized the visitor might be the result of her wondering.

The man stood in front of her knife collection again, his back to her, his hair a long braid down his back. It was exactly like the last time, his posture identical, the door left open the same increment—but this time, Hadrian was with her.

Rania felt as if she had a second chance to get it right.

"Father?" she said and he glanced over his shoulder, a smile in his eyes.

"Daughter," he replied, surveying her.

"A second chance?" she asked and he almost smiled.

"You wondered. That was all it took." His gaze flicked past her and she knew he was studying Hadrian. She knew the moment he spotted his own ring. "You didn't lose it then," he said softly.

"My mate had it," she replied. "It was safe."

Her father pivoted then and offered his hand to Hadrian. "I am Ulrik."

"Hadrian MacEwan."

She watched her father inhale. "More than a man?"

"I am *Pyr*, a dragon shifter."

Her father raised a brow, then indicated the ring. "The stone tells me all I need to know."

"Not everything, Father," Rania said. "Maeve is defeated and the realm of Fae no more."

"I knew this." He nodded. "I felt it."

"I spoke to your mate in the realm of the dead," Hadrian said and Rania watched her father assess him again.

"There is more to you than meets the eye, dragon."

"She misses you."

Ulrik nodded and dropped his gaze. "I miss her, too."

There was such a wealth of love and longing in his voice that Rania's throat tightened.

"She asked me to tell you to dream of her, if I ever met you. She said you can meet in that realm again."

Rania watched her father's eyes light then well with tears. He frowned and nodded, and when he spoke, his voice was gruff. "I thank you for this."

She put her hand in Hadrian's. "We're going to have a son, Father. I hope you will teach him the stories of our kind."

Ulrik smiled fully then for the first time. "A child!" he said softly, his eyes lighting. "Oh yes, daughter mine, I would like very much to have a family again." He opened his arms to her then and she stepped into his embrace, hugging him tightly as her tears rose. She had a family again, thanks to Hadrian. Not just a son on the way, but twelve brothers and a lost father returned to her. From a life of solitude, Rania was surrounded by love—and the greatest love of all was that of her dragon shifter.

"I don't understand," Lynsay said to Abigail. "How can the swan be gone?"

They were standing by the pond at the big house, its turrets and gables towering over them. The older woman shook her head. "There's no saying with wild things, dear. It was healed so it went home. It wasn't banded so it was wild." Her voice softened. "We had no right to keep it captive, dear."

"No, but..."

Abigail patted Lynsay's arm. "You did a good thing, dear, and you made a difference. You'll have to imagine it safely on its way and be content with that."

Lynsay wasn't content with that. She felt cheated, again, denied something important to her. She just wanted to see the swan healed. She just wanted to know that it was okay, to see as much with her own eyes, but Abigail said she hadn't seen it since the previous day.

Another chance for something had slipped through Lynsay's fingers.

She trudged back to the pub, disgruntled and wishing for a change. She didn't even know what she wanted. Great sex? True love? A sense of purpose? A partner? All of the above and more—but that seemed greedy. She knew she was lucky. She owned her own business and her home. She had financial security and good friends. She was healthy and pretty much happy.

If alone.

There was a guy standing outside the pub when the familiar structure came into view.

"We don't open until noon," Lynsay told him, intending to walk right past him. She lived in the small house attached to the pub. It was newer, but still a hundred years old.

He turned and smiled at her, the sight stopping Lynsay in her tracks. Had she ever seen such a great looking guy? His hair was dark and wavy, his eyes were piercing blue. His smile was so radiant that she felt as if she was standing in the sun. He was taller than her and broad-shouldered, if dressed in clothes that seemed a bit shabby and old-fashioned. Simple. He'd look amazing in a suit. She took a good look, figuring it couldn't hurt, not caring if he was offended.

His smile broadened a little more. "Do you live here?" he asked and she couldn't place his accent at all. It was a bit Scandinavian, but not quite.

"I do. I own The Swan & Thistle," she said, but saw that he didn't understand. "The pub. The bar. The restaurant. I have a cook, but it's my place."

He nodded and looked at the old building again, appreciation in his expression. She felt like the sun had slipped behind a cloud when he looked away from her, which just proved how much she needed a date.

"It feels like home," he said softly when she had continued and Lynsay looked back, curious.

"You're not from around here, are you?"

"Not exactly," he said, smiling again.

"Then where?"

"Iceland most recently."

"What do you do?"

"I listen to stories, and I remember them. My mother taught me to do that." He sobered, his gaze trailing in the direction of the big house. "But I have heard so many. I am afraid to forget them. I think I should begin to write them down."

A writer. Well, Lynsay understood and admired that.

"My dad was a poet," she said. "And the unofficial local historian. He wrote down all the stories he heard."

"A kindred spirit!"

"I guess so." Lynsay found herself compelled to elaborate. "He wrote a lot about the big house, the manor house up the way. There's an old story that it was built on the ruins of an ancient castle, one stolen by a barbarian king. It was lost by him when he killed his wife and his twelve sons finally rose against him. Kind of a gruesome story, actually."

"Stories are often gruesome. That doesn't mean they aren't true."

There was a ferocity in his tone then, one that made her wonder what his story was. "You can read my dad's books if you like." Lynsay didn't know what prompted her to make such an offer.

"I would rather you told me his stories," her visitor said. "I like how people tell stories, and you have a beautiful voice." His gaze warmed. "I expect you tell them very well."

"My father always said I'd inherited his gift," she said, feeling herself blush. "Maybe it was the truth."

"There is no harm in a father showing kindness to his daughter," he said firmly.

That was true enough. "You have strong feelings about fathers," she said, keeping her tone light.

"Mine wasn't very kind. I always thought that if I had children of my own, I would spoil them with kindness." He shook his head as if that was foolish.

"I think that's lovely," Lynsay said and their gazes clung for a potent moment. She had a lump in her throat for some reason.

She watched him swallow.

"Kindness can be rare in our world," he said, studying her more intently. "I have the sense that you are a kind person."

"Some people say I'm a pushover, though. Too soft-hearted," she added when he seemed uncertain of her meaning.

"There are worse faults."

True enough. Lynsay started to walk toward her own door again.

"Do you know of a place where I might find work near here?" her visitor asked. "I can work hard and I only need enough of a wage for food and shelter."

"Not saving for a rainy day?" she had to tease.

"It has been and gone. I am simply glad to be alive." He surveyed her again. "And here. I am glad to be here."

"You said it felt like home."

"It does. I would like to stay, if I can find a way."

Lynsay looked around, amazed by the strength of her temptation to help. She heard the delivery truck from the brewery approaching—she could always tell by the way Lukas ground the gears on the corner—and had an idea. "I can always use some brute strength around here," she said, nodding at the truck as it came into view. "There are always kegs to haul and deliveries to be moved."

"I can do this."

"There's a room above the pub you can have. It's usually rented but not right now. And you can eat at the pub."

His smile was warm. "Thank you. This will suit me well."

"And you can collect more stories."

"Yes." He regarded her with a smile. "Will you tell me yours?"

"I might." Lynsay smiled back at him, their gazes locked and the moment stretched into forever. "I'm Lynsay Barnes," she said, offering her hand.

"Trymman," he said, his own hand closing over hers.

"No surname?"

"The past is the past. I am more interested in the future."

And Lynsay found that she felt exactly the same way as she stared into his eyes. Then Lukas honked the horn, making her jump, and there was work to be done.

But there was a bounce in Lynsay's step that hadn't been there before, as well as a sense that Trymman's arrival might be just the change she'd been waiting for.

In the end, it had been ridiculously simple to make a deal with Micah. A Fae sword in exchange for the key to his library. As simple as that.

Sebastian took his time traveling to the continent, knowing it would take a few days for the parcel with the precious key to arrive. He journeyed by night, by train, lingering in London to see the sights he remembered. When he went to Highgate Cemetery, he sensed the presence of other vampires, the few solitary ones remaining, but his reputation undoubtedly preceded him, because they kept their distance.

He ignored the news reports about the unprecedented electromagnetic activity around the North Pole, because he knew what it was. He stood on the roof of his hotel each night though and reveled in the sight of the northern lights, sending all that fucking magick right back where it belonged.

The dragon and the swan had done better than Sebastian could have anticipated.

Of course, much of the credit belonged to him. He had helped them, after all.

His destination was Paris, the city he loved best. Paris was constant in a way that made Sebastian feel young again. It changed, to be sure, but in its heart, the part he loved the best, the pace of change was very slow. His favorite cities shared that trait. Paris. New Orleans. London, to some extent. Budapest. Venice. He really should visit Istanbul again. It had been a long, long time.

He walked down the Champs Elysées at night, savoring the press of people, the sound of music and laughter, the smell of food and women's perfumes. The vivacity surrounding him was thrilling. He'd feasted upon a wreck of humanity, unable to completely abandon Micah's principles by putting a homeless derelict out of his misery. The fresh infusion of blood thrummed through him like a fine wine, giving him an uncharacteristic sense of optimism.

The French loved tradition as much as Sebastian did. The great-great granddaughter of the lawyer he'd hired a century before still managed the family business. Like her forebears, she was amenable to an evening meeting. He suspected that she kept the same excellent brandy in the wood-paneled office.

His step quickened as the hour of their meeting drew near. He moved quickly down the familiar streets, diving deep into the quarter to the townhouse he had visited so many times. The light was on in the office on the second floor, its golden light a beacon to him.

Soon, he would hold the key.

Soon, his sanctuary would be his again.

He rapped on the door and was ushered in by a secretary with downcast eyes and shown to the stairs. "I know the way, thank you," he said in French and the secretary inclined his head, then vanished into an office on the main floor.

He tapped once on the door of the office and heard the lawyer's invitation from inside. He opened the door with a flourish and a smile, only to freeze in astonishment.

The lawyer was there, of course, standing behind the desk every lawyer in her family had used, the walls behind her thick with books bound in leather. She was impeccably groomed as always, dressed in a dark suit, her hair twisted up, tasteful small diamonds at her earlobes. The bottle of brandy was on a small table before the fireplace, but there were three glasses on the tray, the cut crystal catching the firelight.

And Sylvia rose from her seat beside the fire. She looked a bit tired and was dressed more casually than the lawyer. But she smiled at him and Sebastian found himself in awe of her presence.

"I brought the key," she said as the lawyer watched. "Micah preferred a courier for such a precious item and I volunteered."

She held out the antique gold key and Sebastian stared at it. "You shouldn't have," he said, hearing that his tone was brusque.

She laughed a little. "No, probably not, but I couldn't resist the temptation."

"You've done quite well resisting it in the past."

"Time for a change."

He met Sylvia's gaze and was surprised to find her eyes filled with confidence. He wondered how much the lawyer understood: her expression was impassive but he knew she was bilingual.

"Show me your library?" Sylvia asked.

Sebastian frowned and glanced toward the fire.

"It must be very special," she continued softly. "I love libraries. You know that. And I've come all this way."

He moved closer to her, risking the alluring scent of her and his own temptation. "You have to understand that I don't play by Micah's rules anymore."

Sylvia's smile broadened. "But that's why I volunteered," she confessed. He stared at her, amazed that she knew what he was and who he was, yet had come anyway.

He reached for the key, but she withdrew it. "I want your promise that we're done with games and riddles. I want to know the truth, all of it."

"The truth always comes at a price," he warned her.

"Of course. And I suspect it might take a long time to share this particular truth." She held out the key, her eyes filled with a wisdom that hadn't been there when they'd met and he knew that she was prepared for whatever he might show her. He still felt protective of her, but he welcomed the prospect of companionship. "Maybe centuries."

And there it was. He might turn her, but she recognized that and had come to terms with it. Maybe she even welcomed it.

Sebastian frowned. "You can't change your mind about something like this, you know."

"I know. But I need a tutor, and I think you might be the perfect one." She held his gaze and he heard an ancient name echo in her thoughts, a name he'd never expected to be openly associated with him again. *Semyaza.*

She knew. The magick had betrayed him somehow, just as he'd guessed it always would.

But Sylvia knew the truth and she'd chosen him.

And that meant the responsibility for her fate wasn't entirely his own. Sebastian smiled, unable to disguise the pleasure he felt, then lifted the key from her grasp. "We could go there now."

"Yes," she said simply and he closed one hand over the key as he put it in his pocket. He held it there, so glad to have it in his possession again.

Then he took Sylvia's hand in his, ensuring that he controlled his strength. He inclined his head to the lawyer and thanked her, then made a future appointment to review several investments.

The brandy would wait.

His step was light when he and Sylvia stepped into the street together, and Paris sparkled all around them, as filled with promise as a glass of champagne.

"You're sure?" he asked and Sylvia nodded.

"You have a private library," she confessed with a smile, her gaze dancing over him.

"Your ulterior motive," he teased. "You want to catalogue my collection."

"More than that. I want to be with you, Sebastian, in every way. I want to hear all of your story. I want you to teach me everything you know." Her smile turned mischievous. "But we can read when we don't have anything else to do."

And, much to his own surprise, the prospect of that adventure suited Sebastian just fine.

Days and nights passed without a word from Rania's brothers. Rania and Hadrian had chosen to remain in Iceland in the hope that they might appear there. Each night, while Rania slept, Hadrian went outside the cottage and looked at the sky overhead. He'd checked in with the *Pyr* and had been relieved that they were okay. Alasdair had taken Yasmina to his lair in Scotland, and didn't want to be disturbed. Kade had been delivered to Drake for instruction and review. Rhys and Kristofer had retreated to their respective lairs, and Theo was helping out at the Circus of Wonders as they rebuilt.

Hadrian was glad to be alone with Rania for the moment.

Each night, he shifted shape and coiled himself around the cottage in his dragon form, his chin resting on his tail just outside the front door. He could watch the opening in the outer wall from there. Usually, Rania joined him, curling into his claw, telling him stories of all she'd seen and done over the centuries, or just being with him.

It was idyllic, with the exception of Rania's concern for her brothers.

The *Pyr* were planning to gather on the solstice for Hadrian's scale repair, so Rania and Hadrian returned to Northumberland before going to Vermont. On their first morning back at his lair, Hadrian heard a man whistling. It was snowing lightly and the wind was up. The snow had started to fall in the early hours of the morning and it was gathering in the trees. Rania was sleeping deeply beside him and Hadrian was watching the snow fall over the stream. At the sound of the whistle, he felt himself shimmering on the cusp of change, but slipped from the bed and went to the door.

A man was approaching the lair with purpose. He was blond and tall, a handsome man of maybe thirty years of age.

Hadrian opened the door to greet him and the man smiled. "Hadrian!" he said, as if they were old friends, and strode forward with his hand extended. "How's Rania? Is her pregnancy going well?"

"Edred," Hadrian guessed and the new arrival laughed.

"I forgot you wouldn't know, and the big clue is still behind me." He grinned and rolled his eyes. "Lazy bunch of brothers."

Hadrian heard footsteps then and men calling. In moments, he was surrounded by twelve good-looking young men, all healthy and all with the same clear blue eyes as Rania. Each one, when he looked closely, had a mark on his left wrist, as if something had burned the skin. Rania was obviously awakened by their arrival and came out to be greeted with joy, hugged and kissed and lifted off her feet. She was passed from brother to brother despite her protests then surrendered to Hadrian again.

"Where were you?" she demanded of Edred. "What took you so long?"

"We ended up in northern Spain, near our favorite places to stop on migration," he told her, then gestured to himself. "But like this without any of the identification people seem to love now."

"But how did you get here?"

"We stowed away on a freighter that seemed a bit shady, then worked for our passage. Then we hitchhiked north."

"How did you know to come here?" Hadrian asked and the thirteen siblings all smiled.

"We've been here before," Edred said with a mysterious smile.

"When," she asked and he grinned at her.

"Haven't you guessed yet?" Edred asked, his tone teasing. "The ruins in the town near here are from the castle our father stole, all those years ago." He gave her a little squeeze and his voice roughened. "I like that your home is close to where it all began. I like that it all came right in the end."

"Me, too." Rania was blushing and blinking back tears. "You must be starving," she said and urged them inside.

"No millet," one brother said and they all laughed together as they crowded into the house. It was good to see Rania laughing and happy, surrounded by the family she'd lost and found again. Hadrian smiled as he followed, knowing that they were starting their own family, too. The future was bright—because the firestorm had been right all along.

EPILOGUE

On the winter solstice, the *Pyr* gathered at Bones for Hadrian's scale repair. Hadrian and Rania flew to New York from Iceland in her plane. He was impressed with her piloting abilities and already thinking about getting his own license. He liked it much better than commercial travel.

For the first time, there were other shifters in attendance at the ceremony, as well as mortal men. The coven of mercy had left their refuge for the evening to witness the festivities. The wolf shifters of Manhattan were there, along with Wynter Olson and the mortal mates from Alaska. Edred had come with another of Rania's brothers at her invitation and stood a little apart from the throngs of Others. She'd invited her father, too, and Hadrian was a bit disappointed that the swan-prince hadn't chosen to come. The djinns were in a celebratory mood—both Niall and Sloane had been conferring with Yasmina about Alasdair's treatment. Hadrian thought that his cousin just needed more time with Yasmina. Murray and Mel were pouring drinks as quickly as they could, and many from the Circus of Wonders had shown up as well. The bar was crowded and the mood was festive.

When Quinn arrived with Sara and his small forge, there was a welcoming cheer from the *Pyr*. Sara and Quinn's sons had gone to stay with Erik and Eileen in Chicago. Murray shouted to clear the dance floor and it was done more quickly than Hadrian would have expected. Quinn set up his forge and shifted shape, becoming a dragon of sapphire and steel. The sight of him working with such care at the jeweler's forge silenced the Others in attendance. They stood in a ring around the dance floor, obviously fascinated.

Theo was the next to shift, becoming a dragon of carnelian and gold. The Others applauded his transformation and he blew a small stream of dragonfire, to their delight. Thorolf shifted next, becoming a massive dragon of moonstone and silver, followed by Balthasar, who was citrine and gold in his dragon form. Arach left Wynter and the light of their firestorm diminished slightly with distance. Hadrian knew he didn't imagine that Arach took his alternate form with gusto, becoming a dragon of aquamarine and silver. If showing off would help with that firestorm, Hadrian wished him luck.

Alasdair was next, becoming a dragon of hematite and silver. Yasmina stroked his scaled side with admiration and he visibly preened, then swept his tail across the floor. He was looking more vital with every passing day. Would he have a firestorm with Yasmina once he was recovered? Hadrian hoped so. He wanted his cousin to be happy.

Kristofer changed shape next, taking his peridot and gold dragon form. Bree stood beside him, clearly proud of her dragon warrior, and Hadrian thought he could see the start of her baby bump. Rhys was next, becoming a dragon of garnet and silver. He'd catered the scale repair, his team having delivered many huge trays of food for the celebration afterward.

Then Hadrian took Rania's hand. He smiled at her and loved how she smiled back at him, then changed shape in a brilliant shimmer of blue. If he was showing off a bit, too, he thought it was deserved. His emerald and silver scales shone in the light, but when he would have breathed fire, Murray protested.

"Remember the fire code!" the bar owner cried. "Keep the temperature down, please. It's hot enough with so many dragons in here."

The crowd laughed, their anticipation palpable.

Mel gave Quinn the scale that Hadrian had lost, and the Smith of the *Pyr* began to heat it on his forge. Rania presented her *katar* to Quinn for the repair of the scale. Hadrian particularly liked the weapon, a push dagger with gold ornamentation, and liked that it had played a part in breaking Maeve's spell forever. He was honored that it would be fused with his scale, a gift from his mate to ensure that he was armed.

Quinn straightened and turned, the scale glowing red in his talons. "Fire!" he cried, and the *Pyr* echoed the word. "One of Hadrian's affinities, a sign of passion and his very nature." Hadrian made a little plume of dragonfire, despite Murray's earlier protests.

"Earth," Quinn said then and pressed the hot scale into the gap on Hadrian's chest. "Governing his smithing abilities and his practicality." The skin scorched and Hadrian tipped his head back, exhaling dragonsmoke instead of fire.

"Air," Sara said and Hadrian felt Rania blow upon the hot scale. "One of the affinities his mate brings to the union, symbolic of intellect and problem-solving."

"Water," Rania whispered and Hadrian caught his breath as her tear fell on the scale, cooling it. He opened his eyes to find her smiling up at him, her hand on his claw. "The affinity I only regained because of my dragon shifter, who thawed the splinter of ice embedded in my heart. Because of him, I can love again."

The Others cheered at this sentiment and Hadrian shifted shape in a glorious blaze of blue light. He caught Rania up and kissed her thoroughly, knowing that he was the luckiest *Pyr* alive.

The firestorm had made his every dream come true.

ABOUT THE AUTHOR

Deborah Cooke sold her first book in 1992, a medieval romance published under her pseudonym Claire Delacroix. Since then, she has published over seventy novels in a wide variety of sub-genres, including historical romance, contemporary romance, and paranormal romance. She has published under the names Claire Delacroix, Claire Cross and Deborah Cooke. **The Beauty**, part of her successful Bride Quest series of historical romances, was her first title to land on the *New York Times* List of Bestselling Books. Her books routinely appear on other bestseller lists and have won numerous awards. In 2009, she was the writer-in-residence at the Toronto Public Library, the first time the library has hosted a residency focused on the romance genre. In 2012, she was honored to receive the Romance Writers of America's Mentor of the Year Award.

Currently, she writes paranormal romances and contemporary romances as Deborah Cooke. She also writes historical romances as Claire Delacroix. Deborah lives in Canada with her husband and family, as well as far too many unfinished knitting projects.

To learn more about her books, visit her websites:

http://deborahcooke.com
http://dragonfirenovels.com
http://delacroix.net

Printed in Great Britain
by Amazon